Random Tales

Random Tales

Kathleen Moir

with best wishes

Kathleen Moir.

Spiderwize

Random Tales

Spiderwize
Office 404, 4th Floor
Albany House
324/326 Regent Street
London
W1B 3HH
UK

www.spiderwize.com

ISBN: 978-1-907294-97-6

Table of Contents

THE DECORATOR

'**T**HAT'S IT!' Betty shouted to the wall. 'I'll just have it painted as I've already told the decorators— magnolia. At least it will be fresh and clean.' After all, Billy was bringing his girlfriend all the way from America to meet her, not to inspect the house. She sighed. She felt just like the house looked, old and tired, and neglected. It had been two years since Ted had died, and she hadn't done anything to sort out either herself or the house. She always woke up feeling so tired and miserable. She had meant to do things. Billy had suggested some voluntary work, perhaps in a charity shop. The local school was always in need of people, to lend a hand with fund raising. Or perhaps she could go back to the church choir. She had a good voice, and she used to enjoy it. Somehow, she couldn't summon the energy to do anything. Friends kept telling her it was time to move on, but she couldn't do it.

Watching Ted die had first made her feel angry, then horribly hurt, as though he had died and left her on purpose. Now, with Billy having been moved to New York with his job, she just felt numb. She wandered into the living room and gazed at Ted's photo on the coffee table. He looked serious but kind, as he had always done. She kissed her

1

fingers and lightly touched his lips. She had promised him, before he died, that she would get on with her life. She was letting him down, and she felt so guilty.

'Have a bit of fun before it's too late,' is what he'd said.

'Oh Ted,' she whispered. 'If only you were here.'

The doorbell rang. She shook herself and went to answer it. On opening the door, the first thing she saw was light—a blinding white light. She hadn't realised the sun was shining so brightly.

'Hello,' she called, shielding her eyes. 'Who is it?'

'Hi,' called back a high, tinkling voice. 'Decorators!'

'B...but,' flustered Betty, 'I'm not expecting you until next week.'

'No, no,' replied the sing-song voice. 'It says here on my schedule, Betty Mackay, 25th.'

Betty found herself stepping aside and following, into the living room, a person in the whitest, cleanest overalls she had ever seen.

'I'm sorry,' Betty stuttered, 'but I wasn't expecting...'

'I know. I get it all the time. You were expecting a man, weren't you?' laughed the tiny blonde girl before her. 'Don't worry. I'm Angie and I'm a very good decorator. Honestly, I'll do a great job! I've got the paint here,' she trilled, holding up the paint tin in her hand. 'I've always liked yellow.'

'Yellow? I didn't choose yellow,' said Betty, swallowing hard.

'It definitely says yellow on my instructions. A soft mellow yellow.'

Before Betty knew what was happening she was in the kitchen making tea. Minutes later she saw to her astonishment that Angie had the living room ready for decorating. The furniture had been moved to the centre of the room and all the ornaments were safely in a box in a corner.

'How did you manage that?' gasped Betty.

'Oh, I have my ways,' laughed Angie again. 'Now I'll just have my cup of tea and then I'll get started.'

Angie beamed at Betty and quietly shut the living room door. Betty didn't know what to do. She washed some dishes, swept the kitchen floor and tried to read the newspaper. She felt quite flustered but somehow excited at the same time. 'Yellow,' she mused, 'mmm.'

It seemed like no time at all when there was a tap at the kitchen door, and Angie stepped in. She had taken off her overalls to reveal equally white jeans and T-shirt.

'I'm going out for some lunch,' she said, grinning at Betty. 'Why don't you come with me?'

Somehow Angie manoeuvred her into the hall and out of the front door. She steered Betty into a small corner cafe and ordered cheese sandwiches and milkshakes. Betty didn't think she had ever tasted a milkshake, but it was delicious.

'It's good to try new things,' said Angie, eyes shining.

Over lunch Betty warmed to Angie. She told her all about Ted's death, and Billy going to America to work, and how difficult she found life without either of them. She told her about the house, and how dismal and dingy it seemed, and how she had lacked the energy, or the will to do anything about it.

'Ted always liked colour,' she admitted. 'He would have liked a yellow living room.'

On the way home from the cafe they passed a boutique. They stopped and looked through the glass. In the middle of the brightly coloured display was a gorgeous red dress. It looked lovely and soft, with a gently pleated skirt and elbow length sleeves.

'Just your size,' smiled Angie, walking towards the shop door.

'Oh no, I couldn't possibly…,' Betty began to say. But, with an excitement she hadn't felt in ages, she followed Angie inside.

Back at the house with Angie hard at work in the living room, Betty started to feel rather foolish. Why on earth had she let Angie persuade her into buying that dress? It was completely impractical. She didn't know when she would have occasion to wear it. Perhaps the shop would take it back.

At six o'clock Angie knocked on the kitchen door and said the living room was finished. Betty stared in amazement at the transformation. The colour was wonderful! The room seemed so full of life, so vibrant. Angie had also rearranged the furniture, the ornaments and the photographs.

'I hope you don't mind,' Angie said apologetically.

'No, no,' whispered Betty, shaking her head. 'It's beautiful, thank you so much.'

'Just one thing,' said Angie. 'The curtains, I don't think they quite go any more.'

Betty looked sadly at the drab colourless drapes on either side of the window. They looked terrible.

'The shop round the corner from the church does great readymade curtains,' enthused Angie. 'Why don't you go there tomorrow while I put a lick of paint on the hall and staircase?'

Angie left. Her overalls were as clean and unmarked as they had been when she arrived.

The next day Betty came out of the curtain shop with the most gorgeous pair of yellow and gold, leaf patterned curtains, and Angie helped her hang them. The hall and staircase were painted and looked brilliant: yellow, but deeper than the living room.

'I'll be back tomorrow to do the kitchen,' smiled Angie.

Betty was delighted with how the house was beginning to look.

'It's got a bit of life and colour now,' she said softly to herself.

That night before she went to bed she looked at her red dress. She might upset Angie if she took it back. Perhaps she could wear it when Billy came with his girlfriend. She held it against herself. It was really lovely but there was something not quite right with it. She stared at her reflection in the mirror, then it dawned on her. It was her hair. It looked so unkempt, so unruly. She thought with shame that she hadn't been to a hairdresser since Ted had died. When Angie arrived the next morning she had made up her mind.

'I'm going to get my hair done,' she said firmly to Angie.

'Great idea,' giggled Angie, thrusting a card into Betty's hand. 'Why don't you go to my hairdresser? Just tell them I sent you.'

A little while later Betty was hurrying down the high street clutching the card Angie had given her. She found the place—a small insignificant shop, with wigs in the window. She didn't remember ever having seen it before. Betty swallowed hard and went inside. She was greeted by a handsome smiling man with black shiny hair, and beautiful deep brown eyes. At once she felt she could trust this stranger, and before she knew it she had agreed to a chic modern cut with blonde highlights. Betty walked out of the hairdresser with mounting excitement. The hairdo had taken years off her. Rafael, the hairdresser, had even kissed her hand as she left! She hurried home, desperate to show Angie.

When she arrived the front door was locked. Betty unlocked the door, lifting the spare key she had given Angie off the mat. The lightness and freshness and colour of the hall and stairs seemed to envelope her in warmth as she walked through to the kitchen. Here Angie had excelled herself. The kitchen was painted in the prettiest, softest, most beautiful green she had ever seen. Below the plain cornice a lovely leafy pattern had been stencilled, echoing the pattern of the lounge curtains. Betty was amazed. How on earth had Angie managed to do so much in so little time? And where *was* Angie? Betty's eyes alighted on a note on the work surface.

SORRY TO HAVE TO GO SO SUDDENLY, BUT THE BOSS WANTS ME BACK AT HEADQUARTERS. BET YOU LOOK LOVELY. THE POST IS ON THE HALL TABLE. LOVE, ANGIE.

PS I'VE LEFT MY CARD IF YOU NEED ME.

Betty was disappointed that Angie had gone. She wanted her to see her transformation, and to understand how different she felt. The post consisted of an advert for a Salsa dance class which started that night in the town hall. Betty smiled to herself. She pictured the red dress, and her new hairdo. Did she dare?

Late that night she hugged herself in bed. She felt animated, energetic, and happier than she had for a long time. She had met some lovely people. They had been so welcoming, so friendly. She already had an invitation for coffee and a dinner date. She felt too excited to sleep but eventually drifted off.

She was awakened by a persistent ringing noise. Scrambling out of bed she realised it was the front doorbell.

'It's Angie,' she thought excitedly, and ran downstairs and opened the door. She was met by a large figure wearing very dirty overalls.

'Hello love,' said a gruff voice. 'Decorators!'

Betty was taken aback

'Sorry,' she spluttered. 'It's been done. The decorator's been and done all the work. Look, here's the card she left.'

A rough hand with dirty fingernails took the card.

'Never heard of 'em,' snarled the voice. 'Is this a wind-up? D'you want me or not?'

'But it's been done,' protested Betty.

The lumpy figure pushed the card back into Betty's hand and stomped down the path. She shut the door, not quite understanding what was going on. Walking into the bright, light living room, Betty glanced at the card Angie had left on the hall table. She couldn't understand how the mix up with the decorator had occurred. She turned the card over. It was written in gold. In beautiful script, it said

A Gabriel
Decorators Inc.

There was no address. There was no phone number. Betty felt confused.   Her eyes swept round the exquisitely decorated room and alighted on the photograph of Ted. Angie had moved it to a prominent position on the mantelpiece. She looked at the familiar loved face and smiled, and for just a moment she could have sworn that Ted smiled back, and winked at her.

WHEN THE SCREAMING STOPPED

HIS BINOCULARS SCANNED the silent glen again. There it was, the cottage he had seen from the hilltop. A wisp of smoke curled from the chimney. Someone must be at home. He was hungry and cold and tired. He didn't know the exact time, but thought it must be about four o' clock. A familiar feeling of excitement mounted in his stomach. Beads of perspiration appeared on his forehead as his breathing became fast and shallow. He wiped the wetness from his face with a gloved hand. He flicked his tongue over his lips, enjoying the salty taste. His stomach rumbled. It was three days since he had eaten and a week since he had slept in that warm bed. He grinned as he remembered the slender body, and shiny red hair that had hung down past her delicate neck—the neck that had been so easy to snap. Why did she have to scream? He hated it when they screamed. It drove him mad. Mad!—He laughed out loud. That's what they had all said. Even his mother had said it.

'You're mad, Philip,' she had said when they took him away. 'You're mad and there's no help for you. You should never have been born.'

She didn't understand. Nobody did. He wasn't mad. He only wanted to love them, to touch their soft smooth necks. But they always screamed and he had to stop them. Sometimes he stayed with them for days, once for more than a week. What was her name, Wendy, Wanda? He couldn't remember. He could only remember her warm creamy skin. But like the others, when she screamed, he had to silence her.

Shivering, he lifted his rucksack on to his shoulder, stood unsteadily and started slowly towards the white-walled house. He was stiff and sore from sleeping outdoors, but hiding in the hills was a way to stop being caught. He had seen his photo on the front page of the newspapers, so he knew he was being hunted. There was no way he was going back. All that talking to psychiatrists and therapists, and listening to the others moaning on about their abused childhoods. No one wanted to listen to him. He wanted to tell them about his dreams, about silky delicate skin and fragile necks, but no one wanted to know. There was no way he was going to stay in that hospital for the rest of his life. It was bad enough being locked up, but being drugged every day was worse. He soon realised, though. He knew what they were up to, giving him tablets to keep him sedated. He'd tricked them into thinking he was taking the pills. The little blonde nurse had been cute and she'd had such a beautiful neck. But she did scream.

As he reached the cottage his heart hammered in his chest and he echoed its beat on the door. No one came. He walked round to the back. A fat figure was hoeing a vegetable patch, while chickens skittered around his feet. It turned. Small piggy eyes almost hidden in a pink doughy face stared at

Philip. Philip was disappointed to see a boy, but he grinned and the face grinned back. The figure straightened and continued to stare and grin silently with a vacant look that made Philip feel strangely uncomfortable. He felt a touch on his shoulder and spun round to face a fat wrinkled woman with similar piggy eyes.

'I think we've got company, Rob,' she whispered. 'Away in and put the kettle on. '

Keeping hold of Philip's shoulder she manoeuvred him into a kitchen-cum-living room.

After watching him devour a huge plate of freshly baked sponge cakes and a mug of tea, the woman spoke.

'I'm Bella, and Rob's my son. Folk think he's a bit soft in the head, so we keep ourselves to ourselves. We're quite self-sufficient here, so we don't need anybody. We don't get many visitors, but those that come get treated right, so you'll stay for supper, okay?'

Bella frowned as Rob started to laugh. It was more a whimpering animal noise than a real laugh. He pointed to Philip's rucksack.

'What's in it?' he squeaked.

'Not much,' shrugged Philip, 'Just stuff.'

'Don't mind him,' Bella blustered. 'He doesn't mean any harm. He's got a thing about rucksacks.'

'I got lots,' volunteered Rob. 'I'll show you.'

'Enough!' shouted Bella, 'Away out and feed the chickens.'

Rob scowled and shuffled out of the kitchen.

'So you don't get many visitors?' questioned Philip. 'You must feel isolated, but I suppose with television and stuff you keep up to date.'

Bella gave a hollow laugh. 'No reception for television,' she shrugged. 'Same goes for phones, and those mobile things. Mind, I don't hold with them anyway.'

Philip sat and watched as the woman prepared supper. He had already decided to wait around to see what he could steal. He would bide his time. He was in no hurry, especially now, when he knew for certain they didn't know who he was. A pity Rob hadn't been a girl. Now that might have been fun. For now he would have to be content with supper. His stomach growled with hunger as Bella clasped a shiny spoon in a pudgy hand and stirred at something simmering in a huge pan. The smell of it was wonderful. It made his jaws ache with longing. Bella sliced carrots, and potatoes and turnips, with a long pointy knife. Philip found himself breathing in time to the rhythmic chopping of the blade against the table, and was almost mesmerised by the flashing of the steel.

'You don't say much, do you?' questioned Bella. 'You've got family, I suppose? Somewhere to go, someone waiting for you, looking for you?'

Philip jumped at her voice. 'N-no,' he stammered, 'No family, no one at all.'

'Sometimes that's best,' smiled Bella and dropped the knife with a clatter. She nodded in the direction of the pan and licked her fat lips.

'Not long now,' she chuckled. 'Not long now.'

The three ate supper in a silence, broken only by the animal noises of Rob, as he greedily slurped down his meal, allowing the juice to trickle down his chin. The food was delicious. The meat was tender, the vegetables not overdone, and full of a flavour that Philip didn't recognise. He mopped up the gravy with great chunks of bread before pushing his plate away. He leaned back on his chair, his stomach full.

'Good, wasn't it?' Bella beamed at him. Philip nodded and Rob whimpered softly.

Perhaps a change of plan was called for, pondered Philip. This wasn't a bad place. He was sure he could con Bella into letting him stay for a while. He hadn't felt this good in a long time. It was comfortable and quiet, and if Bella's cooking was that good all the time—well, he was sure he could put up with Rob for a while. And then if he got restless, he could move on. He sighed. It was funny, but in an odd sort of a way he felt as if he had come home.

'You cook like that every day?' he asked. Bella nodded. 'Where do you get the meat? What was it—chicken, rabbit? Was it fresh? I didn't recognise it.'

Bella shook her head. 'We keep the freezer stocked,' she said. 'In the cellar.'

'I'll show him, ma,' said Rob, knocking over his chair in his haste to stand up.

Bella's guiding hand on his shoulder again, she led Philip out of the kitchen. 'I'll be there in a minute, you follow Rob. You can see for yourself.' She disappeared back into the house.

Rob led the way out into the garden, down some steps and into the cellar. It was cold and dark. Rob snapped on a light. At the back of the cellar was a large old chest freezer. On one side of it was a battered, stained kitchen table, and under it Philip noticed several rucksacks. Sitting on the table was a meat cleaver and a carving knife.

'You butcher your own meat?' he asked, fascinated by the shiny blade of the cleaver. He had never used a knife. He felt excitement mount in his chest and wetness appear on his forehead and palms. Rob stepped over to the freezer and opened up the top. He pointed inside.

'Look,' he said, grinning. 'Come and look.'

Two strides and Philip was standing beside Rob, his fingers only inches from the gleaming blade lying on the table. He reached for it, at the same time glancing into the deep freeze cabinet.

His heart missed several beats. His body was suddenly stiff and unable to move, as he stared at the contents of the cabinet. Four pairs of eyes looked sightlessly at him, from four disembodied human heads. Underneath were naked bloodied limbs, and pieces of fleshy carcasses. His tongue became wooden and dry in his mouth, as his mind tried to make sense of the horror he was seeing. He was conscious suddenly of someone screaming. The screaming went on and on, and he was vaguely aware of being held by his arms. A quick slice from the carving knife and the screaming stopped.

Bella wiped the knife on her apron and smiled at Rob.

'I hate it when they scream,' she said.

TOM

I BURST THOUGH the hospital door. The receptionist looked up.

'Tom Watkins?' she enquired, eyeing my uniform. 'Second door on the left, room number seven,' she smiled encouragingly. I walked, my heavy boots echoing along the corridor. Number seven, my brain said.

George Best and David Beckham wore number seven shirts.

Seven is the magic number.

Jesus spoke seven times on the cross.

There are seven hills in Rome.

There are seven primary colours.

Seven is the fourth prime number.

Seven is the atomic number of nitrogen.

Sibelius and Prokofiev both wrote seven symphonies.

'The just man falls seven times and rises again but the wicked stumbles to ruin.'

Enough! I told myself. I found my mother's room and walked in.

'Son.' She tried to smile. 'Tom! So they let you come. Bad journey?'

'No,' I lied. 'Plane from Basra to Brise Norton, and then train to Glasgow, and taxi here. It was okay.'

I stared at the face I knew so well, but didn't quite recognise. God! She looked so old, so lined, so ill. Pale. Almost transparent skin was stretched tightly over her protruding fleshless cheekbones. She stretched out a bony hand. I took it in mine. She managed a smile.

'Uniform's a bit mucky.'

'Yeah, I'll get it cleaned.'

I held my mother's hand. We both knew we didn't have long.

She spoke in a whispery voice.

'So how do you feel about this war? Pride, sense of right, honour?'

I looked at my dying mother and I knew I couldn't pretend. She was the seventh daughter of a seventh daughter, and she was Irish. She would know exactly what I was thinking, as she had always done.

'No Mam,' I managed to say. 'I don't feel pride. The thing I feel most is shame. I feel ashamed that I've contributed to the death of hundreds of people. I'm ashamed that I've witnessed the suffering of so many, and not helped them. And I'm ashamed that I've experienced the terrible brutality of war, and not spoken up against it.'

She squeezed my hand.

'That's my boy,' she murmured. Still talking like an academic. 'Maybe once this is all over you'll go back to uni and finish your degree? I'm proud of you, son. Sorry it had to end like this. But remember, you are special. You have a special gift. Use it wisely.' She closed her eyes and slept.

Gift? I asked myself. It's no gift. It's a curse.

As I sat beside her bed, I felt an overwhelming tiredness. When had I last slept, really slept? Even before I joined the army, it was pills that helped me sleep. My mind, my memory just wouldn't stop working.

I was five years old when my mother first took me to see a doctor.

'He's not right,' she whispered. 'He can remember everything. It's just not right.'

I thought everyone was like me. I could recount every conversation, every radio programme, everything that anyone had said to me, as long as I could remember. As I grew older I could summon up facts and figures, and things I had been told, at will. I saw more doctors, and more specialists. When I was fourteen I was told, 'You have an eidetic memory, Tom; not just that, though. You also have hyperthysmestic syndrome. This means that not only are you able to remember almost word for word everything that you have read and that you have been told, but also, you have an autobiographical memory. You are able, when asked, to recall events that you have personally experienced. You can be asked a date and be able to recall the events that occurred that day. You are able to say what the weather was like, what day of the week it was, and everything that happened. Your mental calendar occurs automatically and obsessively. You have little control over it. We can, though, help you to manage it. You are in good company. We think that Mozart, Saint-Saens, Jerry Lucas the American basketball star, and Norris McWhirter, one of the authors of *The Guinness Book of Records*, all had eidetic memory.'

I didn't want to have this memory thing. I just wanted to be like everyone else, but I couldn't. School was difficult. Teachers didn't exactly know what to do with me. The other children thought I was odd. They called me names.

'Tom the swot!' they would shout. 'Teacher's pet!' 'Weirdo.'

They didn't understand. Mam took me out of school and had me home-tutored until I was twelve. I had a go at secondary school, but that was worse. I was resented, for being able to recite the whole works of Shakespeare. It was thought unfair that I could recall all of what I read. I was really seen as some sort of cheat. Mam, worried for my mental health, again had me privately tutored. My father had long gone. Unable to stand the strain of having what he called 'an abnormal son', he left when I was ten.

When I was seventeen I was accepted at Cambridge University to study history. I didn't fit in at all, and after a year I joined the army. For the first time in my life I felt as though I belonged. No one knew about my memory, and if they did they couldn't have cared less. The only thing anyone bothered about in Iraq was following orders and staying alive.

I left Mam's bedside and went home to bed. I didn't pass an easy night. Nightmares of death and destruction disturbed my much needed sleep, depriving me of the few hours of oblivion that I craved. The next few days were themselves a nightmare. I watched my mother shrink bodily until she looked no more than a small child. She slowly lost her frail grip on life and fell into unconsciousness. The staff tiptoed in and out of her room, checking the morphine drip.

Sometimes they wiped her brow or made comforting gestures, by squeezing my shoulder or arm. They would urge me to 'go and have a break', or 'eat a sandwich, and drink some tea'. I would have none of it. I would stay with my mother until she passed on to—I didn't know what. Just as she saw me into my life, I would see her out of hers.

There was no fuss, no bother, no anything. She just stopped breathing and a nurse said, 'She's gone. She's at peace now.'

The next few days passed in a blur. There were friends and relatives to speak to. The house to sort out and the funeral to arrange. I left the organising of the service to the priest and undertakers. There were hymns and prayers. I couldn't sing or pray. My mind remembered and I couldn't control it.

> Give sorrow words. The grief that does not speak
> whispers the o'er-fraught heart and bids it break
> *Macbeth*

> O death where is thy sting?
> O grave where is thy victory?'
> *Corinthians*

> Our life dreams the Utopia
> Our death achieves the ideal
> *Victor Hugo*

> Our dead are never dead to us until we have
> forgotten them
> *George Elliot*

Quotations ran through my mind until I thought I would go mad.

I didn't cry, couldn't cry. I shook hands, ate sandwiches and drank whisky. People I knew and some I didn't, hugged me and patted my back.

'So sorry,' they whispered.

'What will you do now?' some asked.

I shrugged. 'Back to the army. I have to go up to Fort George. Perhaps back to Iraq?'

Iraq. Could I do it again? Could I again be part of the awfulness? It had started out so well. March 19th in the evening, 20 miles from the Iraqi border, we listened in silence to Lieutenant Colonel Tim Collins.

'We go to liberate not to conquer. We will not fly our flags in their country.

'I know men who have taken life needlessly in other conflicts. They live with the mark of Cain upon them.

'If you harm the regiment or its history by over enthusiasm in killing, or in cowardice, you know it is your family who will suffer.

'There may be people among us who will not see the end of this campaign. We will put them in their sleeping bags and send them back. There will be no time for sorrow. Let's leave Iraq a better place for us having been there. Our business now is North!'

My mind recited the whole speech as I sat on the train heading for Inverness. The train was crowded. I felt conspicuous and awkward in my uniform. Several people offered me sandwiches and drinks. Others tried to engage me in conversation. I concentrated on my meditation exercises, but couldn't fall asleep. My brain was full of images, of conversations, of sounds.

I saw an Iraqi child, whose skin and flesh was peeling from her body.

A comrade with no legs screaming for his mother.

A house on fire with a family inside unable to escape.

A soldier with no eyes clutching at my arms.

Men praying, to whom, they couldn't say.

My mouth was dry, my eyes stung, and my heart was thumping as I got off the train at Inverness.

'God bless, lad,' said an old woman.

'You take care now,' said someone else.

'Want a lift to the Fort, mate?' asked another.

'N-no thanks,' I managed to stammer. 'Things to do first.'

I started walking. I didn't know the direction and I didn't care.

I just kept walking, putting one foot in front of the other. Later I realised I was walking on grass. It was rough grass, not like a lawn. I didn't know where I was. I didn't know what time it was. I was very tired. I sat down and leant against some rocks. I slept.

I awoke with a start. It was still quite dark. I felt confused and agitated. Where was I? I turned. There was a plaque on the rocks I had rested on.

The Battle of Culloden was fought on this moor
16th April 1746
The graves of the gallant highlanders who fought for
Scotland and
Prince Charlie are marked by the names of their clan.

I was on Culloden Moor where the Jacobite army of Prince Charles Edward Stuart was defeated by the army of King George. My brain took over. Unable to stop it I remembered that the 27th Regiment of Infantry, a predecessor of the Royal Irish Regiment, fought on the side of the King. The Battle of Culloden proved the death-knell for Jacobinism and the rebellion to overthrow King George II.

I shut my eyes, but couldn't shut my ears. I heard shouting, and terrible screams. War cries of clansmen, intermingled with the discharging of guns and canisters of ball. Metal clanged against metal, as howling and yelling men fought hand to hand, bayonets against broadswords. I opened my eyes. Choking clouds of smoke veiled tri-cocked hats and long coats. Plaided clansmen ran to the sound of the piobaireachd as they were felled by grapeshot and sword.

'I've finally gone insane!' I screamed.

Suddenly all was quiet. Fingers of light started their way through the darkness. I listened to the silence and drank in its peace. And finally the tears fell. I let them fall freely, enjoying the feeling of release. I wept for my mother, and for a father I did not remember. I wept for lost and injured comrades. I wept for all the millions of soldiers, killed and maimed, in all the bloody conflicts and battles, from Culloden to Iraq. I wept for the futility of war, and its senselessness. Finally, I wept for myself, for my loneliness, my 'gift', and for my mortality. I stood and surveyed the moor. I smelt its freshness, its newness of morning. The tears left me.

Feeling strangely strong and elated, I knew what I had to do. I heaved my rucksack onto my back and headed back to Inverness and Fort George.

WALKING THE DOG

'**C**OME ON HAMISH, WALKIES!'
Hamish stood, head on one side, ears erect, and tail wagging furiously.

Emy paused and looked at her reflection in the hall mirror. She wasn't pleased with what she saw. Grey hairs spiralled through the dark brown and lines surrounded her green eyes. God, she looked fifty-eight, not forty-eight! She made a sarcastic face. 'Damn you, Laura! Damn you for being Rob's secretary, damn you for being younger and prettier than me!'

They set out for the dell just as they did every morning and evening. Emy was glad she had taken her father's advice.

'Get a dog, gel. Get a dog! It'll get you out, and you'll meet people. You never know what might become of a chance meeting.'

Emy found Hamish at the dog rescue centre. He had walked up to her, sat, and offered her a paw.

'He's a stray,' apologised the girl at the centre. 'Nobody wants him. He's not very bonny.'

'You and me,' whispered Emy. 'Nobody wants me, either.'

Hamish had a lopsided grin, a black beard and large pointy ears. His provenance was dubious, but Emy loved him with a vengeance.

The dell was unusually quiet. None of the normal dogs and walkers were to be seen. Hamish bounded ahead of Emy. As she rounded the path to the familiar larch tree, she saw him sitting in front of a boy. Emy approached warily, but not too concerned. After all, he was just a boy.

'Crackin' dog,' muttered the boy from beneath his black hoodie. 'What's his name?'

'Hamish,' replied Emy too brightly. 'What's yours?'

'I'm Adam. Dog's good.'

Hamish ran on and Emy started after him.

'I'll come with you!' shouted Adam. 'Is that okay?'

'Yes, fine,' answered Emy with a nervous laugh.

They walked on in silence. Hamish leaped beside Adam, retrieving the sticks that he threw.

'You come here every day?' asked Adam suddenly.

Emy stiffened. 'Yes, morning and evening. But not always,' she added.

'Well, maybe I'll see you again. Bye.' He grinned, and humming a familiar tune he ran off.

Emy was quite rattled. He looked okay, but you could never tell. What was he doing here in the dell? Why wasn't he at school? He was dirty and unkempt. She thought of her own two boys. Joe in Australia, having just left school for a gap year. And James in Glasgow working hard, she hoped, as a first-year medic. Oh, how she missed them! The house was empty and soulless without them, and the never-ending stream of friends they brought round.

He was there the next day, and the next, sitting by the larch tree. He looked different without his hood up; sort of vulnerable. His red hair stood on end and his face was covered with freckles. He didn't say much, but he whistled and hummed the same tune that Emy half remembered. He always played a bit with Hamish and then dashed off.

On the third day Emy decided she had to talk to Adam. Where did he live? Who were his parents? What was he doing in the dell?

He was there, crouched by the larch tree, and whistling that tune. Emy ran after Hamish. She caught her foot on a tree root and fell. A searing pain went through her ankle as she tried to struggle to her feet. Adam was at her side in an instant.

'Don't move. Sit still,' he commanded. 'Maybe broken. Let me have a look.'

Somehow he managed to half carry her home. He sat her on the settee and made her strong sweet tea. He found an elastic bandage in the bathroom cabinet, wound it round her ankle, and topped it with a bag of frozen peas he had taken from her freezer.

'For the swelling,' he explained. 'Don't think it's broke. Done a first aid course and got a sustificate,' he muttered .

'CERTIFICATE,' nagged Emy, unable to help herself.

'Okay, CERTIFICATE!' laughed Adam.

For the next few days Adam took Hamish out for his walks. He did a bit of shopping. Only milk and stuff for a lunchtime sandwich, but he did it willingly and wouldn't accept any payment.

'Nah!' he sniffed when Emy had offered him money. 'I like doing it.'

They got talking. Adam explained that he was an only child. His mother had died of cancer when he was twelve, and his father hadn't stopped drinking since. He had left school as soon as he was sixteen, three months before. 'Was no good at school,' shrugged Adam. 'Was in that special class, you know, for dim kids. Teacher kept shouting. She didn't like me. Mind you I didn't like her either.' He laughed. 'There was twenty-two of us and only one of her. I bet she was glad when I left.'

Adam was easy to talk to. Emy explained about Rob leaving her, and how empty the house seemed with both boys away.

'A younger woman,' she explained. 'Much prettier than me.'

Adam stared at her. 'Must be off his rocker,' he declared. He studied the photos of Joe and James. 'Lucky beggars,' he sighed, 'Having you for a mum.'

Even when her ankle was mended, Adam continued to take Hamish out.

'You've probably got things to do. Maybe people to see? I'll take the dog out. I 'avent got nuffin' else to do.'

Emy didn't tell Adam that she too had nothing else to do. Taking Hamish out morning and evening had given a structure to her day. She didn't dissuade Adam though. She had somehow come to feel responsible for him. She had never worked. Rob hadn't wanted her to. She had brought the boys up almost single-handedly. Rob worked away, often abroad. Sometimes she didn't see him for months. Still, it was a shock when he announced after twenty years of married life, he was leaving her.

'I've moved on,' he explained. 'Fiona understands me. You'll not want for anything. You'll be well provided for.'

He was true to his word. She had the house, enough money, but not much else. Friends at first rallied round, but when they realised Rob wasn't coming back they stopped phoning. After all, who wants a single, nearly fifty woman at a dinner party? Emy was lonely, and bored, but she didn't know what to do about it.

One morning Adam announced: 'What you need is a job!'

Emy was taken aback. 'A job? I'm not qualified for anything. What sort of job would I get?' she bristled. 'And, while we're at it, it's you who needs a job. You can't spend the rest of your life taking Hamish for walks! It's time you pestered them at the job centre. '

Adam coloured and lowered his head.

'Maybe,' he whispered. 'Maybe.'

Adam didn't show for the next three days. Emy scoured the dell. She listened for his familiar whistling and humming, but there was nothing. She was worried but didn't know what to do. She knew he lived on the Oxhill council estate, but not his exact address, and she realised to her dismay she didn't even know his last name.

On the fourth day she decided she had to do something. That evening, instead of the dell, she steered Hamish towards the high rise flats on the unfamiliar estate.

Oxhill was a sprawling mass of concrete. She had no idea where to go. She made for a row of shops. A group of youths were massed outside a chip shop. Hamish, as friendly as ever, bounded towards them and the tempting smell of chips. Emy swallowed hard, and with thumping heart walked up to the group.

'I'm looking for someone,' she stammered. 'Maybe you know him. His name's Adam.'

'And who wants to know?' sneered a voice from behind a scarf wound round a face.

'I'm his friend,' replied Emy boldly. 'I haven't seen him for a while and Hamish here is missing him.'

'Is that right?' said the scarf, and to Emy's surprise he bent down and tickled Hamish behind his ears. The rest of the gang followed suit, patting Hamish and feeding him some chips.

'D'ya mean that ginger kid with the drunk dad?' asked a pock faced lanky lad. Emy nodded. 'We'll tell him you want him. You should go home. S'not safe here, you wandering around. Some rough blokes about.'

Emy thanked them and left.

'Great dog missus!' shouted the scarf after her.

The next morning, just as she was about to go out with Hamish, the doorbell rang. She thought it was the postman but it was Adam.

'Hi,' he whispered. 'Remember me?'

He followed her into the living room.

'Took your advice,' he grinned. 'Got a job.'

'That's wonderful,' she beamed. 'Where? Doing what?'

He giggled. 'Dog walking. The kennels up the road were advertising in the job centre, so I phoned and they offered me the job. A month's trial. It's only part time for now; mornings and evenings. But it's what I want to do.'

Emy was ecstatic. 'That's fantastic! Well done, you! I'm so pleased.'

'Well yea, but like, there's something else,' spluttered Adam. 'It's you. I've found you a job an' all.'

Emy stared at him. What on earth did he mean? How could he have found her a job?

'It was in the Job Centre,' he babbled. 'I thought it was perfect for you. I felt, you know, sort of responsible for you, you bein' lonely an' all, and me goin' to be workin'. Look, I took you the what ya macallits?'

'Particulars?' volunteered Emy.

'That's them,' replied Adam, taking a leaflet from his pocket. He handed it to Emy. She straightened the crumpled sheet.

> OXHILL SECONDARY SCHOOL
> WANTED – CASSROOM ASSISTANT
> LEARNING SUPPORT UNIT
> Experience with boys 14 – 16 desirable

Emilie's heart leapt. It sounded great! Did she dare? Could she possibly apply?

'Tell you what,' laughed Adam. 'You give me a reference and I'll give you one!'

He grinned, fondled Hamish's ears, and hummed his favourite song.

'What is that song!' demanded Emy. 'It's been driving me nuts trying to remember.'

'Rolling Stones,' chuckled Adam. 'It's called WALKING THE DOG!'

A PRESENT FROM SANTA

T HE FRONT DOORBELL woke him. Jack had no idea of the time and his head hurt.

'All right, I'm coming,' he tried to shout as he staggered towards the persistent ringing. His throat was dry and raw, and all his voice could manage was a hoarse whisper. He opened the door, screwing up his eyes against the light, gasping at the freezing December wind that hit him.

'Well, are you going to keep us standing on the doorstep all day?' asked an irritated voice.

Jack opened the door wider and peered at the owner of the voice. There was something familiar about the face that was half hidden by a large hood.

'Bella!' he gasped. 'Auntie Bella! What are you doing here?'

'For goodness sake Jack, wake up and let us in out of the cold!' snapped the woman.

Jack stepped aside as Bella strode into the middle of the room, trailing a small child in one hand and a large suitcase in the other.

'Your phone's been cut off,' she complained, 'and there was no time to write; I couldn't get in touch. Bert's had a stroke and I have to look after him. I need you to take Jenny.

I'm at my wits' end, Jack. I can't cope! I didn't want her to go into care. She needs you now. She needs her Dad.'

Jack glanced down at the child who clung to Bella's hand.

'What? Oh no, I can't. How can I? I'm not ready. I need more time,' he gasped.

'You've had more than enough time, Jack,' replied Bella softly. 'It's been four years since Jean died and you've only seen Jenny a few times. It's not fair on her, Jack. What happened wasn't her fault. You're my nephew, and I wanted to help, but I didn't mean to take on Jenny for ever, only until you got yourself sorted.'

Jack forced himself to look at Jenny. He thought he would feel hatred for the child who had lived while his beloved Jean had died. But he didn't feel hatred. He felt nothing at all, just a great emptiness where his heart should have been. Jenny stared back at him with huge green eyes, her tiny face framed by a mane of red wavy hair. She didn't look like Jean. Jean's eyes had been hazel and her hair a beautiful soft brown. This child was a stranger. She didn't belong to him at all.

'I need to go, Jack,' whispered Bella. 'There's a bus back to Glasgow in half an hour. I have to collect Bert from the hospital this afternoon. They want as many patients as possible to go home for Christmas.'

'Christmas!' echoed Jack. 'I hadn't realised...'

'I'm sorry, but you'll just have to make the best of it. Get your phone fixed and we'll speak. There's things in here for tomorrow.' She pointed to the suitcase. She handed it to Jack and turned to Jenny. 'Now you be a good girl to your Dad and I'm sure Santa will come tonight. I'll come and see you soon.'

Letting go of Jenny's hand she stooped to kiss her, strode to the door and left.

Jenny stared first at the door, then at Jack.

'Are you my Dad?' a clear loud voice asked him.

Jack didn't answer, but turned away, sat in the armchair by the fireplace, and stared into the empty grate. On one side stood a coal scuttle with a dirty brass shovel and poker lying beside it. Jean had always kept them so clean and shiny. On the other side of the fireplace rested a huge basket filled with old newspapers. Four years before it had been full of the flowers he had taken to the hospital the night that Jenny was born; the night that Jean had died.

Jenny tugged at his sleeve. Her green eyes peered into his face.

'Auntie Bella says that my Mummy is in heaven. Can we go and see her?'

The rest of the day passed like a dream for Jack. He managed to make beans on toast for Jenny and set and light the fire. He watched her play with her doll on the mat in front of it. She sang softly, and whispered to it, as if it were a real baby. It grew dark, and Jenny fell asleep on the mat. Wearily Jack picked her up and carried her to his bedroom. He laid her on his bed and covered her with the quilt. Then he went back into the living room and poured himself yet another measure of whisky. He went towards his chair and noticed the fat body of Domino sitting in it. He didn't really like cats but Domino had been Jean's cat, and he hadn't had the heart to get rid of her.

'Where have you been hiding?' he whispered.

He shooed her out of his chair and took a gulp of whisky. Lost in thought, he jumped when Jenny touched his arm. In her hand she held one of her long socks.

'Where will I put it, Dad? Auntie Bella told me not to forget to hang it up.' Puzzled, he stared at her. 'For Santa,' she said urgently. 'He's coming tonight with presents, Auntie Bella said so.'

Through the alcoholic haze, realisation hit Jack. Of course! It was Christmas Eve. Jack looked at Jenny. Her eyes were full of excitement. Bella must have put presents in the suitcase. He would get them later.

'Hang it over the fire,' he slurred.

She was too small to reach the mantelpiece. He watched as she hung it over the handle of the flower basket, and then went back into the bedroom. Jack got up and reached for more whisky.

'I'll ring social services tomorrow,' he mumbled to himself. 'There's no way she can stay here.'

A while later, he took the few presents out of the suitcase, and placed them on the floor beside the hearth. He had nothing to put in the stocking. It remained empty. Eventually he fell into a dreamless sleep on the settee. The next thing he was aware of was his hand being pulled, and a voice shouting. At first he couldn't make out what was going on. It was still quite dark and the fire had all but gone out. He tried hard to understand what Jenny was saying. It was something about Santa and presents.

'I told you he would come!' she babbled. 'Look Dad, look what Santa bringed me for Christmas.'

Jack stumbled to the door and switched on the light. Jenny was kneeling in front of the fireplace. The pile of presents lay unopened beside her. Unsteadily, Jack walked towards her.

'Look Dad,' she whispered. 'Look what Santa bringed.'

Jack looked, and there, inside the flower basket, on top of the newspapers, lay Domino. Snuggling into her were five tiny furry bodies. Above Domino's head dangled the empty sock. Jack knelt down on the rug beside Jenny.

'Look,' she whispered. 'Santa bringed me baby pussies for Christmas.' She stroked one of the tiny kittens gently. 'Don't worry,' she whispered to Domino, 'Me and my Dad will take care of you and the babies. We will, Dad. You and me—we'll take care of them. Won't we?'

As Jack looked in bewilderment at Domino and the kittens, and then at Jenny, something inside him stirred. A long forgotten feeling welled up inside his chest. He took Jenny into his arms. For the first time since Jean died, tears fell freely as he buried his face into the mass of red hair.

'Oh yes, Jenny, we'll do that,' he managed to murmur. 'Together we'll take care of them—forever.'

THE WEDDING

BEN STARED AT THE E-MAIL in disbelief. This couldn't be right. It must be a joke. Wil couldn't do such a thing. But Wil had written:

'Please be my best man on 10th August and try to be happy for me. Please phone. Best love, Wil.'

Ben paced the hotel bedroom. They had an agreement—no commitments until their software company was well established. They were nearly there after working their socks off. Another year or so and—well, who knows—the proverbial world and oyster!

Ben punched the bed. What was Wil thinking of! They worked all over the world. This week it was Hong Kong, next week it would be New York. Business was booming. What the hell was Wil doing? He had thought that Wil was spending a huge amount of time in Scotland. But they were trying to get a foothold in local government, so Ben hadn't thought too much about it.

Ben was beside himself with rage. They had agreed at the outset—no commitments, no serious relationships till the business was a success.

The phone conversation was heated to say the least.

'I'm sorry, Ben, but I couldn't help myself. I love her and want to be with her. I met her last year, when I went home to stay with Mum and Dad for my knee operation,' reasoned Wil. 'Her name's Lucy. She lives next door to Mum and Dad. She's gorgeous, Ben! You'll love her too.'

No amount of talking could persuade Wil. He was marrying Lucy and that was that. He wanted Ben, as his only brother and twin, to be his best man, but if Ben was reluctant, then he would do without him.

A few months later Ben found himself in a taxi on the way to his parents' house. Even though Wil was going to destroy their lives, he had relented, and agreed to be best man.

As the taxi pulled up at his parents' house Ben tried to calm down.

After uni, it had been he who had persuaded Ben to start their own company, and had dragged him away from Scotland. Obviously, it had all been a huge mistake, and he would have to sort it out one way or another. As he opened his parents' front door he knew what to expect. Right away his mother squealed and hugged him, and his father wouldn't let go of his hand. Of course, the aunts were there—the twittering twins his father called his sisters, and boy, did they twitter!

'Isn't it wonderful!' exclaimed Aunt Dot. 'Just you wait. You'll be next!'

'Oh, it's just like a fairy tale!' gushed aunt Vera. 'The girl next door! Whoever would have thought it!'

After a while Ben thought he might vomit, so he excused himself saying he needed some air.

'Good idea,' nodded his father. 'Go down to the church. Lucy's helping with the flowers. She's dying to meet you. You can't miss her. She's the one with long red hair and the biggest smile you could imagine. Wil's gone to organise the music for the reception.'

Ben walked the familiar route to the church. He and Wil had trod the same road every Sunday when they were youngsters. Sunday school followed by a family Sunday lunch. How tedious it had been. Wil hadn't seemed to mind the endless family camaraderie, the same old jokes, the smothering 'familiness' of it all. When he thought back, he and Wil were really nothing like each other at all. Okay, so they were twins, but maybe that's where it stopped. It was a relief that Wil hadn't been called Bill or else they would have been Bill and Ben. Less like flower-pot men they couldn't be. If that's what Wil wants, thought Ben, then that's what he'll get. I'll not stand in his way of family Sundays and mediocre living. I'll see through the next two days and then I'm gone. I'll make a go of the business on my own, and when I'm ready, then who knows?

Ben stopped at the door of the church. The notice read:

ST MICHAEL'S PARISH CHURCH
MINISTER
THE REV M STEWART

He walked into the church and shivered. St Michael's always made him shiver. It was a combination of the cold stonework, the sheer size of the place, and the feeling of age. Centuries of people had worshipped here and it made him feel rather uncomfortable, as if he were an intruder. He had enjoyed the singing when he was a child, but he had never been what you would call a believer. He walked soundlessly on the red carpet, down the aisle past the choir stalls, towards the altar. The steps in front of the altar table were strewn with flowers. Bent over the flowers was a slight figure dressed in jeans and a T-shirt. Ben stopped, uncertain what to do. His father was wrong, he thought. Her hair wasn't red but a rich golden colour. He coughed slightly and she spun round.

'Oh, you didn't half startle me,' she grinned. 'Well, there's no mistaking *you*, is there? Two peas in a pod is what your mum said. But Wil said you were the good-looking one!' She grinned again, extending her hand to be shaken. Her hand was soft and warm but the handshake surprisingly firm. 'You okay?' she asked, opening wide huge green eyes. 'You look a bit pale.'

'Y-yes,' Ben lied. 'I'm fine. Th-the journey, you know, tiring—it's a long way, a long time.' What was wrong with him? Why was he twittering like the aunts? He couldn't think of anything sensible to say. Even if he could, he didn't think he could manage to say it. His jaw felt stiff and his tongue too big for his mouth. He felt queerly sick and his throat was dry. Maybe it was the flowers. Their scent was quite overpowering. Perhaps he was jetlagged. Whatever it was, he couldn't take his eyes off this beautiful and captivating woman.

'We need to talk. About tomorrow. You know, about your role—what you have to do.' She ran her fingers through her hair. 'Sorry, I'm looking such a mess, but I thought I would just lend a hand with the flowers. I scrub up quite well though. I'll look better tomorrow.' She beamed at him, and Ben's heart beat faster than it had ever done. He had never felt like this before. It was exciting but also frightening. He really needed to get away from the church, from the town, and from the whole family thing. He needed to get back to being himself.

The rest of the day passed in a haze of eating and drinking and chatter. The family all gathered at his parents' house for a pre-wedding get-together. Ben had never felt less like partying. The wine flowed, and the jokes grew sillier as the evening wore on. At last Ben was able to escape to bed. His sleep was fitful, and his dreams full of a girl with golden hair and an angelic smile.

Next morning, Wil and Ben were dressed in good time. They wore identical kilt outfits, and their mother pronounced them 'magnificent'.

'Hope the minister marries Lucy to the correct brother,' joked their father. 'I even have a hard job telling you apart!'

Wil gave Ben a self-conscious hug as they entered the church. 'Hope we can still be friends as well as brothers,' he whispered. Ben managed a small smile.

'I hope you'll be happy Wil. I really do.'

As Lucy walked down the aisle the guests rose. Ben kept his eyes firmly fixed on the carpet beneath his feet. He counted the squares and the triangles on the pattern. When the ceremony began he lifted his head and looked, beyond the minister, at the huge stained glass window. He stared at it as the ceremony progressed.

'I, William, take you, Lucy, to be my wife. In the presence of God and before this congregation. I promise to be a loving, faithful and loyal wife to you as long as we both shall live.'

Ben shivered as Wil spoke. It all sounded so final, so forever after. Then it was Lucy's turn. Her clear bell-like voice echoed through the building. He fumbled for the rings, and managed to hand them to the minister without dropping them.

Then it was all over, and they were outside the church in brilliant sunshine, for the photographs. They took forever.

'Now the bride with the bridesmaids. Now the groom with his parents,' commanded the photographer.

Then Ben heard at last, 'One last photo now. Let me have bride and groom, best man, bridesmaids and the minister.'

Ben sighed with relief. Soon he would be released and could go and get on with his life. He stood next to Lucy. He could almost feel her joy, and her delight. She turned and smiled at him. Ben also smiled. Then a sensation came over him. He felt a deep happiness—a tranquil, peaceful, but exciting feeling he had never experienced. He couldn't help himself as he grinned, past Lucy, at the smiling, beautiful, green eyed Rev Mary Stewart.

THE RUNAWAY

'ANY SPARE CHANGE, MISTER?'
The voice was young; the words whispered. He looked at her face as his hands fumbled in his jacket pocket for loose coins. Silently he placed them in the cardboard cup she held.

'Thanks mister.' She smiled at him, crinkling the edges of her green eyes. He stared, then walked away, his leather shoes clicking on the pavement. Through her lashes, she watched him stride off; an old guy in an Armani raincoat that flapped in the wind.

She was there the next day and the next, and the next. Always the same words.

'Any spare change, mister?' and he would stare at her and put money in her cup.

One day he said, 'Would you like a cup of coffee? There's a cafe round the corner.'

She nodded and followed him. She looked better after a cup of coffee and a bacon sandwich. 'Thanks mister,' she murmured.

'Richard, my name's Richard. What's yours?'

'Elizabeth,' she replied, removing her grubby woolly hat and shaking out a shock of blonde curls. 'After my mum, but everyone called her Liz.' He frowned slightly.

'I knew an Elizabeth a long time ago,' he whispered. 'I called her Lizzie.'

His sad eyes gazed at her.

'You can call me Lizzie if you like,' she suggested. He nodded.

'Last name?' he almost demanded.

'Pearson. I'm Elizabeth Pearson.'

'Family?' he enquired.

'None,' she replied. 'My mum died of breast cancer nine months ago. We lived with her boyfriend. He was a rat. He hit her and me and he tried to, to, well, you know, touch me. So I ran away.'

'Father?' Richard persisted. 'What of him?'

'Dunno,' she sighed. 'Never knew him. He ran off before I was born. Mum said he was trying to be a painter, an artist, but he was too interested in drugs to make a go of it. Her parents didn't approve of him. She used to laugh about being born to be a lady but gave it all up to run off with a no good artist, and ended up working in a pub.'

Over another cup of coffee Elizabeth talked and Richard listened.

She had nowhere to go, but the street was better than home. Some nights she was scared. Some nights she didn't care. There were plenty like her, living rough, some existing with drugs and cheap booze. There was no end of company, only she didn't want that sort of company, and she didn't know what to do next. She needed a job but she was only sixteen and didn't know how to go about it. She cried and huge tears coursed down her grubby face.

He took her shaking hand and spoke quietly. 'I've got somewhere you can stay, until you decide what to do. It's better than the street.'

'N-no,' she panicked. 'I couldn't. I don't, you know... I couldn't stay with you!'

'I don't mean that,' he soothed. 'It's a flat I rarely use these days. I have a house out of town.'

The next few days were like a fantasy. The flat was beautiful; full of shiny furniture and rich looking rugs. Richard bought her clothes and food and magazines. She watched television and played CDs and read. She told Richard she liked to draw and he brought her paper and pencils. She didn't dare go out. She thought perhaps she was in a dream and if she went outside she might wake up. She saw him every day. He would come sometimes at lunchtime, sometimes at seven, but would never stay all night. They talked about all sorts of things; music, television, and art, but never about him. Lizzie was curious about Richard. She longed to know about his home, his work, and his family. But he always side-stepped her questions and changed the subject.

'You have a talent,' he enthused, admiring her sketches. 'A real talent. You really need to go to Art College.'

'Yeah! And the band played,' she answered, laughing.

After a while she began to get restless. She needed to go outside, needed to see other people. She said to him, 'Can I go out?'

He said, 'Of course, you're not a prisoner, but I think we need to have a serious talk about your future. We'll talk tonight. I'll be back about seven.'

When he left she put on the fluffy pink jacket he had bought her and with her heart in her mouth, she ventured out and downstairs to the front door. The air felt fresh and clean and she drank in its crispness. She took a few steps along the pavement, and then, panicking, turned back. She didn't want to lose the feeling of safety she had in the flat. She didn't want to lose the cosy warmth she had got used to. She ran upstairs and back inside. She wondered what Richard had meant about her future. Maybe he could find her a job. She thought he must have a good job to be able to afford the flat and all the stuff he bought. Maybe he was a lawyer or accountant. She decided when he came back she would ask him about a job. Maybe there was something she could do in his office. She was good at making tea, and school had taught her a little bit about computers. She sat on the settee and waited.

He didn't come that night, nor the next day. She worried. What had happened? What if he was fed up with her, wanted rid of her?

She couldn't stay in the flat without him. It wouldn't be right. But where would she go, what would she do? The thought of the streets was sickening. The thought of her mother's boyfriend was worse. 'Oh mum,' she cried, 'why did you have to die?'

She lost track of time, sitting on the settee, waiting for Richard to come. Worrying about him, she realised just how fond of him she had become. Then came a knock on the door.

'It's Richard!' she cried as she hurried to turn the key. But it wasn't Richard. She opened the door to a plump middle-aged woman who peered at her through thick lenses.

'I'm Isobel,' she said breathlessly. 'Richard sent me, but it's okay, he's going to be fine. He just wants to see you.'

Elizabeth gazed, puzzled at the woman. 'What? What do you mean?' she stammered. 'What's happened?'

Isobel sighed. 'Sorry,' she apologised. 'I thought you knew. Richard is in the hospital. He's had a heart attack, but he's going to be fine. He sent me to get you. I've got a car waiting outside.'

'Oh,' was all Elizabeth managed to utter. She didn't know what to think or what to say.

'Yes, yes,' carried on Isobel. 'Come on, we'd better not keep the good man waiting. What's your name? I don't think Richard told me.'

'It's Elizabeth, Elizabeth Pearson,' she answered, 'but Richard calls me Lizzie.'

'Ah, thought as much. Thought you must be a relative,' smiled Isobel with obvious relief.

Elizabeth was puzzled. She shook her head at Isobel. 'What do you mean?'

Isobel sighed. 'My boss, Sir Richard Pearson,' she said with some impatience. 'The man who owns this flat, the one who wants to see you pronto. His daughter was called Lizzie, but sixteen years ago she ran away with a no good artist.'

A LOST CAUSE

'THE DOCTOR WILL BE HERE soon, Sheila. He'll give you something to make you more comfortable. He's a new doctor, one we haven't had before. His name is Clutterbuck. Dr Clutterbuck.'

She frowned. She had heard that name before. But where, she thought? She did a lot of thinking nowadays. There wasn't anything much else to do. Her body had given up. Well, what did she expect? The cancer was widespread, and they had told her no more could be done. She was more than ready for the next stage, whatever it might be. She said the name over in her head: Clutterbuck, such an unusual name. Of course! How could she have forgotten Vincent Clutterbuck. So long ago. How long? Must be fifty years at least.

'And this,' announced the headmaster as he opened the classroom door with a flourish, 'is your class.'

The class, as one, stood to attention.

'Good morning class,' boomed the head.

'Good morning Mr Harwood,' chorused the children.

'This is your new teacher, Miss Mason. What do you say?'

'Good morning Miss Mason,' they voiced in unison.

'Good morning children,' she managed to reply.

Truth be told, she was terrified. This was her first job, her first class since graduating, and she was appalled at how she felt. Forty pairs of ten-year-old eyes stared at her. Some were hostile, some were amused, and some looked as frightened as she was. It suddenly hit her, that she was only twelve years older than these children.

'So,' continued the head, 'there are some very good pupils here, and unfortunately, some who will never make the grade. You will just have to do what you can with them.'

With that, he left the room. She looked round with sinking heart. The old desks were in rows, reminiscent of the 1940's. The only things adorning the walls were times-tables posters, and a map of the world. She certainly had lots of work to do.

'Right children,' she said in a bright voice. 'Let's get to know one another. Will everyone please come and sit in front of my desk so we can talk.'

'You mean on the floor, like infants?' asked one.

'We've never done that 'afore,' ventured another.

'There's not enough room,' protested someone.

With patience and persistence, she got them to move the desks back, and make room for them to sit informally in front of her. From there she started to get to know the children in her class. With a lot of persuasion, one by one, they told her their names, a bit about themselves and their family, and what they wanted from school. Their answers were mostly predictable, until she came to Vincent.

'I'm Vincent,' he announced. 'I can't read, and I'm a lost cause.'

She smiled at his assurance. 'What makes you say that?' she asked.

'Oh, all the teachers say so,' he said with a cheeky grin. 'I'm just not able to learn to read, so I'm a lost cause.'

During the next few weeks she sorted out the classroom. She got the children to paint pictures, and she pinned them to the walls. She organised the reading, so that not every child was trying to read the same book. It worked, apart from Vincent who would not, or as she discovered, could not read.

'I told ya.' His cheeky grin was infectious. 'I can't read.' His non-reading didn't seem to worry him at all. He was, however, as Vera discovered, far from being unintelligent. His number work was impressive, and his ability to remember facts and figures, remarkable.

Lost cause or not, she couldn't give up on Vincent, and she sought the help of the other teachers in the school. Everyone had an opinion.

'Look and say, that's the way forward,' said one.

'Syllabification!' proclaimed another.

'No no, a child like that needs phonics, or maybe word attack skills,' intimated someone else.

'Don't waste too much time on him,' cautioned the Head. 'Dysfunctional family, fly by nighters, if you get my meaning. This is Vincent's fifth school. Don't suppose he'll be here for long.'

She was bewildered, and at a loss to know how to help Vincent, but she was determined not to give up.

One Monday morning Vincent didn't appear in class. Apparently, on the Saturday he had been bitten by an adder, and was in hospital. He wasn't seriously hurt. On his return to school on the Thursday, he was treated as something of a hero. He needed no encouragement to tell everyone what had happened to him. Sheila went to the school library and found a book about snakes, and gave it to Vincent. She knew he wouldn't be able to read it, but thought he might like the pictures. The next day at the end of school, Vincent stayed behind. He asked her to read to him out of the snake book she had given him. Every day for the next two weeks, Vincent stayed behind after school. She read to him, and then he started to read alongside her.

Sheila asked him if there was someone at home who could help him.

'Only Michy,' he explained.

'Michy?'

'Yeah, Michelle, my big sister. She's twenty-four. She sometimes helps me.'

Vincent made great strides with his reading. After a few weeks he could read back to her the passages she had read to him. At first she thought he was memorising, but one momentous day he volunteered to read out loud, from a group reading book. He managed perfectly. Vincent didn't need phonics, or syllabification, in order to learn to read. What he did need was a sufficient interest in books, someone to read to him, and time.

Next term Sheila took on a huge project. The music teacher and herself had the idea of producing a musical, for a concert for the end of the school year.

This was quite outwith the norm for the school, but they managed to persuade the deputy head, who in turn persuaded the head, that they should be allowed to give it a go. *Oliver*, the musical, had just been a huge success in the West End, and they thought it would be perfect for the children in their school, to perform. They asked for volunteers from the top two years. All, without exception, signed up. Their plan was to have all the children singing, with narration between the scenes, but they soon realised they would need a few soloists to carry the story.

They auditioned for the main parts and were astounded to find that Vincent had a fantastic voice and would make a great Oliver. Rehearsals went on for weeks. The children were at fever pitch as the great day drew near. Backdrops were painted, costumes were made and tickets were sold out.

The night of the concert arrived. The applause of the audience at the end of Oliver was amazing. The children had excelled themselves and everyone was ecstatic. Sheila found Vincent in the changing room.

'Congratulations!' she gushed. 'You were magnificent. I bet your mum and dad are proud of you.' Vincent looked at her with a wistful gaze.

'Nah, they didn't come. They've gone to the pub. Michy's here though.'

Sheila walked with him to the front door. Michy stood waiting, her blonde hair framing an elfin face remarkably like Vincent's. She looked up and grinned at the small boy.

'You were great. Just great,' she whispered as she hugged him. She looked at Sheila with eyes that glistened with tears. 'You're great an' all Miss,' she stammered.

End of term was looming and the tidying up and paperwork took its time. The last day of term found her class bouncy and full of excitement. They were off to 'big school' after the holidays. That morning Vincent was absent. Sheila was disappointed. Vincent's friend came to her and gave her an envelope.

'Vincent's gone,' he explained. 'Family's done a moonlight. Think his dad owed money, so they've scarpered.'

The envelope contained a card with a picture of a snake drawn on the front. The card said:

THANKS FOR EVERYTHING LOVE VINCENT
AND MICHY (HIS MUM)
XXXXXXXXXXX

'Doctor Clutterbuck's here, Sheila,' someone said brightly.

She was shaken out of her reminiscence. She looked at the doctor, smiled, and held out a hand to be shaken. The good-looking face, the blond hair, the green eyes, and the cheeky grin were familiar, even after so long.

'Is your name Vincent?' she asked.

He shook his head. 'No, I'm called Oliver, but my dad is Vincent.'

'Is he a doctor too?' she had to ask.

'No, he's an accountant, but he's just retired.'

'Please tell him,' she smiled, 'that Miss Mason says thank you for the card, and that she never did think he was a lost cause.'

A BABY BROTHER

'**I WAS JUST WONDERING,**' said Grandad, poking his head round the bedroom door, 'if you would like to come to the park with me.'

Emily nodded and jumped off her bed. She had been hugging Big Ted and sucking her thumb. She wasn't supposed to suck her thumb now that she was seven, but she didn't care. It made her feel better.

'Mum and Grandma are going to bath James,' he said. 'I thought you and I could do with some fresh air.'

Emily put on her red jacket and her blue boots, and tucked her long brown hair under a green woolly hat. 'Good idea,' smiled Grandad. 'It might rain.'

A wailing noise started as they left the house.

'Babies do that,' smiled Grandad, raising his eyebrows. 'They do that a lot.'

Emily said nothing. She held Grandad's hand tightly as they walked towards the park.

'Grandma thought you might have wanted to help to bath James,' chuckled Grandad. 'But I thought differently.'

Emily smiled. It wasn't a real smile. It was a pretend smile. She had done a lot of pretending lately. Ever since Mum and Dad had come home from the hospital with James, she had pretended. She had pretended that he was lovely. He wasn't. He was red and wrinkly, and she thought he looked a bit like a monkey. She had held him, and kissed him, and said she loved him. She didn't. He was wriggly and noisy. He was in the way. He was a pest and she didn't want him in her house.

She didn't want a brother, or a sister. She had been what everyone called 'an only child' for seven years and she had liked it.

It was her friend Sara who had started it.

'Your mum and dad won't want you after the baby is born,' she crowed. 'Mums and Dads always love the baby best. You'll be ignored. They haven't got enough love for you and the baby.' Of course Sara would know, having three younger sisters.

Emily had tried her best to forget about the coming baby, but it was difficult. Mum kept taking her out to baby shops to buy clothes and nappies and stuff. All the talk in the house was about the baby. Dad spent all his spare time decorating a room for the baby. There was wallpaper covered with giraffes, curtains with giraffes, and even giraffes on the cot blanket and on the rug.

'Isn't it lovely?' said mum dreamily. Emily said nothing. She didn't like the giraffes and she didn't like the yellow paint round the door and window. Dad never had any time to play with her like he used to. Sometimes Mum didn't even read her a bedtime story.

'Sorry love, I feel a bit sick. It's the baby, you know. Reading makes me feel worse.'

She felt a bit angry but mostly she felt sad and empty inside.

After James was born the house was always full of visitors, bringing presents for James, and cooing into the Moses basket. Most of them brought her presents too. 'Big sister presents' they all called them. But she didn't want big sister presents. She didn't want to be a big sister.

She watched as Mum and Grandma fussed over James and sang to him, and fed him, and cuddled him, and spoke about him all the time. She wanted to go back to the days before James, when she had Mum and Dad all to herself.

Sara was right, thought Emily. They don't love me now, they only love James.

At the park Grandad pushed Emily on a swing, and caught her as she slid off the chute. He produced slices of bread from his pocket and they sat on a bench and fed some cooing pigeons.

'Babies take a lot of looking after,' said Grandad. Emily nodded.

'They need to have everything done for them at first,' he continued. 'But they do grow.' Emily nodded again, as two fat tears trickled down her cheeks. 'Come on,' said Grandad, jumping up. 'Let's go and have a Pizza and a drink.' Pizza and fizzy drinks were really only allowed on special occasions, but Grandad said it wasn't very often just the two of them went out, so it counted as a special occasion. At the Pizza cafe there was a clown entertaining the children. He was twisting balloons into all sorts of animal shapes. Emily thought he was clever and clapped when he made one long orange balloon into a lion and gave it to the boy sitting at the next table. Then he took a very long brown spotty balloon and twisted it this way and that. It wasn't obvious, at first, what he was making. Then he turned it the right way up, strode over to Emily and handed it to her. She took it and automatically said, 'Thank you.' It was a giraffe.

'I'll look after that, if you like,' whispered Grandad, tucking it inside his jacket. 'I like balloons,' confided Grandad. 'I like the way they start off being small and then when you blow into them they get bigger and bigger. The more you blow, the bigger they get. Did you know that we've all got a balloon inside us?' Emily shook her head and looked at Grandad with wide eyes. 'Oh yes, we've all got one,' continued Grandad. 'It's a sort of love balloon. The more love you need and feel the bigger the balloon gets and more love is stored inside it.'

Emily looked doubtful. 'What happens when the balloon is full?' she asked.

'That can never happen,' explained Grandad. 'There is always room for more love inside us, always enough room in your balloon to love another person.'

Emily thought for a moment. 'So Mum and Dad can love James *and* me?' she whispered.

'Of course they can, and they do,' smiled Grandad. 'They love you both very, very much.'

Emily was quiet on the way home. When they reached the front door she turned to Grandad and whispered, 'Please can I have the balloon?'

He took it from the inside of his jacket and handed it to her. She took it gently and followed Grandad into the house. She stopped outside James's bedroom where she could hear mum and grandma talking, and James still wailing. She turned to Grandad who smiled encouragingly at her. Swallowing hard, she pushed open the door and strode into the room. Mum and Grandma turned and looked at her. A wailing James squirmed in Mum's arms. Emily held up the balloon towards James. He looked at it, and stopped the noise immediately.

'It's a giraffe,' she murmured. 'It's for you.'

James opened his eyes wide, and gave her his first ever smile.

A HAPPY BIRTHDAY

VERA STRUGGLED TO HER FEET and, holding tight to the walking frame, made slow progress to the front door. She thought she had heard the postman, and sure enough, on the mat lay an envelope. She hoped it would be a birthday card. It looked like one. The next trick was picking it up. The pickup stick was in the basket on the front of the walking frame. It was a tiresome procedure, unfolding it and then manoeuvring it under the envelope, but after a few false starts she managed to get a grip on the envelope and lift it off the floor. Exhausted by the time she made it back to her chair, she sat getting her breath back. Sometimes the postman made a mistake and put mail for number six through her door; but no, this was definitely for her. Her name and her address were on the front of the envelope. She opened it carefully and removed the card. A picture of a rose stared at her. Inside were the words HAPPY BIRTHDAY, and underneath some scribbly writing. She put on her reading glasses and peered at the tiny letters.

We'll be round to see you at tea time on your birthday and will bring your present love Jamie and Laura xxxxx.

Well, she mused. That's a turn up. You don't see a grandchild for months and then two turn up at once! She chuckled to herself. Perhaps Jen will come too. She usually popped in on a Wednesday on her way home from work. A present, eh! Vera felt intrigued. What could it be? She hadn't had a present from the twins for years. They didn't really do birthdays anymore. There was a time, she remembered, when birthdays were big affairs—when the grandchildren were small, and she and Dan would drive to Jen's. There would be sparkling wine, fancy nibbles and cake and they all took copious photos. But it all changed when Jamie and Laura were in their mid-teens.

'It's just that they're growing up, mum,' explained Jen briskly. 'They don't want family parties anymore.' So she stopped seeing them on their birthday and sent a card and a cheque instead. She knew they received them all right. Her bank statement confirmed that. It just would have been nice to get some sort of thank you. She still got a card and a present from Jen on her birthday, usually chocolates or flowers delivered to the door.

As if on cue the doorbell rang. When she finally managed to make her way to the door she was greeted by a bored looking delivery boy. 'Flowers,' he mumbled before thrusting them into her arms. The card said,

> *Happy birthday mum*
> *love Jen & Alex xx*

Vera made herself a cup of tea, sat at the kitchen table and surveyed the flowers Jen had sent. They were lovely.

Pink and white roses nestled among greenery and gypsophla. Dan had been fond of roses. Two large tears escaped and fell down her cheeks. Annoyed, she rubbed them away. There's no point in that, she told herself. Feeling sorry for yourself gets you nowhere.

Things would have been different if it hadn't been for the stroke. She was just about coping with Dan's death from cancer when she was struck down. The doctors assured her that she would regain most of her mobility, but at the moment it was difficult. Maria, her carer, came in every morning to help her wash and dress, and once a week two cheerful girls came and did all the cleaning. Thank goodness Dan had left her well provided. She could afford to pay for her help. It was the shopping though that was the worst. Jen did help, but she was always busy, and Vera didn't want to become a nuisance. Instead she made do with the shopping service provided by the council. Every Monday, someone came and did her shopping at the local corner shop. It was just basic stuff—milk and bread and eggs and so on, and every so often Jen stocked her up with more exotic things from Marks and Spencer. She was grateful, but it wasn't the same as choosing and buying for yourself.

Dan had always laughed that her hobby was shopping, and that she should join shopaholics anonymous. She smiled at his photograph on the window sill. His handsome face stared back at her. The photo had been taken eighteen years ago, just before the twins were born. It had been an exciting time, Vera remembered. Jen had been keen to continue with her career as a lawyer, and when Vera was given the chance of early retirement, she hadn't needed a second bidding. The opportunity to look after the twins, to be part of their lives, was a dream come true. How she loved it when they were little. She took them everywhere; to the zoo, museum, botanic gardens and parks. Then later there were swimming lessons, gymnastics and morning nursery. All too soon they had on school uniforms and were into the daily routine of after school activities and homework. She was still needed then, but not so much. As they grew she was needed less and less, until they were suddenly all grown up, and able to look after themselves.

Dan, of course, had worked until well passed retirement age. He used to joke that it wouldn't do to have two idle people in the house enjoying themselves! Now she was on her own in the house, idle yes, enjoying herself, no. She missed Dan more than she could express. She missed the friends they used to have. One or two still kept in touch, but after Dan died, the invitations slowly dried up. It was difficult being a singleton amongst all the couples they socialised with. They used to have good times with friends, especially Jack and Molly Sutherland. Jack had been a friend of Vera's from school. She always had a soft spot for Jack. Dan had always jokingly called him 'Vera's old boyfriend'. They had dinner parties together and theatre outings, holiday weekends at hotels and picnics. For quite a few years they had fun. But things change. Keeping in touch just becomes too difficult. Jack and Molly moved to Spain. At first they wrote and phoned each other. They were invited to Spain of course, but Vera was always too busy with the children to get away. Then the letters dwindled to a note at Christmas time. Last Christmas there hadn't even been a card.

The doorbell woke Vera from her dreaming. She was greeted at the door by two smiling faces.

'Happy Birthday Gran,' they chorused, and giggling, they manoeuvred themselves into the flat, carrying an enormous cardboard box.

'What's all this then?' laughed Vera. 'Hope it's not a kitten or a budgie.'

'No, nothing like that,' grinned Polly.

'You wait in the living room, Gran, and we'll sort the surprise out in the dining room, then you can come in.' Peter chuckled like he used to.

Sitting on the settee, Vera fretted. She couldn't begin to think what on earth was in the box. She hoped the twins hadn't spent a lot of money on whatever it was. They needed all their money. They were going to university after the summer, and that wasn't cheap. After what seemed an eternity Polly and Peter came to fetch her.

'Okay Gran, you can come in now,' they chorused. 'Now close your eyes, and don't open them till we tell you.'

Vera made slow progress to the dining room. Then, at last, she stood at the door, eyes squeezed shut.

'Okay, now you can look,' squealed Polly, as she began to sing 'Happy birthday'.

Vera stared in amazement at what was on the table. She knew what it was. She had never seen one up close, had never laid hands on one, but she *knew*. It was a computer. She stood, speechless.

'Well, what do you think?' asked Peter. 'Looks quite neat in here, doesn't it?'

'It's not new,' Polly hastened to add. 'It's our old one. We've been saving the money you give us for Christmas and birthdays. We've bought laptops to take with us to uni.'

'W-well, it's very thoughtful of you,' began Vera. 'But what do I do with it?'

Polly and Peter looked at each other and raised their eyebrows.

'Well, you know how you like shopping but can't get to the shops?' explained Peter. 'Well, with the computer you can go shopping. Groceries, clothes, curtains or anything at all. You can browse it all on-line, buy it, and it'll be delivered right to your door.'

'And,' continued Polly, 'you can E-mail people. It's a bit like letter writing, only quicker. You can E-mail us when we're at uni and we'll E-mail you back and keep you up to date with what we're doing.'

'Also,' enthused Peter, 'when you're up to it, you can join clubs and groups and chat to people all on-line, and you can even play bingo.'

'This is all very well,' sighed Vera, shaking her head. 'It's so very good of you, but how on earth am I going to learn how to do all the things you've spoken about? I don't know the first thing about any of it.'

'Ah well, that's where mum came in useful,' grinned Polly. 'She put us in touch with an old friend of yours. We've spoken to him. He's a bit of a whizz on the computer. He said he would be delighted to come and see you and give you lessons. His wife died last year. He used to live in Spain, but now he's home for good. You must remember him, Gran? His name's Jack Sutherland.'

BLACKPOOL

JEAN SNAPPED HER SUITCASE SHUT. There, she was done. Everything was sorted, and she was ready to go. The doorbell rang. Her neighbour, Mike, stood grinning.

'Ready?' he asked

'Yes thanks,' she replied.

They drove to the airport in relative silence.

'So good of you to give me a lift again,' she ventured.

'Not at all,' beamed Mike. 'So glad to be of service. So it's the South of France this year?'

'Yes,' confirmed Jean. 'Nice.'

'Thinking of going on holiday myself,' he ventured. 'Not sure where to go, though. I don't really like flying. Not like you,' he chortled. 'You must have clocked up a fair few flying hours.'

Jean smiled, but said nothing. He dropped her off at departures.

'Have a good holiday. Come back with a suntan.' He waved and was gone.

Mike was a good neighbour. Since Reg died he had become a good friend. He did odd jobs around her house, and cut the grass. He declined any sort of payment, saying that he was glad to be useful.

'I expect he's lonely,' suggested Sylvia, her daughter. 'You know, what with him being on his own, and his son and family miles away.'

Jean agreed. Nevertheless it was a good feeling to have someone like Mike near at hand.

Jean wandered into the airport. There was a good bookshop upstairs. She took the lift up. Her case was too big for the escalator. She bought three books and then went for a cup of coffee. An hour later she exited the airport and hopped into a taxi.

'The bus station, in town please,' she instructed the driver.

'You bin' somewhere nice?' he nosied.

'Yes, thank you,' answered Jean abruptly.

'Well,' beamed the coach driver, when she entered the coach. 'We thought you weren't going to make it this year, Mrs Davidson. Welcome aboard the Blackpool express.'

Jean found her seat and tried to relax. She did enjoy her holidays. When she first mentioned she might holiday in Blackpool, her friends and family didn't like the idea at all. They thought it was downmarket.

'Full of kiss-me-quick hats, and candy floss,' declared her daughter. 'You can't possibly be serious about holidaying there!'

'Not terribly middle class, is it?' sniffed Molly her sister. 'It's all hen nights and drunkenness, from what I've read.'

'I hear Blackpool is full of drug addicts,' asserted a neighbour. 'Wouldn't catch *me* going there.'

But Jean had seen a television programme about Blackpool and thought it looked like fun. There seemed to be lots to see and do, and she had been determined to go and experience it all for herself. So she had thought up a plan. For the last few years she had travelled all over the world. Not really 'travelled' the world, but sort of virtually. Every year she sent for lots of travel brochures and decided on a holiday destination. She read up about the place and then told all her friends and family about it. One year it was Athens, another Rome. One year she even ventured as far as New York. But it was all only make-believe. She only did it to please other people. The fact was that she loved Blackpool. She adored its beach, the tower, the amusement park, the aquarium, and even, dare she say it, the Bingo sessions. She enjoyed meeting her favourite celebrities in Louis Tussauds. She marvelled at the acts in the Tower circus, and took great pleasure in strolling in the park and the model village. She had been going to Blackpool every year since Reg had died. Maybe it was silly to pretend about going abroad, but it seemed to please everyone, so she kept doing it.

'I don't do postcards and souvenirs,' she had explained. 'If you need me you can reach me by mobile.' Sylvia, her daughter, seemed relieved when Jean said she wanted to holiday alone.

'No, no, you need to holiday with Mike and the children,' she had replied, when Sylvia, somewhat tentatively, suggested the year that Reg had died that she might want to go to Majorca with them. 'You need time with your family. I need my own space too. Perhaps we could do a weekend or something together, later.'

As the coach neared Blackpool, Sylvia's excitement grew. She stayed at the same hotel each year. It was small, but very comfortable, and the people were very friendly. She was greeted like an old friend, and made to feel right at home. Her room was large, and a balcony overlooked the seafront. Sylvia sighed with contentment and prepared to enjoy two weeks doing all the things she relished.

She was careful, though, not to become too friendly with other guests. She had heard people exchanging addresses, and promising to visit when they got home. That would never do. She was polite, but not overfriendly. She didn't care if people thought she was snobbish and standoffish. She couldn't take the risk of becoming too involved with other folk. If she did, she knew that sooner or later the cat would be out of the bag, and her Blackpool holidays would be over. She couldn't let that happen.

The next few days were wonderful. She slapped on the sun screen, bought a big floppy hat, and sat on the beach. She admired the expertise of the jet skiers, and smiled at the ice cream cries of the children. She giggled quietly at the young girls as they posed and postured themselves in the briefest of bikinis, while boys, with their tanned and muscled bodies, strolled admiringly amongst them.

Before the evening meal she sat on the balcony watching the waves gently lapping the sand while she sipped a fruity glass of Chardonnay. The hotel provided great meals. The waiters tried to get her to sit with other people, but she politely refused. Every night, after eating, she took a stroll along the sea front, delighting in the cool breeze. Later a bath and a book beckoned, after which Jean slept like the proverbial baby.

It was on the sixth day of her holiday that things started to go wrong. First the weather took a turn for the worse. The beaches lay empty and the indoor attractions became unbearably full. The shower in her room developed a leak, and she was transferred to a much smaller room with no view. The hotel people were sorry, but they were full and there weren't any other unoccupied rooms available.

Jean fretted. The thought of wandering about in the rain didn't appeal. Neither did squashing in with the crowds at the aquarium or zoo. Perhaps she would just stay in the dismal room and read. Maria, the chambermaid, had other ideas.

'You not to sit here lonely,' she scolded in her Spanish accent. 'This not good room. You go out and meet people. The ballroom in the Tower. There is music and dancing in afternoon. You go and enjoy.'

She had always avoided the tea dances in the Tower. She had never relished the prospect of being asked to dance and having to make polite conversation.

'Who am I kidding?' she asked her reflection in the tiny bathroom mirror. 'Who would want to dance with an old bird like me?' Still, partly to please Maria, and partly because she was curious about the tea dance, she combed her hair, applied a bit of lipstick, put on her best dress and set off for the Tower. Outside the notice read:

Romantic Tea Dance
Accompanied by the music of the
Mighty Wurlitzer Organ

Inside, the ballroom was packed. Jean found a seat in a relatively quiet corner, and watched the dancing. She enjoyed the music and found herself humming along to familiar tunes. After about half an hour, tea, sandwiches and cakes were served. Jean almost left then, but feeling rather peckish, decided to stay. There was an empty seat beside her, but to her relief no one seemed to want it. She was tucking into a second sandwich when she heard a voice enquire: 'Is this seat taken?' The voice sounded familiar. She turned and gasped. Grinning down at her was Mike, her neighbour!

'A long way from France, aren't you? Would you care to dance?' Still smiling, he led an astonished Jean onto the dance floor. 'I don't like going abroad either,' he confided, grinning at her worried face. 'Blackpool suits me much better. But please don't tell anyone I said so.'

THE FOLK NEXT DOOR

S AM WATCHED WITH DISMAY as the removal van was slowly emptied. Half of the contents of the van seemed to be toys. 'Good grief, how many children do they have?' he asked himself. Over a cup of tea he fretted. Next door had been empty now for two years, ever since old Mrs Peters had died. He was used to peace and quiet, he liked peace and quiet, he needed peace and quiet. What he didn't need was a hoard of screaming kids rampaging about in the back garden next to his, probably shouting and bawling in the street out in the front. They would have footballs, no doubt, and be kicking them off his car. Oh, but they wouldn't get away with it. No! He would watch them like a hawk. At the first sign of trouble, he would complain to the parents, and if they wouldn't do anything, then it would be the police. He wasn't about to let his quiet, calm street be turned into some hooligans' playground.

Sam had lived in Maple Street for fifty years. The day after he and Muriel got married, they moved in. There was no money for a honeymoon in those days. In those days folk worked for everything they had. There was nothing handed on a plate back then. There were no free hand-outs from the state. When Hazel was born, Muriel stayed at home and looked after her. That's how it should be. He nodded to himself. Turned out all right, did Hazel. She did them proud, going to university and becoming an accountant. Of course it was a blow, when she and her husband emigrated. They had been home a couple of times—the first time when Muriel died, and then again after their first son was born. He hadn't even seen his second grandson. They kept on at him to visit, but Australia was so far away.

Sam's dreaming was disturbed by a baby crying. He looked out of the kitchen window. There in the long grass of next door's garden was a pram. A small boy was rocking the pram, to no avail. Sam sighed—it looked as if his peaceful old age was over. Ah well, at least there seemed to be only two children, and at the moment, they were small enough not be causing any problems.

During the next few days Sam watched the goings on next door, from behind his curtains. He saw a thin young woman pushing the pram towards the shops. The small frail looking child he had seen in the back garden accompanied her, hanging on to the handle of the pram. There had been a man too—a large burly type who arrived one day and left the next in a taxi. 'Hmm, that's all we need,' grumbled Sam to his cat Victor. 'She's obviously one of those single parent families with a dozen boyfriends, and living on benefit.' Victor rubbed himself along Sam's leg and purred.

'Seems a nice lass,' cooed Mrs Bain from down the street, when Sam met her. 'The bairns are always clean and tidy. I must ask her in for a cup of tea.' Sam said nothing. You wouldn't catch him asking her in for tea.

There was activity next door. Sam watched as men arrived and cut the grass at the back. They cleared lots of rubbish. Rubbish, that poor Mrs Peters must have left. Next, the men erected a swing and then a slide, and then, of all things, a climbing frame with a sort of shed under it.

'Well fancy,' tutted Sam. 'She must have money to spare.'

Taking a walk that afternoon, Sam came face-to-face with the threesome from next door. He would just have walked passed, but the woman stopped him.

'Hello,' she smiled. 'I'm Heather, your new neighbour.' She extended a hand to be shaken. Sam took her hand. He was a bit flustered, not sure what to say.

'I'm Sam,' he managed. 'Hope you've settled in.' He knew he should have added that if there was anything he could do she should let him know, but he didn't. He didn't want to become involved.

'This is Alex,' she continued, pointing at the small pale boy. Alex stared silently at Sam. 'The baby's called Ewan.' She paused, waiting for him to say something. Realising nothing was forthcoming, she began pushing the pram. 'See you then, bye.' The baby waved as they went on their way.

A few days later Sam was feeling a bit under the weather. He had lost Victor, and he had had an intense discussion on the phone with Hazel.

'There's no way we can come home in the next couple of years, Dad,' she explained. 'It would be easier for you to come here. The boys are growing fast and we want them to get to know their Grandad. Please Dad,' she pleaded. 'Give serious thought to coming to Sydney. The other thing is that we don't want you to come for a holiday; we want you to come for good. We want you to come and stay here, with us.'

As he looked for Victor in his overgrown garden, he gave serious thought to what Hazel had said. It wasn't as though he couldn't afford it, but it was a non-starter, he argued. At his time of life, moving and living in another country? No no, it was impossible! Feeling very tired and old, he went inside and sat in his favourite chair.

A persistent knocking on his front door woke him.

'Sorry to disturb you,' said a distraught Heather. 'But please, can you help me? Please, can you look after Alex for half an hour? He won't be any trouble. He'll just play in the garden. I have to take Ewan to the doctor. Mrs Bain said she would look after Alex, but she's gone out. She must have forgotten.'

'N-no, I couldn't, can't,' spluttered Sam. 'Surely someone else could, or can't you take him with you?'

'No,' she cried. 'I don't know anyone else. Ewan isn't at all well, and I'm not allowed to take Alex into the surgery because of infection. Please, please help me.'

He wanted to ask what she meant about infection, but as tears coursed down the woman's face, Sam relented.

'Okay, I'll watch him, but don't be long.'

He went next door and out into the back garden. Alex was sitting on the grass. Victor was on his knee enjoying being stroked.

'I know he's your pussy,' he said in a surprisingly strong voice. 'But he likes coming here.'

'That's okay,' answered Sam. 'How old are you?'

'I'm four and a half,' answered Alex. 'Can you bark?'

'Don't think so, I've never tried,' smiled Sam. 'Why do you ask?'

'Mrs Bain said your bark was worse than your bite. Do you really bite?'

'No, I don't,' laughed Sam. 'Do you go to school?'

Alex considered the question.

'Not until I'm better,' he shook his head. 'Hope I get better before we go to see Micky Mouse. I've got keemia.'

Sam frowned. 'What have you got?'

'I've got LOOKEEMEEA.' He said it very slowly as if talking to a small child. 'I go to the hospital a lot. It makes me tired.'

Sam's heart skipped a beat. Did this tiny child really have Leukaemia? It hardly seemed possible, yet he did look unwell. He was pale and frail, small for his age, and the hair on his head was sparse. 'So you're going to see Micky Mouse?' said Sam brightly.

'Yep,' answered Alex. 'Dad said so.'

'Dad? Where is he?' questioned Sam.

'He is working for money, so we can see Micky.'

Alex suddenly appeared tired so Sam stopped the questions. He watched as Alex played with Victor. He had, to his shame, never played with his cat.

Heather arrived home with Ewan in her arms. 'It's only a virus,' she explained. 'Nothing serious.'

Over a cup of tea Heather told him about Alex. Leukaemia had been diagnosed two years ago. The doctors were hopeful of a cure, but weren't giving any assurances. They had moved house to be nearer the hospital, and Andy her husband had taken a well-paid job down south. It meant being away from them, which they all hated, but he hoped to have enough money saved, by the end of the year, to take them all to Florida.

'Alex loves Micky Mouse,' she explained. 'So Andy said we must take him to Disney, before, before... But it's so difficult on my own.' Large tears fell down her pale face.

'I understand.' Sam nodded, and patted her hand.

Later at home Sam paced the living room. His brain buzzed. He had decisions to make. He fiddled with the telephone book and scoured the pages beginning with T. He found what he was looking for and dialled the number. A helpful girl answered.

'Yes,' he said. 'This is what I want. A holiday in Florida for two adults and two children. As soon as possible, please, and the hotel must be near Disney. Oh, and while you are at it, I need a one-way ticket to Sydney, Australia.'

DISPOSABLE INCOME

ELLA LOOKED UP FROM THE LIST and chewed on the end of the pencil. She had already written FILLET STEAKS, MUSHROOMS, PEPPERS, PAVLOVA, RED WINE.

Jeff looked over the top of his newspaper. He eyed her shopping list.

'You off to the shops, love? Honestly, I don't know how you do it. You're a genius. Our standard of living doesn't seem to have changed at all since we were both made redundant. It just goes to show, having a reduced disposable income isn't so bad, as long as you're careful where you shop, and look out for bargains.'

'You can speak, Jeff,' Ella beamed. 'You must have squirrelled away a tidy sum, to pay for all those holidays we've had, not to mention the new television, and the drop head Mazda. Joan was green with envy when I told her we had ordered a new leather suite. She asked me if we had won the lottery or something.'

Jeff grinned. 'Well, we're not exactly destitute, and you can't take it with you, as they say. Anyway I think we deserve to treat ourselves.'

Ella smoothed her reversible coat round her. It was large and comfortable, with huge pockets. She loved that coat. It had been a present from Jeff.

'I'll just see if Joan fancies meeting me for a cup of coffee later,' she muttered, waving the phone in Jeff's direction. Frowning, she replaced the phone in its cradle. 'Something wrong with the phone, love. Can you do something? Must be a fault somewhere. I'll get Joan on my mobile. She isn't half jealous I've got a Blackberry. I'm off then,' she smiled. 'See you at tea time.'

'Okay love. Think I might look at more travel brochures. D'you fancy a cruise next year?'

'That would be great—if we can afford it of course,' Ella laughed.

She parked the Mazda in Sainsbury's car park and picked up a hand basket at the front door. Vegetables first, she thought. She popped a large red pepper in the basket and followed that with a bag of mushrooms. She strolled to the fresh meat aisle and surveyed the fillet steak. Gosh, it was even more expensive than last week! She took her time examining the packs. Choosing the largest one, she turned and swiftly scanned the aisle. She clutched the steak in her right hand, handbag over her right shoulder and the basket on her left arm. She walked purposefully to the end of the aisle, and at the same time slipped the pack of steak into one of the inside pockets of her coat.

She passed the time of day with the chatty check-out girl, paid for the pepper and mushrooms and went back to the car. She would go to the Co-op next, and then perhaps Waitrose. She chuckled to herself. It was only fair to shop at different places. It wouldn't do to always go to the same shop. At the Co-op she paid for some potatoes and a small carton of cream, and walked slowly to the car, being careful not to squash the Pavlova which nestled in one of her large pockets. She took her time in Waitrose, examining the shelves of wine. She picked out a cheap bottle of Vin de Pays. 'That'll do nicely for cooking,' she smiled to herself. As she passed the rows marked 'Fine Wines' she quickly pulled a bottle of Chateauneuf du Pap from the middle shelf and popped it inside her coat. She was glad the pockets were not only wide but also deep.

Depositing her shopping in the boot of the car, she pulled out her Blackberry and phoned Joan. She stroked its sleek body as she listened to the ringing of Joan's phone. The mobile had been her birthday present from Jeff. He was really clever with money. She had never had to worry about bills and holidays and buying new things for the house. Ever since they got married twenty years ago they had an agreement. She would buy all her own clothes and the day-to-day things like food, from her salary, and Jeff would see to the rest. Of course she didn't make nearly as much as Jeff, and she couldn't save at all. Not that she had to, of course. Jeff was clever with investments and shares, and stuff that she didn't really understand. But now things were different. She couldn't tell him that she had spent nearly all her redundancy money. She had to do the best she could; couldn't let the side down. Things would work out. She was sure she would get another job soon and everything would be okay.

There was no answer from Joan. Drat! She couldn't wait to tell her about the cruise. She would be beside herself with jealousy. Looking at her watch she saw it was only eleven o' clock, too early to go home. She might as well start looking for cruise wear.

In the department store she found what she was looking for. Floaty dresses for evening. Long shorts and designer T-shirts for day wear, and trendy swimwear. She made her way to the changing room with an armful of clothes. There was no one on duty at the door. She smirked to herself. No one to count how many things she was trying on. Taking her time, she tried the dresses first. She especially liked one, a bright pink halter neck in a very fine material. It wouldn't take up much room in a suitcase, she thought, nor in one of her coat pockets. The shorts and T-shirts came next. She was glad she had been strict about keeping her figure, unlike Joan who was now rather overweight. She wouldn't look good in shorts.

She pulled her skirt and jumper over a smart pair of blue linen shorts and a white and blue T-shirt.

'Not suitable madam?' asked a bored assistant as she handed her the rest of the clothes.

'No, I'm not sure,' smiled Ella. 'I'll have another look round.' She pretended to look again at the dresses, then took the escalator to the ground floor, and then walked smartly out of the front door.

In the car she smoothed out the dress and put it in an empty shopping bag. That was probably enough for today, she nodded to herself. No point in being greedy. There were plenty more shops. She would try again tomorrow. She drove home feeling very pleased with herself. Jeff need never know about her lack of funds.

What's all this then, she tutted to herself as she manoeuvred the car into her street? Two police cars, a large removal van with a posh looking car behind it, were outside her house. What on earth was going on? She parked and got out. Two men in overalls were putting her plasma screen television into the van. Jeff was standing by the police cars. His face was as white as a sheet.

'What's going on, Jeff?' she demanded.

Jeff opened his mouth but no sound came out.

'Right, we'll get the suite next!' shouted one of the overalled men. 'And we'll have the keys to that Mazda too, if you don't mind.'

'W-what?' spluttered Ella. 'Will somebody please tell me what is going on?'

'Sorry,' said one of the policemen. 'They've come to reclaim your stuff. It appears it hasn't been paid for.'

Ella exploded. 'Jeff, what has happened?'

Jeff looked at her with an ashen face. Tears started to stream down his cheeks.

'S-sorry, love,' he managed to stammer. 'It's just that you wanted so much, expected so much, always needed to be better than everyone else. All the expensive holidays you wanted. Only I didn't have the money, see. It's all the credit cards. I couldn't keep up. Now it's all gone. I owe so much. Might even have to sell the house.'

Over Jeff's shoulder she could see Joan looking out from behind her net curtains.

Ella pulled herself up straight. She patted the posh dress still nestling in her inside pocket. She looked Jeff in the eye and winked. 'It's all right, love,' she cooed. 'We'll be okay, you'll see. We'll think of something. Come inside and we'll have a little talk.'

She put her arm round his shoulders and, waving in Joan's direction, manoeuvred him into their house.

THE WINDOW CLEANER

'**O**KAY, SO YOU IN OR NOT?' snapped Larry.

'I dunno. I mean, it's a risk, init?' questioned Rick.

'Na, it's foolproof. Nobody's gonna take any notice of winda cleaners. Big Mick's countin' on you.'

'Okay, I suppose, I'm in,' shrugged Rick. 'Tell Big Mick I'm good.'

'Right, so Big Mick says we just go for the posh houses. You know, the ones with the high walls and the big gardens. My brother, he'll tell us when the folk are away on holiday. He delivers papers an' knows when they cancel. We can't fail. It'll be fine.' Larry grinned. 'All you 'ave to do is shin up your ladder, look into the rooms an' make sure the coast's clear, no cleaning ladies, or anybody about. Big Mick and his boys, an' me, we'll do the rest.'

Rick felt uncomfortable. He didn't really want to be in on this scam. He had done his fair share of thieving in the past, but not for a long time, not since he had been with Marsha. Marsha had told him, 'Any funny business Rick, and I'm gone. I don't do prison visiting.'

Now though, Big Mick and his gang had moved into the area. Rick sighed. He wasn't sure what to do. He couldn't go to the police. That would be like signing his own death warrant. He couldn't just walk away. What was he supposed to do? To tell the truth, he was a bit frightened of Big Mick. He would just have to go along with it for now. Big Mick was a thug. Rick knew that. He was up to all kinds of dirty tricks, and he knew that to cross him would be a mistake, but he would need to find a way out. There was no way he was becoming one of Big Mick's gang. He'd had his fill of gangs. After Sid the Slicer had been put away, he had decided that enough was enough. Sid's real name was Sidney Cut, but everybody called him Slicer. He had been top dog in town for years, the chief villain. No one had dared to stand up to him, but the police had caught him red handed, with stolen money from the bank robbery. Since then Rick had been clean. He had a good life with Marsha and he wanted it to stay like that.

The funny thing was, Rick liked cleaning windows. He liked the way they sparkled and gleamed when they were done. He was proud that all the shining windows in the High Street were down to him. He enjoyed working on the huge windows of the department store, in the shopping centre. He liked his private customers, too. They were mostly old folk, too old to do their own windows, and so grateful. You would think the way some of them spoke, that Rick was doing them a big favour.

'There you are, son. £5? Na, have £6! You don't charge enough. I'm dizzy even watching you climb up so high.'

'Cup of tea Rick? I'll just put the kettle on.'

'I've just made some fruit cake. Have a slice. Go on, take some home with you.'

He liked his work. He didn't want Big Mick barging in and spoiling things.

'Five o' clock,' puffed Rick to himself, stowing his ladder on top of his van. 'Think I'll just pop round to Grans, do her windows, then it's home to Marsha and tea.'

He reached the row of shabby old cottages and waved in at Gran's window. She came to the door a bit flustered and red in the face.

'Oh, I've had such a day!' she twittered. Rick smiled. Gran had a story. He was going to be a bit late for tea.

'It's the roof, see. It was a good job that chap came and saw it. Nice as ninepence, he was. Said he could do the work right away, but he needed supplies. He was ever so kind. Took me to the bank, in his car he did, so I could get him the money. He's coming back tomorrow to do the job.'

Alarm bells rang in Rick's head as he tried to make sense of what Gran was saying. £800! She had given some cowboy £800, because he said her roof was in a dangerous condition! Not only that, he had conned her neighbours out of similar amounts. Old man Henderson had given him £600. Maisie Tompson only had £500, but he said that would be okay, as her roof wasn't as bad as the rest. Rick spoke to all the neighbours. Altogether some crook, some unspeakable rat, had taken over £3000 from a group of vulnerable pensioners.

Rick was so livid he could hardly speak. Gran cried when she realised the truth.

'Sorry Rick,' she kept repeating. 'He seemed such an honest bloke, in a big black car. I even admired his lovely red hair. How could I have been such a fool! Should we call the police?'

'The police? Na!' Rick would come up with a better idea. Black car and red hair, eh? He would see about that. He gathered the neighbours together. He told them there had obviously been a mistake, and to leave it with him. He would get their money back.

At home Rick was beside himself with fury as he told Marsha what had happened.

'Careful love,' advised Marsha. 'Don't get yourself into trouble. Maybe it would be better to have the police involved.'

'No, s'alright. I know what I'm doin'. I've got a plan. I'm goin' to get that scumbag crook, to give Gran and her neighbours their money back.'

'So you're just going to ask him politely then?' laughed Marsha.

'Somethin' like that. Yeah,' grinned Rick.

Next day Rick phoned Larry. 'Right, so when do we start with Big Mick's idea?'

'The word is it's Thursday, eleven o clock.'

'Fine, but tell Mick I need t'see him beforehand, sort out a few details, like. Tell him I'll be in Murphy's snooker club s'afternoon 'bout three.'

Rick flicked through the Yellow Pages till he found what he was looking for. 'Yeah, that's what I need,' he told a bored sounding girl on the end of the phone. 'Plain white van with ladder clamps on top. Yeah, I'll pick it up 'bout 12. Only need it for the afternoon. Ta.'

At eleven o' clock Rick took a bus to the van hire depot on the other side of town. He drove the van to his house, took his spare ladder out of the garage and secured it to the top of the van. Then he drove the half mile to the Northfield housing estate and parked in the Co-op car park. He timed himself. He walked back home in four minutes. He had plenty of time before his meeting with Big Mick, so he made himself a sandwich and a cup of tea, and tried to calm down. There were risks involved in what he was about to do, but the thought of Gran and her money made him determined.

At a quarter to three he drove his own van the half mile to Murphy's. He drove slowly into the car park. He needed to park in just the right spot. He manoeuvred the van to within a couple of inches of Pat Murphy's Merc, and smiled to himself. So far so good. Big Mick was already inside. He was with some of his yobs, and by the way he was staggering around, he had obviously been there some time and had drunk more than a few glasses of beer.

'Well, if it isn't little Ricky,' he slurred. 'Come on, buy uncle Mickey a drink and tell me what you want to know.'

His entourage laughed as Rick went up to the bar. 'A round of drinks for the gents,' he said to Pat Murphy. Pat frowned. He knew Rick didn't usually associate with the likes of Big Mick. As he poured the drinks, Rick patted his pockets.

'Well, that's stupid of me,' he said loudly. 'I've forgotten my wallet.'

'It's okay,' Pat shrugged. 'Pay me tomorrow.'

'No, no,' insisted Rick. 'I'll just nip to the bank and get some money from the machine. Won't be long.' He was just leaving when he stopped and turned to Pat. 'Here!' he shouted, as he threw his van keys to Pat. 'You might need to move my van, if you want your car out. I've parked right in front of it.'

Outside, Rick broke into a run. He was fit so it only took him a few minutes to reach the Co-op. He got in the hire van, changed into the old red jacket and baseball cap he had left inside, and drove round the corner to Northfield Place. He parked outside number forty-three. There was no one about in the shabby street apart from a couple of grubby kids and a spaced out teenager sitting on a doorstep. He got the ladder off the van and took it round the back of the two-story semi. He was in luck. One of the bedroom windows was slightly open. In no time at all he was standing in the dingy, untidy lounge. He started searching. He mustn't be too long. He went quickly through the cupboards and found nothing. He also drew a blank with the chest of drawers. He was becoming frantic. He was taking too long. Where would someone not very bright hide three thousand quid? Top of the wardrobe? No. In the oven? Not there either. He upturned a bed. There it was, under the mattress in a Co-op bag! He put it inside his jacket and exited the house the same way as he had entered. With the ladder safely back on its moorings, he drove to the Co-op, and reparked the van in the same spot. He changed back into his black leather jacket, and with the money safely zipped inside, sprinted to his house, handed the money to an astonished Marsha, and ran back to Murphy's. How long had he been gone? Probably less than fifteen minutes.

'So, what kept ya?' sneered Big Mick 'Bank run out of money?'

'Na, machine wasn't working,' explained Rick. 'Had to wait in a queue.'

Next morning he was summoned to Murphy's. Big Mick looked as if he was about to explode. He poked Rick in the chest.

'I've bin robbed!' he snarled. 'I've bin robbed an' I think you had a hand in it!'

'Me?' questioned Rick. 'How's that then?'

'I was robbed and I was here. You left here an' I was robbed. Mrs found the place done over when I was here. Three grand down the toilet an' I think it was you! Got in wi' a ladder, they did, just like a winda cleaner. Somebody saw a geezer in a red jacket. What ya got ta say?'

'If you remember,' said Rick calmly, 'I left here to go to the bank, and I left my van keys with Murphy. My van was here all the time. And I was wearing a black leather jacket. It couldn't have been me, could it?'

Grudgingly Big Mick agreed. Inside Rick was shaking, outside he appeared quite bold.

'Thing is,' he lied, 'I hear that Sid Slicer's got his boys looking for som'dy. Seems like this bloke did Sid's old mum out of hundreds, for a non-existent roof repair. Sid's not happy. Even from the inside he can get things done.'

He stared at Big Mick's piggy eyes. Big Mick seemed to have gone very pale. 'He's going to make a big thing of it.'

'Oh Rick!' gasped Gran on the phone. 'I think you must have been wrong about the red haired chap. We got our money back. We've all had an envelope with our money in it put through our doors. A message with it said: '*Sorry for any inconvenience, won't be able to do your roof.*'

'That's great Gran,' replied a smiling Rick. 'Glad it all worked out. Won't be seeing you for a couple of weeks. I think I'll take Marsha to Spain for a holiday.'

IRENE

IRENE AWOKE WITH A START. Instantly alert, she listened hard, but there was no sound, save the soft hum of the central heating and the ticking of the alarm clock. The clock rang, and Irene stretched out a hand and tapped the top of it. The harsh ringing stopped instantly. Irene counted to twenty. She felt okay so she pushed the blanket from her, swung her legs over the side of the bed, and stood up. No sweating, no panicky sensation, no shortness of breath. That was good. She would write that in her medical diary. She was due to see the doctor next week. He would be pleased with her. Fourteen years, she mused, and she was just about able to live a normal life. Fourteen years since the shock of becoming pregnant at 40. Fourteen years since the start of the panic attacks and the start of OCD.

She well remembered her first panic attack. She was looking at the biscuits in Marks and Spencer, when she started to feel strange. She couldn't decide which biscuits to buy—chocolate or shortbread, caramel wafers or ginger crumbles? Making a choice suddenly became overwhelming. She couldn't do it. She started to cry and felt sick and dizzy. There was a roaring sound in her head, and a pain gripped her chest. 'I'm having a heart attack,' she said to herself.

Terrified, she found herself unable to move. Her leaden legs felt glued to the floor. Fear of passing out gripped her and she held on tight to a shelf. The confused noise of shoppers buzzed round her. No one stopped to help. She must have seemed like a crazy woman. She felt she needed to get home, away from the noise and the smell of people. She needed to get home and go to bed. After what seemed like an eternity, she managed to let go of the shelf, and abandoning her shopping basket, escaped outside. The dizziness subsided, and somehow she managed to find a number 6 bus to take her home. Later that day, the doctor had, to her and Bert's astonishment, pronounced Irene pregnant.

She opened the curtains and peered out. A weak ray of sunshine brushed the bareness of the garden. Flowerless borders hugged the grey stone wall, and leafless bushes looked forlorn in the cold winter morning. 'A long time till Spring,' said Irene to herself, sighing deeply. She hated Winter. She knew some people loved it and would wax lyrical about the beauty of snow and robins, and Christmas, but not her. Even as a child she had hated Winter. She had hated the cold that numbed her feet and hands, hated the snow that the other children revelled in. She never understood why her friends would want to play in the cold, icy wet stuff, sledging and making snowmen, flinging themselves on top of great piles of it, and throwing it at each other. She remembered soggy gloves from falling over, and red weals around the calves of her legs where wellington boots had rubbed, and the agony of chilblains on her toes, from warming her feet too quickly in front of the fire. Of course they didn't get the snow nowadays like they used to.

Even if they did she couldn't see today's children playing in it. They were all too busy with computers and iPods, and all sorts of technology, to bother about playing outside. But there was still this Winter to get through, and she supposed she would manage this one, just as she had for the last fifteen since Helen had died.

She went into the bathroom, turned the egg timer over and brushed her teeth until the sand ran out, then she splashed her face with cold water and patted it dry. Her clothes were laid neatly over the bedroom chair. She had chosen them with care last night, before she went to bed (a navy pleated skirt and a white jumper with a navy flower motive on the front), just as she had done every night for years. She dressed quickly and ran a comb through her thick grey hair. A dab of lipstick and she was done. Taking a deep breath, she glanced in the mirror. What she saw didn't fill her with glee. It was a tired lined face that looked back at her, grey and tired. Her eyes had a sadness about them. There was no spark, no life, no joy in them. A familiar feeling of apprehension started in the pit of her stomach. 'Stop it, Irene Forbes!' she said sternly. 'Pull yourself together. It's not every day you turn fifty-five. Behave!'

She walked slowly downstairs, breathing evenly as she had been taught. As she passed the front door, she glanced at the doormat. There was no mail. She hadn't really expected any but she had hoped that Rob would have remembered her birthday and sent a card. 'He'll come round later,' she thought out loud. 'Yes, that's it. He'll come round during his lunch break, or perhaps even after work. I expect he'll bring a surprise present.'

She had laid breakfast in the kitchen the night before. She spooned six heaped spoonfuls of bran flakes into the white china bowl. She took milk from the fridge and carefully poured it on top of the cereal, until it came to the edge of the blue stripe that ran along the inside of the bowl. Coffee followed the cereal—one level teaspoonful of instant, one sweetener and three-quarters of a mug of just boiling water. Breakfast over and the dishwasher filled, Irene turned her attention to the task of the day, the writing of the Christmas cards.

She studied her list. She had always written Rob's name at the top of the list. Well, she would, wouldn't she? Rob was the most important person in her life—always had been. But of course now there was Joanne. Not that she was unhappy about Joanne being Rob's wife. She was a nice lassie and always made Irene feel welcome. But now Rob had to put Joanne first. Well, he would, wouldn't he? He had promised to love and honour her. In front of everybody in the church, her Rob, her baby, her man, her friend, her everything, had promised himself to Joanne.

She could remember every detail of how he'd looked that day, five years ago. He was so handsome in his kilt outfit. She remembered how the pleats of his kilt sat perfectly straight, their creases like knife edges. She herself had polished his shoes on the morning of the wedding, buffing the leather until she could see her reflection looking back at herself. A sad crumpled face, not crying, but wanting to. And she hadn't cried, couldn't cry. Just as she hadn't cried when Helen died. Gripping her handbag tightly in the church, she had concentrated throughout the ceremony on

Rob's broad strong back, and a while later even managed a small smile for the photographs. Joanne of course had looked beautiful. Everyone had said so. But all that Irene could remember about Joanne was that there were forty-eight flower motifs, sewn in sequins on the long train that fell from her shoulders.

Everyone said it was a wonderful wedding. In the line-up before the meal when she shook hands with all the guests, they all said more or less the same thing:

'Lovely couple—don't they look well together—you must be very proud' etc. etc. She wondered if they rehearsed what to say. Did they all stand in front of their mirrors that morning and ponder, 'What will I say to Irene? Should I mention Bert? Will he even be there?'

Of course Bert was there. But only for the ceremony, and the Champagne. He didn't stay for the meal and the speeches. She had been grateful for that. Rob had been adamant.

'Of course he's coming, Mum,' he had said in a strange, strained voice that Irene had not recognised. 'I can't get married without my Dad being there.'

And Bert had come to the church, and sat in the front row beside her, and beside him had sat his wife Isobel, and their daughter Kate.

'She is my half-sister, after all,' Rob had argued, and Irene had felt too numb, too defeated, too tired, to even protest.

How she had got through the day she would never know. It all seemed so unreal, so dreamlike. That morning she had made Rob his breakfast as usual—a bowl of Corn Flakes, two slices of toast with butter and marmalade, and a cup of strong tea. They had both been in their dressing gowns and very subdued. Bob had tried to be light hearted.

'Come on, Mum,' he had chided. 'I'm getting married, not executed.'

Irene had forced a smile and ruffled Bob's hair, but then gone into the bathroom and looked in the mirror in complete despair. What was she going to do? She had never been by herself. Never had spent a night alone! Even in the hospital there were lots of people she could call on, could rely on. Now she would be by herself, and she felt desperate. But she couldn't let Rob down, so for his sake she dressed in her neat new navy blue suit and pink hat, and was ready when the taxi came to drop off Mike, who was the best man, and to take her on to the church.

It was Bert who had taken her by the elbow and steered her to her place in the photographs. He had seen her into the taxi, with the bridesmaid and best man after the service, and had brought her a glass of champagne when they got to the hotel for the reception. Before he took his leave he even kissed her lightly on the cheek.

'Good bye, Irene,' he had said in a gruff whisper. 'If there's anything I can do, you know—don't hesitate.' Before Irene could think of a reply he was gone, his wife at his side. Their daughter looked bored and sulky, the way that only thirteen-year-old girls can. Irene had felt sick and dizzy but managed to hold herself together, by counting the empty champagne glasses left on the table by the door of the dining room.

The rest of the day passed in a haze of food, speeches, wine, more photographs, music, dancing and laughter. She especially remembered the laughter. Everyone had been so happy. Everyone happy, she thought except herself. But she managed a smile when Rob and Joanne drove off from the hotel. Rob had kissed her.

'Bye Mum, thanks for everything. I really mean that,' he had whispered in her ear. Thanks for everything? Thanks for what, she thought? Thanks for not being there when I really needed you? Thanks for being in a psychiatric ward when I was sitting my finals? Thanks for not coping with life so badly that Dad left us for another woman? And last but not least, thanks for being such a terrible mother that you let my sister die?

Someone saw her into a taxi, and she found herself at home—alone. She took off her wedding clothes and put on Rob's comfy dressing gown that he had worn that morning. Pulling it around her she sat, closed her eyes and thought of Rob.

She thought of the day that Rob was born. It was August. She'd had a model pregnancy. No morning sickness, no excess weight gain, no mood swings. She had loved every minute of it. It was as though she had been born to be pregnant. She spoke to the baby, hand on bump at every opportunity. And she sang to it and lovingly caressed it. It seemed the natural thing to do although her mother thought it very odd.

'You'll soon know all about it, my girl,' proclaimed her mother through clenched teeth. 'It's no picnic, you know, giving birth. Why do you think you've got no brothers or sisters? I tell you it's hell on earth.'

But Irene found her mother to be wrong. She gave birth to Rob after five hours of gentle labour. He appeared, serene, blond and beautiful and she immediately fell in love with him, as did his father, his grandmother, and anyone else who laid eyes on him. The staff at the maternity hospital cooed over him, almost falling over themselves to hold him. Irene had felt great, but still had to stay in hospital for seven days as was the custom then. It was also vogue at the time to bottle feed, and Irene was given no encouragement to do otherwise. Rob was the perfect baby. He fed every four hours and slept through the night after three weeks. He was a happy smiling baby, and grew into a happy smiling toddler. No one could find fault with Rob. He was perfect. Bert had been as smitten as anyone else and had often only half joked to Irene that another three or four like Rob would be no bad thing. But it was not to be.

Of course Bert had been ecstatic when she fell pregnant with Helen. She had just felt numb, as though it was happening to someone else. She had a dreadful pregnancy. The morning sickness, or rather the all-day sickness, lasted the whole nine months. The panic attacks continued, and the obsessive, compulsive disorder made her clean the house over and over. Rob, at fifteen, tried to help, but more and more he retreated to his room, till Irene hardly saw him at all. Bert was doing well in the police force, but long hours and shifts meant he was not at home as much as Irene would have liked.

The clock struck ten. Irene started from her dreaming.

'Come on,' she said sternly to herself. 'This is no way to get these cards written.' She gripped the pen and underneath

To Rob and Joanne she wrote, *Have a lovely Christmas, love mum x.*

Next on the list were Vivienne and Joe. She wondered what she would write on their card. Vivienne would enclose one of those word-processed letters as usual, boasting about holidays in the Greek Islands, weddings attended, and how well Steven and Michael were doing in the bank. If you believed what she wrote, they ran the Bank of Scotland between them. Then she would add stuff about people Irene had never met: 'Olive and Harold invited us to spend the summer in their villa in France' or 'Beatty and Larry want us to go on a cruise with them this summer'. Who were these people? She hadn't a clue. But Vivienne had been her childhood friend, and her bridesmaid, and had tried to help during those awful days after Helen died. She had made endless cups of tea, answered the door to the doctors and police, had steered her through the dark week of questions, weeping and despair, and had dressed her for the funeral. She had seen that Rob and Bert had food enough in the fridge, and had been a rock without whom, Irene doubted, she could have survived. But afterwards she had slowly distanced herself. She had explained to Irene that she couldn't cope with the grief any more, but Irene knew that it was the whispering and rumours that Vivienne couldn't cope with. But she had stayed in touch even though it was now just a Christmas card.

Vivienne and she had known each other since Primary School. They always went around arm in arm whispering secrets and laughing together. Even on a Sunday they were with each other, sitting closely on a hard pew at Sunday

School. Vivienne and Irene had been inseparable, and as the
years went on they became, as her mother used to say,
'Joined at the hip.'

Teachers at school used to call them Tweedle Dum and
Tweedle Dee. They had both gone from primary school to
the Academy. They liked school well enough, but they didn't
shine academically. They did okay, each gaining five O-
levels before going on to the commercial college, to learn
shorthand and typing. Irene's Dad was keen for her to
become a secretary.

'You'll never be without a job,' he used to say. 'If you've
got shorthand and typing, and a bit of common sense, you'll
be fine.'

He was anxious for Irene to do better than he had done.
'Education,' he would spout, usually on a Saturday night
after his customary couple of pints in the local pub,
'Education is the way out of poverty.' Not that they were
poor exactly. They always had plenty to eat and good
enough clothes. But a house that they owned, holidays every
year—that was beyond them. They lived in Orchard Street, a
quiet dark street of grey granite tenements. They had two
rooms and an outside toilet, which thankfully, unlike some
families, they didn't have to share. The big room had a sink
and a cooker, a dining table and chairs and a couple of
armchairs set beside a coal fire. A bed recess housed a large
high bed where her Mum and Dad slept. The other room was
Irene's bedroom. It was tiny. There was room enough for a
single bed, a chest of drawers and a wardrobe, where they all
kept their clothes. She supposed they had been happy
enough. Dad worked long hours as a gas fitter and went to

the pub on a Saturday night, and church on a Sunday. Sometimes he went out on a Friday night for a drink at the local pub. Mum, like most wives at that time, didn't have a regular job. She did the housework, shopping and cooking and sometimes went up to the west end to help her friend Molly clean other people's houses, in places like Rubislaw Den where the posh folk lived.

Irene was allowed to go to the Girls Guildry on a Friday night. It was held in the church hall, and either her father or mother took her there and back. It was a bit boring really—a few games, singing and listening to someone droning on about being a good Christian—but it was better than being at home when Dad was there. He would want her to sit and read one of the encyclopaedias he had bought from a man who came round the doors selling them from an enormous suitcase. She enjoyed reading, but her dad got angry if he caught her reading what he regarded as trash. Enid Blyton, for example, was regarded as rubbish. But Irene adored The Secret Seven, The Famous Five, and the Adventure Stories. She could lose herself for hours in an adventure book, but if her Dad found out, there was hell to pay. Not that he ever laid a hand on her. It was the cold disapproval, the anger in his gruff voice that scared her to death. It was lucky for her that Dad worked shifts, often starting work at seven in the evening which left the coast clear for her. Mum didn't mind what she read. She wasn't sufficiently interested. Most evenings when Dad was working, her mother would sit by the fire and listen to the radio. Mum loved popular music programmes, plays, and scaring herself to death listening to Journey into Space.

Irene smiled. 'Tame stuff compared with now,' she mumbled to herself. Sometimes when her Dad was working Vivienne would come round, and the two of them would sit on Irene's bed and talk about what they would do when they grew up. Vivienne always said the same things. Marry someone rich and travel round the world. Irene's plans were quite different. She wasn't going to get married. She was going to get a good job and buy a bungalow and live by herself. She would write stories in her spare time, and maybe even become famous like Enid Blyton. The two girls would always end up laughing and giggling, until Irene's Mum came in and told Vivienne it was time to go home. Funny how things never work out the way you planned.

She knew that Maggie's card would say the same sort of thing as Vivienne's, only in a more roundabout way. Probably along the lines of 'Where do the months go? Another year gone by and we've not met up. Do give me a ring when you're free and we can arrange to meet.' Irene knew that Maggie didn't have the slightest intention of 'meeting up'. As sisters-in-law, Maggie and Irene were once very close. Maggie was Rob's godmother, and at one time they would see each other at least three times a week. She wasn't married, and spent a lot of time babysitting Rob, so that Irene and Bert could go out to the pictures, or the police social evenings.

When he was older, Rob spent a lot of time at Auntie Maggie's, and Irene had been very happy for him to do so. It had come as something of a shock when right after Helen died, Maggie stopped phoning and coming to the house. 'Just like Vivienne,' thought Irene out loud, 'only more immediate.' She had seen Maggie only once since Helen's funeral, and that had been at Rob's wedding. She supposed that Maggie saw a lot of Bert, his wife Moira, and their daughter Kate. Perhaps she was Kate's godmother too. She didn't know.

It hadn't taken Bert long to sort himself out after he left her and Rob. Two years later, and he was married with a baby. It was soon after the birth of the baby that Irene was hospitalised again. Rob had just started uni, but when she was allowed home, Rob had cared for her; shopping, cooking meals and some days, even washing and dressing her. It was Rob who took her to the hospital, for her appointments with the psychiatrist, and who talked her through the bad days. Money hadn't been a problem. Bert had been left decently off, after the death of his parents, and provided well for her and Rob. It was a relief not to have to worry about money, but it was small consolation for being deserted. She'd had no inkling at all that Bert was going to move out. It was the year after Helen died that he came home from work and told her.

'I just can't take it anymore,' he explained. 'The grief, the guilt, the sheer awfulness of everything. I'm sorry, Irene, but I just can't live with it all anymore. I'm leaving. There isn't anyone else, if that's what you're thinking. There's no joy left between us. It's better if we both make a fresh start.'

'A fresh start?' Irene had screamed. 'How do I make a fresh start knowing that I let my baby die?'

But Bert had gone, and she knew that if it hadn't been for Rob she would have killed herself.

Rob had been an astonishing help when Helen was born. After an excruciating 36-hour labour, Irene was left exhausted and drained. When she was allowed home, it was fifteen-year-old Rob who had made bottles, helped with the nappy changing, and even pushed the pram round the neighbourhood, baby in one end, and a big pink teddy he had bought her, in the other.

Bert was working more than ever. There was promotion on the horizon and he was out of the house more than he was home. Helen was a sickly baby who cried all the time and was difficult to feed. After two months things weren't any better and Irene was at her wits' end.

The night it happened Bert was on nightshift. Helen was crying with a pitiful mewing sound, and Irene didn't know what to do. She was worn out, and wept with tiredness.

'Go to bed Mum,' urged Rob. 'I'll see to Helen. Go on, it'll be okay.'

Gratefully Irene had gone to bed, and drank the warm milky drink Rob had given her along with two sleeping pills. The next thing she remembered was Bert shaking her.

'What happened!' he was screaming. 'What have you done?'

Stumbling, she followed him to Helen's room. There in the cot lay Helen, still and serene, as though she was asleep. Her skin had a waxy look and her lips were blue. Helen wasn't asleep, she was dead.

For Irene the next hours passed in a blur. The house seemed to be full of people. Policemen and doctors asked endless questions, most of which Irene was unable to answer. No, she didn't think she had got up to Helen in the night. No, she didn't remember hearing her cry. She had gone to sleep. She had been so tired. Yes, Helen was a difficult baby. Bert had wept. She had never seen him in tears before. Rob didn't cry. He just held his mother tight and kept saying, 'I'm sorry mum, so dreadfully sorry.'

Rob explained that he had given Helen her night time feed, and put her down to sleep. His mother was already asleep when he went to say goodnight. The next thing he knew, was his father screaming that Helen was dead.

The next few days were a nightmare. Doctors, policemen and officials came and went. Irene was questioned, again and again, as was Rob. Vivienne and Maggie made endless cups of tea and sandwiches which no one ate. The official pronouncement was Cot Death.

Bert and Rob carried the tiny white coffin between them to the funeral. The church service was short, and Bert held Irene as they lowered the coffin into the grave. The house was silent for months. No one spoke much and no one laughed. Visitors became non-existent. Irene felt as though her life was over. It was Rob who gently coaxed her back to life. He took her out for short trips and eventually managed to get her back to some semblance of normality. Bert worked all hours. He hardly came home, and when he did he didn't speak much. Irene knew that he blamed her for Helen's death. That was bad enough, but the fact was she blamed herself. Try as she might, she couldn't remember what had happened that night. Had she gone to Helen in the night? Had she heard her cry? Could she have done anything to prevent what had happened? She had no memory, no answers.

Tired of reminiscing and card writing, Irene filled the kettle. Perhaps Rob would come soon. He would like a cup of tea. Almost on cue the doorbell rang. Irene opened the door to Rob. His face was white.

'What's wrong?' demanded Irene. 'What's happened?'

With shaking voice Rob tried to speak. 'It's Joanne,' he croaked.

Irene's heart leapt in her chest. She took hold of Rob's shoulders. 'Tell me,' she urged.

'It's Joanne—she's pregnant,' stammered Rob.

Irene looked at him in disbelief. 'Pregnant? But that's great...' she began.

Rob stared at her as tears started to pour down his cheeks. 'I thought you knew, Mum, I thought you always knew it was me. I couldn't stand what Helen was doing to you, to us. I just took the pink teddy and put it over her face, just to stop the wailing, the crying, the noise that was destroying us. I just wanted it to be back the way it was, with just the three of us. Don't you understand, Mum?' He screamed: 'I killed my sister!'

Irene stared in disbelief. 'You didn't, you couldn't... I always thought that maybe it was me.'

'No Mum, it was me, and now my wife is pregnant, and what if the baby turns out like Helen? Do you think I might do it again? I'm a murderer, Mum, and you'll have to help me.'

Irene breathed deeply. Suddenly a strange calm come over her. She felt in control, and stronger than she had done in a very long time. She took her son into her arms and caressed his head as she had done years ago. She made soothing noises, as she contemplated the enormity of what she had to do next.

Touching Base with Trauma

Reaching Across the Generations:

A Three-Dimensional Homeopathic Perspective

Elizabeth Adalian MCH MARH

Touching Base with Trauma

Reaching Across The Generations:
A Three-Dimensional Homeopathic Perspective

by

Elizabeth Adalian

ISBN: 978-0-9955748-1-6

This book is produced by Elizabeth Adalian in conjunction with **WRITERSWORLD**, and is produced entirely in the UK. It is available to order from most bookshops in the United Kingdom, and is also globally available via UK based Internet book retailers.

Copy Edited by Meg Brinton and Ian Large

Cover Design by Jag Lall

WRITERSWORLD
2 Bear Close Flats, Bear Close, Woodstock
Oxfordshire, OX20 1JX, England
☎ 01993 812500
☎ +44 1993 812500

www.writersworld.co.uk

The text pages of this book are produced via an independent certification process that ensures the trees from which the paper is produced come from well managed sources that exclude the risk of using illegally logged timber while leaving options to use post-consumer recycled paper as well.

DISCLAIMER

The content of this book is intended for information purposes only.

It is not a substitute for professional medical advice, nor is it to be used for purposes of self-diagnosis or self-treatment.

Homeopathic treatments should only ever be taken under the direct guidance and care of a properly and fully trained homeopathic practitioner.

Neither the publishers nor author will accept any responsibility for any ill effects resulting from the use or misuse of the information contained in this book.

CONTENTS

ACKNOWLEDGEMENTS

A certain alchemy takes place when a concept which has been fertilised in the mind is transferred to print. This 'transmutation' would not have been possible without the support of Kristina Buravcova and Nigel Hargreaves, PhD. They brought their wizardry to the task of formulating and drafting the material with their expert skills at every stage of the book's development.

I should also like to pay tribute to my fellow editorial team members of the Alliance of Registered Homeopaths from whom I have received so much encouragement for my contribution of articles over the years for their flagship magazine, *Homeopathy in Practice*. In fact, it is through the research I undertook for these articles that I felt inspired to write this book.

In the final stages, I called upon my colleague, Meg Brinton, to undertake the copy editing. She carried this out with great vision and clarity to support the task of delivering the contents in a cohesive and comprehensible manner to the readers.

On a personal front, family members and many friends cheered at the sidelines. I dedicate this book to my personal friend and colleague, Sara Da Silva, who has been unremitting in her devotion throughout the years. It was only through her dogged determination to ensure I saw the project through that I persisted till the very end.

INTRODUCTION

Some years ago, after the war in former Yugoslavia, I worked in Bosnia and Croatia as a homeopath contributing to the recovery of the community from collective trauma of the conflict. What became startlingly clear to me when taking the patient's history was that the dominant influence upon the case was, not so much what the individual endured as a result of the war, but what they brought to that suffering from their primal life experience. I realised that this message came especially from the impressionable years of infancy where susceptibility is so deeply rooted.

Since then I have adopted this understanding in my clinical practice because I realised it is not necessary to have undergone exposure to war to feel traumatised. In my practice, I have observed that the vicarious effects of trauma can percolate through at least three generations. This is especially true when there has been a collective trauma (such as the Holocaust), which is often suppressed. This made me see how important the unexpressed emotions from the unconscious are in dictating the health of present and future generations. Applying the results of this approach to my cases was quite startling as well as lasting in its effects.

My aim in this book is to connect transgenerational healing to current modes of expression of disease in contemporary society. This requires a three-dimensional case analysis that includes the capture of patterns passed through generations in order to more fully decode the presenting trauma in the patient.

According to Judith Herman in her seminal book, *Trauma and Recovery*: "Traumatic events are extraordinary, not because they occur rarely, but rather because they overwhelm the ordinary adaptations to life." [1] She continues: "There is a spectrum of traumatic disorders ranging from the effects of a single overwhelming event to the more complicated effects of prolonged

---

1   Herman, Judith (1997), *Trauma and Recovery*, Basic Books, New Ed Edition.

and repeated abuse." In fact, any event which remains protracted or repeats itself, whether based on abuse or not, could be considered a trauma. Sometimes, in the case of abuse, the perpetrator may be totally unaware that their attitude has caused distress. If, however, the actions were carried out wittingly on the part of the abuser, then the damage would appear to be much more intense and lasting for the sufferer. This means that a natural disaster or an accident – however distressing at the time – would have much less intense impact in the longer term than abuse which has been perpetrated deliberately.

This book is laid out in two main parts. Part 1 – Tracing the Trajectory – details the meaning behind transgenerational healing. Part 2 – Materia Medica – highlights aspects of remedies that I have found particularly applicable in cases of *transgenerational trauma*.

As a result of the research I have undertaken for this book, I have come to realise that, when teaching homeopathy, there needs to be less focus on the subjective and objective symptoms of the case, and more on what 'informs' them – the *third dimension*. Looking into this more deeply, I propose this 'informing' to be a foundational layer, which is rooted in the primal period of life. If the patterns making up this foundational layer are not addressed, they become recycled in consequent layers in a different but related theme each time a similar *trigger* or stimulus occurs. This then compounds the presenting patterns until they eventually lead to deep pathology.

Nowadays, parents are guided to instil self-confidence in their children, but this was not so common in previous generations. This could result in a lack of self-value which perpetuates the influence on the next generation and can then become the uppermost 'lesion' in subsequent generations. This then needs to be addressed as an initial layer in the treatment of the patient in accordance with a *transgenerational case framework*. In order for the patient to alter their lens on such an aspect of themselves, they may also require much additional support from the homeopath and, as they then recover their self-confidence, those around them will also need to adjust to this new perspective. This in itself can create further stress and disruption and possibly reveal other buried layers of distress. I have noted that when there has been extreme duress in the history, the personality often becomes halted at the actual age when the stress impacted. Therefore, sometimes, after giving a successful remedy to remove the lesion layer, an additional and often related remedy needs to be given to support the maturing process in the patient. This is expanded upon in 1.1 Setting the Scene.

By learning materia medica according to causation, whether emotional or physical, it is possible to apply the exact remedy based on this methodology for transgenerational treatment. However, the 'pivot' of the distress may not lie within the consulting patient but in a relative of theirs, living or deceased. I describe this concept further in Part 1. It reinforces the importance, when learning materia medica, of paying attention to the vital *'ailments from'* rubrics in each individual remedy picture. For example, an overview of *'abuse, ailments from'* or *'deception, ailments from'* – both very disabling triggers on an emotional level – and *'injuries, head, blows, ailments after'* or *'vaccinations, reactions, ailments from'* on the physical level, could indicate the need to anchor the case in this triggering context.

Respectively, the possibility of physical symptoms dictating outcomes on the mental or emotional level should not be overlooked. In these cases, the hierarchy according to the Eizayaga Model should be reversed unless the symptoms are emotionally triggered in the first place. [2] This is particularly valid in relationship to the gut which, when diseased, has profound emotional effects. This is due to the fact that the gut has as many, if not more, nerve receptors than the brain and is even considered to be the second brain. [3]

---

2   Eizayaga, Francisco X. (1991), *Treatise on Homoeopathic Medicine*, Ediciones Marecel, 1st Edition.

3   Gershon, Michael D. (1999), *The Second Brain – Your Gut Has a Mind of Its Own*, Harper Collins Publishers.

This transgenerational framework of understanding exemplifies the emphasis on how the unconscious can transmit the patterns underpinning the distress in the presenting patient. The symptoms resulting from a transgenerational trajectory can then be incorporated into the analysis of the case to establish the exact simillimum needed within its true context. A key observation by the practitioner during case-taking may be the avoidance of eye contact when discussing certain family members or different situations experienced in the past. This could point to the 'uncompensated state' of the patient – revealing where the true core of the issue lies, although it may be unconscious to them.

As a conceptual architecture for understanding cases, the transgenerational healing framework translates into other therapeutic disciplines as an approach to healing. Psychotherapists may identify with this. A book which greatly influenced me along this path is *Biogenealogy: Decoding the Psychic Roots of Illness – Freedom from the Ancestral Origins of Disease.* [4] Although this is not a homeopathic book, one can see its relevance from the following quote: "It is possible to trace the root cause of an illness to our ancestors: their unresolved psychic distress can become part of the cellular memory we inherit. Until addressed, it will continue to trigger illness in the generations that follow." Obissier continues: "Illness is a physical response to a past emotional trauma, either experienced by the patient or an ancestor." He refers to '*occulted emotions*' and this expression really struck a chord with me. I see that the word 'occult' evokes a hint of mystery as well as hiddenness from the patient. This represents the underpinning issue creating a block to true cure and is therefore requisite of the transgenerational healing approach for resolution of cases.

My aim is that this work on the transgenerational healing framework of understanding will inspire homeopaths to not only gain lasting cures, but also support their patients to better perceive their life journey in a healing context. Of course, such influences as birth trauma, drugs, both medicinal and recreational,

4   Obissier, Patrick (2005), *Biogenealogy: Decoding the Psychic Roots of Illness –
     Freedom from the Ancestral Origins of Disease*, Healing Arts Press.

head injury, and viral infections play a role, but I believe it is the family dynamics and role models that need to be addressed before lasting cure can be achieved in each case.

I trust the reader will be encouraged to think 'beyond the box' and target healing at its true source. In this way, prevention of the onward flow of negative transmission can occur and future generations can be released from this type of bondage.

The rubrics mentioned in this book are based on those listed in Robin Murphy's *Homeopathic Clinical Repertory*. [5]

The materia medica is distributed throughout the text, with remedy names in italics which, I hope, makes them easy to spot, in addition to the individual entries in Part 2.

In order for the reader to refer to individual chapters in isolation, it is inevitable that there is a small amount of overlap between them. This is intentional so that a cohesive view can be gained without having to navigate the greater text in the situation.

The cases which are mentioned throughout the text come from my practice both in the UK and overseas. Details have been adjusted in order to protect the anonymity of the patients.

5   Murphy, Robin (2005), *Homeopathic Clinical Repertory*, Third Edition, Lotus Health Institute.

PART 1

TRACING THE TRAJECTORY

1.1 SETTING THE SCENE

If the physical body is regarded as a reflection of the human mind, and the patient treated accordingly, then healing can take place at a deep level. Symptoms are not random but actually symbolise subtle messages – often transmitted from the unconscious – to describe the triggering mental/emotional state.

When treating physical pain, practitioners may recognise that it symbolises 'somatisation' – a projection of unexpressed emotions onto this plane. In the remedy *Kali carbonicum*, for example, where deep physical pathology can take over, the patient is often out of touch with their emotions. In the course of recovery, the patient, in order to fully heal, needs to express the contributing emotional symptoms. Prior manifestation of these symptoms was often totally unfamiliar to them or their close family, so the patient needs to alter their emotional expression in order to recover physically. This can mean a very radical shift takes place which needs a lot of support from the practitioner, especially in certain cultures where verbal expression of emotions is often discouraged. Anger may be the main emotion the patient is comfortable with. This displaces 'heartfelt' feelings that have become 'concretised' in the symptoms as a type of 'armouring' – in the case of *Kali carbonicum*, often affecting the heart and lungs. This level of 'stuckness' can also be seen in *Conium maculatum* and *Plumbum metallicum*, both remedies where serious pathology can occur on all levels as a result.

In Traditional Chinese Medicine (TCM), the lungs are associated with grief and the bladder with fear. [6] These examples of the mind/body connection are useful pointers to the background of the presenting pathology. Is it any coincidence that many old people die of pneumonia? As age creeps up, regrets can accumulate and eventually contribute to the final demise of the patient, culminating in this particular physically-manifested outcome.

---

6   *Causes of Illness – 7 Emotions*, www.sacredlotus.com/go/foundations-chinese-medicine/get/causes-illness-7-emotions.

The expression 'no pain, no gain' means that pain, like any other symptom, acts as a defence mechanism of the organism to signal awareness to both the sufferer and the observer of their underlying state. Homeopathic treatment can target the contributing behaviour, thus removing the need for the pain signal.

When a disease process is ongoing, a negative attitude only intensifies the force of this decline. Once the 'mind shift' occurs, reversal of pathology can ensue, thereby resulting in a full recovery. In fact, sometimes the illness is perceived, albeit in retrospect, by the patient to have guided them into reclaiming their true nature, which had got lost along the way.

It may be the first time a window of opportunity for recovery has appeared in the individual's life. Not only does the sufferer need to adopt a more positive attitude, but so do the surrounding family members in turn. The observations and attitude of the homeopath are therefore key to support a healthy outcome for the patient and also this ongoing shift towards growth. When energy is no longer obstructed in the body by negative emotions, the 'vital force' can regain its equilibrium. This frees up the creativity of the individual to realise their full potential.

As previously mentioned, it is noticeable that, when there has been extreme duress in the history, the personality often arrests at the actual age when the stress originally impacted. It is therefore important, after giving a successful remedy to remove this layer, to prescribe a related remedy to support the maturing process. I observed this after prescribing *Morphinum* for a 64-year-old patient who remained locked in her two-year-old mindset when a major early life trauma occurred. Jan Scholten refers to *Lactic acid* as "the girl that never grew up". [7] After receiving *Lactic acid*, she was able to embrace her adulthood and make up for all the years of lost time, much to the bemusement of those around her.

I have become increasingly interested in treating children and

---

7   Scholten, Jan (2007), *Homeopathy and the Elements*, Alonissos Verlag.

adults with autism and related 'States on the Spectrum' and, although certain remedies are recommended for these 'states', I have seen that it is often the life experiences and resulting attitudes of family members towards the compromised member that has a marked bearing on the choice of optimal remedy.

For example, one child had reached the age of seven before his father accepted that he was autistic. His mother was tormented by carrying this burden of awareness alone, realising that time was ticking by and the child was becoming increasingly alienated from family and peers, as well as himself. The father finally and reluctantly agreed for the child to be homeopathically treated but did not appear at any of the consultations despite encouragement from myself and the other family members. The father's sense of shame was based on what other people would think, which served as a 'maintaining cause', promoting the child's condition and prolonging his agony and that of the collective dynamic. *Thuja* unblocked the case as this burden upon the child, projected from the parent, was encompassed within the remedy picture as the stumbling block preventing the child from opening up. After treatment, the child started to make eye contact and reach out to others. The tensions within the family also eased as the effects of the treatment filtered through to other members in a vicarious way.

The concept of 'primal wounding' introduces possible complications when treating adopted children. Whatever the history in each individual case of adoption, the issue of 'rupture in the attachment process' is universally present and, of course, if signs are evident, should be addressed during treatment. Nancy Verrier, MA, presented a paper at the American Adoption Convention in California, as the guardian of a baby adopted when three days old, saying: "I believe that this connection, established during the nine months in utero, is a profound connection, and it is my hypothesis that the severing of that connection between the child and biological mother causes a primal or narcissistic wound which often manifests in a sense of loss (depression), basic mistrust (anxiety), emotional and/or behavioural problems and difficulties in relationships with significant others. I further believe that the awareness, whether conscious or unconscious, that the original separation was the result of relinquishment affects the adoptee's sense of self, self-esteem, and self-worth." [8]

Naturally, if a child has been adopted into a loving family, any initial damage to the brain structures caused by the absence of bonding may be modulated through this ongoing affirmative influence. Boris Cyrulnik believes that damage from such early loss can in fact be reversed, based on his own experience of the trauma of losing his parents in the Holocaust. [9]

Saccharum officinale is a remedy that holds the specific theme of adoption in its picture, and scores highly in the choice of remedies where damage has occurred. The 'occulted' emotions are often destructively acted out in children needing this remedy, especially if their primal history was one of abuse, which can unfortunately at times be true. How many children discover by chance that they are adopted or perhaps they have been misled regarding their paternal origin? The rubrics **'deception, ailments from, friendship, deceived'** and **'grief, deception, from'** apply here. This could be the picture of the *Magnesium* group of remedies which portrays the 'orphan theme' in their reaction to the world.

The pattern of attachment is often passed down through the generations. It is well documented that abuse may perpetuate this pattern of destructive behaviour in the offspring. [10] However, there are instances where the pattern of relating is consciously opposed to that of a role model. Hilary Boyd's novel is a good example of this. [11] It concerns a woman of a certain age who embarks on an affair ten years after her husband left the marital bed without explanation. It is only when the wife is forced to 'out' the affair to her husband that he breaks down and reveals the hidden background to his decision. It transpires that, on that

---

8   Verrier, Nancy, MA (April 11-14, 1991), *The Primal Wound: Legacy of the Adopted Child. The Effects of Separation from the Birthmother on Adopted Children*, American Adoption Congress International Convention, Garden Grove, California.

9   Cyrulnik, Boris (2009), *Resilience – How Your Inner Strength Can Set You Free from the Past*, Penguin.

10   Miller, Alice (2008), *The Drama of Being a Child: The Search for the True Self*, Virago.

11   Boyd, Hilary (2012), *Thursdays in the Park*, Quercus.

fateful day, he had bumped into the perpetrator of the childhood abuse he had suffered. More significantly, he had never spoken about it. This pattern resembles that of the remedy *Opium*, where a memory is triggered by a 'resonant' impetus. It also serves as a reminder of how toxic these types of secrets can become when maintained in this way.

To proceed: their daughter chooses a partner who suffers with Asperger's syndrome – which may not be a coincidence! Things start to 'unravel' when he ignores a head injury their small child suffers in the playground. It is then possible to see how the repercussions of the 'toxic secret' permeate the forthcoming generations – denial increasingly becomes a byword in this type of hidden family dynamic. Later, it is revealed the 'heroine' of the book had lost a brother when they were both young and the family had never spoken about it. It is possible to see the 'law of attraction' operating here throughout the generations on so many levels. The narratives of realistic life stories such as portrayed in this novel help to see the often unrealised patterns in real life and are particularly relevant to expressions of transmitted trauma.

In another case which presented for treatment, a patient resisted abortion all her reproductive life. This was strange to her as she was not someone who took the moral high ground on this issue. It was only after her mother's death that she learnt, quite casually from her older sister, that their mother had experienced two abortions between their respective births. She realised at this point why she had always had such a strong aversion to succumbing to this fate herself, and went into shock and needed homeopathic treatment to recover. As inferred above, her sister was completely unaffected, illustrating the varying individual susceptibility within the same lineage given the exact same trigger.

According to Bessel Van der Kolk, traumatic experiences may be encoded differently from memories of ordinary events, which is why they can become so embedded in the psyche. [12] One could

---

12   Van der Kolk, Bessel (1998), Trauma and Memory, *Psychiatry and Clinical Neurosciences*, 52(S1):S52-S64.

speculate in the above scenario that the younger sister became afflicted due to the awareness – conscious or not – that she was therefore unwanted and this explained the reason for the dysfunctional relationship she had always experienced with her mother, which she had never previously fathomed.

The whole theme of this treatise is worthy of consideration for illnesses which are prevalent in certain cultures – for example, Ashkenazi Jews have a predisposition to breast cancer, ovarian cancer, and a rare central nervous system genetic disease called Tay-Sachs. [13] African and Afro-Caribbean people are disposed to sickle cell anaemia, [14] and Cypriots to thalassaemia. [15] When one considers the collective cultural unconscious prevailing in these different races, it may be that their overlapping history of oppression could be a component in this phenomenon of 'disease attraction'. This means that there could be a 'genus epidemicus' remedy for these different states based on this theory. Remedies such as *Carcinosin* and *Staphysagria* are relevant here on a miasmatic level. *Carcinosin*, specifically, is an important remedy for auto-immune disorders where the roots are deeply embedded in the cultural and family history. These remedies could not only support the active suffering but, even more validly, serve as a prophylactic to entering such a trajectory of disease. This could apply not only to the patient but also their children, by stemming what attracts the disease in the first place – the transmission of the inherited sense of violation which is perpetuated unrelentingly through the generations.

---

13 Brandt-Rauf, Sherry I., JD, Mphil, et al. (November 2006), Ashkenazi Jews and Breast Cancer: The Consequences of Linking Ethnic Identity to Genetic Disease, *American Journal Public Health*, 96(11):1979–1988.

14 Booth, Catherine et al. (January 2010), Infection in Sickle Cell Disease: A Review, *International Journal of Infectious Diseases*, 14(1):e2-e12.

15 *Cyprus: How One Nation's Culture Influences Its Genes* (2010), www.geneletter.com/cyprus-how-one-nations-culture-influences-its-genes-16/.

1.2 INCORPORATING THE TRANSGENERATIONAL FACTOR WHEN TEACHING HOMEOPATHY AND CASE-TAKING

My intention in writing this book is to illustrate the need to be more focused on what 'informs' the case and less focused on its subjective and objective symptoms. Indeed, the fundamental layer of the case structure is often rooted in the primal period of life. If these patterns are not addressed, they become 'recycled' in a different but related format each time a similar 'trigger' or stimulus occurs. This then compounds the lesional patterns until they can eventually lead to the occurrence of deep pathology.

Severe pathology such as auto-immune disease may be rooted in a background of extreme trauma. Through a transgenerational framework of understanding, the pathology can continue unremittingly along its destructive trajectory especially if the patient remains exposed to strong 'maintaining causes'. These 'maintaining causes' can often be derived from the way the family dynamic is expressed. [16] The patient and their ancestors would have experienced this trauma to a degree commensurate with the depth of the resulting physical symptoms.

When learning materia medica, it is important to identify the 'ailments from' rubrics in each individual remedy, whether on an emotional or a physical level. For example, 'abuse' or 'deception' are both very disabling triggers on an emotional level, and 'head injury' or 'vaccination' significant on the physical level, so it is vital to understand the case in its true triggering context. We should never overlook the relevance of physical symptoms which dictate outcomes on the mental level. In these cases, one should reverse the hierarchy unless, of course, it was emotionally triggered in the first place. [2]

---

16 Dube, Shanta R. et al. (2009), Cumulative Childhood Stress and Autoimmune Diseases in Adults, *Psychosomatic Medicine*, 71(2):243-50.

Taking the time-line into consideration, therefore, it is possible to see a whole new meaning to case-taking and resulting homeopathic treatment. Even if the causative trauma afflicted past generations, it can be included in the anamnesis of the individual patient. Often, when a parent's time-line is superimposed upon that of a presenting patient, one can perceive peaks of stress at similar stages of life development in the overlapping cases. It is as if these triggers became encoded at a cellular level in the offspring ready to be activated according to their individual susceptibility because the latter has informed the level of resulting damage in the case. As it may skip a generation, this might not necessarily be apparent in sequential ones.

Of course, the homeopath needs to gain the patient's trust in order to work in this way, and it may take time before the patient is comfortable enough to give the relevant information. The ideal is to treat all family members in order to benefit from a combined synergistic effect and each individual member will contribute according to their presenting picture. However, it is not always possible to do this directly although the individual relatives' contribution to the presenting patterns can be incorporated in the patient's background. This can be achieved by including key rubrics which reflect the major impacting influences on the case. The results in one patient can filter vicariously through to other family members as healing percolates through the layers of suffering. For example, if someone who has fathered a child was, in his early history, a victim of abuse, he may now be concerned about passing on the damage to his child. This indicates that, as the possible 'pivot of distress' in this new dynamic, he is the one ideally to be treated. This would release not only the child but also the other family members who, hitherto, had remained in the 'firing line' of his sense of violation.

The practitioner should take into account the combination of inherited characteristics, through either the miasmatic or the 'epigenetic' link. Consideration should also be given to the intra-uterine effects on the development of the brain of the child, acquired through trauma in pregnancy. These influences should be incorporated into the hierarchy of rubrics when assessing the outcome in the choice of remedy.

If a patient becomes irrationally upset by inoffensive remarks of others during case-taking, the practitioner could suspect that this has triggered a 'wound' experienced earlier in life. These feelings may not even relate to the presenting patient, but represent a reflex from an experience of their parents (or grandparents, or even great-grandparents) despite the fact that the original DNA may not have been passed on. This is quite a revelatory factor when one considers how it may affect the whole theory of miasms in one's homeopathic understanding.

If materia medica is learnt according to causation – whether emotional or physical – the exact remedy can be selected based on this methodology of transgenerational understanding. The specific neural conduit which becomes honed in this way is likely to have been passed down through the generations. This is the result of repeated ruminations on the part of the sufferer. This shows how significant role models are. However, the genetic inheritance which penetrates the psyche through negative emotions (such as fear and guilt) leads to a similar response. The 'unconscious' attracts the same resonant situations into the patient's life unless this propensity can be identified and addressed accordingly.

Nowadays, the legacy of war is never far away from our patients. This means that, as the descendants, they carry a vulnerability to this contributing trigger when similar reminders arrive. The *Iodum* patient, for example, may have had to go on the run, become afraid of starvation and for their very existence itself. Thus, a patient who eats voraciously to their own detriment may have such a history if the background of their case is explored deeply enough. Nothing in their own story could explain their impulsivity around food. Therefore, applying this approach to case-taking could open up a whole new vista of lasting cures on both an emotional and corresponding physical level.

This concept begs the question on how to resolve issues residing in the patient's imprinted blueprint rather than randomly entering their mind. Homeopaths often ask questions around specific ailments but, if they were to probe around family trauma, this might throw up subtle responses. Finally, with the support of the simillimum, the patient can become free from this influence for the first time in their life and shed the burden they have carried till then.

1.3 THE RELATIONSHIP BETWEEN TRANSGENERATIONAL HOMEOPATHY AND THE MIASMS

Miasms in homeopathic terms represent an inherited chronic undermining in the expression of health of the individual. Their manifestation could be interpreted as a reflection of the underpinning transmitted unconscious belief systems which infiltrate the ancestral lineage.

Psora is the fundamental miasm underlying all the other ones mentioned here. Through the lens of *Psorinum*, the nosode of psora, one can appreciate the background of abandonment and deprivation. It is all about survival, which is a universal human instinct explaining why psora underlies all the other miasms. The anxiety manifested in this miasm can lead to panic attacks or even disturbance in the heart rhythm.

The sycotic miasm, represented by the nosode *Medorrhinum*, shows the patient is unable to look inwards to nurture themselves but always needing external stimulation. This attitude could have been inherited through role models; conversely, it could be intrinsic to the patient due to adverse early life experience – even occurring while in the womb or during the birthing experience. The excessive personality can manifest in a hyper-kinetic state and indulgence in hedonistic as well as materialistic pursuits without concern for their own welfare. The way this miasm attacks the bodily structure is by affecting mucous membranes which link the innermost with the outermost. The excess in mucous is a direct reflection of the emotional state described above.

The syphilitic miasm, represented by the nosode *Syphilinum*, is easily passed down the ancestral line in the form of alcoholism, birth defects, depression, insomnia, Parkinson's disease or strokes. These diseases start to destroy the structure of the body, which can be irreversible. The organism has no longer the energy to repair itself. Given the accident-prone nature of this miasm, men seem to comply more with it than women from my observation in practice.

The cancer miasm, represented by the nosode *Carcinosin*, is the sum total of the psoric, sycotic and syphilitic miasms. As a result of my experience of using this remedy, I now believe *Carcinosin* is the main nosode associated with transgenerational trauma, as borne out by the overwhelming number of references to it throughout the text. The patient feels they need to justify their existence as a result of their ancestral inheritance. They do not let themselves express anger or strong emotions, which means they often have problems with boundaries and take on the moods and sensitivities of others rather than feeling and expressing their own. This may result in deep pathology such as diabetes, mental illness or inflammatory disease, culminating, as the end result, in cancer. In order to prevent this negative habitual trajectory, early treatment of such cases is essential. Once the patient takes *Carcinosin,* they can start to voice their feelings and find their rightful space in their family and friend groupings. The family may struggle to adjust to this change but, at some level, will realise its benefit to the patient. This often occurs in cases of anorexia where the patient becomes more vocal in their needs in order to embrace their newly-gained adulthood, having been stuck in victimhood for so long.

In *Motherland,* her mother's biography, Rita Goldberg refers to her family's history of Holocaust survival as 'a crushing burden'. [17] She mentions that, for second-generation survivors, making sense of their background is especially difficult, because it has sometimes been obscured, especially where parents have been unable to talk about their experiences. The very ability to cut off from the pain, which enabled survival, is the exact issue which afflicts future generations, unless addressed. These survivors also felt, albeit mistakenly, that it was relevant to withhold this information from their children. Hence, one sees in *Carcinosin* a strong sense of silent grief where the grief is actually hidden from the sufferer due to the context of its origin. Goldberg said, when speaking of the strength of the audience response at a London

17   Goldberg, Rita (2014), *Motherland: Growing Up with the Holocaust*, Halban Publishers.

28

reading: "I was startled by it and am beginning to see how many of my generation were defined by their parents' history, even though they did not live through it."[18]

The importance of Goldberg's book, when seen through a 'homeopathic filter', is the significance of the need for children of survivors to understand the origin of their own suffering. For example, teenagers may not feel able to voice their anger and anxieties in order to protect their parents, especially if their ancestors were victims of true suffering and threat to their very survival. Suppression of emotions, which is so key to the cancer miasm, is fuelled by such a history.

In *Descendants of Holocaust Survivors Have Altered Stress Hormones*, based on the work of Rachel Yehuda, an Israeli researcher in the field of epigenetics and the intergenerational effects of trauma, the author explains the vicarious but unconscious related suffering of the ancestors. [19] Yehuda and her colleagues studied mass trauma survivors and their offspring, and found that descendants of people who survived the Holocaust have different stress hormone profiles than their peers, which perhaps predispose them to anxiety disorders. Their research established that survivors have lower levels of cortisol, the hormone that supports the body in returning to normal after trauma; and those who suffered post-traumatic stress disorder have even lower levels. The theory even suggests that this adaptation happens in utero. An enzyme which is present in the placenta would normally protect the foetus from the mother's circulating cortisol. The epigenetic factor beyond the classic genetic mechanism for transmission plays out here as it could be argued the paternal influence has less of a role in this interplay. This is an important factor for homeopathic case-taking and analysis. Could it also be possible that these descendants, who are prone to post-traumatic stress disorder, may also be at risk of such diseases as age-related metabolic syndrome, including

---

18 Goldberg, Rita (March 18, 2014), London Reading, Waterstone's Bookshop, Hampstead High Street.

19 Rodriguez, Tori (2015), Descendants of Holocaust Survivors Have Altered Stress Hormones, *Scientific American Mind*, 26(2).

obesity, hypertension, and insulin resistance?

The miasm theory, with its ancestral connection to disease, teaches the value of treating both parents before conception where possible. This way, the homeopath can address the ongoing trajectory of disease through the generations from recurring in different manifestations in future offspring. After all, the roots of so many pathologies are laid down both before and after conception.

1.4 RECENT DEVELOPMENTS IN NEUROSCIENCE

The awareness of the importance of the role of the unconscious coincides with the recent developments in neuroscience: it has been established that brain structures can easily be undermined as a result of prolonged fear, neglect and, in extremis, abuse. The more intense the triggering factor, and the younger the victim at the time of impact, the more the brain structures become modified or damaged. The amount of cortisol released during such stressors is what creates this modification.

For example, the remedy *Alumina*, which is often prescribed for Alzheimer's disease, has in its picture a possible background of early family chaos which impacts on the brain structures. The gradual build-up of cortisol causes damage to the hippocampus, the specific brain structure responsible for memory. Homeopathy is one system of medicine that can work retrospectively to reconcile these pattern-forming influences and, accordingly, restore function to the affected brain structure. Of course, 'maintaining causes' also need to be removed.

Affection received in infancy shapes babies' brains, impacting the receptors in the brain which influence how the adult later responds to stress. This, in turn, can translate into disease later in life. In *The Biology of Love*, Arthur Janov describes how love begins in the womb, literally shapes our brains, and determines how we think, feel and act throughout life. [20] He even declares that love determines the state of our health and the length of our lives. This explains why early trauma leaves such an indelible mark, especially when no conscious recollection of the related events remains. The brain structure which is so affected by this interaction is the amygdala – that part of the limbic system where mood is regulated. If the amygdala has been primed in this way, later along their life trajectory, panic attacks, free-floating anxiety, or possible irrational phobias can afflict the patient. This governs

---

20   Janov, Arthur (2000), *The Biology of Love*, Prometheus Books.

the adrenal system's ability to control the fight or flight response. The amygdala is the one brain structure which seems to be fully formed at birth. [21]

This is why it is possible, by taking the full timeline into consideration, to adopt a whole new meaning to case-taking and resulting homeopathic treatment. Even if the causative trauma afflicted past generations, it can be included in the anamnesis of the individual patient.

---

21 Adalian, Elizabeth (Winter 2010), Sculpting the 'Software' – Targeting Specific Brain Structures, *Homeopathy in Practice*.

1.5 PSYCHO-PHYSIOLOGY –
THE BRAIN AND THE LIMBIC SYSTEM

The limbic system is where the mood is modulated and bonding takes place. The brain structure, the amygdala, is intrinsic to the limbic system, reaching maturity more quickly than the other structures. The amygdala can be seen as the 'emotional barometer' which can be 'calibrated' by the mother's experience and handling of stress in pregnancy. This reinforces the value of treating a pregnant woman during this vulnerable time, if not before. The two hormones – oxytocin and prolactin – are released at birth to foster the bonding experience and, in turn, to boost the brain area. Breastfeeding augments their action by its very nature as these hormones act positively on the amygdala. [21]

Brain structures are very much compromised in schizophrenia and other related 'States on the Spectrum' such as addiction, eating disorders, personality and dissociative disorders. These are examples of illnesses where, unless one explores the roots in the history of the case, there can be no resolution. It has recently been discovered that, due to their plasticity, damaged brain structures can be returned to their healthy form. [22] It is a principle underpinning this finding that homeopathy can contribute to their restoration. The word 'spectrum' indicates that these 'states' can vary considerably in their manifestation. This means that some sufferers are entirely limited and defined by it, whereas others operate in the 'mainstream world' with very little awareness either from themselves or others that they may be compromised by the restrictions this inevitably places on them.

22   Doidge, Norman (2007), *The Brain that Changes Itself,* Viking Penguin Publishers.

1.6   EPIGENETICS

In recent years, 'epigenetics' has become a 'buzz word' in the field of neuroscience. This implies that the effects of traumas are passed on through the generations at a cellular level and become attached to the DNA of the patient. At the same time, they do not change the DNA code itself. This is why people with the same DNA, such as identical twins, may have different health challenges. Identical twins' experience in the womb is completely different, even though the twins may look the same on the outside. Different positions as embryos or experiences during the mother's labour can create lasting epigenetic effects. This transmission is often through an emotional link, but can equally be due to such factors as chemicals or drugs. An example of this is bisphenol-A (BPA), which is an endocrine disruptor affecting neurological development. This influence could affect not only the individual but also a transgenerational contagion both on a physical and mental/emotional level. [23]

In this context, research into the long-term effects of the birth control pill on future generations, not only on a hormonal level, but also on a psychic level, would be valuable. One theme of the remedy *Folliculinum*, beyond its hormonal influence, is of non-individuation, a theme commonly observed in children who have grown up with autism. This begs the question of an epigenetic link between 'States on the Spectrum' and a history of the use of 'the pill' in the mother leading up to conception. [24]

The most startling aspect of the concept of epigenetics is that less than 2% of the population is born with a genetic condition. [25] The rest of the population succumbs to illness due to lifestyle and behaviour which means that, just by making changes on these levels, it is possible to control genes which govern the majority of

---

23   Negri-Cesi, P. (April-June, 2015), Bisphenol A Interaction with Brain Development and Functions, *Dose Response*, 13(2):1559325815590394.

24   Strifert, Kim (2014), The Link Between Oral Contraceptive Use and Prevalence in Autistic Spectrum Disorder, *Medical Hypothesis*, 83(6):718-25.

25   Hall, S. (2012), Journey to the Genetic Interior, *Scientific American*, 307(10):80-4.

disease manifestations. However, if an individual is locked into negative thinking based on adverse memories from the past, this is likely to result in a similar reaction to future resonant events. Stress, a byword of current times, is one of the greatest triggers to epigenetic change. Trauma can manifest on a physical level as well as an emotional one, especially when the trauma has been suppressed; and specific physical ailments such as stomach ulcers, heart conditions and insomnia are known to be rooted in stress.

Traumas, whether emotionally or physically induced, are often unexpressed in one generation but acted out in subsequent ones unless they are dealt with in the interim. The way this hidden 'wound' is expressed and received relates to the individual susceptibility of subsequent generations. I have seen this in practice where children have been denied knowledge of their true origins. Articulation of trauma by the sufferer to the descendant – however painful – should be encouraged at the level of understanding of the recipient of this information at the time. This dialogue can be amplified as the child develops and becomes ready to hear the full story. Needless to say, a sensitive approach by the homeopath and the family is essential. Homeopathic treatment can really open up these avenues of communication. This is because valuable insight is gained in the process of recovery, which hitherto was hidden to the patient. In fact, this insight starts to develop during the consultation when the focus of attention is often projected onto this issue within a safe and confidential environment. Unfortunately, Western societies do not generally encourage such discussion of past events due to the desire to avoid exposure to criticism by showing weakness or shame.

It has recently been documented for the first time that a mother's diet in pregnancy can change the expression of genes in her unborn child, and that this can have an impact upon the child's development right up to adulthood. [26] This means it is not just what happens to the parents before, during, and after conception

26   Dominguez-Salas, P. et al. (2014), Maternal Nutrition at Conception Modulates DNA Methylation of Human Metastable Epialleles, *Nature Communications*, http://www.nature.com/articles/ncomms4746.

that affects the 'epigenetic imprint' upon the child, but also the nutritional status of the mother during gestation. This research opens up a whole new arena beyond the influence of emotional factors. Apparently, most of the switching on and off of genes through the epigenetic factor, whether emotional or nutritional, takes place early in life, if not in utero.

In recent times, with the invention of ultrasound technology, the womb can be regarded as providing an evolving environment enabling the foetus to respond to music or the sound of the mother's voice. This demonstrates that this organic and emotional interaction is vital for the baby's development and survival. In addition to the birth itself, these factors dictate the baby's resilience. This understanding has only recently come to the fore with the advent of epigenetics. As epigenetic factors are not 'soldered' to the DNA of the individual, this suggests that they are more easily addressed than genetic ones when appropriate treatment is given. Nowadays, more and more advice is given to patients in mainstream medicine to enhance their 'epigenome' through lifestyle changes such as, for example, the adoption of mindfulness and meditation on an emotional level and healthy eating habits and exercise on a physical one.

These days, emphasis is placed on the importance of the mother's health leading up to conception, as well as during pregnancy, birth and after. While such environmental challenges as diet, drug abuse and chronic stress experienced by mothers have been shown to affect the neuro-development of the offspring and increase the risk for certain diseases, the influence of the pre-conception father's state on his child is less well understood or even mentioned in the literature. This is about to change due to recent research carried out by Professor Tracy Bale and her team at the University of Pennsylvania in the *Journal of Neuroscience*, which shows that sperm does not appear to forget anything. [27] Stress experienced by a man, whether as a pre-adolescent or adult, leaves a lasting impression on his sperm that passes on a

---

27   Rodgers, Ali B., Bale, Tracy L. et al. (May 2013), Paternal Stress Exposure Alters
     Sperm MicroRNA Content and Reprograms Offspring HPA Stress Axis Regulation,
     The Journal of Neuroscience, 33(21):9003–12.

blunted response to stress to his offspring. The type of stress described is linked to several mental disorders. This points to a newly discovered epigenetic link to stress-related diseases such as anxiety and depression, passed from father to child, even though that stress may have occurred many years earlier.

Stress placed on pre-adolescent and adult mice induced an epigenetic mark on the sperm that reprogrammed their offspring's hypothalamic-pituitary-adrenal axis – a region of the brain that determines the response to stress. Both male and female offspring had abnormally low reactivity to stress due to the resulting inhibited brain development.

Practitioners should therefore consider the combination of inherited characteristics through the 'epigenetic' link, perhaps even more than through the miasmatic one, and bear in mind the intra-uterine effects on the development of the baby's brain acquired through trauma in pregnancy. It is important to incorporate these combined influences into the hierarchy of rubrics during remedy selection.

1.7   PSYCHOTHERAPY

In *Pieces of Light: the New Science of Memory*, Charles Fernyhough stresses how important it is, for the sake of children's development, to talk about the past within the family dynamic. [28] He believes this enhances autobiographical memories as it is these types of memories which contribute to one's life narrative. He says: "Talking together about the past seems to be vitally important in children's creation of a self that extends through time." Teenagers who have been exposed to this early dialogue have been found to produce earlier memories to make sense of their lives than those denied this advantage. It is important to remember, however, to guard against assigning symptoms to a patient unless they are genuinely applicable.

Bert Hellinger created the concept of 'family constellations'. [29] This relates to the unconscious role each member of a family plays. Birth order, of course, plays a part, but beyond this it is often one particular parent or close family member at any one time who is the 'pivot of distress', and a specific child who 'carries the can'. This child can act it out through dysfunctional behaviour and corresponding physical ailments which represent a manifestation of the unexpressed dynamic operating within that system. Targeting the treatment at the 'pivot of the distress' is the ideal, where possible, as this releases the whole collective dynamic.

The visionary educator, Rudolf Steiner, spoke of the scripts being 'written' by the age of seven. [30] As the child cannot control this programming of the brain, this sets in place the self-sabotaging beliefs which can affect all aspects of future life unless consciously recognised and addressed accordingly. Carl Jung said: "*Everything*

---

28   Fernyhough, Charles (2012), *Pieces of Light: The New Science of Memory*, Profile Books.
29   Hellinger, Bert (2001), *Love's Own Truths: Bonding and Balancing in Close Relationships*, Zeig, Tucker and Theisen, Pheonix, USA.
30   Steiner, Rudolf, Bamford, Christopher, and Fox, Helen (1995), *The Kingdom of Childhood*, Steiner Books, Inc., Foundations of Waldorf Education, USA.

that has not been revealed expresses itself in the form of fate." His emphasis was on the 'collective unconscious'. [31]

In 1909, Sigmund Freud wrote: "A thing which has not been understood inevitably reappears; like an unlaid ghost, it cannot rest until the mystery has been solved and the spell broken." His emphasis was on the 'personal unconscious'.

Leopold Szondi, a contemporary of Jung and Freud, linked both their different ways of thinking through the 'familial unconscious'. [32] This suggests that hidden genetic characteristics are based on the individual experience of life and on the interactions within the original family structure, and that the act of choosing is completely conscious, but the reason for the choices remains encrypted in the 'familial unconscious'. This last theory is the closest to the concepts in this book and is resonant with the concept of 'occulted emotions' mentioned in the Introduction.

31 Stirt, Joseph A., MD (2002), *Quantations: A Guide to Quantum Living in the 21st Century*, iUniverse, USA.
32 Kiss, Enikő Gyöngyösiné, *Personality and the Familial Unconscious in Szondi's Fate-Analysis*, www.szondi.pte.hu/document/fate-analysis.pdf.

1.8   ATTACHMENT THEORY

John Bowlby's 'attachment theory' was influenced by Lorenz's study of imprinting (albeit in young ducklings), which demonstrated that attachment was innate. Bowlby then translated this into human behaviour, showing its consequent survival value. [33] This infers that children enter the world biologically pre-programmed to form attachments with others.

Bowlby believed that any conditions which threaten closeness to the primary caregiver (usually the mother), such as separation, insecurity and fear, will induce a negative response. If this attachment is severed during the vital first two years of life, significant negative consequences, such as emotional and social issues can result, culminating in reduced intelligence, depression, increased aggression, delinquency and what he calls 'affectionless psychopathy'. Homeopaths might infer from this that the more extreme the primal deprivation, the more extreme the resulting negative emotional reaction.

33   Holmes, Jeremy (1993), *John Bowlby and Attachment Theory (Makers of Modern Psychotherapy)*, Routledge Publishers.

1.9   CREATING A SHIFT IN
A NEGATIVE MINDSET

The individual mindset is very much influenced by miasmatic inheritance combined with the example of the role model. If these factors prove negative, it takes much encouragement from the practitioner and steadfastness on the part of the patient to shift this mindset into a more positive gear. A type of 'armouring' slips in and can become 'concretised' in the body. This occurs, for example, in *Conium maculatum*, where hard tumours can arise as a result of the emotions shutting down, which is a typical mindset in the background of auto-immune diseases as a whole. Other remedies where 'armouring' takes place are *Kali carbonicum* (affecting the heart and lungs) and *Plumbum metallicum*. All three remedies involve serious pathology.

When a disease process is ongoing, a negative attitude only intensifies the destructiveness of this decline. Once the 'mindshift' occurs, reversal of pathology can ensue, resulting in a full recovery. In fact the illness may be perceived, albeit in retrospect by the patient, to have guided them into reclaiming their true nature that has got lost along the way, as referred to earlier.

1.10 MIND-BODY CONNECTION

The thyroid is an example of an 'emotional' organ, often afflicting women during times of hormonal changes. These are times when they often feel they have not got a 'voice'.

Thyroid disease often goes unrecognised in men but, when men feel increasingly disempowered in today's culture, they can suffer equally with this disease. *Baryta carbonica* has an interesting rubric relating to the mind/body connection, ***'delusion, legs, cut off, are'***. In Robin Murphy's *Nature's Materia Medica*, *Baryta carbonica* is said to have 'numbness from knees to scrotum', 'burning pains in lower limbs', and 'pain in the knees, while kneeling'. [34] These physical symptoms represent the withdrawal and retardedness of the patient needing this remedy – in other words, the patient is physically impeded from going forward. When the remedy is given based on the physical symptoms alone, not only do they become addressed, but also the corresponding emotional picture becomes integrated and restored at the same time. To take the logic one step further, the reason for slowing down on all levels could be because the thyroid is under-functioning, even to the point of 'cretinism', a condition dating right back to birth. This means that treatment outcome can cover all these different aspects of the case in its ability to work retrospectively in this radical way.

Another example could be a case of duodenal ulcer which has been inherited from a parent; not only will the targeted remedy deal with the physical pathology, but also the emotional roots behind it. Duodenal ulcer is widely documented to be linked with anxiety. [35] So, by addressing both the roots of the illness plus the pathology, one circumvents the onward transmission of such an ailment through the generations. Not only does the treatment address this specific ailment, but related and deeper ones which can create both emotional and physical turmoil.

---

[34] Murphy, Robin (2006) *Nature's Materia Medica*, 3rd Edition, Lotus Health Institute.
[35] Goodwin, R.D., et al. (2013), A Link Between Physician-Diagnosed Ulcer and Anxiety Disorders Among Adults, *Annals of Epidemiology*, 23(4):189-92.

Persistent states of anxiety often lie in the background of 'States on the Spectrum' which are a growing issue in today's culture. Exploring the history of previous family members could be the key to preventing the onset of these 'states' in the individual. In other words, by withdrawing the flame, the cauldron is extinguished. At the same time, the role model of defeating attitudes is diffused, so no longer remains as a 'maintaining cause' to fuel the ongoing state. Additionally, patients with 'States on the Spectrum' – both adult and children – often suffer with a compromised gut as part of their specific syndrome. This is because the gut holds a reflective resonance with the brain through the vagus nerve. [36]

---

36 Schmidt, Charles (March 2015), Mental Health May Depend on Creatures in the Gut, *Scientific American Mind,* 312(3).

1.11 STRESS

Stress has become a byword of the 21st century. John F. Kennedy observed that the word 'crisis', when written in Chinese, consists of two characters – one represents danger, and the other represents opportunity. Homeopaths can appreciate this concept and work with their patients to transform their experience in this way.

How a person responds to stress is very individual – depending on miasmatic influences and learned methods of reacting within the original family. In fact, the breakdown of families seems to be one of the main adverse influences operating nowadays in society. This, in turn, increases isolation as family members become disseminated across distant locations and countries.

So much depends on the value of resilience as a way to maintain balanced health, as described in the remedy pictures of *Silica* and *Strontium carbonicum*, which are given to support people in achieving this. We learn early on in our study of the *Silica* patient that 'they lack grit'.

During Samuel Hahnemann's lifetime (1755-1843), the word 'stress' did not exist and it was only in the 1930s that Hans Selye coined the expression based on his observation of the trends existing at the time. He noted that his observations of rats could be compared to the human experience. He discovered that one of the first targets of stress is the pituitary gland which, in turn, affects all the major endocrine glands such as the thyroid, the thymus (often damaged by vaccination) and – most significantly – the adrenals, which are strongly interlinked with the thyroid gland. [37]

We may therefore wonder if it is any coincidence that women, after childbirth, may manifest thyroid disease at a time when emotions and hormones are thrown into absolute disarray. In this

---

[37]   Wilson, James L. (2002), *Adrenal Fatigue: The 21st Century Stress Syndrome*, Smart Publications.

process, adaptability to changes is severely threatened. The endocrine glands are compromised by stress at the best of times, but especially at this vulnerable time.

The adrenals, during stressful situations, release excessive levels of cortisol in the initial phase until they become depleted. This process, in turn, affects many functions, including bone renewal and memory.

Is it any coincidence that there is an epidemic of osteoporosis and Alzheimer's disease, for example, as well as such states as allergies, autism, asthma, fibromyalgia, M.E. and cancer? The phenomenal rise in incidences of these illnesses is commensurate with the increased awareness of stress impacting everyone's lives. I believe the degree of unresolved trauma operating within the family structure, and how this impacts on the individual, compounds the marked inability to adjust to the modern world.

Where trauma is not expressed in the family, children may act it out unconsciously in destructive ways. Secrets in families can also manifest in this way, so such rubrics as *'deception, ailments from friendship, deceived'* and *'grief, deception, from'* can operate here.

As sleep is one of the first characteristics to be affected by stress, it is important to explore a patient's quality of sleep to ascertain the impact the stress is exerting on the individual. During sleep, a person reveals their 'uncompensated state' – that which cannot be distorted. Dreams often reflect the core of the issue at stake. Reflecting this back to the patient can be useful if they are ready to explore their deeper meaning. As the patient becomes more integrated through treatment, it is often the dreams that show coherence with this process before other symptoms, especially where patients are not emotionally articulate.

Opium and *Stramonium*, both well known for trauma, often reveal themselves through sleep disturbances. In *Opium*, for example, sleep apnoea may occur and in *Stramonium*, the well-known symptom of nightmares. Both remedies are in the rubric *'sleep-walking, somnambulism'*. All the remedies in this rubric include trauma in their picture: *Aconite, Anacardium, Cannabis indica, Hyoscyamus, Kali bromatum, Natrum muriaticum, Opium, Stramonium, Tarentula, Veratrum album,* and *Zincum metallicum*. This implies that this symptom mirrors both disorientation and repression at the same time illustrated through the range of remedies listed. People with a history of intense trauma often do not recall their dreams. As they become healthier through homeopathic treatment, they can start to access and work with their dreams to guide them towards cure.

1.12 THE LINK BETWEEN DOPAMINE AND CORTISOL

A certain level of stress can be used to fuel the focus to achieve life goals. However, when stress goes beyond an endurable level for each individual, the amount of cortisol released during the initial phase of the stress response triggers a dopamine surge. This becomes addictive until a state of high alert takes over and, as the dopamine level reduces, cortisol again takes over. When this occurs, after a protracted length of time, the feel-good factor that is associated with dopamine rapidly dwindles. At this stage, all incentive for achieving any goals disappears completely. This pattern of behaviour is rooted in the primal years when it becomes encoded in the responses of the individual. It could be that a lack of oxytocin (the bonding neuropeptide) is the underpinning factor which underlies many of the disease states covered in this book. Influences on the mother that enable this to occur include issues from her own childhood, her experience of pregnancy, the birth itself and breastfeeding. 'States on the Spectrum' are often rooted in this type of history, especially addiction, where the 'substance' becomes a substitute for the missing mother – the 'true mother' and also the 'archetypal mother', who is so sadly lacking in culture today. [38] The 'substance' itself, whatever it is, reduces oxytocin even more, thus setting up a never-ending cycle in the balance between dopamine and cortisol. This whole cycle is conditioned by epigenetics: through recognising the pattern of behaviour which conditions this type of response, the practitioner can gain the insight to treat accordingly.

Children who are born by Caesarean section may lack oxytocin as they do not experience the surge of this neuropeptide released by travelling through the birth canal, as occurs in a vaginal delivery. Also, during Caesarean births, the brain is not moulded by the bones of the pelvic cavity as the infant passes through. This is an

---

[38] Jung, Carl G. (1991), *The Archetypes and the Collective Unconscious (Collected Works of C. G. Jung)*, 2nd Edition, Routledge.

important factor in the birthing process for the healthy development of the brain structures. Caesarean births also have a shock factor due to sudden exposure to bright lights and a sanitised environment. Mothers are less able to cradle their infant until the wound heals due to the effects of the surgery in such a delivery.

Premature babies are also disadvantaged when it comes to oxytocin as they are placed in incubators away from the loving touch of a parent and often attached to machines for their very survival. Once they are reunited with their parents, the link may therefore be more tenuous because the often unexpected early arrival, and resulting under-development of the infant, may affect the parents' belief in its long-term well-being and survival. The parents' own thwarted expectations of how the experience should have been for both them and the child may also affect the bonding. The shock of premature birth experienced by both infant and parents is an added contributor to any bonding issues which may quite understandably result. On top of this, symbiosis is jeopardised by the limited time the baby has spent in the mother's womb where the primal bond is first formed. [39]

The background of such trauma could form an epigenetic link affecting future generations, such is the assault on the cellular memory of the organism. As parents have to take over the care of the child as soon as they are discharged from hospital, there may be no space for them to process their reactions to such an unforeseen event in their lives.

IVF, which often results in multiple births, is frequently sought when pregnancy does not ensue spontaneously. These infants may be born pre-term and are placed in incubators until they are formed enough to control their own survival functions and catch up with their latent development. It would be an interesting study in years to come to monitor the epigenetic effect resulting from these children's early life traumas. In these cases, not only is there the effect of the trauma, but also the drugs involved in the process

39 Bell, Michele (2003), *The Effects of Prematurity on Development: Process Studies: The Premature Birth*, www.prematurity.org/research/prematurity-effects1c.html.

to enhance the mother's fertility, which would act to form part of that epigenetic transfer.

Oxytocin is produced in the pituitary gland which is the governor of all the different endocrine systems and dictates the overall health of each one. If oxytocin becomes deficient for whatever reason, this could affect the endocrine system of the body which can so easily become imbalanced. Even if the delivery was normal and the child was born at full term, any stress experienced in pregnancy could have been transmitted to the child and the effects may not be immediately visible. The gut may often be the first sign that the child has been affected. A compromised gut is often a concomitant to different 'States on the Spectrum' and could be the first sign of the incipient mental 'state'. [3] Sleep disturbances can equally be a precursor to the development of a later 'State on the Spectrum'. This is why, during case-taking, it is important to explore the conditions prevailing in pregnancy and in the parents' history leading up to conception which could have created an adverse effect on the child.

A disease such as polycystic ovary syndrome, for example, which has a link with diabetes, can be fuelled by irregular eating and resulting cortisol surges. This can easily trigger the dopamine/cortisol circuit. Once mealtimes are regulated, a major 'maintaining cause' is removed, the increase in well-being is noticeable, and the trajectory towards diabetes is averted in the process. Needless to say, diabetics are urged to eat regularly to keep their blood sugar levels steady. As cortisol is kept in balance by doing this, the feel-good factor of dopamine is experienced and that increase in well-being can fuel recovery from the disease.

1.13 VICTIMISATION

In former times, bullying supported young people to find their way in the 'pecking order'. Nowadays, there is a whole new dimension to this type of behaviour. In extremis, this can involve people being driven to suicide by taunting through the Internet – commonly known as cyber-bulling. These teenagers are caught up in this type of addictive behaviour as much as the perpetrators of this atrocity. This pattern of co-dependency is instilled from childhood where the 'victim' depends on the abuser. One sees this in *Carcinosin* and *Staphisagria*, where the suppression of anger induced by this early dynamic can repeat itself in the later pattern of relationships formed along the life trajectory. This is why, when such remedies are given, the victim may instigate a severance of the unhealthy relationship they have maintained until such time as they become more individuated and able to fend for themselves in the process of cure. In this way, the pattern of inter-generational co-dependency is broken once and for all, or at least in the instance of the co-dependent relationship operating at the time.

According to Professor Louise Arseneault from the Institute of Psychiatry at King's College, London, the impact of bullying can last a lifetime and affect physical and mental health even 40 years later. [40] The research quoted in the article even states that children who have been bullied are more likely to experience anxiety, depression, suicidal thoughts, and poor physical health by the age of 50 than those who have not been subjugated in this way. She continues: "When we compared the effects to other childhood adversities such as being put into care, abuse by an adult, or neglect, it is of the same scale. Some children will be set on a pathway towards problems for the rest of their lives." This is an extreme comparison but, when one looks into such a background through a homeopathic lens, it makes complete sense. Arseneault concludes: "Bullying really gets under the skin and

---

40   Smith, Rebecca (April 18, 2014), Bullying at School Affects Health 40 Years Later, *The Telegraph*, www.telegraph.co.uk/news/health/children/10772302/Bullying-at-school-affects-health-40-years-later.html.

affects the biology at a cellular level. The word recall test indicates bullying victims were showing signs of early ageing."

Lycopodium is the quintessential remedy for premature ageing and certainly shows signs of exposure to early bullying in its symptom picture. It would appear that the onslaught of perpetual bullying activates the adrenals and this is what contributes to the acceleration of the ageing process. Not only is academic work likely to suffer as a result of bullying, but also the ability to sustain relationships in later life, not forgetting the social support structure. Memory may be compromised regardless of the sufferer's IQ. There are only two remedies in the rubric **'memory, weakness, fear, from'**: *Anacardium* and *Cuprum metallicum*. It would appear from this rubric that the adrenals in these remedies have been constantly agitated to finally afflict the memory in this way. *Anacardium* is the only remedy in the rubric **'memory, weakness, humiliation, from'**.

Possibly related to the impact of bullying, dyslexia is a condition where the sufferer struggles to read and to make sense of conventional learning. This means that they frequently experience humiliation in the classroom setting. This in turn feeds the low self-esteem the condition already engenders and can affect the attitude of the teacher and fellow pupils towards the sufferer. By addressing this dynamic through homeopathic treatment, energy is released to acquire the skills to concentrate on the academic challenges presented to them. In this way, the dyslexic can tap into their true creative potential which so often goes hand in hand with this challenge.

Sensitivity to bullying is shown in the rubric **'unhappiness, prolonged, due to others'**. The main remedies listed are: *Aurum metallicum* (the main remedy for suicidal thoughts), *Carcinosin, Lycopodium, Natrum muriaticum, Nitric acid, Sepia* and *Staphisagria*. The rubric **'affected, easily'** lists: *Calcarea carbonica, Ignatia, Lyssin, Medhorrinum, Mercurius vivus* and *Phosphorus*, in addition to *Carcinosin, Natrum muriaticum and Nitric acid*, which also appear in the first rubric.

Other rubrics to consider for bullying include:

- *'abuse, ailments from'*
- *'admonition, agg., ailments from'*
- *'domination, by others, ailments from'*
- *'humiliation, mortification, ailments from'*
- *'punishment, ailments from'*
- *'anger, reproaches, from'*, with only *Colocynth*, *Ignatia* and *Staphisagria* appearing.
- *'crying, weeping, reproaches, from'*
- *'fears, phobias, reproaches, of'*
- *'scorned, ailments, from being'*
- *'sensitive, reprimands, to'*

Lycopodium is the only remedy in the rubric **'insanity, reproaches, others'**, which suggests that the bullied becomes the bully unless the transmission is arrested through treatment.

Constitutional homeopathic treatment early in life is the best way to prevent a vulnerable individual from becoming a victim of bullying. This builds up the resilience and supports them from becoming prey to this form of attack. If not addressed, it can become part of the 'epigenetic transmission' and afflict future generations as they enter the social arena along their life trajectory.

1.14 ALIENATION AND ISOLATION

Alienation and isolation are an increasing problem in our society and take a considerable toll on health. I include the materia medica for these issues here rather than in Part 2 as the differentiation in the chosen remedy pictures is key to targeting this frequently vital characteristic.

The theme of *Hura brasiliensis* is expressed in the concept of the 'leper's remedy', which is a feeling that AIDS patients may experience or patients who feel equally ostracised. The accompanying skin symptoms in AIDS, such as Kaposi's sarcoma, comply with the pathogenesis of *Hura*. This symptom represents the theme of being repellent to others in the psyche of the patient.

Pertinent rubrics to states of alienation and isolation treated by *Hura* include:

- *'delusion, friend, thinks she is about to lose a'*
- *'delusion, alone, world, that she is'*
- *'delusion, deserted, forsaken, being'*
- *'delusion, despised, that he is'*
- *'delusion, repudiated by relatives, thinks is'*
- *'isolation, feelings'*
- *'reproaches himself'*

In *Hyoscyamus*, the trigger is often disappointed love, even to the point of suicide, as shown in the rubrics **'love, disappointed, ailments from'** and **'jealousy'**. The patient can become quite murderous from rage in their jealous state. Mania is heightened after childbirth and can reach the stage of insanity, often manifesting in lascivious behaviour. *Hyoscyamus* is in the rubrics: **'abuse, ailments from'**; **'complaining, supposed, injury, of'**, where it is a single, italic, remedy (these patients can claim rape or attack, as well as *Lilium tigrinum*, *Lyssin*, and *Tarentula hispanica*); **'fear, betrayed being'**; **'delusion, persecuted, that he is'**;

'delusion, poisoned, thought he had been'; *'delusion, he, has suffered, a wrong'*, where it is a single, black type remedy; *'hysterical, behaviour'*; *'mania, alternating, with frenzy'*, where it is the only remedy; *'mania, rage, with'*; and *'mania, puerperal'*.

In *Lyssin*, the adrenals are considerably compromised as a result of persistent strain on the patient. In fact, they remain balanced until they sense they are at the point of being attacked, which is like the rabid dog, the saliva from which the remedy is derived. Because their senses are in a heightened state of alert – see the rubric *'offended, easily'* – it does not take much for them to experience this.

Pertinent rubrics to states of alienation and isolation treated by *Lyssin* include:

- *'abuse, ailments from'*
- *'anger, suppressed, ailments from'*
- *'delusion, impelled to recklessness'*
- *'delusion, tormented, thinks he is'*
- *'humiliation, mortification, ailments from'* including both *'mental/emotional problems, from'* and *'physical problems, from'* – these two sub-rubrics suggest somatisation due to inability to express the appropriate emotion when provoked.

A child had suddenly become paralysed with fear in his own house for no obvious reason and had not responded to indicated remedies. His mother and younger brother also came for treatment. The younger brother, uncharacteristically, did not require a remedy, such was his resilience and robustness in life. This demonstrates that susceptibility within the family often resides more acutely with one particular member, according to their individual vulnerability.

Patients are the practitioner's greatest teachers and this applies very poignantly here. Some time into their treatment, the mother suggested that the child's father was the 'key' due to his alienation from the family but that he would never be able to recognise or address this. However, she finally managed to persuade him to seek treatment, ostensibly for his hay fever, as a way of persuading him to fill in the 'missing part of the equation', as she perceived it. In fact, when exploring his history, he spoke quite openly about the family wound. What transpired was very profound: at the same age as when his older son became afflicted, he was expelled from his country of origin and had never spoken about it. Once the father was treated for this trauma and he was able to make the connection, the child began to recover spontaneously. It seems that, unconsciously, the father had 'frozen' his son in time as a way of protection, and needed to release him at a cellular level. Although *Natrum muriaticum* was the obvious remedy, the curative remedy was *Natrum carbonicum* due to the degree of removal from his immediate family and the marked sensitivity in the case.

This induction into 'vicarious healing' through the guidance of the patient proved illuminating in understanding the importance of the family dynamic in unravelling the 'maintaining causes' within homeopathic cases. It demonstrates that a trauma undergone by parents before the birth of their children, especially if not articulated, can nevertheless shape the manner in which the child later experiences life events. This case demonstrates that the more silence prevails, the worse is the resulting suffering projected onto other family members. Therefore, rubrics such as *'grief, silent'* and *'grief, undemonstrative'* are so vital, even if serving as a vicarious symptom in the presenting case.

1.15 BEDWETTING (ENURESIS)

This is treated as a physical symptom in the homeopathic repertory but the rubrics do not actually take into account the emotional component of this symptom. Practice has shown that there is often a difficulty on the part of the child to 'individuate' and the bedwetting maintains them in their babyhood and protracted neediness. The parent may – for whatever reason – maintain an unconscious grip on the child, so preventing them from reaching their milestones in the appropriate manner and breaking away. Once a remedy is given to loosen this enmeshment, the child heals and makes a quantum leap in their development in the process. If there is an inherited pattern to this symptom, it could be that a similar dynamic operated in the previous generation which is being replayed here.

Bedwetting is often a vicarious symptom – a vent, perhaps – for an unexpressed trauma in the family. In this type of symptom, the 'symbiosis' between child and parent should never be overlooked. An example of this is a case of a 5-year-old girl who only recovered when her mother received *Natrum muriaticum* for her suppressed grief about the death of a close friend of the family. It was as if the girl was expressing the tears through the bedwetting which the mother could not voice. This is a true example of transgenerational healing and indicates how different family members sometimes need to be brought on board to target the trigger to the distress. *Folliculinum* is also a good remedy to cut across the over-identification between child and parent and can be given to both parties to loosen that tie.

Causticum is another significant remedy for bedwetting. It has a special affinity with the bladder and the child's fear often intensifies in bed at night. There is a foreboding in their make up which is based on marked grief. Due to their sympathetic nature, this grief could again easily reside in the parent and be unwittingly transmitted to the child. According to Chinese medicine (TCM), the bladder symbolises the emotion of fear [6], so it is no surprise that such remedies as *Causticum* and *Natrum muriaticum* will manifest this type of corresponding physical symptoms.

The rubric *'bedwetting, enuresis'* in the Bladder chapter of the *Repertory* overlooks the strong type of emotional component which is often the trigger on the time-line in such cases. When the parent can let go, the child heals. Conversely, when the child heals, the parent can loosen their grip on them. This is a demonstration of vicarious healing and validates the importance of addressing the family dynamic rather than the presenting symptom as an isolated 'lesion'.

1.16 PUBERTY ISSUES

Puberty is a time of individuation and forging one's own identity. When stepping out from the protection of the family, the world can appear quite hostile. Peer group pressure asserts itself vociferously at this stage of development and nowadays the Internet means that this pressure is not only in the individual's immediate circle, but out there 'at the touch of a key'. It is necessary to become not only resilient, but sure of boundaries in order to resist this influence.

Historically, such 'rites of passage' were celebrated in ceremonies and 'elders' were regarded as mentors to the growing offspring. Sadly, this support system is rare in today's world and Samuel Hahnemann, the founder of homeopathy, would not have recognised the current 'disease state' at this very vital stage of life. In addition to this, male role models in today's family structures are often absent. In fact, today's society seems to frown on teenagers during what should be a stage of maturation rather than marginalisation.

Males feel the pinch even more than females as feminism has created a backlash against them. It is as if the roles have become reversed, and this is illustrated in a recent surge in suicides amongst this age group. [41] Depression at this stage of development can present in a more chronic way than in adults and is more resistant to allopathic medication.

Homeopathic treatment can circumvent this eventuality if teenagers are encouraged to recognise the need for such support. Although they may present with a surface condition such as acne or a discharge, there is often a tumultuous mindset behind this façade – as in the syphilitic remedy *Kali bromatum*, which is a major remedy for pustular acne with a very nihilistic emotional state behind it. At puberty, not only the syphilitic, but also the sycotic miasm can be evoked; boundaries can become weakened

41 Bilsker, Dan and White, Jennifer (December 2011), The Silent Epidemic of Male Suicide, *British Columbia Medical Journal*, 53(10):529-34.

at this stage in development and it is easy for the sycotic mindset to creep in. Society almost enhances this with its negative messages on the Internet and in popular youth culture publications.

As well as potential family dysfunction, academic pressures, combined with society pressures, often act as ongoing 'maintaining causes'. Teenagers may complain that their parents expect too much of them in their studies and fail to understand the other pressures they are under.

It is now known that huge internal changes occur in brain chemistry during puberty and that brain structures continue to form way after birth, especially during the teenage years. Influences such as trauma and exposure to computer screens could compromise these structures at this time, as well as such influences as alcohol and drugs.

The way one reacts to this developmental stage is very much based on the level of attachment secured as an infant. If one has been made to feel safe, then that protection fuels the responses as the individual matures. Ongoing parental responses also play an important role. If the message stems from one of danger, then the outlook will be afflicted accordingly. Lack of boundaries can conversely mean a teenager knows no restraint, in which case they can easily fall victim to addiction to various degrees. This plays out according to the level of 'unease' they sense as a result. They may need the 'substance', whatever it is, in order to 'feel'. One sees this in the remedy *Mercurius vivus*.

Anacardium is the most important remedy in my practice for psychic states during puberty. This remedy spreads right across the 'spectrum' from ADHD to learning difficulties, OCD, schizophrenia, and Alzheimer's. The causative factor is often domination – see rubric **'domination, by others, ailments from'** or, at worse, abuse – see rubric **'abuse, ailments from'**. The effects of these influences create a split where the boundaries become weak. Underneath a great feeling of weakness is a front of bravado where the patient may adopt crude language – see rubric **'cursing, swearing'** and **'violent, behaviour'**. They lose their moral code and there is lack of awareness of the repercussions of this – see rubric *'unfeeling, hardhearted'*. As a result of their early behavioural and learning difficulties, they may miss out from school. To compensate, they may start showing off and, in the process, fall in with the 'wrong crowd'. The outcome can be possible addiction or unruly behaviour as the syphilitic miasm unfolds. Obviously, the earlier these children can be treated – when the first signs of dysfunctional responses manifest – the easier it is for them to avoid entering this trajectory. The ideal would be to treat the parents before conception to iron out the inherited aspect of this type of susceptibility.

The hardness in *Anacardium* can progress towards paranoia. They may direct violence towards others, and can also turn the violence against themselves and commit suicide (usually by shooting or throwing themselves from a height).

Helleborus niger is a remedy with two main causations: 1) disappointed love on the emotional level and 2) brain diseases such as encephalitis and meningitis or head injury on the physical level. Consider this remedy (as well as *Aurum metallicum*) for depression, especially at puberty. The depression presents as a coma-like state where nothing can be enjoyed or reacted to, as if someone has hit them over the head with a frying pan! This state can be seen in orphanages where the child may resort to head-banging to relieve irritation in the brain as part of a ritualised pattern of behaviour.

There is a feeling of helplessness and indifference to loved ones in *Helleborus* – see rubric *'indifference, loved ones, to'*, where it appears in black type alongside *Phosphorus* and *Sepia*. This symptom is a more exaggerated *'Sepia'* state. The mindset in *Helleborus* may build up so gradually that it can easily be missed by loved ones. A notable symptom is *'depression, first menses, menarche'*, where it is the only remedy in the rubric. This feeling is worse before periods once the cycle becomes established. *Kali bromatum* is another important remedy for 'ritualistic' behaviour but theirs is manifested in a restless way. Both *Helleborus* and *Kali bromatum* share a feeling of great guilt. In *Kali bromatum*, there is early loss of memory and insomnia with deep depression. These symptoms, combined with the 'ritualistic' behaviour, connect it to the syphilitic miasm. There can also be a history of abuse in the background.

Hyoscyamus is a major remedy for puberty; this is fitting as it is a time when sexuality becomes aroused. This patient, as a result of disappointed love (as in *Helleborus*) or after possible abuse in early life (as in *Anacardium*), can turn to precocious and promiscuous sexuality. In my experience, this is especially true in males, and this remedy helps to provide the boundary to stand back from this propensity. The patient may even flaunt themselves by appearing naked in public.

The mania in this remedy could be brought on by any of these fundamental triggers in isolation or by the use of pleasure drugs (fuelled by these types of emotions). Anorexia can be a cry for help with this type of background.

Lac humanum, being made from mother's milk, is a very emotive remedy. A picture of addiction is often in the background, especially anorexia or over-eating. This addiction is based on the theme of primal feeds being unavailable to them. This remedy is not represented in repertories of traditional materia medica but it can be regarded as a major polychrest for this age group. There may have been a 'lack of humanity' (a play on words based on the name of the remedy) shown to them in their 'primal' life and there may have been learning difficulties earlier on. The patient then progresses along the 'spectrum' to such behaviours as addiction. Apart from food issues, other addictions include alcohol, drugs, or sex ('love' addiction). Being a very hormonal remedy in females, symptoms are worse around the time of menstruation.

Saccharum officinale is another remedy poorly represented in repertories. Along with *Lac humanum* (milk), another basic nutrient of childhood, there is dysfunction at this phase of development. These children have often been adopted from an abusive background or had 'emotionally absent' birth parents. As a result, a pervasive state develops where all possible boundaries are challenged. There may be a seductive quality, which is manipulated to gain attention, albeit often at an unconscious level. This is an aspect of their 'bottomless pit of need' which contributes to the exasperation and concerns of their parents or carers. Their lack of boundaries translates into sexual precocity where there is lack of awareness of the provocation this behaviour causes. *Hyoscyamus* and *Mercurius vivus* have more awareness of the effects on others of their precocious sexuality.

In the *Saccharum* history, there is often an addiction to sugar. This is the 'tip of the iceberg' which, if unbridled, can lead to the development of more dangerous addictions later. This early need for sugar supports the release of dopamine in the brain – the 'happy neurotransmitter'. Again, this is a sign of the lack of nurturing in the history and the type of depression seen in the syphilitic miasm. The destructive undercurrent links right back to their ancestry.

Carcinosin is the most common remedy for eating disorders in puberty. There may be a history of prolonged fear, suppression, or trauma in the immediate family or past generations. This is the 'good child' – they cannot experiment and may sublimate through sports or travel addiction. The remedy enables the patient to express their rightful anger to access their true selves. The whole family needs to adjust around this shift within the individual being treated. This is not an easy matter and one which needs marked support from the prescriber. It may be necessary to advise the family to embrace this as a sign of necessary positive individuation.

There may be a history of glandular fever, a common illness in puberty, which is very common in the picture of this remedy. This illness leaves a lasting effect on both emotional and physical energies. These teenagers may have spent years nursing a sick loved one and/or losing sleep as a result. There may be a history of Holocaust survival in the family where the victim felt a state of prolonged fear and resulting survivor's guilt. This combination of factors can seep through generation after generation if not addressed.

There are polarities within the remedy *Medorrhinum*. The patient may be mild and sensitive while, at the same time, being easily influenced by aesthetic influences. Equally, they can be wild with an enhanced sense of hedonism which can lead them to engage in dangerous pursuits such as perverted sexuality and/or violence. These patients do not need a lot of sleep and, in fact, come alive at night. The sycotic miasm emblematic of this remedy is highlighted in impulsive patients who show a tendency towards alcohol or drug abuse. It is all part of the excessive personality driven towards enjoyment at all personal costs. Nervousness may manifest in anticipatory anxiety and/or nail-biting. They may have failed in school due to poor concentration and memory. Their presentation may be very dreamy.

In *Syphilinum*, various symptoms can exist in isolation or combine together to burden the patient. These symptoms include: impenetrable depression, possible ritualistic behaviour such as repeated hand-washing, anxiety about health, fear of insanity, and poor memory. This nosode, when used as a remedy, is anti-social, whereas other comparable ones, such as *Carcinosin* and *Medorrhinum*, are keener on company. It is easy to pick up the negative energy of a *Syphillinum* patient and the prescriber can use this as a pointer to this remedy or one belonging to the syphilitic miasm.

Alcohol and drug addiction are based on the self-destructive aspect of the syphilitic nosode, whereas, in *Medorrhinum*, these addictions are much more based on the patient's hedonistic instincts.

Tuberculinum is often more indicated in the early part of childhood than during puberty, but can apply during this stage of development. There is a romantic longing combined with a feeling of unfulfillment leading to restlessness and a desire to travel. The patient wants to burn the candles at both ends. They can be abusive with swearing and destructiveness. This last set of symptoms is shared by *Anacardium*, so a differentiation needs to be made when deciding between these two remedies. *Anacardium* veers more towards the syphilitic aspect of behaviour, whereas an entrenched optimism underlies the *Tuberculinum* state.

1.17 INFERTILITY

A further example of transgenerational influences upon disease is shown in the field of fertility, where experts are realising more and more that obstacles to conception are more than just nutritional or structural. They are even speaking of adverse messages passed down through the generations regarding sexuality and childbirth. This means that, by promoting discussion within the family regarding previous ancestral traumas, the child can grow up to integrate them without acting them out in such negative ways that they become an impediment to their own individual attitude to procreation. This parallels the psychotherapeutic concept of 'wounding'. [42]

In polycystic ovaries, a masculinisation of the female might take place, with: absence of menstruation, weight gain, deepening of the voice and excessive face/body hair. There may even be an unconscious intention on the part of the sufferer not to claim her sexuality and therefore remain a child in the eyes of her parents. Here, a cultural component can come into play. The *Baryta* remedies as well as *Bufo* could be indicated in these cases.

In endometriosis, which is becoming increasingly common in young women, the effect on the lives of the sufferers is intense, not only when it comes to fertility. The amount of pain and discomfort can be crippling and often prevents sexual relationships. Together with marked physical limitations, the prevailing mood is equally compromised. Beneath such intensity of symptoms, there is often a strong emotional trigger underlying this state which undermines the very core of the woman's being. Tracing this back along the time-line is the only way to underpin the case and bring freedom from such struggle. There may be an inherited aspect to this disease and the implicit message about femininity and motherhood due to the miasm or the epigenetic factor. Nosodes come into play due to this aspect but also

---

42 Harville, Emily W., PhD, and Boynton-Jarrett, Renee, MD, ScD, *Childhood Social Hardships and Fertility: A Prospective Cohort Study*, www.ncbi.nlm.nih.gov/pmc/articles/PMC4100793.

indicated remedies according to the acquired mindset.

Cuprum metallicum is known for its cramping and could be a remedy to affect the suppression of emotions which have led to such a marked reflection on the physical level. Not only could it help address the uppermost symptoms, but also the reflective bowel disturbance and resulting weakness.

If the nosode *Carcinosin* is indicated in a case, combining it with *Cuprum metallicum* in the form of the remedy *Cuprum cum carsinosin* could be a good way to start treatment – to address not only the inherited factor through the *Carcinosin*, but the cramping nature through the *Cuprum metallicum*. Both remedies are indicated for marked suppression of emotions which can translate onto the physical body in such a virulent manner.

If there is a background of chlamydia, the nosode *Medorrhinum* could apply, as well as other sycotic remedies such as *Thuja*.

When the mood becomes increasingly desperate due to infertility, the syphilitic miasm can come into play. *Syphilinum* matches the degree of despair often manifested in these cases and *Aurum muriaticum natronatum* is a specific remedy to match, not only this resulting despair, but also both the physical disease process and the mood state.

Supportive remedies such as *Agnus castus* and *Ustilago* may be needed to dampen down the oestrogen overload which could apply in these cases. *Ustilago* has the symptoms: 'suppressed menses without cause' and 'vicarious menstruation' – both of which cover endometriosis, which often needs immediate physical relief before deeper treatment can take effect. This frees the energy for healing and balances the hormonal element which is so predominant. A history of using the birth control pill may contribute to the disease state in these cases. Of course, *Folliculinum*, which is derived from the ovarian follicle, can work well to unblock the action of the birth control pill if this is the direct trigger.

The current marked increase in cases of endometriosis could be due to the amount of xenoestrogens in the environment. These can be found in, for example, parabens in cosmetics, plastics, food dyes and preservatives, fertilizers and weed killers. An exponential rise in the number of cases of endometriosis may therefore be due to this increased production of xenoestrogens. Patients should be advised to avoid exposure to these influences as much as possible – otherwise, they may act as a maintaining cause in their infertility or that of their future offspring. [43]

43 *Xenoestrogens Increase the Risk of Endometriosis* (March 3, 2015), www.bioidenticalhormoneexperts.com/xenoestrogens-increase-the-risk-of-endometriosis.

1.18 PREGNANCY AND BIRTH ISSUES

Programming of lifetime health going right back to the experience in the womb is as important as, if not more important than, our genes in determining individual mental and physical performance. [44] This implies that susceptibility to chronic disease can develop as the result of adverse environmental influences experienced as an embryo and can then become perpetuated through early life and beyond. This is where the epigenetic factor comes into play.

If a mother loses a parent while pregnant, and the child she is carrying is not treated for this loss, then recovery from any presenting ailment could be limited. It is as if the residue of the vicarious grief acts as a 'maintaining cause' in the case. At least, if it is expressed to the child by the affected parent, then it can be gradually integrated in a healthy way and over a period of time. As a result, recovery can take place.

Trauma during the birth process is recognised to contribute to difficulties down the line in the life of the affected child. [45] However, the mother's state in pregnancy is also relevant and often overlooked in case-taking. Given that the gestation period often contributes to the future health of the developing child, especially in 'States on the Spectrum', this oversight could lead one astray when it comes to analysing and treating the case. For example, a mother might be in a state of fear during pregnancy because of a previous stillbirth or fear of the actual labour. This protracted fear can have an enduring effect on the baby's internal stress monitor (the brain structure called the amygdala) which might in turn lead to issues such as ADHD, depression, impulsivity, phobias, and sleep issues in the child as they develop.

If the child was unwanted by either parent, this ambivalence can be acted out in a type of reticence in the child, as seen in a remedy such as *Magnesium carbonicum*, the orphan's remedy. The child's

---

44 Nelson III, Charles A. PhD (October 2012), The Effects of Early Life Adversity on Brain and Behavioral Development, *Brain in the News*.

45 Van der Zee, Harry (2009), *Miasms in Labour*, Homeolinks.

sense of identity and self-value is tarnished by this ambivalence, whether the patient is aware of this or not.

Of course, the effect of exposure to chemicals and drugs in the womb plays a role, the embryo being especially sensitive to any toxicity the mother may be exposed to. However, it is hard to track down their specific influence as any resulting problems tend to manifest much later in life. Even mild exposure to alcohol or tobacco can lead to learning difficulties and behavioural problems, which are becoming increasingly common these days. The practitioner should therefore take into account the combination of inherited characteristics (through the miasm or through the 'epigenetic' link) and intra-uterine effects on the development of the brain of the child and then incorporate these influences into the hierarchy of rubrics when treating the case.

The reason why behaviour could be determined from birth or even conception is due to the effects on brain development of various contributing environmental and genetic influences in the embryonic stage of life. These behaviours include 'States on the Spectrum' covering attention deficit disorder, addiction or schizophrenia. In a case in my practice, I used the rubric *'chaotic, behaviour'* as the first rubric in the hierarchy of a child where the mother had felt out of control with her domestic situation during pregnancy. This led me to the remedy *Agaricus muscaris,* which had an immediate effect on the presenting learning difficulty. If I had not used this rubric, my analysis might have been thrown off course and onto a false lead.

The symbiosis between mother and child is key to the long-term health of the child. [46] By increasing bonding through remedies such as *Saccharum officinale,* this aspect can be integrated retrospectively to liberate the patient from this constraint which has impeded them up to the point of the treatment.

---

46 Swaab, Dick (2014), *We are our Brains – From the Womb to Alzheimer's,* Allen Lane.

1.19 POST-NATAL DEPRESSION

This is often a hidden state – both to the patient and often to the prescriber – and can last for many years unless addressed.

Author Tim Lott's article, *The terrible effects of postnatal depression*, starts with the words: "I have never suffered from postnatal depression." [47] According to a report issued by the Maternal Mental Health Alliance, up to 20% of women experience mental health problems in pregnancy or in the first 12 months after birth. [48] Lott continues: "That's a shocking figure, not merely because of the huge number of women involved. It's the corrosive consequences trickling down the generations." As anybody who has read his memoir, *The Scent of Dried Roses*, knows, he is a lifelong sufferer from depressive illness. [49] He spent many years trying to work out why, and has come up with many possible explanations. To date, the most convincing one he can find is that his mother unwittingly 'gave' it to him, possibly through her genes, but more likely through the tragedy of her own post-natal depression. It was only after she committed suicide 30 years later that he discovered this through tracing and reading it in her medical records.

Lott speculates that the unresponsiveness of a depressive mother who cannot 'mirror' her baby can lead to the development of a depressive child. The quoted report rightly recognises this, noting the effect "over decades on their children's prospects, both in terms of development in the womb and during the crucial early years". He says the lack of recognition of post-natal depression is not merely a scandal for the poor victims who suffer it, but also for their children. If those children are women, we might expect it to lead to another loop of mental illness if they give birth themselves.

---

47 Lott, Tim (October 24, 2014), The Terrible Effects Of Postnatal Depression, *The Guardian.*

48 Bauer, Annette et al. (October 20, 2014), *Costs of Perinatal Mental Health Problems*, Centre for Mental Health, UK.

49 Lott, Tim (2009), *The Scent of Dried Roses: One Family and the End of English Suburbia – an Elegy*, Penguin Modern Classics.

Had his mother's state been recognised and treated at the onset, Tim Lott could have been saved from a lifetime trajectory of depressive illness. The remedy that might have helped a mother at the time may still be the remedy to help a child after many years of unresolved suffering.

Future mothers tend to have such high expectations of the anticipated result of her pregnancy. The birth may not go according to plan, or perhaps breast-feeding does not turn out to be as easy as one's ideals expected. At a time when hormones are in great flux, the mother has to adapt to the responsibility of caring for a newborn whose needs are initially hard to identify. In addition, sleep deprivation may be the last straw. This impasse puts great strain on the new mother and she often feels unable to ask for help. At this time in our history, there is more isolation in communities; family members may be spread out and cannot be on call to support the new domestic status quo.

By treating the mother during this critical time, crucial bonding is ensured for the long-term psychological health of both her and her child. Many children who turn out to be 'on the Spectrum' have been denied this vital period of 'turning on the brain'. They may also have been subject to possible neglect as a result of the mother's inability to function.

Anacardium is beneficial where the patient feels torn in two and unsure how to respond to motherhood. If the mother lacked nurturing when she was young, she might find it hard to find warm feelings for her own new baby. Ultimately, the child can end up with compromised brain structures and resultingly with learning difficulties. This remedy can be under-recognised for post-natal depression.

Aurum metallicum is suggested when high ideals have been dashed and the perfectionist make-up of the patient cannot possibly maintain these standards under the duress of motherhood. She may be disappointed that she can no longer compete in the 'testosterone-driven' business world out there. Her failure to breastfeed, for whatever reason, might plunge her into dark despair.

Sepia unconsciously switches off her mothering instinct. This is often due to poor thyroid function since the birth process. The relationship with the father of the baby may not be working and the pregnancy unwanted in the first place. The cuttlefish, from which *Sepia* is derived, sends out a cloud of ink which obscures the offspring from sight. This image symbolises the feeling around the post-natal *Sepia* state.

Other remedies appear in the rubric **'depression, sadness, childbirth, after'**, but the examples above illustrate the possible development of post-natal depression.

According to Terri Apter in her book, *Difficult Mothers: Understanding and Overcoming Their Power*: "A mother's prolonged emotional absence affects the physical and chemical make-up of a child's brain. Positive emotional exchanges stimulate the growth of cortisol receptors that absorb and buffer stress hormones. At three years of age, children of depressed mothers are more limited in their ability to use expressive language." [50] She infers that, by age five, children of mothers who suffered post-natal depression are significantly more likely to be disruptive.

Many remedies overlap when cross-referencing rubrics **'depression, sadness, childbirth, after' / 'insanity, childbirth, after'**, and **'attention deficit disorder' / 'hyperactive, children' / 'learning disabilities, studying, reading'**. These include: *Anacardium, Baryta carbonica, Hyoscyamus, Lycopodium, Mercurius vivus, Phosphorus, Sepia, Stramonium, Tuberculinum,* and *Veratrum album*. This is no coincidence as there is a direct link here between 'cause' and 'effect'. The remedies listed are of major significance in 'States on the Spectrum' and related conditions.

Therefore, if it is possible to treat the mother before symptoms develop, not only the patient can be saved from suffering, but also the next and future generations. Otherwise, their lives could be adversely affected long-term without this early intervention at

---

50   Apter, Terri (2012), *Difficult Mothers: Understanding and Overcoming Their Power*, W.W. Norton and Company.

source. If homeopaths consider they are treating children with such a background, they should look at rubrics relating to the mother's 'post-partum state', such as: *'depression, sadness, childbirth, after'* or *'insanity, childbirth, after'*, according to the description of her state at this very vulnerable time both for her and her child.

This is true prophylaxis for future generations who otherwise could continue to inherit this often hidden disabling burden. By incorporating such causative rubrics in the case, even though not emanating directly from the child, true resolution of an often intractable state can finally ensue.

1.20 THYROID MALFUNCTION

Thyroid disease, which often goes unrecognised and may manifest in the form of anxiety disorders, depression, or even bi-polar disease, can also cross the generations. This fits the understanding that our learned reactions often stem from our original family dynamics. This is where anti-miasmatic prescribing is so vital in 'cracking this code', especially by using the nosodes in these cases. 'States on the Spectrum' in the child may even be a reflex from compromise to the mother's thyroid, which may not have been obvious in pregnancy or immediately afterwards during lactation.

As the thyroid gland represents the gland of the emotions by providing the link between the brain and the 'emotional voice', emotional symptoms may take precedence over physical symptoms in a presenting case. The thyroid gland can become compromised at such times of hormonal turmoil as puberty, after childbirth, and in menopause. These are times when a woman must be able to ask for her needs to be met and it may not be possible for women in today's society to reach out in this way. This is rooted in early life influences due to negative dynamics afflicting the sense of worth in the individual.

A typical background for hyperthyroidism is when a patient feels insecure and has a history of having to act as caretaker in the family, which is typical of the cancer miasm. In *Carcinosin*, suppression of anger drives the disease and, once the anger can be expressed, the voice can flow in a beneficial way to both the sufferer and those around them, and the thyroid is relieved of its burden. Other significant remedies for suppressed anger include *Lycopodium*, *Magnesium muriaticum*, *Natrum muriaticum* and *Staphysagria*. Remedies with a strong sense of duty such as those in the *Calcarea* and the *Ferrum* groups also rank highly here.

In hypothyroidism, a type of 'hiding' may have occurred in order to avoid forging ahead in life. The primal message may have been one of failure and it is hard for them to change this mindset. The *Baryta* group of remedies, *Bufo*, and *Graphites* are examples of remedies which can support this process and relieve the thyroid of the resulting toxicity creating the disease state. These remedies share weak identity and a tendency to prevaricate.

Low libido is part of the thyroid picture, especially in hypo-cases. This can compromise the sufferer's relationship and could make the patient feel guilty as a result. *Sepia* is the obvious remedy, but it could equally be a case of *Natrum muriaticum*, among other remedies, according to the prevailing mindset and thyroid state at the time.

Spongia, a major thyroid remedy which is also used as a support in constitutional treatment, has in its picture great timidity as well as loss of sexual excitement. Of course, this remedy contains a lot of iodine, which is an important component of the thyroid gland.

Resentment is a highly toxic emotion, especially when carried over from childhood, and can be a maintaining cause in the case. The *Ammonium* remedies markedly cover this emotion, the *Muriaticum* derivative acts better for hyperthyroid states and *Carbonicum* more for hypothyroid states. Note that 'resentmentment of the mother' complies with *Muriaticum* and 'resentment of the father' with *Carbonicum.* [51]

In an *Ammonium carbonicum* case, where the goitre was threatening to cut off the air supply to the throat, the patient avoided surgery with the intervention of this remedy. Her history included a father who never allowed her to individuate and 'have her say'. By 'gaining her voice', her thyroid was saved and she could confront the family dynamic in a much healthier way.

All the *Iodatum* remedies have an affinity with the thyroid. *Ferrum iodatum* is a lesser-known remedy for middle-aged women with this dysfunction. At menopause, when the periods cease, exophthalmic goitre can develop. As this is a time when women are particularly vulnerable to 'going off the rails', this may not only be an emotionally-triggered symptom. Cessation of menses can trigger this disease as there is a direct correlation between the base chakra (the womb) and the throat chakra (the thyroid). After

51 Scholten, Jan (1993), *Homoeopathy and Minerals*, Stichting Alonissos.

hysterectomy, when menstruation is suddenly arrested, this is again a time when thyroid disease can creep in as a compensation for this outlet, and is what is known as a 'vicarious symptom'.

The *Iodatum* remedies, with their theme of escape, fit in well with a common aspect of modern day society which plays out in the life of refugees who cannot throw off their history of the subjugation they had to endure in their country of origin. They have lost their voice and vital choices have been denied them. Is it any wonder, then, that thyroid disease can be the resulting outcome?

The thyroid can easily be compromised in anorexia, as it is the gland of growth, metabolism, and emotional expression. However, which came first? Was the thyroid out of balance and then depression emerged? The latter, in turn, could have triggered anorexia in the patient or, conversely, anorexia could have led to the thyroid losing its balance. As mentioned above, the mother might have suffered thyroid disease in the past or during and after the pregnancy. Behind thyroid disease, there could even be 'post-traumatic stress disorder' either within the family history of anorexics, and/or in their own background of development.

Thyroid disease is under-diagnosed, especially in men in society as a whole. This may be because, at a time in our history when women have gained considerable inroads in society, the backlash created in men could create a feeling of powerlessness which can manifest in this, very often, hidden disease. The *Aurum* group of remedies and *Lycopodium* are examples which feature here.

Note that the Broda Barnes Temperature Test is a recommended reliable way of checking thyroid levels. [52]

---

52   *The Barnes Basal Body Temperature Test,*
     www.regenerativenutrition.com/content.asp?id=574.

1.21 HYSTERIA

It is hard to define hysteria, as the word 'hysteria' can be mistakenly used to describe any type of extreme behaviour. This can manifest in an over-the-top emotional response, as seen in the remedy '*Moschus*' where the sufferer may 'scold until the lips turn blue'. The hysteria may be projected onto the physical sphere, especially when the patient is out of touch with their mindset. This is known as 'dissociation', and is illustrated by the remedy *Tarentula hispanica*, when the patient can feign paralysis, particularly when being observed.

According to Adam Zeman: "Sufferers report higher rates of adverse childhood experiences, especially sexual abuse. Hysterical episodes are often triggered by injury of some kind, especially injuries that cause panic at the time. Depression and anxiety are commonly present." [53] This is not well brought out in the provings of the major hysterical remedies, but is useful for homeopaths to include in their exploration of suspected hysteria cases. The hysteria represents the defence mechanism's way of dealing with intolerable situations. Some people develop hysteria as a way of coping whereas others may, conversely, develop alexithimia, which means they cannot articulate their suffering at all. It all boils down to the individual susceptibility of the patient and the effect of role models who influenced them during childhood.

The word 'hysteria' comes from the Greek word for 'womb' which explains why it is mostly women who develop hysteria, despite the increasing numbers of men developing it nowadays. This could be explained by today's increasing number of factors impacting the developing embryo during the mother's pregnancy which contribute to this overlap between the genders. Women's hysteria is often worse at times of hormonal flux, such as puberty, after childbirth, and at menopause. This is no coincidence when the actual meaning of the term is considered.

---

53   Zeman, Adam (2009), *A Portrait of the Brain*, Yale University Press.

Lasciviousness may co-manifest with hysteria, which again ties in with the womb connection. Remedies with these joint symptoms include *Ambra grisea, Crocus sativa, Hyoscyamus, Lachesis, Lilium tigrinum, Moschus, Platina, Stramonium, Tarentula hispanica* and *Veratrum album*. As this list includes many of the well documented remedies for hysteria, it illustrates that enhanced sexuality is often a concomitant in women going through hormonal flux at these crucial stages of their lives. Hysteria is where attachment to disease becomes apparent, and often a physical ailment such as asthma or paralysis results. In other words, there is some investment in the attention the 'disease' gains, albeit usually at an unconscious level. This can be seen in the remedy *Tarentula hispanica*, where the aetiology of 'disappointed love' is so strong that the manipulation it triggers in the patient can be quite startling to the observer. Interestingly, *Tarentula hispanica*, despite its extreme reaction, appears only in plain type in the related rubric. This compares to *Ignatia* – the best known remedy for hysteria – also rooted in disappointed love – which appears in black type in this rubric. It is unusual to find remedies such as *Anacardium* and *Argentum nitricum* in the rubric for hysterical behaviour (where they both appear in italics). It could be that this is reflected in the very distinctive physical symptoms both these remedies manifest.

1.22 INFLAMMATION

According to Khandaker et al, chronic physical illness such as coronary heart disease and type 2 diabetes may share a common mechanism with mental illness. [54] They state that people with depression and schizophrenia are known to have a much higher risk of developing heart disease and diabetes. Children with elevated levels of Interleukin 6 – a protein released into the blood in response to infection – are more prone when older to develop depression and psychosis.

Khandaker et al also found that inflammation may be a common mechanism that influences both physical and mental health. It is possible that early life adversity and stress lead to persistent increase in levels of Interleukin 6 and other inflammatory markers in the body which, in turn, increase the risk of a number of chronic physical and mental illnesses. Indeed, low birth weight, a marker of impaired foetal development, is associated with increased levels of inflammatory markers as well as greater risks of heart disease, diabetes, depression and schizophrenia in adults. They conclude that inflammation could be a common link between chronic physical and mental illness.

When I discovered this research, I saw why *Carcinosin* is so well indicated in the above-mentioned illnesses as well as other inflammatory childhood diseases. Given the background of inherited trauma in this remedy, it is no wonder that *Carcinosin* is the essential nosode with such a combination of factors. In addition, people needing this remedy often have marked suppression on both a physical and mental level when young, or in their case history. Auto-immune disease and ultimately cancer are often the end results of such a disease trajectory triggered in early life.

---

54   Khandaker G.M. et al. (2014), Association of Serum Interleukin 6 and C-Reactive Protein in Childhood With Depression and Psychosis in Young Adult Life: A Population-Based Longitudinal Study, *Journal of the American Medical Association of Psychiatry*; 71(10):1121-1128.

How anger is controlled is very much dictated by role models in the family structure. A recent study found that angry people may suffer from an excessive inflammatory response and even names this syndrome 'intermittent explosive disorder' or 'IED'. The findings in the article "suggest a direct relationship between plasma inflammatory processes and aggression in humans." [55] Professor Emil Coccaro, of the University of Chicago, Chairman of the Psychiatry and Behavioural Neuroscience Department who led the research, concludes that it is not known if the inflammation triggers aggressive feelings, or aggressive feelings set off inflammation.

With this conclusion in mind, it is interesting for homeopaths to look at a remedy such as *Lyssin* (*Hydrophobinum*), which is reputed to match extreme aggression as well as the severe pathology of auto-immune disease, and in which it is clear that aggressive feelings come first. This law of cure fits homeopathic philosophy and demonstrates that anger management, whether through homeopathic treatment or other targeted protocols, can save the patient from damaging effects being projected onto the physical sphere in such an extreme and life-threatening way.

55   Coccaro, E.F. and Coussons-Read, M. (2013), Elevated Inflammatory Markers in Individuals with Intermittent Explosive Disorder and Correlation with Aggression in Humans, *Journal of the American Medical Association of Psychiatry*, 71(2):158-65.

1.23 AUTO-IMMUNE DISEASE

Due to overwhelming emotions taking over, normal functioning of the organism can be prevented from occurring. The auto-immune disease becomes the somatisation of this process instead of a healthy immune response. Modern lifestyle alone could be blamed for the significant increase in auto-immune disease, but susceptibility, as always, is often rooted in childhood, if not pre-birth. The fact that the origins go back so far explains why the major nosodes *Carcinosin*, *Psorinum*, and *Syphilinum* appear in the rubric **'auto-immune, diseases'** in the 'Clinical' chapter of the repertory. As nosodes are not usually well represented in the repertory and, given the fact that there are only 17 other remedies in this rubric, this validates their importance in supporting these cases. Among the other remedies, *Arsenicum album*, *Lac caninum*, and *Lilium tigrinum* appear in italics. What these remedies all share is a strong sense of disconnection, which is so emblematic of today's world.

A remedy which does not appear in the rubric but I have found useful for auto-immune disease is *Lyssin* (*Hydrophobinum*). The idea of the body attacking itself complies with the 'Doctrine of Signatures' of this remedy (its derivation is the bite of a rabid dog). *Lyssin* is sensitive and can easily feel provoked, like *Staphysagria*. However, their reaction is markedly more intense, to the point of the most extreme violence. The 'wound' could emanate from childhood abuse and that sense of violation is projected outwards towards others, thus perpetuating the cycle. These patients also cannot tolerate witnessing violence against others – hence the rubric **'sympathetic, empathy, feels same pains as others'** where *Phosphorus* is the only other remedy. This is a 'strange, rare and peculiar' symptom, given the overall characteristics of the mental/emotional state of the patient needing this remedy.

It is interesting that 75% of auto-immune cases arise in women. However, when men do succumb to these diseases, they experience more intense and more painful symptoms. [56] I wonder why women are so much more susceptible; the hormonal factor may, of course, be relevant – but, on the other hand, women are better able to offload their stresses to others. It may be that denial of self plays a role combined with an inability to embrace life's challenges. This could be due to early conditioning as well as a resulting sense of restricted vision for the sufferer's life trajectory.

56 Fairweather, Delisa and Rose, Noel R. (2004), Women and Autoimmune Diseases, *Emerging Infectious Diseases*, 10(11):2005-11.

1.24 INSOMNIA

Sleep is a great leveller and I have found that patients usually describe their sleep patterns accurately. A useful way to assess the response to a remedy is to explore changes in sleep patterns, especially with people who find it difficult to assess their emotions more directly. A good response to homeopathic treatment is when the patient falls asleep more easily and wakes during the night less often but the dreams become more distinct and meaningful to the patient. In an *Opium* case, the dreams took on a whole new resonance. After a series of buried traumas, their resolution took place in a sequence of dreams in reverse order of when the traumas occurred. Each dream integrated the past trauma: as the dreams unfolded, they became less and less threatening until they no longer held any torment whatsoever. The patient was then able to restart their life and embrace their hitherto blocked potential. This phenomenon was an eye-opener in a very closed case where perhaps the sufferer would not have worked through the traumas in any other way.

The traumas behind sleep dysfunction could represent an unexpressed ancestral issue which the patient acts out in this very undermining way. When the dreams become more integrated and the patient starts to make sense of them, the effects of this breakthrough can percolate through to other family members. In this way, tensions are unlocked and healthy channels of communication open up to free the dynamic in the relationships.

When a patient cannot escape from a recurrent but disturbing dream, it is often because the trauma behind it has not been brought to the conscious mind of the sufferer for them to process. Remedies can be used to look beneath this 'stuckness' and liberate the patient from the recycling of the trauma, thus making sense of the suffering it entails. The adrenals are relieved of the resulting stress which has been compounded by the recycling of the dream. High cortisol levels result from loss of sleep as well as disturbing dreams. Physical ailments that can result from this overload include allergies, arthritis, auto-immune disease including diabetes, fibromyalgia, heart disease, infections/inflammations, obesity, osteoporosis, thyroid disease as well as cancer.

If dreams cannot be recalled, challenging traumatic memories cannot be 'translated' into more soothing ones. It could be that dreams serve to renew the connections between the neurons and, especially in cases of post traumatic stress disorder, the patient cannot fully move forward without the outlet of this facility.

1.25 CANCER

As one can gather from studying *Carcinosin*, the cancer nosode, many cancer patients have a history of suppression. This can relate to the physical sphere in the form of fevers, as well as repeated inflammatory diseases. The emotions may also be affected, often in the form of an inability to hold their ground. The symptom of suppressed anger is an important keynote in the picture of the patient requiring *Carcinosin*. As in the remedy picture where the patient finds it hard to recognise their boundaries, in the disease process of cancer, the organism cannot contain its spread.

There is a heavy 'ancestral load' in the history of the *Carcinosin* patient's family, where a combination of oppression and isolation has often played a significant role. This takes its toll on the organism and, combined with the inflammatory nature of this remedy, can result in such illnesses as arthritis, diabetes, or extreme mental health issues. These background elements can converge to create an unhappy childhood in the cancer patient. This may be due to the relationship between the parents leading up to conception and the subsequent birth of the child, as well as the relationship between the child and the parent(s). The child may have experienced isolation at birth due to the mother's inability to bond with them or perhaps due to separation at birth.

Susceptibility in these cases thrives on this bedrock of early dysfunctional relationships when the patient is at an impressionable age. Many toxic influences may impact the patient but it is this emotional background that invariably triggers the disease state, which can act as a 'maintaining cause' if not addressed, and then the patient can remain powerless about resolving its increasingly morbid effect on the organism.

A remedy related to *Carcinosin* in cancer cases is *Conium maculatum*. The grief in the background to this remedy is such that the patient finds it hard to trust their natural instincts and, as a consequence, a hardening takes hold. This in turn is reflected in the disease process of cancer. Like *Carcinosin*, the *Conium* patient may have spent years taking care of others and in the process has lost the ability to connect with themselves.

There are many other remedies with an affinity to cancer which include this similar disconnection from self which allows the disease to take hold.

1.26 OLD AGE ISSUES

During a recent holiday to a rural area of Italy, I was struck by how healthy the elderly are there. This may be, in part, because of fresh air and sunshine, but I believe their strong family connections and support systems are a bigger reason. With an ageing population in the UK at a time when families often move away from each other, this type of structure is sadly lacking here.

Old people often regress and, like infants, cannot always express their symptoms, which is why observation is so important. It is therefore vital for the homeopath to glean information from relatives and friends about the early life of the patient because, hard as it is to believe, what emerges in old age is often a throwback to childhood, including any unresolved issues from that time.

Brain structures are often compromised by the time old age is reached. This can be due to early abuse or neglect. A history of abuse, however, is not always identified in old people because their generation may not have recognised abuse in the same way as it is perceived today. 'Putting up and shutting up' was very much the order of the day when they were young.

Drugs – medicinal or recreational – can also compromise brain structures. So, damage from drugs or possible early abuse or neglect can lead to depression and memory loss, manifesting in old age as possible resulting mental states. The two brain structures involved here are the amygdala (the emotional barometer) and the hippocampus (the memory 'bank'). These structures are heavily interlinked so it is rare for one to be affected without the other. Similarly, expression of emotions such as anger and grief was often not encouraged during the childhood of these patients, which is why *Carcinosin*, *Natrum muriaticum*, and *Staphysagria* are common remedies for the older generation.

If isolation is an issue, the patient needs support if possible. There might have been a rift with family or friends. Breakthroughs can be made with the support of remedies such as *Manganum aceticum* (representing the emotion of resentment which can literally eat the patient away). This in turn can lead to weakness, wasting, and possible hearing problems. *Manganum* is complimentary to *Psorinum* with its lack of reaction and weakness, in which case, if *Psorinum* has not worked or fails to hold, *Manganum aceticum* should be considered. This is especially the case if resentment is an overriding issue. In *Psorinum*, the issue is more to do with abandonment.

After a healing response to a remedy, the patient is more likely to reach out to others. They may even, as a result of treatment, feel prepared to reconcile old hurts from the past. This means they are no longer alienated from the original support structure they may have had in place and frees up the energy for healing to begin.

1.27 STATES ON THE SPECTRUM

Persistent states of anxiety often lie behind 'States on the Spectrum', which are a growing issue in today's culture. These 'states' include: attention deficit disorder, autism, obsessive compulsive disorder, addiction, schizophrenia and Alzheimer's disease.

The word 'spectrum' indicates that these 'states' can vary considerably in their manifestation, meaning that some sufferers are entirely limited and defined by their diagnosis, whereas others operate in the mainstream world with very little awareness either from themselves or others that they may be compromised in this way.

Factors such as birth trauma, drugs (medicinal and recreational), head injury, vaccinations and viral infections play a role. However, I have found that it is invariably the history undermining the family dynamics and attitude of the role models which needs to be addressed before lasting relief can be achieved in such cases.

ATTENTION DEFICIT DISORDER

When combining the rubrics for **'hyperactive, children'** and **'restlessness, mental, children, in'**, three of the half-dozen or so black type remedies in each are nosodes: *Carcinosin*, *Medorrhinum* and *Tuberculinum* in the first rubric, and *Bacillinum*, *Medorrhinum* and *Tuberculinum* in the second. This is remarkable as, in general, nosodes are not well represented in the repertory. In the time-line of the nosodes, the presenting issue is rooted in both the ancestry and early life of the child, which confirms the view that attention deficit disorder, like other 'States on the Spectrum', extends far back into the history of the family. The stress reaction is set far back in time, which should dictate how the case is treated. The other black type remedies in the combined rubrics are *Arsenicum album*, *Hyoscyamus*, *Mercurius vivus*, *Rhus toxicodendron*, and *Stramonium* – all syphilitic remedies. The total number of remedies in both rubrics suggests that attention deficit disorder relates to all the miasms.

In the history of these remedies is a strong sense of anticipation as if there is a vague sense of danger hanging over them. This combines with a type of confusion which did not previously exist. Therefore, the child is likely to fail in what they set out to do, which compounds their profound awareness of their actual under-achievement. To make matters worse, the parent often feels threatened by this as a projection of their own inadequacies and reflects this, as an added strain, onto the already fearful child. For a sensitive child, as seen in *Carcinosin* and *Medorrhinum*, this could affect their sleep pattern, setting off yet another cycle of adrenal exhaustion. In these cases, such 'maintaining causes' should be removed as much as possible through the tactful intervention of the homeopath.

These combined remedies also hint at: abandonment, anger which can culminate in a desire to fight, childishness (children often regress after experiencing trauma), emotional excitement, fright, grief, hysteria, and mania.

The rubric **'chaotic, behaviour'** may be relevant in these cases as the chaos in attention deficit disorder is often a reflection of that in the original family's collective dynamics. Better known remedies in this rubric are *Anacardium, Belladonna, Hyoscyamus, Medorrhinum*, and *Mercurius vivus*, and lesser known ones are *Agaricus, Androdoctonus, Bovista, Stramonium*, and *Zincum metallicum*.

If the pressure on the child persists, then deeper 'States on the Spectrum' can slip in, such as addiction and schizophrenia in the teenage years and possibly Alzheimer's at the extreme end of life.

AUTISM AND ASPERGER'S SYNDROME

The roots of both autism and Asperger's syndrome are thought to be laid down in the womb – they could be described as 'embryonic disruptions'. Martha Herbert and Karen Weintraub, in their book *The Autism Revolution: Whole Body Strategies for Making Life All It Can Be*, say that, for many years, most doctors considered autism to be a genetic problem in the child's brain, and that the resulting troubles would remain forever. However, the authors say that autism is frequently a 'dynamic process'. [57] The rise in autism cannot be explained by genetic factors alone and, according to them, inflammation blamed on environmental factors is often implicated, which can date back to the time the baby was in the womb. This susceptibility to inflammation could also be attributed to the 'load' each parent contributes from their earlier life experiences.

Symptoms of autism and Asperger's syndrome usually lie dormant until the second year of life, by which time various influences such as chemicals in the environment, food colourants, or vaccinations could begin to trigger the susceptibility. It is therefore important, when treating these cases, to explore the pre-birth stage of life as much as, if not more than, post-birth. There may have been ambivalence on the part of a parent regarding the pregnancy, the mother may have lost a child previously or perhaps there was a threatened miscarriage or a stillbirth, resulting in insecurity about the long-term outcome.

If use of the contraceptive pill leading up to the pregnancy might have affected the outcome for the child's development, the remedy *Folliculinum* can neutralise the resulting damage to the child and support their individuation from the mother, which is so vital in these cases.

One reason why nosodes in general are so applicable in 'States on the Spectrum', and especially in autism and Asperger's syndrome,

---

57   Herbert, Martha and Weintraub, Karen (2013), *The Autism Revolution: Whole-Body Strategies for Making Life All It Can Be*, Ballantine Books, Inc.

is their origin in the pre-birth experience. *Carcinosin* comes up strongly here given its remedy picture as well as because it is a composite of the other three major nosodes, *Medorrhinum*, *Psorinum*, and *Syphilinum*.

Simon Baron Cohen presents a theory in *Extreme Male Brain Theory of Autism*, that autism and Asperger's syndrome are left-brained conditions, and he attributes their prevalence to the fact that women are now operating in a testosterone-driven world. [58] This means a mother may not engage with her foetus, instead focusing intently on her work in a competitive marketplace. There could therefore be a compromise in the bonding process, which undermines the formation of the brain structures. *Lac humanum*, a remedy derived from mother's breast milk, could apply here to redress this rupture.

---

58   Bligh, Rebecca (2008), *Simon Baron-Cohen's Extreme Male Brain Theory of Autism*, www.academia.edu/2033271/Simon_Baron-Cohens_Extreme_Male_Brain_Theory_of_Autism.

OBSESSIVE COMPULSIVE DISORDER

In obsessive compulsive disorder (OCD), thoughts tend to focus on a restricted but related number of themes. David Adam, in his instructive autobiographical book on the subject, says that up to one third of sufferers attribute their fixation to contamination with dirt and disease, and many others to a fear of doing harm. [59] This can be exaggerated due to their sense of personal responsibility, which could have been instilled in them when growing up and culminates in this particular outcome in the patient. Others have a need for patterns and symmetry, and perfection in their own body image. The need to control this aspect of their lives makes them feel in control. Combining the rubrics *'fear, control, losing'* and *'superstitious, behaviour'* brings up *Argentum nitricum* (black type in both rubrics), *Arsenicum album*, *Carcinosin*, *Medorrhinum*, and *Thuja*. Many obsessions are hidden due to shame. A sense of shame is a very 'sycotic' feature, although *Anacardium* and *Aurum metallicum*, which tend to be more syphilitic, also appear in the rubric (as well as *Opium* and *Staphisagria* in black type). These could relate to sexual or violent urges against others, or blasphemous thoughts. Remedies relevant to the presentations of this state occurring later in the development of this case include: *Arsenicum album*, *Kali bromatum*, and *Thuja*.

The trigger to OCD could be an external one, perhaps sparked off by a certain odour – a 'Proustian moment', if you will. An internal trigger could be a stress reaction, poor mood, or a subconscious emotional shift. Whether the trigger is external or internal, the response comes from within. This response is conditioned by epigenetic factors going back to early life and is what needs to be treated in these cases. It is vital to realise that it is not intrusive thoughts themselves which drive OCD, but the way in which they are interpreted and acted out by the individual sufferer.

If the role model in the family manifests OCD in their behaviour,

---

59   Adam, David (2014), *The Man Who Couldn't Stop – OCD and the True Story of a Life Lost in Thought,* Picador.

that example becomes the norm for a child growing up in that environment. As the condition runs in families, it can be perceived primarily through the epigenetic model which then slots into the miasmatic one.

Presenting symptoms could be withdrawal of interest in usual hobbies and becoming selfish and detached from the distress of others around them. *Helleborus*, *Opium* and *Sulphur* are black type remedies for **'indifference, pleasure, to'** and also appear in black type in the rubric **'ideas, fixed'**. *Helleborus* is black type in **'indifference, loved ones, to'**, *Sulphur* appears in **'indifference, others, towards'**, and *Opium* is so detached from their real feelings that they cannot emote with others' painful feelings.

Helleborus is not known for hysteria and mania but can manifest these 'states' as a result of self-blame for their tortured mindset. See the small rubric **'mania, demoniac'** where this remedy appears in italics. This rubric teaches one the polarities in different remedies as *Helleborus* is a remedy generally noted for its impassivity.

Women are especially vulnerable to OCD after childbirth due to the marked emotional, as well as hormonal adjustment which takes place in the process. If traits existed beforehand, the birth can trigger an exaggeration of the pre-existing state or herald a new one, often about the safety of the child and their own ability to take care of them. *Platina* is an interesting remedy which covers both the disturbed mental state after childbirth and emotional detachment from their offspring.

Other possible triggers are: too much responsibility being placed on the OCD sufferer when young, or a background of betrayal by trusted family members. *Hyoscyamus* and *Veratrum album* are interesting remedies that can comply with the trigger of betrayal.

Kali bromatum is a key remedy for religious fanaticism, especially when the obsession is tinged with guilt. It is a single, black type remedy in the well-known rubric **'delusion, vengeance, thinks he is singled out for divine'**, and this shows the impact this feeling has on the psyche.

Paediatric auto-immune neuropsychiatric disorders (PANDAS) can be triggered by a physical disease such as a streptococcal infection. [60] The *Streptococcinum* proving includes 'tormenting thoughts and anxiety, obsessions', and 'thinks that he will become mad'. This emphasises the need to take the time-line in these cases on both a physical as well as a psychic basis. The possible trigger for these disorders is a real eye-opener.

OCD overlaps with many other 'States on the Spectrum', especially addiction, attention deficit disorder, autism and Asperger's syndrome, eating disorders, and schizophrenia.

---

60   National Institute of Mental Health, USA,
     www.nimh.nih.gov/health/publications/pandas/index.shtml.

ALEXITHIMIA

This comes from the Greek for having no words for emotions (a=lack, lexis=word, thymos=emotions). Alexithimia can have a profound effect on surrounding family members, especially when it is part of the make-up of a parent. [61]

In one case, a 17-year-old boy became violent and started committing crimes with no obvious explanation. It transpired that his father suffered from alexithimia and was unwittingly acting as the 'pivot of distress' in the family. The lack of communication with him had created an impasse in the boy's life and he could only express his frustrations by acting out in this way. Although the boy was unaware of the trigger to his state, the homeopath can establish where the pivot lies by observing or treating other family members. In the above case, the missing link between father and son could be elicited in this way, and although the traditional parental role model seemed absent, deep down, he may have been present in his own way. This condition could easily fall under the umbrella of 'States on the Spectrum' with its communication issues and emotional distance.

According to Tori Rodriguez, alexithimia is co-morbid with multiple mental disorders, including obsessive compulsive disorder and addictions. [62] Diabetes, heart disease, hypertension and certain gastrointestinal disorders are all linked with the trait. *Saccharum officinale* has a particular mental symptom, 'painlessness', which could apply to alexithimia cases where the patient is so out of touch with their emotional state that this transfers to the physical sphere. By the time the patient realises they have marked symptoms, pathology has already set in. Of course, *Saccharum officinale* can be a major remedy for addictions, not just for sugar, but for hard drugs as well. *Opium* and *Stramonium* also experience 'painlessness'. No explanation

61 Ornstein, Robert (1998), *The Right Mind: Making Sense of the Hemispheres*, Harcourt Brace and Company.
62 Rodriguez, Tori (July 2014), Emotional Ignorance Harms Health, *Scientific American Mind,* 25(4).

needs to be given for *Opium* due to its obvious derivation. *Stramonium* has such a marked background of abandonment and possible abuse that physical pain may no longer be experienced by the sufferer. Although this was originally a protective measure by the defence mechanism, if unaddressed, serious disease may be ignored by the patient on this level.

Remedies such as *Chelidonium*, *Kali carbonicum*, *Mercurius vivus*, and *Natrum sulphuricum* can open people up to communicate so the disruptive dynamic between the generations can be eradicated in a healthy way and the resulting rupture repaired. A marked symptom of *Kali carbonicum* is that the patient is so out of touch with their symptoms that, by the time heart pathology arises, they are completely unaware of its severity, as mentioned earlier. It is not that *Kali carbonicum* does not experience pain; it is just that the 'dis-connect' is so strong that they are unaware of its significance. Such is the strength of their 'somatisation' (subconsciously transferring unrealised emotional symptoms onto the physical sphere) that it translates into the form of pathological states.

It is interesting that one of the most emotionally closed remedies, *Natrum sulphuricum* (and *Natrum muriaticum* to a lesser extent) is also one of the most suicidal in their intentions. If there is a vent for expression of intimate feelings, this tendency is averted. Once, through treatment, the patient is able to access this tool, these negative feelings no longer come to the fore.

Aurum metallicum is also markedly suicidal in its orientation and appears black type in **'talking, indisposed to'** (*Natrum sulphuricum* appears in italics). The patient needing *Aurum* often channels their emotions into work. For them, their success in life is defined by work achievement: this becomes an unconscious distraction from an inner life. They may have received the early message of 'work ambition to the exclusion of other goals' when growing up from their role model. Accessing inner feelings then becomes more difficult if this capacity was denied them in early life.

Suicide is a growing phenomenon these days, especially among young men. [41] With the current increasing empowerment of women, men continue to be at risk right up to middle age. A defence is often maintained by the patient who shows a 'persona' to the outside world. *Mercurius vivus* tends to use alcohol to allow communication to flow, which serves as an unconscious distraction from facing their true selves. More information about alexithimia is given in the entry for *Mercurius vivus*.

DYSLEXIA

In 2014, the *Guardian* newspaper reported on research by The Dyslexia Research Trust, *Could eating oily fish prevent dyslexia?*, which expanded on research into the visual and auditory difficulties of this 'state'. [63] It reports that 50% of people who possess the particular genetic make-up have no difficulties reading, but merely have a certain vulnerability to the disorder. However, the difference between those who do and those who do not manifest this trait may rest on environmental factors before and after birth. The article continues that gene-related defects that occur early on in development may be a consequence of which genes remain active and which do not, which could all be down to the epigenetic factor.

Some dyslexic people experience visual issues, such as problems controlling eye movement, which I have found to be the case in *Agaricus* and possibly *Bovista* – both remedies which could be considered for dyspraxia, a related syndrome affecting the coordination. In other cases, sustained difficulties in learning to read have been put down to problems with phonics (being able to split words into their constituent sounds and match them with the letters).

According to John Stein at the University of Oxford, many dyslexics hear the sounds but cannot access them in the right sequence because their auditory nerve cells do not work fast enough, and it is believed this is because of a lack of certain omega-3 fatty acids. [63] It could also be due to the messages between the different brain structures being misdirected.

One needs an acute auditory processing system and nerve membranes which react fast to pick up on the differences in words that contain similar sounds. Stein says something of great interest to homeopaths: "If the child doesn't get enough exposure to sounds while they are in the womb, the membranes will not

63   Cox, David (November 2, 2014), Could Eating Oily Fish Help Prevent Dyslexia?, *The Guardian*.

function properly." He concludes: "Your language abilities piggyback on your auditory processing abilities." This suggests that the symbiosis between mother and child is set in place during this vital phase and communication between them starts in the womb, and affects later outcomes such as learning difficulties like dyslexia.

Baryta carbonica, *Calcarea carbonica*, *Mercurius vivus*, *Phosphorus*, and *Silica* form the building blocks of remedies used in early childhood and beyond. Their prevalence in the rubrics for both dyslexia and hearing problems indicate these issues may have existed from the very start of life.

Causticum can mispronounce words and may make mistakes in saying names of objects. This can be due to paralysis of the auditory nerve. Reverberation of sound can occur in *Causticum* and also in *Mercurius* and *Phosphorus*. In the background of *Causticum*, there is often a marked history of grief and disappointed love.

Silica can have hearing difficulties and can also be indicated for dyslexia. A strong symptom is dull hearing due to swelling and catarrh of Eustachian tubes and tympanitic cavity. (*Calcarea carbonica*, *Lycopodium*, *Mercurius*, and *Phosphorus* are other remedies indicated in dyslexia which also suffer catarrh of the Eustachian tubes).

Silica children may have been born prematurely so the brain structures could have been compromised since birth. Therefore, if their failure to thrive is due to prematurity, the younger a child can be given a remedy, the better. This can be very significant to prevent the later development of such limiting issues as dyslexia. The sufferer is worse living in damp conditions and the hearing impairment may follow on from measles (*Mercurius vivus* shares this symptom). *Tuberculinum* can also have impaired hearing from birth, being closely related to *Silica*, and therefore may have to be given in the same case to give enduring effects to the single remedy treatment. *Carcinosin* and *Hyoscyamus* are known for making mistakes while reading, and both appear in the rubric **'dyslexia, general'**.

Natrum carbonicum, although not in the rubric for **'dyslexia, general'**, is known for transposing words. Like *Silica*, they may suffer recurring earache which undermines their quality of hearing. The remedy can refine their memory, which is often weak, and help them to focus.

A peculiar symptom in which *Natrum carbonicum* is the only remedy is **'illusions, hearing, sounds appear to come from left side when they really come from the right'** in the 'Hearing' chapter of the repertory. This could mirror some scrambling in the messages passing between the different brain structures.

The nosode *Medorrhinum*, although not well represented in the repertory, is also a remedy for weak memory and concentration problems. Patients needing this remedy also experience an illusion of hearing and the remedy features in the rubric, **'illusions, hearing, sounds seem double, whistling'** (as the only remedy appearing in the rubric) in the 'Hearing' chapter of the repertory. They may have enlarged adenoids, like the remedies *Baryta carbonica*, *Calcarea carbonica*, *Lycopodium* and *Mercurius vivus*, which are also indicated in dyslexia. *Mercurius vivus* can confuse left and right (which may account for its indication in many 'States on the Spectrum', including autism).

Lac caninum shares with the above remedies an affinity for the throat. It also has difficulties with hearing where noises reverberate and a sensation that they are speaking in a large empty room; sounds seem as if far off. They can call things by the wrong names – a symptom also seen in *Stramonium*, which may reverse words and, famously, say plums when they mean pears! – see rubric **'mistakes words, wrong words, using, says, plums, when he means pears'**, where it appears in italics, with only two other remedies, *Dioscorea* and *Lycopodium*, in plain type. Confidence issues are key to *Lac caninum* as in most of the remedies mentioned here, and the hearing impairment can be hereditary. Even the nosode *Medorrhinum* is in the rubric **'confidence, lacking, no self esteem'**.

As mentioned under the Victimisation entry, *Anacardium* is the remedy I have found to be needed most often in 'States on the

Spectrum', and dyslexia is no exception. Of course, in the background is also a strong lack of self-confidence. As reflected in the polarities observed in their emotional state, hearing can be acute at times but also, conversely, weak at other times. Dyslexia can lead to marginalisation in the classroom setting which can have a life-long effect on the sufferer as it feeds into any low self-esteem they may already struggle with. One often finds great creativity in the dyslexic brain which is just waiting to be unleashed. In fact, I have heard that some art colleges prefer to accept dyslexic candidates than those who are 'neurotypical' because of the degree of latent creativity acknowledged to exist in these students.

Dyslexia sufferers may have had to endure persistent bullying and marginalisation from peers as well as teachers. This is especially the case if awareness of the condition has not been made sufficiently available to them. These children need a lot of encouragement and parents as well as teachers may unwittingly feel disappointed by the limitations dyslexia presents in the classroom. Following on from this, it is easy to see that low self-confidence could be significant in underpinning dyslexia. Once the indicated remedy is given and the confidence is restored, the patient can start making the necessary brain connections to overcome this learning difficulty. At the same time as their confidence builds, they can more easily tackle any stumbling blocks which prevent them from moving forward.

A remedy which is known for 'mutism of childhood' is *Agraphis nutans*. This remedy has adenoids, with enlarged tonsils creating much mucous. Although few mental symptoms are noted, perhaps those which exist could be creating a physical block to speech. Once cognition is cleared through the release of this blockage, the learning process can start to flow. As soon as any resulting speech impairments are cleared on a physical basis, if dyslexia is a direct result, it can be addressed with *Agraphis*. Similarly, remedies such as *Hydrastis* and *Kali bichromicum*, by removing catarrh, can free up the airways so the faculties can flourish. This indicates that dyslexia is not always rooted in a mental/emotional trigger. At the same time, by removing the related physical block, the mood can be freed up in those affected in this way, and herald better cognitive ability.

With dyslexia's relationship to schizophrenia and other 'States on the Spectrum' through the compromise of the relevant brain structures, it is no coincidence that the indicated remedies for dyslexia cover many of these 'states'. Therefore, as with other 'States on the Spectrum', treating parents before conception is the ideal to wipe the slate clean. Otherwise, at best, treating mothers during pregnancy to facilitate gestation and also birth itself, is key to preventing behavioural as well as learning difficulties. A picture of drug use – medicinal or recreational – in the parents' history is an example of an epigenetic factor which could influence such outcomes as dyslexia. A recent study shows that cannabis can shrink the brain as its use reduces the grey matter, which is linked to decision-making and empathy. [64] Those brain structures affected – the cerebral cortex and the amygdala respectively – are often compromised in 'States on the Spectrum'.

The study also found that supplementation of omega-3 fatty acids support dyslexia cases and other related 'States on the Spectrum'. The remedy *Lecithin*, in low dose repeatedly, could facilitate the same process as omega-3 fatty acids as an adjunctive remedy to the constitutional one given in the case. It tones up the mood and energy as well as acts on the enhancement of the cognition.

---

64 Filbey, Francesca M. et al. (2014), *Long-Term Effects of Marijuana Use on the Brain*, www.pnas.org/content/111/47/16913.full.

ADDICTION

Addiction is a disease affecting the brain which influences the sufferer to become enslaved to obtaining and misusing a 'substance' or accessing a 'destructive behaviour' regardless of the risks involved. Teenagers easily succumb to the lure of addiction due to peer group pressures as well as the escapism it offers them. As their main brain structures are still 'under construction', they are especially defenceless when it comes to resisting the effects of these influences, whatever they may be. It is well documented that cannabis can trigger schizophrenia in the vulnerable brain. [65]

Brain chemistry can be altered as a result of the misuse of 'substances' and accessing 'destructive behaviours'. The reward centre – the amygdala is especially affected. [66] This is because the pleasure neurotransmitter – dopamine – is produced here. In addition to the damage created in this way, both adrenaline and cortisol released as a result of the chronic stress underlying addiction adds to this 'load'. This makes it particularly difficult to renounce the 'habit'. A vicious cycle ensues as dopamine becomes further depleted.

The remedy *Medorrhinum* reflects the constant seeking – partly for enjoyment, but also for the habitual effect of the addiction. The sycotic miasm, representative of this remedy, is so easily evoked during the teenage years when excessive behaviour and excitement are so alluring. In this remedy picture, there is often a history of a difficult birth or issues in the pregnancy which undermine the longer term emotional and physical health of the resulting child.

The syphilitic miasm also comes into play here, as it represents the self-destructiveness of the habit and the resulting spiral towards death.

---

65 Collingwood, Jane, *Cannabis May Cause Schizophrenia-Like Brain Changes*, www.psychcentral.com/lib/cannabis-may-cause-schizophrenia-like-brain-changes.

66 Lewis, Marc (2011), *Memoirs of an Addicted Brain: A Neuroscientist Examines His Former Life on Drugs*, PublicAffairs.

The sufferer may be a victim of foetal alcohol syndrome, where the addiction has lain dormant since embryonic life. This is a true example of transgenerational transmission where the habit is often exacerbated by a role model while growing up. Therefore, the younger the age at which a child can be treated in these cases, the more advantageous the outcome. Often, the whole family needs treatment to circumvent the 'enablement' of the addiction.

It is hard to treat addictions with any discipline of healing or therapy as, to start with, the person has to admit that they have an issue. It can take years of homeopathic treatment or other therapy before a patient gains the insight to acknowledge this, even to themselves. Once this breakthrough happens, it is possible to commit to long-term treatment. (Also, modern media holds addiction in high regard in its portrayal of famous role models in society today.)

The substance or focus of the addiction becomes the one factor the victim can control as, often, they have been unable to control their basic 'feeding' in their early life. ('Feeding' refers to both food and nurturing.) The remedy, *Lac Humanum*, is pertinent here as it is derived from human breast milk, which contributes to the bonding pattern between mother and child. Also, it taps into the amygdala through its transmission of oxytocin – fondly known as the 'cuddle hormone'.

This lack of control often leads to role reversal, and it is the focus of the addiction, whatever that may be, that governs the victim rather than the other way around. Remedies with a history of domination that often come up in addiction cases are: *Anacardium*, *Carcinosin*, *Cannabis indica*, and *Thuja*. The last two remedies are in the rubric **'delusion, superhuman, control, under, is'** which, sadly, is not just a delusion in an addict's case, but their reality.

Other related remedies which are actually derived from pleasure drugs, such as *Anhalonium*, *Morphinum*, and *Opium*, veer towards addictive behaviour as a way of coping with the lasting effects of trauma the sufferer has endured when young. This can so easily be re-evoked if not dealt with in the meantime.

Anhalonium has a picture of splitting off as a survival mechanism with a susceptibility to schizophrenia which can push the individual towards addiction. In turn, the substance – whatever it may be – can serve to reinforce the schizoid state. Hence, a vicious cycle occurs which is hard to arrest. The patient can be so cut off from reality that it is hard for anyone to make contact with them. This remedy is often given based on observation rather than subjective symptoms proffered by the patient. Visions, if present, can be so graphic and extraordinary that they are hard to relinquish, as they act as a safety net for the prevailing neurosis.

Morphinum is as useful as *Opium* for trauma which has been suppressed. *Morphinum* has, however, extreme sensitivity to pain, which is the opposite modality to *Opium*. The addiction therefore serves to quell this reaction and the patient may easily overdose, such is their need to 'feel' normal. The homeopath needs to take into account that this patient may lose moral judgement and distort the truth, maybe even more than in *Opium*.

Reflecting on the opium dens which were once so common in China in times of pestilence and serfdom, the idea of domination can be seen to be applicable to the addictive state generally. This ties in with the whole idea of the 'Doctrine of Signatures' which, in this example, can guide one to comprehend a pattern of behaviour which still persists today, albeit in a less exaggerated manner in all addictions across the board.

War veterans can easily become hooked on substances to assuage symptoms of 'post traumatic stress disorder' and when they return to civilian life, they find it hard to renounce the addiction. These 'wounds' are often invisible and can only be eased through the use of substances. Post traumatic stress is conditioned by early life experiences, so not every returning soldier suffers in this way. This propensity is based on the level of resilience which has been imbued in them since young and is what needs to be addressed through treatment.

Blast injuries, especially to the head, can feed into this scenario. *Natrum sulphuricum* can support such a patient and help deal with the resulting depression, as well as *Lyssin* which is particularly sensitive to noise.

It is no coincidence that opium grows near battlefields, as in Afghanistan and in Belgium in the early part of the last century. Think of the famous poem, *In Flanders fields, the poppies blow.* [67] In the *Opium* picture, the original hurt is so great that the memory wipes it from the conscious level. However, the unconscious is re-triggered every time a resonant reminder occurs. This is when addiction can raise its ugly head as a way of blotting out the pain. Pain may not be felt in *Opium* on a physical level, such is the level of numbing, but sorely on a mental/emotional one.

Instant gratification demonstrated in addiction could relate back to a Caesarean birth when no fight was needed to struggle through the birth canal. *Saccharum officinale* is a remedy where the child may push all the boundaries, often culminating in 'pervasive personality disorder'. [68] This state could also arise in cases of adoption or fostering where early 'rupture' has occurred with lasting damaging effects.

In the process of cure, a stronger addiction may be replaced with a milder one as the patient responds to treatment; for example, sugar might replace alcohol. The patient may see this as a negative reaction but – as long as it is a passing phase – and maybe a return of an old symptom – it can be seen as a positive step. It is therefore best to avoid follow-up prescriptions during this transition.

These rubrics suggest a link between issues of childhood rejection and domination, and alcoholism in adulthood, and are followed by a discussion about the main remedies in the combined rubric:

- *'love, disappointed, ailments from'*

- *'domination by others, ailments from, children, in'*

- *'domination by others, history, of, a long'*

---

67   McCrae, John (1915), *In Flanders Fields, the Poppies Blow.*

68   Matson, Johnny L., Sturmey, Peter (2011), *International Handbook of Autism and Pervasive Developmental Disorders (Autism and Child Psychopathology Series)*, Springer.

- *'abandoned, forsaken feelings'*
- *'helplessness, feelings'*
- *'homesickness, nostalgia, general'*
- *'pining, away from mental and physical, anxiety'*
- *'alcoholism, dipsomania'* (in 'Clinical' chapter)

Six of the 11 black type remedies in the combined rubric are: *Aurum metallicum, China officianalis, Lachesis, Nux vomica, Sulphur* and *Veratrum album*, and 15 of the 28 remedies in italics: *Antimonium crudum, Calcarea carbonica, Capsicum, Carcinosin, Cocculus indica, Hyoscyamus, Ignatia, Kali bichromicum, Lycopodium, Natrum carbonicum, Phosphorus, Rhus toxicodendron, Sepia, Silica*, and *Stramonium*. This research displays how important it is, where possible, to trace the time-line in addiction cases from the very early stages of life, as well as the miasmiatic influence in the case.

A type of autism or Asperger's syndrome which has remained unrecognised may contribute to addiction and enhance the trajectory which pushes the sufferer into the habit. If addiction is perceived as being part of the same spectrum as autism and Asperger's syndrome, it would easily creep in further along the line of similar pathological development. This later suffering can be averted, however, if the early state is recognised and addressed soon enough. *Mercurius vivus*, which hides behind alcohol as a way of opening up channels of communication, is relevant here. These channels can remain totally blocked without this type of remedy intervention.

EATING DISORDERS

Attitudes to food and eating disorders are often strongly affected by early influences and role models in this area when young. If, for example, someone has a history of starvation, as in a war situation, it is understandable when they become a parent to imbue food with considerable meaning when offering it to their offspring. If the child does not clear their plate, the parent may take this as an insult. Conversely, if the parent had an eating disorder themselves, they may inflict this neurosis onto their child in the message they project onto the food they offer. It is therefore important to explore the background in the primal period of growth when taking the case where there is an eating disorder, to uncover the true 'underpinning trigger' to the patient's specific disorder.

In the *Vanadium metallicum* picture, the child strives to be perfect without knowing why. [69] The child may focus on food – one area they can control – sub-consciously avoiding growing into the form pubescence brings, so that they no longer need to meet the aspirations of the parents by remaining a small child in their eyes. This demonstrates how eating disorders can be a family issue, the pivot often residing in a parent rather than the child who acts out the collective dysfunction in this way. It is no coincidence that the remedy *Vanadium metallicum* appears in the rubric **'childish, behaviour'**.

I believe *Vanadium metallicum* will be a major polychrest for new generations because of today's parental pressures for academic excellence, which are often applied to a child regardless of their individual interests and potentials. This is on top of the 'cult of Facebook'. Here, the messages of a narcissistic society impact the vulnerable individual fighting to find their place in, what seems to them, an ever unattainable world. One psychiatrist is quoted as saying that the 'achievement focus' – amassing A*s and looking

---

69 Luthar, Suniya (2003), The Culture of Affluence: Psychological Costs of Material Wealth, *Child Development*, 74:1581-93.

good – is more toxic for children than divorce'. [70] In her article, Cavendish states: "Many schools fear they will be labeled if they own up to the scale of eating disorders or self-harm among their pupils." The two states often go hand in hand.

The 'herd culture' which fosters eating disorders in the size-zero ideal promoted in today's media is a further impetus. *Carcinosin* gives boundaries for those who find 'going along with the mainstream' is the easiest option. Often, in the background of this remedy, is a history of suppression to the point of non-individuation. The remedy can then give the sufferer a voice to stand out from the crowd. When this occurs, this can rock the boat with the family – especially when permission is not overtly given to do this. Subsequently, the whole family has to reshuffle their roles to enable the child to liberate themselves from this unwitting tyranny.

In one case, the mother of a morbidly obese patient was herself the child of an anorexic mother. This is known as an 'epigenetic transmission', even though it manifested in a polarised way across two generations. The mother invested in over-feeding her daughter as a vicarious way of assuaging her own sense of deprivation. The habit became entrenched and culminated in severe pathology.

Individuals who find it difficult to express their feelings and physical needs may suffer more with eating disorders than other members of the population. Attitudes to eating are an unconscious way of masking their feelings or avoiding them at all costs.

Recent statistics show that obesity is a rising phenomenon in UK society. [71] Fast food and a sedentary lifestyle are often blamed, but I believe it is fundamentally the unconscious mind and the emotions attached to eating, which stem from childhood, that dictate one's attitude to food.

---

[70] Cavendish, Camilla (March 15, 2015), Parents are Inflicting Psychological Harm in an Educational Arms Race, *The Sunday Times*.

[71] Waumsley, J.A., Dr, Chairwoman (2011), *Obesity in the UK: A Psychological Perspective*, The British Psychological Society.

According to the *Observer* newspaper, some people are emotional over-eaters, as they 'eat their emotions' in the form of food to comfort themselves in times of stress and this is why they gain weight. [72] The issue which is highlighted in the article is the additional burden of 'venom, disgust, and outright cruelty' that the victim has to deal with in public. The article even implies that this form of repudiation only compounds the over-eating issue. With the current emphasis on the 'body beautiful', it is no surprise that the unconscious message which has perpetuated from childhood exacerbates similar wounds – adding insult to injury.

Antimonium crudum has this level of sensitivity, combined with the urge to over-eat. In the background is a level of disappointed love/grief which contributes to this emptiness. Even though their digestion is impaired, this is no barrier to the habit. *Calcarea carbonicum* is equally sensitive and also combines 'gluttony' with delicate digestion. *Hura brasiliensis* carries the sense of ostracisation suggested in the *Observer* article, although this is not a remedy generally associated with over-eating.

Staphysagria can be indicated for over-eating when there is a background of suppressed anger and inability to express feelings. In cases where there is a history of abuse, the patient may turn to food or cigarettes to push everything down, and the oral cavity becomes the sphere where this often happens.

Staphysagria may have a background of sexual suppression, in which case there is no stimulation of the hypothalamus to release the hormones which calm the appetite. Is it any surprise, then, that the *Staphysagria* patient is so orally based when it comes to 'stuffing things down' in this way?

Just as anorexia enables sufferers to avoid womanhood, obesity can provide a security blanket so that others do not find them sexually available. This can happen after abuse or when, for whatever reason, they do not wish to attract the attention of the opposite gender, often sub-consciously. When treating such cases,

---

72   Ellen, Barbara (July 13, 2014), The Overweight Deserve Help, not Sneers or Malice, *The Observer*.

the unravelling can be quite rocky as others around them adjust to their reclamation of the self.

Any eating disorder can be both triggered and fuelled by oppressive family dynamics. This means the cure may come when the sufferer leaves the 'nest' and gains their autonomy, which is all that is required. The defence mechanism no longer relies on the protection the disorder allows them. This is an example where the philosophy of 'maintaining causes' holds so true in homeopathy.

As eating is such a primal function, any imbalance shows the true 'uncompensated state'. The source could even go back to a grandmother, for example, and what she ate in pregnancy. If there was a famine, as occurred in Holland in the war years, the effects could manifest in the third generation's nutritional status, and predispose them to later diseases such as schizophrenia or cardiovascular disease. [73] Food represents reward in this scenario, and so there can never be enough to satisfy the appetite.

When the public learns to appreciate the epigenetic factor which plays out in an eating disorder, their attitude could completely change towards the unfortunate victim. This could equally apply to any 'State on the Spectrum', which is why exploring the time-line according to the concept set out here can be so important.

---

73 Bastiaan, T., Heijmans et al. (2008), Persistent Epigenetic Differences Associated with Prenatal Exposure to Famine in Humans, *Proceedings of the National Academy of Sciences of the United States of America*, 105(44).

BODY DYSMORPHIA

Body dysmorphia is a recent phenomenon in society which arises when there is distortion in the eyes of the sufferer about the shape and size of their body. This delusion is accompanied by contempt of the body and, often, a compulsive need to assuage the feelings by over-dieting and/or over-exercising. It is not helpful that society has become so image-based that, unless one complies with this albeit misjudged ideal, one can feel rejected and reviled by one's peers.

Thuja, with its need to maintain a perfect image despite feeling inadequate inside, is a significant option for addressing body dysmorphia. However, *Sabadilla* – a related remedy to *Thuja* – is a smaller and lesser-known specific remedy for this state. Both remedies belong to the sycotic miasm with its fixedness and sense of shame. Many of *Sabadilla's* specific symptoms relate to the dysmorphic state: **'delusion, deformed, some parts are'**, **'delusion, erroneous, ideas as to the state of their body'**, and **'delusion, body is withering'**. This mindset can apply to men as much as women in the modern world. Like *Thuja*, the patient can be unresponsive to questions and their sleep can be disturbed due to their preoccupations. *Sabadilla* is more restless than *Thuja*.

Thuja needs to project a manufactured image to the world, such is their sense of inadequacy and guilt. The delusions in *Thuja* overlap with *Sabadilla*, but the self-contempt in *Thuja* is more exaggerated. *Sabadilla* is less likely to feel suicidal as a result of their neurosis than *Thuja*.

Anorexic cases often have a strong sense of body dysmorphia and, even if the sufferer is painfully slender, they often see themselves as fat or ugly. The first breakthrough in treatment comes when the patient can finally grasp the reality of their situation and stop hiding behind this delusion. *Thuja* has the type of mindset which can lie behind anorexia. By hiding their true feelings (see the rubric **'hides, true feelings'**) the sufferer can act out their distress in this way.

Lac caninum, with its marked self-contempt, is also worth considering for body dysmorphia. Their confidence is so low that the patient can easily hide behind this neurosis as an unconscious way of avoiding progressing in life. See the rubric *'delusion, looked down upon, that she is'*, where *Lac caninum* and *Platina* are the only remedies which appear and the rubric *'delusion, diminished'*. *Sabadilla* is also in this rubric, *Thuja* appearing in the sub-rubric: *'thin, is too'*. As with *Sabadilla* and *Thuja*, there is fixedness about their ideas. In the rubric, *'disgust, body, with one's own'*, *Lac caninum* appears alongside *Thuja*. However, *Lac caninum* does not care what others think in the way that *Thuja* does – the latter being more image-conscious with its strong relationship to the sycotic miasm. *Lac caninum* is a more syphilitic remedy.

SELF-HARM

This phenomenon can occur at any stage of life but is especially prevalent during puberty.

The rubric, **'mutilate, body, inclination to'**, contains many remedies, including some of those discussed already: *Anacardium, Hyoscyamus, Lac humanum, Syphilinum* and *Tuberculinum*. Self-harm often accompanies anorexia, but can also exist in isolation. *Lyssin* and *Mancinella* are both remedies which comply with the ethos of modern day culture in their different themes. Self-mutilation is a type of behaviour which links these two very polarised remedies.

Lyssin is made from the saliva of a rabid dog, and the patient needing this remedy literally 'bites back' under provocation. This is similar to the theme of *Staphisagria*, but the reaction is much more marked in *Lyssin*; in fact, both the trigger and the reaction are more extreme in *Lyssin*. The senses are hyper-acute, so even the sound of someone eating can drive them into their typical 'supercharged' over-reaction. They are desperate about their plight, a mental state which matches the remedy's affinity to the syphilitic miasm. There can be aggravation from seeing or thinking about water. Apart from emotional provocation, the state can be brought on by being bitten by a dog. Their abusiveness could overlap with *Anacardium* and, to a lesser degree, *Tuberculinum*. The *Lyssin* feeling of being insulted can be imagined by the affected individual, such is the depth of their original 'wound'. A rare symptom, given the main theme, is empathy for others' pain, such is their sensitivity. The rubric is **'sympathetic, empathy, feels same pains as others'** – where the only other remedy is *Phosphorus*.

Mancinella is reputedly made from the forbidden apple in the Garden of Eden, so it is no surprise that it has mystical qualities. The patient is impressionable and has a background of poor role models, which means they are easily led to find and follow cult heroes. These can be pop singers – often with satanic tendencies. This is where self-harm comes in. There is often a background of one emotionally harsh parent and, conversely, and in compensation, the polarity of another who is overly tender. This is confusing for the growing child and can lead to identity issues, especially regarding their sexuality. This remedy is in the rubric *'fear, homosexuality, of'*. Their feminine side is often over-developed. This symptom is also found in sycotic remedies such as *Medorrhinum, Pulsatilla, Staphysagria* and *Thuja*, which share with *Mancinella,* *'memory, weakness, of'* and *'thoughts, vanishing, of'*. *Mancinella* has fear of insanity, as the patient soon realises they are 'on the edge'. It is valuable to study the different and contrasting manifestations of these symptoms in these comparable remedies.

SCHIZOPHRENIA

Schizophrenia often manifests during the late teenage years and may go unrecognised for some time. This is because any teenager can easily cut themselves off from others, perform poorly in school, become hostile and be attracted to addictive substances – all features which can indicate the very disease itself.

Even mainstream medicine recognises that schizophrenia may be related to trauma – especially in early life – which undermines the vulnerable patient. [74] To extend the time-line retrospectively, the trauma may even originate within the womb when the trigger may not necessarily be an emotional one but a physical one such as insufficient blood supply reaching the placenta.

The sufferer may have been raised in an institution where the nurturing factor was completely absent. In these children's cases, if the case could be traced far enough, we may see that the deprivation dates right back to the time of conception. Even malnutrition or hypothyroidism in the mother's pregnancy could contribute to this mental state developing later in the child's life.

On a physical level, the patient might have suffered a blow to the head, which is a major causation of such states, given the emotional susceptibility. This injury may go almost unnoticed at the time but, if an accurate history is taken, this information may be uncovered. Banging one's head against the bars of a cot as a means of stimulation could be enough, if repeated sufficiently, to create such a lesion. *Helleborus* is a remedy which complies with the trigger of brain injury, and the possible result of dissociation.

A recent study has found that not only can cannabis trigger schizophrenia but also, conversely, people with a tendency to schizophrenia are more likely to use cannabis than other members of society. [75] This is intriguing for the homeopathic

---

74 Sideli, Lucia et al. (June 2012), Do Child Abuse and Maltreatment Increase the Risk of Schizophrenia?, *Psychiatry Investigation*, 9(2):87-99.
75 Kelland, Kate (June 24, 2014), Study Finds Genetic Links between Schizophrenia and Cannabis Use, *Reuters*, US Edition.

mind with our understanding of the 'law of similars'. If we look at the 'proving' of *Cannabis indica*, we see that it contains more delusions than any other remedy – and that these delusions are all rather outlandish, such as one may discover inside the extreme schizophrenic mind.

ALZHEIMER'S DISEASE

The reader may wonder why I include Alzheimer's disease under the heading of 'States on the Spectrum'. This is because its roots could be laid down in the mother's pregnancy due to emotional triggers such as shock or physical factors. These could be in the form of nutritional deficiencies or the consumption of alcohol or drugs for medicinal use or pleasure. They interfere with dopamine levels in the brain and, as these levels become depleted, the more the neurotransmitters lose their ability to function in an optimal manner.

The effects of smoking should also not be forgotten as these can be as harmful to the developing brain as other substances already mentioned. Their impact depends on the susceptibility of the individual. This means some people will develop learning difficulties in childhood and others will remain cognitively aware all their lives until a marked stressor (or combination of stressors) accumulates and overwhelms the victim. Then they could be plunged into Alzheimer's if the impetus is sufficient at this time of vulnerability.

Exploring the history of previous family members could be the main key to preventing the onset of these 'states' in the individual. At the same time, the role model of defeating attitudes is dispelled, so the 'maintaining cause' no longer fuels the ongoing 'state'. Also, patients – both adults and children – with 'States on the Spectrum' often have compromised guts as part of their specific syndrome. If this is not addressed through treatment with appropriate support remedies, there will be no improvement in the accompanying neurological state.

In an article in the *New Scientist*: 'Keep the Body Well to Slow Alzheimer's', based on research into Alzheimer's disease by Hugh Perry of the University of Southampton, we learn that staying free of 'lifestyle diseases' and infections could put the brakes on

Alzheimer's. [76] These bodily ailments create inflammation that ultimately spills over into the brain, sending its immune cells into a hyperactive, destructive state. This principle applies to any severe outcome of pathology, such as diabetes or heart disease. Therefore, by tackling the underpinning emotional state early on, these physical pathologies may be ruled out and the passage through old age will be eased.

An article in the publication, *Memory*, documents that amnesia begins at the age of seven and is very much conditioned by the experience of early childhood. [77] This ties in with the rationale that Alzheimer's is on the same 'spectrum' as such 'states' as autism and schizophrenia. Equally, in these 'states', early childhood or even 'embryonic' experiences, determine the specific outcome on the 'spectrum'.

Isolation plays a role in all 'States on the Spectrum', but I believe it plays the greatest role in Alzheimer's disease. It is as if isolation has an epigenetic effect on the brain cells and decreases oxytocin, which is vital in remaining 'connected'. It must be no coincidence that many remedies in the isolation rubrics are also indicated in 'States on the Spectrum'. One of the first responses to a curative remedy is reaching out to others and being more receptive towards them. This supports improved functioning of the brain structures, which have hitherto remained compromised and contributed to the disease condition.

Trends in today's society have led to an increasing sense of isolation in many individuals. Before the advent of so much technology, face-to-face encounters were a regular feature of most people's lives. If communication is through a computer, this very vital form of personal interaction cannot be replicated. It could be that the effects can be experienced even beyond the course of one generation.

76 Coghlan, Andy (April 2014), Keep the Body Well to Slow Alzheimer's, *New Scientist,* 222(2966):10.
77 Bauer, P., Larkina, M. (2014), The Onset of Childhood Amnesia in Childhood: A Prospective Investigation of the Course and Determinants of Forgetting of Early-Life Events, *Memory,* 22:907-24.

In non-industrialised societies, it is the custom for the community at large to offer support to the ageing individual which acts as a protection for longevity as well as against the development of Alzheimer's and demonstrates the importance of emotional support as a protection. In a case from my practice, once the family realised the sufferer needed their care and acted upon this, the sufferer regained her clarity in a most remarkable way, demonstrating how isolation can remain a 'maintaining cause' unless addressed. The sense of isolation can originate from triggers such as early abandonment, deception, or the example of the role model when growing up.

In the article, *Oxytocin for Frontotemporal Dementia*, the authors say that a squirt of oxytocin – the cuddle hormone – could tackle symptoms of dementia. [78] This is because oxytocin improves emotional expression processing, empathy, and cooperative behaviour. In dementia, there is emotional blunting, lack of empathy and social behavioural decline. Oxytocin is an important mediator of social behaviour, potentially enhancing emotional expression and prosocial behaviour. This research suggests that oxytocin links dementia with autism, another 'State on the Spectrum', through its bonding effect – in which case, offering *Oxytocin* as an adjunctive remedy to constitutional treatment in 'States on the Spectrum', could help these patients to open up.

The influence of head injuries should not be overlooked – even if they occurred years before – as they can trigger the later development of Alzheimer's. The picture of *Helleborus* can be used as an example to see the effect on the brain of such a trigger. In addition, exposure to certain toxins such as DDT and both medicinal and recreational drugs play a role in this disease.

There is often a history of sleep disturbance, which increases the release of cortisol and results in dopamine reduction in these cases. The appropriate remedy needs to take this into account in order to prevent the brain from becoming increasingly toxic. Sleep disturbance is also often a precursor to other 'States on the Spectrum', especially autism.

---

[78]   Finger, Elizabeth C. et al. (January 2015), Oxytocin for Frontotemporal Dementia: A Randomized Dose-Finding Study of Safety and Tolerability, *Neurology*, 84(2):174-81.

GENERAL COMMENTS ABOUT 'STATES ON THE SPECTRUM'

Wherever the sufferer is on the 'Spectrum', as the case unravels during the treatment, the deeper 'state' may be replaced by a milder 'state'. In one case, an autistic child became hyperactive as he became more engaged through treatment. This could be perceived as a retrograde step, but actually indicates the case is going in the right direction according to homeopathic philosophy. Parents and carers therefore need to be alerted to this progression to avoid rushing in with the Ritalin and 'throwing the baby (of progress) out with the bath water' in the process.

Not only is Alzheimer's markedly affected by toxins, but also attention deficit disorder, autism, Asperger's syndrome, bipolar disorder, and depression in general.

Patients who are on the 'Spectrum', whether in the form of a brain problem or a learning issue, are usually in a state of 'sympathetic fight-or-flight'. Without this being addressed, any chance of resolution is blocked. This state usually originates in childhood where the axis of the hypothalamic and pituitary stress response is calibrated.

Often, these 'states' co-exist within one patient, e.g. attention deficit disorder, Asperger's Syndrome and dyslexia. Regardless of the combination of 'states', the treatment should always be mapped out on a timeline to locate the fundamental triggering factor(s) to be addressed.

PART 2

MATERIA MEDICA

Agaricus muscarius

This remedy is made from fly agaric, a type of mushroom with almost mystical properties in folklore. I have found it to be useful for – among other issues – dyslexia, where the sufferer describes the letters jumping out from the page. There seems to be a 'disconnect' between the way the words are seen and how the brain interprets this visual information. The technical name for this condition is Meares-Irlen syndrome. [79] It can occur in patients suffering with such conditions as ADHD, autism, epilepsy, myalgic encephalitis and multiple sclerosis. It can even occur in isolation of any of these states.

Given that there is often a background of dyspraxia in *Agaricus* – see rubrics *'size, incorrect judge of'*, *'awkward, mentally, drops things'* and *'awkward, stumbling when walking'* (*Agaricus* appears in black type in the last two), one can perceive a lack of spatial awareness running through this remedy which translates into the way messages are received through the senses.

Coupled with this background on the mental/emotional level, there are many rubrics under *'vision'* in the repertory which lead to *Agaricus* for this particular aspect of dyslexia. See rubrics *'vision, dim, focal distance changes while, reading, first longer then shorter'* where *Agaricus* is the only remedy. Also, *'moving vision, letters'* and *'reading, inability from weak eyes, type seems to move'* – again, *Agaricus* is the only remedy in the last rubric. In fact, it was the visual symptoms that first led me to this remedy for dyslexia, an increasingly common condition.

The theme of this remedy includes: 'mental confusion while reading' and the symptom of dullness with sluggishness. Mental exertion makes the patient feel worse – see rubric *'exertion, worse mental'* and a type of forgetfulness can occur of words while speaking – see rubric *'memory, weakness, words, for'* and *'memory, weakness of, children, in'* (where it is the only remedy

---

79   *Meares-Irlen Syndrome*, http://www.dyslexiasw.com/advice/all-about-dyslexia/meares-irlen-syndrome.

apart from *Baryta carbonica*). The rubric *'memory, weakness, expressing one's self, for'* relates to the way visual information is received. The patient may be heedless and inconsistent and resist lessons when the mind needs to be applied. See rubrics *'thinking, aversion, to'* and the symptom of mental aversion to work as well as *'work, prolonged, aggravates'* – the latter where *Agaricus* is the only remedy.

This problem of the lack of conscious reflection can be observed through the visual field as well as auditory channels. A condition called 'auditory processing disorder' has recently been identified, where a similar 'disconnect' occurs. [80] This time, it manifests through the hearing channel rather than the visual one. This could equally apply to the *Agaricus* patient, given that the same brain structures are likely to be compromised as in the visual field.

There may be a background of alcoholism in a parent or a history of punishment. Anger can escalate to a point where strength is increased, as in the remedy *Lyssin* (see rubric *'anger, vexation, ailments from'* and *'rage, fury, strength increased'*). Note that *Lyssin* could be added to the latter rubric. The *Agaricus* patient is very easily offended, like *Lyssin*, and affected by reproaches – these aspects can provoke the type of response mentioned here.

In one case, I put the rubric *'chaotic, behaviour'* first in the hierarchy of symptoms even though this related to the mother's state during pregnancy. It is so easy to overlook this vital aspect, bearing in mind that so much of a case is 'informed' during the gestation period, as highlighted in the Introduction.

The trauma layer must be marked to create the 'soil' for sleep-walking, which is another key feature of *Agaricus*. In cases where this is a feature, there is often a history of suppression of expression of emotions in the background. This early trauma is often unidentified and unarticulated, which feeds into learning difficulties so commonly seen in this remedy, which could be a major polychrest for the learning difficulties so commonly found today.

---

80 *Auditory Processing Disorder*, www.nhs.uk/conditions/auditory-processing-disorder/Pages/Introduction.aspx.

Remedies such as *Agaricus* can release the underlying emotional symptoms so that full healing can occur on all levels. This can have a vicarious effect on other family members as the pressure is released from the collective dynamic which so often has, albeit unconsciously, become embroiled in the surrounding drama these issues promote.

The brain structure which could be primarily affected in *Agaricus* is the cerebellum – which contributes to agility and balance, as well as supporting coordination and cognitive integration. If undermined, these aspects combine, leading to delayed thinking. When damage occurs to this structure, the patient becomes disconnected and cannot learn regular routines. Dyspraxia (a condition affecting the coordination) falls under this brain structure, and often lies behind the specific learning difficulty in the case example mentioned above.

Alumina oxydata

(Other main derivatives include: *Alumina phosphorica* and *Alumina silicata*)

Alumina is reputed to be a simillimum for Alzheimer's disease. However, in order for this remedy to fit the case, the seeds must have been planted early in life, when the young child may have witnessed violence within the family. This leads to a 'splitting off', culminating in the type of disconnection seen in Alzheimer's disease. The brain structure which becomes undermined through this process, as in the case of *Agaricus muscarius*, is likely to be the cerebellum, which is responsible for cognitive integration as well as the capacity for coordination. This remedy illustrates that childhood trauma cultivates dissociation; this very early formative stress inhibits the growth of new neurons. The brain then becomes less adaptable and the speech resultingly slow. Trauma percolates to physical structures in a most destructive way in *Alumina*, highlighting its very 'syphilitic' nature. Alzheimer's disease may then remain dormant and be triggered in old age, or earlier. *Alumina* is only indicated for Alzheimer's disease if this particular brain structure is compromised; *Helleborus* and *Nux moschata*, lesser-known remedies, may also be applicable here. The use of recreational drugs and/or alcohol can also create the type of dissociation seen in *Alumina*.

One reason why *Alumina* has become such a 'polychrest' in this 'state' is its ability to antidote effects of aluminium. It is only in recent years that aluminium has been phased out of cookware and utensils; however, it may still be contained in some allopathic medications and, in many cases, there is a strong medication layer which exists in the background.

Both *Alumina* and *Nux moschata* have dryness running through them, shown in lack of perspiration, dry skin eruptions, feeble menstruation, and thirstiness. These symptoms indicate that dehydration has a major effect on the functioning of the brain – as the brain is composed of 80% water. [81] Even the restless sleep seen in this remedy may be simply due to dehydration.

Alumina is a syphilitic remedy, and has more depression than *Nux moschata*, as demonstrated in the rubrics, **'smiling, never, smiles'** and **'repulsive, mood'**. The emotional causation could be scorn – see rubric **'scorned, ailments, from being'** as opposed to **'love, disappointed, ailments from'**, reflected in *Natrum muriaticum* – another remedy with dryness running through its picture.

There is less timidity in *Alumina* than in the *Baryta* salts, which are more often indicated in the passive state of dementia. There is a sense of disorientation in *Alumina,* the *Barytas* and *Nux moschata*. In *Alumina*, one sees **'delusion, unreal, everything seems'**. In the *Baryta* salts, there is **'delusion, changed, thinks everything'** and **'delusion, strange, familiar, things, seem'**. In *Nux moschata*, this delusion is more exaggerated, as expressed in **'delusion, familiar, things, seem, ludicrous'**.

Plumbum metallicum is closely related to both *Alumina* and the *Baryta* salts. The *Metallicum* remedies are known for their marked level of weakness; so, if the patient is very weak and has not responded to indicated remedies, it is worth considering *Plumbum metallicum*. Note that *Plumbum* is in the rubric **'repulsive, mood'** with *Alumina*, *Ambra grisea* and *Conium maculatum*, the last two remedies also being indicated in Alzheimer's disease.

If there is physical pathology, *Plumbum metallicum* is more likely to affect the upper extremities, whereas *Alumina* relates to the lower extremities. The stasis seen in *Plumbum metallicum* reflects on the bowels in an even more extreme way than seen in *Alumina*, as well as *Ambra grisea* and *Nux moschata* (these last two remedies also being known for constipation).

'Errors of personal identity' are more extreme in *Plumbum metallicum* than in *Alumina* and *Kali bromatum* – see rubric **'delusion, identity, errors of personal identity, thinks she** (this could read 'he' too!) **is someone else'**. *Alumina* and *Nux moschata*

---

81 *Memory and the Brain*, www.human-memory.net/brain.html.

are averse to company, whereas *Plumbum metallicum*, like the *Baryta* salts, dislikes being alone.

The rubric **'imbecility'** includes *Alumina* and other remedies indicated for Alzheimer's disease: *Ambra grisea, Conium, Hyoscyamus, Nux moschata*, and *Opium*.

As the dementia state progresses in *Alumina*, the patient may not recognise their friends or relatives – as seen in *Anacardium*, the *Baryta* salts, *Hyoscyamus, Opium* and *Plumbum metallicum*. This can be disconcerting for those who care for them – see rubric **'relatives, ignores his'**.

On a physical level, the theme of stagnation runs through *Alumina* – often demonstrated in the form of constipation, as referred to above – along with the other remedies discussed here. This illustrates the marked degree of toxicity which needs to be removed, as only then can the patient attain optimal health.

With its marked focus on the gut and strong emotional triggers, we can see that dementia could fall under 'States on the Spectrum'. Children needing this remedy often show malabsorption in the form of eating pica – **'pica, desires to eat sand, slate, earth, etc.'** and **'indigestible things, desires'**. [82] (Pica is the persistent eating of substances such as dirt or paint that have no nutritional value.) These two rubrics are in the Food chapter of the *Repertory*.

Zincum metallicum is a good follow-on remedy in *Alumina* cases when malabsorption remains entrenched. In fact, zinc deficiency can play a significant role in all 'States on the Spectrum', anorexia nervosa being the main one where zinc deficiency is highlighted. [83]

Zincum metallicum may also have a chaotic background, as in *Alumina*. If causative factors cannot be elicited (at any level) in an

---

82 Hambidge, K. and Silverman, A. (1973), Pica with Rapid Improvement after Dietary Zinc Supplementation, *Archives of Disease in Childhood*, 48(7):567-8.
83 Bakan, R. (1979), The Role of Zinc in Anorexia Nervosa: Etiology and Treatment, *Medical Hypotheses*, 5(7):731-6.

Alzheimer's case, observation can still lead to the indicated remedy, as it is the manifestation of the disease state which expresses the true 'uncompensated state' of the patient. Each remedy acts out the distress in its own inimitable way. A dementia patient, after all, is not able to feign their sickness.

Alumina has its place in this 'disease', but so do a myriad of other comparable remedies, each propelled along their own trajectory until the individual expression of the 'state' is exposed for treatment. So, *Alumina* only touches the 'tip of the iceberg' – an iceberg which is on a collision course with this rapidly approaching 'juggernaut'. This applies not only in the western world, but also increasingly in the developing world at large.

Anacardium orientale

(Other main derivative: *Anacardium occidentalis*)

Anacardium, and other remedies in 'States on the Spectrum' (especially schizophrenia), have strong emotional root causes such as abuse, business failure, grief, jealousy, and mortification. Remedies falling under this influence, in addition to *Anacardium*, include *Aurum metallicum, Hyoscyamus, Kali bromatum, Lachesis, Stramonium, Tarentula hispanica,* and *Veratrum album.*

Anacardium, Chamomilla, and *Veratrum album* are the only black type remedies in the rubric **'delusion, voices hears'**, which indicates the extreme extent of the triggers underlying this state. The more extreme the symptoms, the more extreme the nature of its trigger is likely to be.

As mentioned in Part 1, *Anacardium* is the Number 1 remedy in my practice for 'States on the Spectrum', confirmed by its prolific representation for these conditions. There is often a history of domination or humiliation or, at worst, abuse (or any combination of these influences) in the patient's life. This creates a split within the patient which, if left untreated, could lead to schizophrenia. [84] See rubrics **'domination, by others, ailments from, in children'** / **'domination, history, of, a long'**, **'humiliation, mortification'**, **'abuse, ailments from'** and sub-rubrics such as **'with anger'**, **'with indignation'**, **'from punishment'**, **'from sexual abuse'**, and **'from violence'** – *Anacardium* being in black type for the last entry, alongside *Arnica, Carcinosin,* and *Staphysagria.*

This background leads to great undermining of the patient's self-confidence. Concentration and memory can become impaired from a young age, compounding the pre-existing low self-confidence. The brain may become weakened by the overuse of alcohol or recreational drugs, the need for which is a reflection of

---

84 Wood, Janice (2012), Childhood Trauma Linked to Schizophrenia, http://psychcentral.com/news/2012/04/20/childhood-trauma-linked-to-schizophrenia/37610.html.

their avoidant tendencies.

In ADHD, the patient is unable to focus their attention and becomes tense and anxious. This can afflict the function of the adrenals as well as the thyroid. They can then become defiant and resentful – other remedies with similar compromise include *Argentum nitricum, Lachesis, Nitric acid*, and *Stramonium*.

Dyslexia is increasingly recognised these days, and *Anacardium* is a significant remedy as it matches learning difficulties in the early stages. However, if the case is left to progress with ongoing duress from either the parent or main carer, the child could develop schizophrenia as they grow towards adulthood. In fact, psychoanalyst R.D. Laing, in the book, *Sanity, Madness, and the Family*, co-written with Aaron Esterson, maintained that schizophrenia is a social, rather than a medical phenomenon. [85] This conclusion is based on the record of interviews with 11 schizophrenics and their relatives. The authors state that: "The fragmentation of the person is an intelligible response to an intolerable pressure," suggesting that this pressure usually comes from the primary caregivers.

More recently, this view has been increasingly validated in medical circles. [86] In an example of one female patient, her parents interpreted any expression of autonomy as 'her not being herself' and therefore part of her illness. Independent thought was labelled 'being difficult'. There was a background of subterfuge regarding their gestures towards her, and this combined approach was described as 'an invitation to paranoia if ever there was one' – surely a true *Anacardium* situation.

The possibility of an inborn susceptibility to psychosis is validated in L.A. Sass's article which suggests the syphilitic tendency of this remedy and others related to schizophrenia. [87] *Anacardium* is close to *Mancinella venenata* – they share a history of domination

85 Laing R.D. and Esterson, Aaron (1990), *Sanity, Madness and the Family: Families of Schizophrenics*, Penguin Books Ltd.
86 Sass, L.A. (1998), Schizophrenia, Self-Consciousness, and the Modern Mind, *Journal of Consciousness Studies*, 5(5-6):543-65.
87 Shariatmadari, David (August 25, 2013), A Book that Changed Me, *The Observer*.

and isolation (although *Mancinella* does not appear in the relevant rubrics, being under-represented in the repertory). These remedies also share a resemblance in their lack of barriers to filter out what belongs inside, and what belongs outside themselves.

The hardening in *Anacardium* is reflected onto the emotional sphere, and is usually due to the effects of alcoholism (*Hyoscyamus*). Note that the hardening seen in *Conium maculatum* could be due to the loss of sexual activity, or loss of property (the latter also seen in *Aurum metallicum* and *Kali bromatum*).

Anacardium can have a delusion of being pursued – as can *Hyosyamus*, *Kali bromatum*, and *Plumbum metallicum* – as paranoia starts to slip in. The patient may then not recognise his relatives – a state sometimes seen in Alzheimer's (*Alumina*, the *Baryta* remedies, *Hyosyamus*, and *Plumbum metallicum*).

Anacardium has an affinity with the gut, a common concomitant in dementia cases. This patient is always relieved emotionally and physically by eating. The remedy also acts on the joints which can easily become contracted (a reflection of the emotions) and the tendons injured or strained. This shows its close affinity to *Rhus toxicodendron*; the neurosis reflects onto the skin in the form of severe itching, resembling the effects of poison oak. *Mancinella venenata* has even more marked skin irritation as a reflex from neurotic triggers. On a mental level, both *Anacardium* and *Rhus toxicodendron* have learning difficulties and depression.

Like many remedies mentioned in my article, *Beyond the Constraints of Alumina*, there can be marked constipation in *Anacardium*. [88] A marked plug/band-like sensation, often located in the bowels, is typical of this remedy.

As the dementia state progresses in *Anacardium*, regression and incoherent speech can occur, alongside a degree of paranoia – like *Hyosyamus*, *Kali bromatum*, and *Plumbum metallicum*.

If marked aggression 'kicks in' to a dementia case, this remedy

---

88 Adalian, Elizabeth (Winter/Spring 2013), Beyond the Constraints of Alumina: Unlocking the Key to Dementia, *Homeopathy In Practice*.

could come into its own. There is also a tendency for patients to use foul language.

Head injury may play a role at any stage of development (like *Cicuta* and *Helleborus*, among lesser-known remedies). In extreme cases, Tourette's can occur – again, at any stage of development (alongside *Agaricus*, *Hyoscyamus*, *Lycopodium*, and *Stramonium*).

There is a hysterical element to the asthma this patient presents, the lungs being emblematic of emotional distress. Other important remedies with this symptom include: *Arsenicum album*, *Moschus*, *Nux moschata*, *Pulsatilla*, and *Valeriana*. From my own practice, I have observed *Tarentula Hispanica* to be applicable here.

Kali phosphoricum is the closest mineral analogue to *Anacardium* and may be a useful support when nervous tension persists due to anticipation in the build-up to any examination or ordeal the patient is facing. A comparison between *Anacardium* and *Argentum nitricum* appears under the entry for the latter remedy.

Androdoctonus amurreuxi (*Scorpion*)

There are few more emotive animals in the materia medica than the scorpion. As a species, the scorpion evokes revulsion in the onlooker, and this could be a hint for the prescriber at the choice of remedy as this is a feature of the syphilitic miasm, and *Syphilinum* is a closely related remedy. Snakes have a similar effect as well as the tarantula spider. The latter, as a remedy type, could also be on the 'Spectrum'. However, the tarantula would manifest their symptoms in a less intense and less alienated manner than the scorpion.

Brain structures responsible for mood regulation and impulse control are especially damaged in *Androdoctonus*. However, it is a remedy which, it could be speculated, transcends all the different brain structures when it comes to early damage in their formation (along with *Agaricus*, *Anacardium*, the *Baryta* remedies, *Carcinosin*, *Helleborus*, *Hyoscyamus*, *Lyssin*, *Saccharum officinale*, and *Stramonium*). This could indicate a history of extreme duress endured by the mother in pregnancy or by both parents before conception.

This remedy is useful in certain addiction cases, especially where the predilection for video games is so entrenched that social interaction with others is totally ruled out, which might be an escape from what seems like a hostile world around them. In extremis, they can become quite paranoid. This habit affects their sleep pattern so deeply that their circadian rhythms become completely unsynchronised, which just serves to compound the already compromised brain structure. It is as if they are struggling with permanent jet-lag.

The brain becomes dull and the outlook becomes increasingly gloomy. This occurs at the crucial stage of brain development when the dreaded influences of the teenage years take their toll.

The imbalanced lifestyle, panic, and temper outbursts which can appear quite unpredictably can lead to adrenal imbalance. As a reflection of the emotional state, the gut becomes impaired in the form of queasiness, alternating stools and anxiety affecting the abdomen. With the backdrop of the lifestyle described, a regular eating pattern is often precluded, which serves to compound the pre-existing adrenal imbalance and compromised gut.

Robin Murphy's *Nature's Materia Medica*, in the entry for this remedy based on Allen, Clarke and the proving by Sherr, states: "Felt detached, very interested in little things, felt disconnected from the human race, as if everyone were another species." [34]

The patient may be struggling with Asperger's syndrome which has possibly been unrecognised within the family and/or school, thus compounding their already present sense of alienation.

Argentum nitricum

(Other main derivative: *Argentum metallicum*)

In Jan Scholten's analysis of the Periodic Table, the 'silver series' is all to do with performance, and the *Argentum* remedies are the protagonists here. [7]

There is, therefore, a strong sense of anticipation with loss of emotional balance and a risk of panic attacks due to consequent hysteria (this remedy is not always considered for hysteria but appears in the related rubric in italics). This is mirrored onto the physical level in the form of injuries affecting the bones, especially the periosteum, and cartilages. The sacro-iliac joint can become loose and, as a result, the coordination can become compromised.

Comparison between *Anacardium* and the *Argentum* remedies:

Anacardium resembles the *Argentum* remedies in anticipation. The self-confidence is so low that the patient almost invites their own downfall. The overlap between the remedies is shown in the strong sense of abandonment in the background as well as hysteria (*Anacardium* is also not always highlighted for hysteria but also appears in the related rubric and in italics). With the strong sense of anticipation these remedies share, insomnia can easily be a concomitant symptom. The learning process becomes affected and concentration is affected, especially when performing under stress. There may be a history of recreational drugs which have contributed to the state.

Anacardium also resembles *Argentum metallicum* in its action on joints and muscles. In *Anacardium*, the joints can easily become contracted (a reflection of the emotions) and the tendons injured or strained. *Kali phosphoricum*, a close mineral analogue, may have to be given if nervous tension has built up during training for a performance or sporting event. Gut reactions in *Argentum* remedies lead to diarrhoea whereas, in *Anacardium*, the bowels are more likely to feel plugged up, with difficulty in passing stool.

So, there is a marked overlap with this remedy, but also marked distinguishing features between them.

Argentum nitricum is known for impulses and is more compulsive than *Anacardium* to the point of ritualistic behaviour. However, *Anacardium* is black type in the rubric **'impulses, morbid'**, whereas *Argentum nitricum* is in italics, as are *Androdoctonus, Causticum, Hepar sulphuricum, Lachesis, Nux vomica, Stramonium*, and *Thea*. In *Argentum nitricum*, it is a benign impulse, whereas in *Anacardium*, it has more to do with violent intent – being a more syphilitic remedy. The *Argentum* remedies are more sycotic.

Other physical symptoms under *Argentum nitricum* include arteriosclerosis, menstrual irregularities, asthma, adrenal imbalance and skin disease. There is a parallel in these symptoms with *Anacardium* but with different manifestations according to the nature of each remedy's derivation.

Rhus toxicodendron follows both the *Argentum* remedies and *Anacardium* well, especially when the joints and/or muscles are affected. The connection between *Rhus toxicodendron* and *Anacardium* shows how remedies of the same family can combine together in one case or across different generations of the same family. *Dysentery co.* is the bowel nosode most closely related to the *Argentum* remedies and to *Anacardium*.

In the age of high academic expectation, it is no wonder so many students need the *Argentum* remedies, where performance is key to acceptance – see rubric **'anxiety, time, is set, if a'**, where only three other remedies appear: *Gelsemium, Medorrhinum*, and *Natrum muriaticum* – *Argentum nitricum* and *Natrum muriaticum* being the only ones in italics. This projection of perfectionism from parents and grandparents is often an unconscious compensation for their own perceived inadequacies.

Homeopathic pharmacies may combine *Anacardium* with *Argentum nitricum* for exam focus, adding other indicated remedies such as *Gelsemium* or *Lycopodium*.

In my experience, *Argentum metallicum* and *Argentum nitricum* are interchangeable if the action of one is incomplete or fails to impact in any way, especially with overlapping indications.

Arsenicum album

(Other main derivatives: *Arsenicum bromatum* and *Arsenicum iodatum*)

Arsenicum album is a huge polychrest and its keynotes are very distinctive. However, it is easy to miss related remedies which have a subtle difference in their application.

When it comes to sleep disturbances, *Arsenicum* remedies come into their own, especially when physical conditions such as allergies, asthma, epilepsy or skin disease are triggers (*Kali bromatum* and *Mercurius vivus* share this background).

There is a neediness in the *Arsenicum* remedies which is often manipulated by the patient, reminding one of *Thuja*, a related remedy. This can culminate in hysterical or manic behaviour leading to panic attacks or – in extremis – paranoia or psychosis. Medicinal drugs or recreational drugs can induce this mental state in the patient, throwing the adrenals out of balance. This can have a severe effect on the hormones, affecting the libido and creating fertility issues. The gut is a template of the emotional symptoms in this group of remedies more than any other. The emphasis is on the 'anxious stomach', leading to, in extremis, pathological states such as cancer if there is prolonged and unaddressed stress in the background of the case.

The trauma in *Arsenicum* is often based on more vague emotional foundations than other remedies discussed here. Anxiety, grief and isolation are the main triggers mentioned in the repertory. In my experience, physical symptoms such as those mentioned above are often a somatisation of unexpressed emotional distress. This is often seen in cultures where there is no appropriate language (see Part 1, 'alexithimia', having no words for emotions). When patients gain relief from their physical ailments, they may find it hard to embrace any anger or grief unleashed in the healing process. However, this is the only way to relieve the reflected corresponding physical symptoms which they often present with in practice.

The *Bromatum* and *Iodatum* elements overlap to some degree: they share a sense of escape and restlessness. However, *Bromatum* carries more guilt. In *Iodatum*, of course, there tends to be more body heat. *Arsenicum iodatum* carries a fuller proving than *Arsenicum bromatum* and is reputed to be a significant remedy for allergic responses.

Many polychrests such as *Aurum metallicum, Calcarea carbonica*, and *Natrum muriaticum*, can be combined with *Arsenicum* (*album*) if there are indications of both remedies in the picture, e.g. *Aurum arsenicum, Calcarea arsenicosa*, and *Natrum arsenicosum. Calcarea arsenicosa* has a more comprehensive picture in its own right than these other combinations.

Aurum metallicum

(Other main derivatives: *Aurum muriaticum* and *Aurum muriaticum natronatum*)

There is no more emotive substance in all cultures than gold, the substance from which *Aurum metallicum* is derived. The degree of competitiveness is extreme and anything which hinders this strongly developed ambition can lead to the deepest depression. Failure, therefore, is not an option for this patient, and loss of business renders them ruthless in maintaining their leadership status. Their sense of responsibility and duty is highly developed. Perfectionism is very much an issue of current times so this remedy, alongside the *Argentum* remedies, may increasingly become more indicated than it is already. The parents may have projected their thwarted ambition onto their children and it is acted out in this specific way.

Being a syphilitic remedy, the depression is almost palpable, based on the unique symptom that the patient actually feels happy contemplating their own death. See rubric *'cheerful, feelings, death, while thinking, of'* where it is the only remedy, such is the unusual aspect of this attitude. Another reminder of the connection to the syphilitic miasm is the night-time aggravation. They have insomnia with tormented dreams which reflect their overly developed conscientiousness. Like *Conium maculatum*, a hardening takes over and can manifest in the form of arteriosclerosis – *Aurum muriaticum* being the recommended remedy in this case.

Disappointed love combined with guilt matches the *Aurum* state, as the emotional state is rooted in some form of primal abandonment in the history. The sense of guilt can be so strong that it can lead to a type of paranoia or psychosis. Religion can become an outlet for the patient's desperation and they can hold extreme views (commensurate with the strength of the early triggers experienced). Music often provides solace for these patients. The use of recreational drugs or alcohol can sometimes induce the *Aurum* state if the susceptibility is aroused.

There is a danger that *Aurum metallicum* is considered such a strong polychrest remedy for marked depression that other remedies are ruled out. However, like any other state, depression needs to be traced back on the time-line as far back as possible. *Hura brasiliensis* and *Syphilinum* are remedies with 'horrible depression' rooted in feelings of early abandonment. Also, *Aurum metallicum* and *Hura brasiliensis*, once relieved of their depression, look back on this state with incredulity, such is their confidence in their newly-gained joyful emotional state.

Aurum metallicum, like *Mercurius vivus*, is sycotic as well as syphilitic. Therefore, *Aurum* could be indicated with symptoms such as fibroids (a symbol of 'overgrowth'). The derivative *Aurum muriaticum natronatum* may be the better simillimum because it contains the *Muriaticum* element, which covers the female sphere. James Compton Burnett stated that *Aurum muriaticum natronatum* has more power over uterine tumours than any other remedy, and this has been borne out in today's cases as much as during his time. [89] The depth of action of this remedy is summed up in 'carcinoma on a syphilitic base' – therefore, female cancers such as breast and uterine can be indicated in this remedy.

The need for heat and sunshine is so strong in the *Aurum* remedies that there is often a rapid decline in mood at the onset of winter. One only has to consider the 'Doctrine of Signatures' to appreciate why this is the case.

89 Boericke, William, Dr. (1999), *Pocket Manual of Homoeopathic Materia Medica and Repertory*, B. Jain Publishers Pvt Ltd.

Baryta carbonica

(Other main derivatives include: *Baryta iodata*, *Baryta phosphorica*, and *Baryta sulphuricum*)

One may wonder where the trauma in the *Barytas* is seated as no definitive mental/emotional trigger is mentioned in the materia medica. However, the compromise seen in this group of remedies suggests a degree of damage to the main brain structures. This could date back to the pre-birth period when the mother may have had a physical pathology such as underfunctioning thyroid or experienced an undocumented trauma. The *Baryta* remedies are well known to be indicated in infancy and old age. Towards the end of life, they are indicated in passive states of dementia – see rubric **'childish, behaviour, elderly people, in'**, where *Baryta carbonica* appears in black type, with the only other remedy – *Sulphur* – in plain type. *Anacardium, Belladonna, Cicuta,* and *Hyoscyamus,* as well as *Baryta carbonica*, are black type in the more general rubric **'childish, behaviour'** – *Kali bromatum* is only plain type here, but shares the regression of the *Barytas*; note that in *Kali bromatum*, it is accompanied by a sense of foreboding. When an inability to recognise their relatives is reached, it can be disconcerting for those affected (see *Alumina*). However, if the family members appreciate that this could indicate a brain disturbance, they can accept it better and not take it personally.

A recognised symptom of the *Baryta* remedies is hiding (often behind a carer or relative); see rubric **'hide, desire to'**. There may be accompanying physical pathology such as hypertension or sclerotic changes (the latter appearing especially in *Baryta muriatica*), and these physical symptoms can appear without the accompanying compromised mindset.

The timidity in the *Baryta* remedies is more marked than seen in *Alumina*. There is, however, a similar sense of disorientation, which is also found in *Nux moschata*. In *Baryta muriatica*, there is **'delusion, changed, thinks everything'**, and **'delusion, strange, familiar, things, seem'**. (In *Alumina*, the comparable rubric is **'delusion, unreal, everything seems'**.) In *Nux moschata*, this delusion is more exaggerated as expressed in *'delusion, familiar, things seem, ludicrous'*.

Imbecility can take over – *Conium maculatum* can secure the work of the *Barytas* if their action does not hold or work in the first instance. The type of emotional paralysis seen in the *Barytas* matches the sclerotic state of *Conium maculatum*, hence showing the strong complementary nature of these two remedies. Both remedies share their indication in old age.

Both *Plumbum metallicum* and *Alumina* share with the *Barytas* a dislike of being alone – but *Alumina* and *Nux moschata* are averse to company. In *Plumbum metallicum*, there is much more weakness in the presenting picture than the other remedies mentioned here. The *Metallicum* element signifies weakness as a major theme.

Even on a physical level, for example in dental disease, the retractive emotional state seen in *Baryta carbonica* can be projected onto the gums. The teeth are sensitive and sore to the touch (mirroring the patient's state of mind).

The main delusion of the *Barytas* sums up the patient's inability to go forward, illustrated in the rubric *'delusion, legs, cut off, are'*. This can manifest in the form of sciatica, although it is not an obvious remedy for this condition. The well-known inflammatory throat symptoms indicate the same theme of lack of power to project oneself.

In children, before pathology develops, the symptoms are likely to revolve around delayed development, both emotionally and academically. The throat is often afflicted, which contributes to the patient's lack of ability to move forward and individuate.

In one ten-year-old girl presenting typical *Baryta* symptoms – repeated tonsillitis with swollen glands – I observed that she was under-developed for her age, both emotionally and physically. She lived with her parents and her grandmother who was deaf. Despite the mother's protestations, the grandmother did everything for the girl. Due to the mother's restriction from an ongoing illness and the grandmother's disability, the girl was very much confined to the house, thus compounding the already existing *Baryta's* love of familiar territory and dependence on another family member. In such cases, one could easily question if perhaps it is the parent or other close family relative who is unconsciously maintaining the lack of individuation in the child for their own benefit. At this stage in the girl's development, hiding behind her youth was feasible but, as she might have progressed (without the intervention of the remedy), her immaturity would be likely to increase her sense of alienation. This is a true case of transgenerational transmission and shows a link between the *Barytas* and *Folliculinum*, which has over-enmeshment in families, and could easily be the indicated remedy to support the mother and the grandmother to relinquish their control. [90] This intervention could also release the child from the bondage the family dynamic had – albeit unconsciously – inflicted on her.

The final prescription for the child was *Baryta muriatica*. I chose the *Muriatica* element to neutralise the strong matriarchal influence on the case, matching the marked influence of the female lineage of dysfunction.

---

90 Assilem, Melissa (September 1990), *Folliculinum: Mist or Miasm?*, www.homeopathyhome.com/reference/articles/follic.shtml.

Bufo rana

Animal remedies such as *Androdoctonus, Apis, Bufo, Cantharis*, and *Lyssin* manifest very basic behaviour. *Bufo*, made from toad poison, suffers 'low states of disease'. It is known for 'brain softening' which is accounted for by damage to the anterior cingulate gyrus, the part of the brain structure that stimulates primitive emotions. This often triggers an unbridled knee-jerk reaction to perceived threat. This area can be affected due to low levels of serotonin, which might relate back to the mother's pregnancy when marked depression could have left its mark on the growing embryo. Like *Androctonus*, the brain impairment is marked in *Bufo*, famously resulting in illnesses such as epilepsy – a disease afflicting all levels of health.

As a result of this degree of brain impairment, the patient's behaviour is unconscious and indelible. The tendency towards imbecility seen in this remedy is such that the patient may strike out randomly against others. A much maligned and related symptom is 'desires solitude to practise masturbation'. Despite their sluggish appearance, these patients are sexually minded and may also indulge in inappropriate sexual contact with others. Their lack of awareness of boundaries would explain how this behaviour could be possible.

Patients needing this remedy may have low thyroid conditions – which could exist in the presenting patient or could have existed in the mother during pregnancy. This not only directly impacts the child's development, but also affects the bonding process between mother and child, such is the possible degree of detachment induced by the condition. In extreme cases, unless thyroid hormone is given to the child at birth, cretinism will result – this is a true *Bufo* situation. It is often the syphilitic miasm in the background that contributes to these states in children.

A helpful confirmatory mental symptom of *Bufo* is **'anger, misunderstood, when'**, like *Anacardium* and *Ignatia*. This represents a reflection of the 'Doctrine of Signatures' of the toad's responses. *Bufo* is the main remedy for a dislike of animals, even though it is an animal remedy. Its excretions are often very toxic-smelling, particularly the perspiration and flatus. This can be part of the thyroid picture in the case. The odour can be so strong that the room needs to be ventilated before anyone else can enter. The general picture of *Baryta carbonica* can look quite similar, but it is less self-reliant, more bashful and less toxic than *Bufo*. Both remedies have the physical concomitant of salivation in their presenting picture.

The results from taking *Bufo* can be quite startling – in one case, the patient transformed from a 'cretinous' adolescent to a fun-loving and responsible adult. She went on to get married and give birth to healthy children. She managed the family well, something which would not have been previously possible. Not only did she improve in her overall development, but her physical appearance changed noticeably, according to those around her. The effects of the remedy were not only protective of her, but also her children in their future development.

In another case, a 22-year-old female ballooned to 16 stone despite moderate eating. She had probably always suffered from a toxic thyroid condition, but this only came to light through her irregular menses and huge recent weight gain. Such is the poisonous nature of *Bufo* that it is a significant remedy for lymphangitis when the infection spreads rapidly up the offending limb. This can threaten infiltration of the major organs such as the heart or kidneys.

So the remedy *Bufo* could be considered to be the 'neglected old toad' and I hope, by including it here, to elevate it from its 'lowly' status in the homeopathic arsenal of remedies.

Calcarea carbonica

(Other main derivatives include: *Calcarea arsenicosa, Calcarea bromata, Calcarea fluorica, Calcarea iodata, Calcarea muriaticum, Calcarea phosphorica,* and *Calcarea sulphuricum*)

We all learn that *Calcarea carbonica* (the quintessential *Calcarea* remedy) needs security, but where does this need come from? Given the causative factors of fright or shock in the background of this remedy, it could relate back to an early experience in the life of the patient. Conversely, it could go back to a trauma which affected their parents at an earlier stage in their lives and was transmitted to the child at a subsequent time in their development.

We also learn that the *Calcarea* state is a very healthy one, and that not many people remain in this remedy state all their lives. A symptom which stands out is 'horrible things affect her profoundly', which translates into the rubric: **'horrible things, sad stories, movies, ailments from'**. The sub-rubric: **'horrible things, nightmares, from'** shows *Calcarea* as the only black type remedy. This sensitivity can be explained by the formative rubrics of both **'bad news, ailments from'** and **'fright, ailments from'**. These influences must affect the brain structures with all the resulting confusion and learning difficulties documented in this remedy.

Calcarea phosphorica is a much more upbeat derivative and more tubercular in its nature, even after experiencing grief. The nature of this remedy is fierier and the patient is likely to be more emotionally expressive, which gives them a healthy vent for their frustrations. This remedy is often indicated at a young age, whereas *Calcarea carbonica* may be indicated across the age cycles if the patient remains in a basically healthy state. Note that *Calcarea carbonica* should not be repeated too often in old age and can act very well when insomnia takes over.

Most of the remedies under the nightmares rubrics relate to

trauma, so tracing the nightmare on the time-line often reveals the origin of the relevant trauma. When verbal expression is limited, the impact has to come out in some way. If resentment clouds the *Calcarea carbonica* picture, it may be necessary to switch to *Ammonium carbonicum* or, perhaps, *Nitric acid* – both related remedies. The *Bromata* element supports the emotion of guilt more strongly than *Carbonicum* so, if guilt is the overwhelming emotion, *Calcarea bromata* may work better. According to Abdur Rehman, *Calcarea fluorica* stands between *Calcarea carbonicum* and *Calcarea phosphorica* and supports the glands and bones more profoundly than the latter two corollaries, being more syphilitic in its action. [91]

So, despite *Calcarea's* reputation of being very healthy, fears can take over and afflict the emotional and mental state of the patient for a long duration before eroding the physical structures. One may then have to turn to such derivatives as *Calcarea fluorica* with its affinity for the bones and tissues of the body as the pathology becomes more syphilitic. After all, the tubercular phase cannot last forever, particularly when the organism is under intense emotional distress.

91   Rehman, Abdur (1997), *Encyclopedia of Remedy Relationships in Homeopathy*, Haug Verlag.

Carcinosin

It may seem surprising that this is the only major nosode in this section. One reason is that it comprises the sum of all the other nosodes but, more importantly, it is because its background of suppressed emotions is so significant. This, combined with its reputation for matching auto-immune diseases as well as 'States on the Spectrum', ranks it as the key nosode, in my experience, in cases of 'transgenerational trauma'. As mentioned previously, behind every deep pathology are strong psychic triggers which need to be uncovered and addressed. It is well known that release of anger after the administration of this remedy heralds a curative response in these cases: the patient's family may be unused to this expression of emotion so it can be challenging to support patients through this response. It may seem counter-productive to 'rattle the cage' with their nearest and dearest, but this should be perceived as a necessary breakthrough.

Emotional outbursts often happen in cases of eating disorders where patients need to open up emotionally to relieve their symptoms. This may be perceived as threatening to others who are unused to such expression from them. Family members who might have become 'enablers' to the disease would find it especially difficult to accommodate this shift in the patient and may well need homeopathic treatment themselves in order to make the necessary transition.

Sleep symptoms may guide the practitioner to this remedy as it is highly indicated in chronic insomnia. When unravelling such cases, one often discovers a history of prolonged tension with little outlet for verbal expression which could have occurred before the child has been able to access language. Hence, rumination takes place at night and often a strong factor of guilt creeps in. This could easily be inherited through the family history of trauma or as a result of being made to feel unworthy.

When reflecting upon cancer, the disease upon which this nosode is based, one sees a theme of lack of barriers. It is as if the diseased cell merges with surrounding cells and has no self-protection against this phenomenon. This can be translated into the behaviour of the *Carcinosin* patient when their boundaries are blurred and they take on too much from others without any ability to refuse. This illustrates why it is such an eye opener to those surrounding the patient when they finally stand up for themselves after taking this remedy and show their true identity for the first time. It is as if they have, up to this time, had to justify their existence by suppressing their true feelings just to stay alive.

In the early 1990s, the disease 'vulval vestibulitis' was first recognised. Beyond the hormonal link, mostly in the form of the contraceptive pill, I ascertained from patients I treated that emotional trauma plays a great role in triggering the symptoms. The blood supply to the pelvis deteriorates, leading to burning of the walls of the vulva and intense soreness of the surrounding area. The symptoms can be so intense that no penetration can be tolerated whatsoever and even the friction created when wearing trousers cannot be endured by the sufferer. Walking any distance may cause exacerbation of the symptoms so one can see how the patient is limited on many fundamental levels. Unless the underlying trauma is addressed, these symptoms can persist till tissue alterations take place, culminating in possible cervical cancer.

On considering the psychological implications of this disease which afflicts a woman in her most personal area, one can appreciate that the systemic approach can never address the suffering. Without a holistic understanding of the case, no cure is possible. Sometimes, the patient can be regarded as hysterical and tranquilisers may be prescribed. In order for such a virulent disease to take hold, there must be a strong fundamental trigger, as borne out by the remedies which have proved healing. They include *Ammonium carbonicum, Carcinosin, Cyclamen, Folliculinum, Hura, Lac caninum, Platina, Pulsatilla, Staphysagria*, and *Thuja* on a constitutional level. These remedies are all both emotional and hormonal, and demonstrate a history of abuse, rejection, humiliation, confusion of identity, and competing in a male world, all issues affecting women literally 'below the belt'. A woman's hormonal system, with all its cyclical characteristics, represents the interface between her emotions and her physical body.

The dominant miasm in vulval vestibulitis appears to be *Carcinosin*. There is obviously a strong sycotic component with the guilt and shame, as well as syphilitic with the destructive quality of the disease, and *Carcinosin* addresses both these miasmatic components. *Hura brasiliensis* is the only remedy for 'lancinating pain in the vagina' and matches the sense of repudiation seen in this type of disease. *Platina* has vaginismus as a concomitant to this disease – a symptom emblematic of this remedy's cramping nature.

It is immensely rewarding to treat this disease successfully. Not only does the jump in her level of health allow the patient to feel more in control of her health, but also she and her partner can, at last, benefit from a full relationship, which had till then often proved impossible. Also, the use of a nosode such as *Carconocin* can avert an onward trajectory towards the possible outcome of cancer, not only in the presenting patient, but in resulting female offspring as well.

Conium maculatum

This remedy matches the state of endemic materialism which pervades many elements of today's society. In the age of the 'selfie', *Conium maculatum* might represent the quintessential remedy for the increasingly narcissistic generation growing up in today's world. This phenomenon could be attributed to the lack of spirituality which often prevails. Parents who buy into this lifestyle often misguidedly demonstrate a false value system to their children.

Many influences come into play when it comes to cancer, a disease for which this remedy is well reputed. Could it be that the hardening brought about by the materialistic lifestyle has an effect? Other possible interrelated factors which may contribute to cancer in this remedy picture, in addition to suppression of emotions, include contaminated food and pollution as well as drugs – both medicinal and recreational. Drugs are known to flatten the emotions once they take hold and this can remove any connection the users have with themselves, as seen in *Conium*.

The patient may wear their best clothes and buy or even steal useless objects. They do not care for things and waste money accordingly. Insecurity resulting from actual loss of property may trigger this drive, like *Aurum metallicum* and *Kali bromatum*, or the effects of alcoholism – also seen in *Anacardium* and *Hyoscyamus*. The history of loss of property or alcoholism could relate back to the experience of the parents or antecedents rather than the presenting patient.

Equally, there can be a background of disappointed love, showing an overlap with *Natrum muriaticum*. Guilt plays a role, as in *Aurum metallicum* and *Kali bromatum*. Obsessions and compulsions take over, leading to ritualistic behaviour – such is the nature of the unconscious and almost robotic behaviour manifesting in these patients. A hardening supervenes – a shut-down state where the organism becomes 'sclerotic' – invading the tissues and creating such deep states as cancer as well as irreversible auto-immune diseases. Of course, the best known symptom of the plant from which it is derived, hemlock, is the 'ascending paralysis' experienced by Socrates.

The inclination to sit – rubrics **'sitting, inclination to'** and **'slowness, motion, in'** also relate to *Plumbum metallicum*. Another resemblance between *Conium maculatum* and *Plumbum* is the severe constipation, such is the prevailing stagnation in the organism.

Aristotle Onassis suffered with myasthenia gravis and, despite his gargantuan wealth, the only way he could keep his eyelids open in the end was, ironically, by propping them up with matchsticks – this could represent a true *Conium maculatum* situation.

It is a deep and long-acting remedy and may arrive at the cancer miasm through the progression of the fun-seeking *Medorrhinum* or *Tuberculinum*.

The patient may age prematurely due to having followed a hedonistic lifestyle when younger. This suggests the link between *Conium* and both *Medorrhinum* and *Tuberculinum*. Premature senility is seen in the remedy *Selenium*, as well which also complies with the later stages of life as the organism starts to close down.

The *Conium maculatum* 'proving' shows how cancer can creep in when a sexual life is suddenly interrupted, as when someone is widowed. It is no coincidence that the cancer experienced in this remedy often afflicts the sexual organs – the breast or cervix in women and the prostate in men.

In one case, a middle-aged woman presented with arthritis originating in the knees. It transpired that her husband was impotent and she was grieving his loss as a sexual partner. Not only did the arthritis resolve with the use of *Conium maculatum*, but she became more integrated in her attitude to her thwarted sexuality. She was a compulsive swimmer and, when one considers the restless nature of *Tuberculinum* and the relief from exercise of *Carcinosin*, perhaps *Conium maculatum* should be added to the rubric **'exercise, mental symptoms, ameliorated, by** *physical'*, where *Carcinosin* appears in italics and *Rhus toxicodendron* and *Sepia* in black type. This demonstrates the polarity found in *Conium* based on its better known sedentary nature.

The release of endorphins achieved by exercise can become a substitute for the release of tension and sacrifice of intimacy. The sexual deprivation contributes to a dull, uninspiring state of mind. The mind can become weak, speech difficult and comprehension fails. The patient dreads being alone but is worse for company. They are nervous, depressed, timid, and indifferent to daily business or study. This shows how it is related to *Baryta carbonica* and more closely to *Baryta muriatica* with the hardening of the vessels. The deterioration is gradual – like the paralysis mentioned – until they become feeble on all levels. This indifference to the environment, as seen in the remedy *Helleborus*, becomes difficult to penetrate.

Mirroring the tubercular miasm, the patient loses flesh while eating well. Weight loss is of course a recognised sign of cancer. This last symptom is also seen in *Abrotanum, Iodum, Natrum muriaticum*, and, of course, *Tuberculinum*.

Conium maculatum often needs to be preceded by another remedy in order for it to work well, *Baryta carbonica* or *Baryta muriatica* are the best indicated, but also *Causticum, Phosphorus, Silica*, and *Thuja*.

Symptoms are not easily elicited in the initial consultation and often only manifest after trust has been built up between patient and practitioner. *Conium maculatum* is a subtle and important remedy for the contemporary world, especially where so many people opt to live in isolation and leave relationships behind – not forgetting the lack of spiritual life so endemic to modern-day life.

Whereas *Tuberculinum* is indicated in outdoor types, *Conium maculatum* patients often lead sedentary lives. If they sit in front of a computer all day, the moving images can compound their pathology, such is the delicate state of their vision – photophobia being a major symptom.

Injuries to the breast and uterus comply with this remedy, especially after *Bellis perennis* has been given and may not have acted or held. It is also a major remedy for cataracts developing from a blow to the eye – a deeper state than seen in *Symphytum*. It acts well on contusions of the testicles – in this case, low doses given repeatedly work well after well-indicated remedies have not acted or held.

As there is no comparison today with the number of people who achieved longevity in Hahnemann's time, it is a good idea to look afresh at this remedy in light of current social phenomena. To summarise, the essence of *Conium maculatum* can be seen in the slogan 'absence of love in a material world' which, unfortunately, so markedly prevails in modern times.

Crocus sativa

Crocus sativa is a little discussed but significant remedy for today's world. This is because it is one of the most unstable in its reactions of all the homeopathic materia medica, being emblematic of the sycotic miasm.

As a herbal remedy, research in Iran (the country to which the plant is mostly indigenous) has shown that it is as effective as antidepressants such as Imipramine and Prozac in the long-term treatment of depressive illnesses. [92] After such drugs are withdrawn, the highs and lows so often apparent, especially in manic depression (currently known as 'bi-polar disorder'), become exaggerated.

The herb, *Crocus sativa*, is derived from saffron – the most expensive of all herbs. In fact, it takes hundreds of thousands of flowers to create just one kilo of the herb! This shows its true value: records of the herb date back to the volcanic eruption in the ancient world at Santorini. The frescoes uncovered there depict saffron as the closest herb in the vicinity of the image of the deity – again signifying its value. But I highlight here information from the Iranian research that focuses on the deeper state of *Crocus sativa* – a remedy waiting to be excavated from the ruins of what many consider to be the true ancient site of Atlantis. [93]

The *Sativa* component in the name indicates neurosis and hysteria, as well as possible drug use. These elements in *Crocus sativa* compare with other *Sativa* remedies such as *Avena sativa* and *Cannabis sativa*. This link could come through the malaria miasm due to these remedies' combined pictures of both intensity of symptoms and emotional dependency operating at the same time. [94]

92 Bratman, R. (2007), *Complementary and Alternative Health: The Scientific Verdict on What Really Works*, Collins Publishers.
93 Ferrence, S. and Bendersky, G. (2004), Therapy with Saffron and the Goddess at Thera, *Perspectives in Biology and Medicine,* 47(2):199-226.
94 Sankaran, Rajan (2002), *An Insight into Plants, Volume I*, Homeopathic Medical Publishers.

Avena sativa often has a history of drugging, either medicinal or recreational, and is used to wean the patient off the drugs. *Cannabis sativa* often has experimentation with drugs, leading to possible de-personalisation in the user. Trauma alone can induce this picture, as in other related drug remedies such as *Opium*. By addressing the imbalance in the early stages in the *Crocus sativa* patient, later memory and mental function impairment can be prevented. This remedy covers the full range of ages from teenage years right through to senescence.

The focus is often on the female organs – a reflex from the unstable emotional state. According to the 'Doctrine of Signatures', the stigma of this plant represents the female reproductive organs, which means it can greatly enhance the female fertility potential. The proximity of this herb to the goddess depicted in the Santorini frescoes suggests the importance of this herb above others, especially in this type of pathology. Apparently, female oestrogens – both steroidal and otherwise – have been found to coexist within the plant.

There are many parallels between *Crocus sativa* and *Lilium tigrinum*, and also *Platina*. As in the case of the *Lilium tigrinum* and *Platina* patient, a male practitioner should not examine a *Crocus* patient alone, as this patient can also make hysterical allegations as a way of getting attention. Incidentally, hysterical men could also respond to this remedy. See rubric **'hysteria, man, in a'** where it appears with three other remedies, *Carcinosin*, *Medorrhinum*, and *Moschus*, all in plain type.

An early manifestation of the emotional disturbance can be seen in anorexia – an illness which is increasingly creeping into the male sphere these days. *Crocus sativa* is in the rubric **'eat, refuses to'**, but not in the one for **'anorexia, nervosa'**.

Some important rubrics to clinch the picture of *Crocus sativa* (with related parallel remedies mentioned) include:

- **'delusion, business, unfit for, that he is'** ('he' could be replaced by 'she'), in which it is the only remedy

- **'delusion, pregnant, thought herself'** (other remedies in italics include *Opium*, *Sabadilla*, and *Veratrum album*)

- **'eat, refuses to'** (*Hyoscyamus*, *Ignatia*, *Tarentula hispanica*, and *Veratrum album* are other hysterical remedies sharing this symptom)
- **'impressionable'** (there are many remedies in this rubric – *Crocus sativa* absorbs the mood of others and then reacts in their own impulsive and inimitable way)
- **'impulsive, behaviour'** (*Argentum nitricum*, *Ignatia*, and *Pulsatilla* are black type remedies)
- **'kisses, everyone'** (*Hyoscyamus* and *Veratrum album* are the other main remedies)
- **'mental states, alternating with physical symptoms'** (*Ignatia* and *Platina* are black type remedies)
- **'music, ameliorates'** (*Aurum metallicum* and *Tarentula hispanica* are black type remedies)
- **'offended, easily'** (Note: *Lilium tigrinum* is the only remedy in the sub-rubric **'takes advice as criticism'** and *Ignatia* and *Natrum muriaticum* are the only black type remedies in the sub-rubric **'takes, everything in bad part'**)
- **'quarrelsome, alternating with cheerfulness/laughter'** (*Lachesis* and *Staphysagria* are the other main remedies)
- **'rage, alternating, with affectionate disposition'** (*Crocus sativa* is the only remedy)
- **'remorse, repents, quickly'** (*Anacardium* is another remedy of polarity in this rubric)
- **'sexuality, nymphomania, in women'** (*Hyoscyamus*, *Lachesis*, *Medorrhinum*, *Origanum*, *Platina*, and *Stramonium* are black type remedies)
- **'singing, alternating with anger'** (single remedy)
- **'wildness, evening'** (this is a more marked state than seen in *Pulsatilla*)

These rubrics illustrate the remedy's affinity with the sycotic miasm and have particular parallels with three other significant remedies of this miasm – *Cyclamen* for endometriosis with clotted menses, and *Pulsatilla* and *Thuja*.

As illustrated in these rubrics, *Crocus sativa* is more violent in its mood changes than *Pulsatilla* and has a more overt sexuality – even bordering on nymphomania (see rubric **'sexuality, nymphomania, women'**). However, *Pulsatilla* finds it hard to refuse, given their nature. Conversely, *Crocus sativa* is narcissistic and does not need the approval of others, as *Pulsatilla* does.

Crocus shares with *Thuja* the delusion that something is alive in the abdomen but this symptom is better known under *Thuja*.

Incidentally, *Sabadilla* is a key remedy for body dysmorphia, an increasingly recognised condition across the genders where the sufferer has a distorted sense of their own image. This is seen in the accompanying rubric **'delusion, body, erroneous, ideas as to the state of his'** ('his' could be replaced by 'her'), where it is a single, black type remedy.

Cyclamen and *Thuja* carry marked guilt, which is not so apparent in *Crocus sativa* and *Pulsatilla*. Indeed, one of these other remedies may have already been given without results. However, when the hysterical element is defined, *Crocus sativa* could easily be the simillimum.

The *Pulsatilla* element of *Crocus sativa* becomes marked when the patient becomes needy of their partner. This is because the typical delusion is that they are unfit for business. Maybe this remedy should be added to the rubric **'clinging, behaviour'** on this basis. By addressing this fundamental inadequacy, the patient can become autonomous and no longer co-dependent (a type of addiction increasingly recognised these days).

Due to low self-confidence in the *Crocus sativa* patient, like the snake remedies – especially *Naja tripudians* – they need to look attractive to feel worthy. This is compounded by the message disseminated by aspects of the current media. *Tarentula hispanica* is another comparable remedy with love of bright clothing, which also has impulsiveness and delight from music. *Crocus sativa* enjoys singing aloud – a symptom often seen in patients in a manic phase of psychotic illness. This could be a concomitant in these cases to heightened and indiscriminate promiscuity.

To conclude, this remedy may not only be ideal to wean patients off anti-depressants, but often has an overlap with the theme of the case based on its marked instability. With bi-polar disorder becoming so much more common, or maybe more recognised, this remedy could be a major polychrest whose time has come. High potencies are advised with repeated repetition as the energy is directed to the emotional level – even if expressed physically through somatisation.

It was through the discovery of the Iranian research that I was inspired to focus on the deeper state of *Crocus sativa* – a remedy literally waiting to be 'excavated' from the ruins of what many consider to be the true ancient site of Atlantis.

Helleborus niger

The main reaction to trauma in this remedy is shown in difficult understanding and a marked indifference to the environment. The extreme state manifested here is almost coma-like – as shown in the rubric *'stupefaction'*, where it appears in black type. Head injury, brain disease such as encephalitis, epilepsy, meningitis, a stroke, or recreational drugs can induce this state in this remedy picture, and the comparable emotional trigger could be disappointed love.

All these triggers could collide in one patient in, for example, a child raised in an orphanage. There will be disappointed love in the background and also a possible history of head injury as these children often have a certain ritualistic behaviour which involves banging their head against the bars of the cot for stimulation or in an attempt to assuage an injury inflicted on them earlier in their life. Head injury in this remedy can lead to insomnia which might date right back to the birth process. Other remedies such as *Cicuta* and *Natrum sulphuricum* share this history, and all three remedies manifest sleep disturbances as a concomitant. By addressing the sleep symptoms, considerable energy is released, which supports a radical improvement in the mood of the patient. *Cicuta* shares with *Helleborus* regression after head injury.

In one case, an elderly patient had been abused by her husband and had possibly suffered a head injury as a result. After his death and after taking this remedy, coupled with a loving carer, her revival was quite startling.

There is a parallel with *Aurum metallicum* which is often given when a remedy such as *Helleborus* is better indicated. Both remedies have a background of disappointed love but, of course, there is more ambition in cases needing *Aurum*. Both remedies, surprisingly in the case of *Helleborus*, are better for occupation. They both suffer isolation, low self-confidence, absence of enjoyment, and a feeling of worthlessness and powerlessness. However, *Aurum* does not lose energy in the same way as *Helleborus*. *Helleborus* seems so defeated that they become resigned to their situation. *Aurum* is the only remedy which gains solace at the thought of their own death.

In Alzheimer's disease, the tendency is to give *Alumina* as a routine prescription but, again, alongside other remedies, *Helleborus* may be indicated, with its complete lack of recall and marked depression. As seen in *Hyoscyamus*, the *Helleborus* patient may pick at the bedclothes. Like *Opium*, there could be the background of a stroke.

Sepia shares the indifference to loved ones but is generally a more hormonal remedy than *Helleborus*. However, *Helleborus* has the distinctive symptom of amenorrhoea from disappointed love, like *Ignatia, Natrum muriaticum*, and *Phosphoric acid*, as well as being the only remedy in the rubric **'depression, first menses, menarche'**.

Like *Apis*, in encephalitis or meningitis, there can be shrieking during sleep ('cri cerebrale'). If *Helleborus* is indicated in such a state and the case does not respond, *Zincum metallicum* may have to be given to arouse the vitality into reaction.

Sankaran says *Helleborus* belongs to the 'typhoid miasm'. [94] This is indicated by an initial intense pace of disease which the victim resists by closing down, as seen in the state described here. Sankaran claims that the initial excitability – arousing anger – is often overlooked in this remedy, where it appears in italics in the rubric **'rage, fury'**.

Hura brasiliensis

This remedy comes from the sandbox tree. It is a member of the Euphorbia family, like *Mancinella venenata*. The *Hura* genus is known as Assaku among the indigenous people of the area where it grows in Brazil. When the nut ripens in a dry atmosphere, it bursts with great force, accompanied by a loud, sharp crack like the sound of a pistol. [95]

Some nut-derived remedies, such as *Anacardium* and *Nux vomica*, have become major polychrests but *Hura brasiliensis* – sometimes known as 'the leper's remedy' – is very much neglected in practice. Perhaps, it is because the remedy picture is one of extreme deprivation, to the point of ostracisation. It could also be because the remedy picture is hard to detect – as the patient does not always present with the extremely dark syphilitic picture of other remedies belonging to this miasm – this can easily throw the practitioner off course. In addition, it is not well portrayed in the provings; it was only after reading the rubrics ascribed to this remedy that I saw its true state, which is based mainly on feelings of extreme alienation.

Hura is known as the 'leper's remedy' due to the deep sense of self-loathing the patient carries within, which causes them to feel they must live on the edge of society. This may be because they carry a primal sense of 'not belonging', 'primal' being the operative word because this feeling is deep-rooted and stretches back to early childhood. A definitive event will have occurred at that time (a 'rupture' in the life force), which sets the compass of life. Having said this, life-changing responses to this remedy are often more profound than in the case of any other remedies I have seen – they can be startling and transformational to the life trajectory of the patient.

This fundamental feeling of alienation can be demonstrated, for example, in homeless people who are forced onto the streets,

---

95   Vermeulen, F. (1996), Hura Brasiliensis, *Synoptic Materia Medica II*, Merlijn Publishers.

often due to an insult they received within their original family. Having become the black sheep of the family, these victims' only survival is on the edge of society where they can fall into self-abuse such as drug addiction and prostitution, both reflecting the syphilitic miasm to which this remedy belongs. This semblance of 'society' becomes their family, rather than their original family that they feel they never belonged to.

Going back to the 'Doctrine of Signatures', although *Hura* is the hardest nut to crack, it has the softest centre. We see this in the language of the patient – they are often articulate and self-deprecating in their portrayal of their history. *Hura* could be added to the rubric **'amativeness'** – a true description of their combined animation and expressiveness. It appears in **'affectionate, active'**, with *Hyoscyamus* as the only other remedy. These rubrics suggest a buoyant demeanour in *Hura*, which is untypical of the syphilitic miasm where the patients usually drain the energy of the practitioner. Thus, this characteristic becomes a 'strange, rare and peculiar' symptom even if it acts as an unconscious defence mechanism on the part of the patient. At the same time, this can throw the practitioner off course when it comes to selecting a simillimum. All the cases I have observed, despite their intense suffering, have been extremely charming and fun to be with.

Although their turn of phrase is engaging, the sense of revulsion they feel about themselves is often projected onto other people in public. In one particular case, the skin phase was fully developed: this is a major area of suffering which is also quite disfiguring as a projection of the emotional state. People would stop the patient on the street in order to spit at her, as well as revile and jostle her which, of course, made her life a complete misery. The sense of violation she already felt was compounded by the attitude she constantly encountered in public. After receiving *Hura*, she became increasingly integrated in her outlook, her skin symptoms receded and were no longer a reminder of her sense of self-loathing which was so deeply rooted in her psyche.

AIDS victims could respond well to *Hura* and the skin symptoms, such as Kaposi's sarcoma, may alert the prescriber to this remedy. These skin symptoms can be distressing to the patient, and the typical 'hide-bound' state of their skin may act to create the very negative mindset seen in *Hura*. At the same time, the diagnosis itself can create the remedy state in the patient, especially as the misconception that AIDS can taint others runs deep in society.

Another female patient from a deeply religious family was reviled by her family as a result of having been raped as a young teenager by a complete stranger. As a resulting defence mechanism, she lost her femininity (became androgynous) and developed severe and disabling endometriosis. Not surprisingly, the vital force expressed its disease at the core of her female organs. After treatment, not only was her physical state healed, but it became apparent that she was no longer shut down to her attractive feminine side, which had occurred as a direct result of the initial trauma, later compounded by her family's attitude. One can hardly imagine the double blow of first being raped; and then, if not worse than the original insult, the family blaming and ostracising the unwitting victim. She had become a true leper not only in their mind, but also and more importantly in hers. The umbilical cord was brutally severed and the patient was inevitably left with a pathological fear of close relationships. In my experience, in cases needing *Hura*, the 'wound' usually emanates from the original family of the patient.

A male patient, on announcing his homosexuality to his family, was again reviled and, in desperation, felt he had to leave his country of origin to reclaim his self-esteem. After receiving the remedy and working through the corresponding issues it evoked, he felt strong enough to return home to his family, despite their enduring bigoted attitude towards him.

The American author, James Baldwin, could be seen as a quintessential *Hura*. Not only did he suffer as a black person, but also as a homosexual. He became a voice for black people at the time of the ghettos in 1950s and '60s America. He was bitter about his marginalisation in society due to both aforementioned factors in his make-up. He articulated his feelings beautifully in his writing, which is typical of the *Hura* patient. He was also very charismatic, which should be underlined as a strong feature of this remedy. He escaped to Paris to find acceptance and further his creativity but, unfortunately, he died of cancer before his time in great isolation and with extreme rancour. His books include *Go Tell it on the Mountain* [96] and *Giovanni's Room*. [97]

In another case, a woman complained of having lost touch with her feminine side. As in the rape case discussed above, there is a strong theme of androgyny in *Hura* cases, which is usually a reaction to the original 'wound' and becomes a safety valve for future protection. Two months after taking *Hura*, the change was startling, not only to the viewers (it was a college video case), but also to the patient. She expressed a new interest in dress-making and wearing elegant clothes, factors which she would not have contemplated before treatment. She mentioned that she even enjoyed the attention she had now started to attract from the opposite gender.

Her history was of being brought up in a family of males. In her early teenage years when she started to express her individuality, a time when the emotional pathology of the remedy often 'kicks in', her father very uncharacteristically lashed out at her in a sudden and ferocious manner. From that time on, she made a decision to cut herself off from him, and this was when she shut down her feminine side as a deflection. Interestingly, after receiving *Hura*, she was now in touch with this aspect and wanted to address its effect on her general functioning. Her presenting symptom was horrible depression, sounding significantly like that experienced by *Aurum metallicum* patients. She saw no point in living. After receiving *Hura*, as in *Aurum* cases, she looked back at the bleak days with incredulity.

In some cases, it may be necessary to give a corresponding nosode – for example, *Syphilinum* – as an intercurrent remedy to sustain the cure, especially where 'maintaining causes' are strong. Other comparative remedies, as well as *Aurum metallicum*, include *Lac caninum* and *Lac humanum* for their sense of rejection from being

---

96   Baldwin, James (1953), *Go Tell it on the Mountain*, Alfred A. Knopf.
97   Baldwin, James (1956), *Giovanni's Room*, Dial Press.

cut off at source. *Manganum aceticum* compares with its embitterment plus anaemia and weakness, which are both lacking in *Hura*, as well as *Natrum muriaticum* and *Nitric acid* for their unforgiving nature. Another comparison is the new remedy, *Berlin wall*, which is so repelling that it cannot even be stored in the same cupboard as other remedies; this also reflects the theme of *Hura* with its deep sense of not belonging and creating revulsion in others.

In addition to the strongly-developed skin symptoms in *Hura*, there are a wide range of different pathologies which can comply with it, as evidenced by the endometriosis case mentioned above.

Considering the degree of alienation and ostracisation evident in culture today, it is easy to see *Hura* as a polychrest for our time – alongside some of the other remedies discussed in this book. See the following rubrics for *Hura*:

- *'abandoned, forsaken feelings'*
- *'delusion, friend, thinks she is about to lose a'* – *Hura* is the only remedy
- *'delusion, friend, affection, has lost the'*
- *'delusion, alone, world, that she is alone in the'*
- *'delusion, confidence, in him, his friends have lost all'* – where *Hura* and *Aurum metallicum* are the only remedies
- *'delusion, deserted, forsaken, being'*
- *'delusion, despised, that he is'*
- *'delusion, lost, fancies herself'*
- *'delusion, repudiated, by relatives, thinks is'*
- *'delusion, unfortunate, that he is'*
- *'isolation, feelings'*, *'unfortunate, feels'* and *'wretched, feels'*

In conclusion, these findings have generated a lot of interest in this remedy, and in the positive and lasting changes it has brought about in the patients who received it. This may be the 'hardest nut to crack' but, when cracked, let's shout 'hooray for *Hura*' from the hilltops in recognition that its time is here!

Hyoscyamus niger

The *Hyoscyamus* state, like *Helleborus* and many other remedies discussed here, could be induced by disappointed love. However, in *Hyoscyamus* (unlike *Helleborus*) there could also be a history of abuse. The patient may have been damaged due to alcoholism or drug addiction – habits the sufferer may easily have adopted to assuage this unpalatable early history. The state can result in foolish hilarity, with possible jealousy and suspicion; the latter two symptoms reminding one of *Lachesis*. In the full-blown *Hyoscyamus* state, imbecility is unfortunately a natural progression. The patient may refuse to take any medicine, such is their suspicion; again, this reminds one of *Lachesis*. This symptom can be translated into the rubric **'eat, refuses to'**. Note that *Arsenicum* has a similar background. Anorexia and/or bulimia tie in with *Hyoscyamus* when there is a history of verbal abuse and self-destructive behaviour. These states can affect the mouth and throat in the process. After tooth extraction, there can be violent pain with possible twitching of the facial muscles, such is the sensitivity of this patient's nerves. General twitching is a known physical concomitant to the emotional state in this remedy. Many physical symptoms in this remedy, such as coughs, gut impairment, or sleep disturbance, are a direct result of the emotionally charged state of the patient.

The *Hyoscyamus* state can be manic with erotic overtures, leading to exposure of the genitals. *Saccharum officinale* and *Mercurius vivus* can also behave inappropriately when it comes to sexual boundaries, but go less far than *Hyoscyamus*, their remedy pictures being less hysterical.

In *Hyoscyamus*, *Belladonna*, and *Stramonium*, the mania can be so extreme that the patient does not recognise anyone and tries to escape. This shows the triad's close relationship in the 'Doctrine of Signatures', all being members of the Solanacea family of plants. *Hyoscyamus* and *Stramonium* are so close that they can be regarded as two sides of the same coin, states often flitting between the two pictures.

After childbirth, extreme psychosis can erupt and *Hyoscyamus* may match this 'unhinging' of the brain. Suppression of the lochia (the bleeding experienced for two to four weeks after birth) or the milk supply can trigger the mental state. If this state goes untreated or is suppressed by heavy medication, the child may become afflicted by the mother's resulting behaviour. This accounts for a possible trigger to 'States on the Spectrum', as these 'states' may often be a direct and symbiotic projection from the mother's condition at this vulnerable time in the bonding process. These 'states' are usually set in motion in the 'primal' period of life, either in the womb – an 'embryonic disruption' as it were – or in the very early bonding stage of life.

Like all disease, the 'state' represents a defence mechanism for the sufferer. I have seen *Hyoscyamus* to be a useful remedy for promiscuity resulting further along the timeline, especially in young men with this background.

Major trauma remedies feature highly in the treatment of the three major sleep disturbances: apnoea, sleep-walking, and snoring. In *Opium*, the memories are deeply buried; *Zincum metallicum* also releases suppressed emotions, especially after lack of reaction to indicated remedies such as *Hyoscyamus*. When the specific sleep disturbance is addressed, the contributing trauma can subsequently become resolved. Note that sleep reflects the 'uncompensated state' of the patient – the one which is unlikely to be contrived by the patient.

Damage to the temporal lobes of the brain might have occurred in *Hyoscyamus*. This may be from emotional disappointment or, in extremis, abuse – which creates the strong sense of paranoia and suspicion seen here. Also, head injuries can contribute to this state in this remedy, see rubrics **'injuries, head, blows'** and **'concussion, head'** – *Hyoscyamus* appears in italics in both rubrics in the Repertory.

Lyssin shares with *Hyoscyamus*, *Belladonna*, and *Stramonium* the fear of being bitten by wild animals, hydrophobia, and foaming of the mouth.

Like *Crocus sativa* and *Lilium tigrinum*, it could be risky for any practitioner to examine a *Hyoscyamus* patient without a third party present.

In one case, the patient presented naked from the street, believing she was Lady Godiva riding on horseback through the streets of Clapton! With the use of remedies *Hyoscyamus* and *Stramonium*, she was released from her state. When in the *Stramonium* state, she recognised the betrayal which had led to this action and her need for it to be addressed. This is where the relationship of remedies comes in and demonstrates how different related layers need to be addressed as they emerge in such critical cases.

Kali bromatum

(Other main derivatives include: *Kali arsenicosum, Kali bichromicum, Kali carbonicum, Kali iodatum, Kali muriaticum, Kali nitricum, Kali phosphoricum*, and *Kali sulphuricum*)

Kali bromatum shares with all *Kali* remedies a type of fixedness. *Kali carbonicum* is the main remedy in the group known for this characteristic, but it spreads across the board of all the *Kali* remedies.

There are many different triggers to the *Kali bromatum* state, ranging from strokes on a physical level to business failure, death of friends, loss of property, or reputation, on an emotional one – here, there is an overlap with the *Aurum* remedies. However, the outcome is completely different in these two different sets of remedies.

Identity crises often become an issue in the teenage years. This is a time when image is very important, especially in modern times. The *Kali bromatum* teenager may have disfiguring acne which can contribute to this whole sense of questioning and can propel the psyche into a state of breakdown where the individual feels condemned to suffer in this way – *'delusion, vengeance, thinks he is singled out for divine'*. The rubric suggests a theme of religious revenge being wrought on them. Nothing can change their mind as the fixedness is so entrenched, being perhaps 'hard-wired' since early childhood. Here, one sees the true syphilitic nature of the stuckness of this set of remedies.

What is often not highlighted is a type of regression that occurs in *Kali bromatum*, as in the *Baryta* group of remedies. This explains why both groups are susceptible to Alzheimer's disease, when regression can be a startling feature of the illness. In *Kali bromatum*, this regression is accompanied by a sense of foreboding, seen in the rubric *'delusion, doomed, being'*. *Aurum metallicum* features strongly here and shares a tendency towards suicide with *Kali bromatum*. When paranoia accompanies the regression, *Anacardium, Hyoscyamus,* and *Plumbum metallicum* share this concomitant – again all these remedies are indicated in Alzheimer's disease.

A physical symptom such as asthma or epilepsy may disrupt their sleep patterns – see also other syphilitic remedies such as *Arsenicum album* or *Mercurius vivus*. Nightmares can be severely disruptive and may result in sleep-walking, such is the driven state of unresolved trauma in *Kali bromatum*, which may be seen in young children right through to teenagers.

There is a restlessness in this remedy, mainly derived from the *Bromatum* element. It specifically manifests in fidgety hands in the case of *Kali bromatum*. Despite the energy displayed here, the general organism is weak. As mentioned, there might be a history of a stroke, which could explain the startling lack of memory often perceived in patients needing this remedy.

The fear of breaking down under stress mirrors *Calcarea carbonica*. However, *Kali bromatum* is more vulnerable in how they manifest this. *Calcarea carbonica* would show a passive form of reaction, whereas *Kali bromatum* would be quite driven in their presentation of this response.

In one case, a patient was brought to my practice after being found wondering around a graveyard in a desperate state. When he was first brought for treatment, I saw that he was wringing his hands in an exaggerated manner, which is a distinctive concomitant in *Kali bromatum*. At the same time, he could only express a very few words. Such was his turmoil that he sought solace in the only place he felt destined to reside. After receiving *Kali bromatum* (10M potency), he recovered his usual form; it later transpired that his business had hit the rocks – a typical trigger to the *Kali bromatum* breakdown. However, he was completely unable to articulate this background to his state when he first presented for treatment – only the 'uncompensated state' revealed it. One could surmise that he found it hard to recover from such a loss due to the reinforcement of the value of success and always 'getting it right' imbued in him since childhood.

Lachesis muta

(Other major snake remedies include: *Bothrops lanceolatus*, *Cenchris contortrix*, *Crotalus cascavella*, *Crotalus horridus*, *Elaps corrallinus*, *Naja tripudians*, and *Vipera berus*)

Snake remedies and *Scorpion* (*Androctonus*) are highly symbolic. The main known characteristic of snake remedies is their tendency to lie in wait and then bide their time before they pounce, demonstrated in symptoms such as jealousy, loquacity, paranoia, and suspicion.

Lachesis is the commonest snake remedy administered in homeopathic practice. However, it is often interchangeable with related ones such as *Bothrops, Cenchrix contortrix, Crotalus horridus, Elaps corrallinus, Naja tripudians*, and *Vipera berus*. *Lachesis* features mainly at times of change and, given that it is a very hormonal remedy, its predominant time of surfacing is pre-menstrual, post-partum, and especially during the menopause. At these times, not only are the hormones in tumultuous flux, but the woman has to tackle all the complex emotions these significant times bring up for her.

The snake remedies often capitalise on their sexual allure so, at the time of the menopause, the patient can be in turmoil about her perceived fading beauty. *Naja tripudians* relates well to this aspect and, at the same time, is a noted heart remedy like *Aurum metallicum*. It also shares with *Aurum* its sense of doom accompanying the pathology.

Sepsis is an important feature of the snake remedies, *Crotalus horridus* being the most extreme in this aspect, even reaching the stage of gangrene. All the snake remedies are known for their blood-clotting properties, but this remedy is key in cases of haemorrhages and lymphangitis. In fact, *Crotalus horridus* often completes the cure when *Lachesis* ceases to work in general snake cases, such is its depth of action.

Crotalus horridus comes into its own in dementia cases when the memory deteriorates rapidly and the patient cannot express themselves in a comprehensible way. This state could come on after the shock of sepsis or, if this remedy is given during the septic phase, it may prevent any possible resulting dementia. Other snake remedies that have an affinity with memory loss – especially in old age – include *Bothrops lanceolatus*, *Crotalus cascavella*, and *Elaps corrallinus*.

Lachesis is notably left-sided, or symptoms spread from left to right (it appears in black type in both these rubrics). *Naja tripudians* appears in italics in the rubric for left-sidedness. *Crotalus horridus* is opposedly right-sided (appearing in black type in this rubric). *Elaps corrallinus* appears in italics in the latter rubric.

Circulation is affected in the snake remedies, demonstrated in hot flushes and high blood pressure. Constriction aggravates the patient, as does any type of suppression. The throat is especially vulnerable and is often a reflex from distress in the gynaecological sphere, these being the two main chakras affected. Other significant modalities are aggravation from sun and alcohol.

Grief affects the snake remedies markedly and *Lachesis* appears in black type in the rubric **'grief, ailments from'**. The grief may go way back into the background of the case or even be connected with the parents' history. It may not, however, be the first remedy to consider for this causative factor. *Crotalus cascavella* and *Crotalus horridus* appear in this rubric in plain type.

Aggravation from changes is demonstrated in the transition experienced when waking from sleep, leaving the patient quite out-of-sorts. *Cenchrix contortrix* is the snake remedy which suffers the most at this time, and sleep apnoea could represent a somatisation of buried trauma. The patient can go into a coma-like state from which it is difficult to be aroused. Is it any wonder that this snake remedy, along with *Elaps corrallinus*, is in the rubric **'fears, stroke, apoplexy, of having a'**? Such is the snake's sensitivity to change that even changes in the seasons can aggravate them, especially that from winter to spring and summer to autumn. These changes can even trigger mania in extreme cases.

As the *Lachesis* state progresses, and if there is a history of abuse, there may be damage to the frontal lobes of the brain, which leads to the strong sense of paranoia and suspicion seen in this remedy. These last two symptoms are shared by *Cenchris contortrix* and *Crotalus horridus* among the snake remedies. Religion – to the point of fanaticism – can become a saviour to these patients when pushed to this extreme, especially in the case of *Lachesis* – see rubric **'religious, affections, fanaticism'**, where it is the only snake remedy and appears in italics alongside *Anarcadium* with *Veratrum album* in black type.

The pre-menstrual tension which is so typical of the snake remedies emanates from the anterior cingulate gyrus – the brain structure that stimulates primitive emotions. There is often an unbridled knee-jerk reaction to what is seen as a threat, and this could be interpreted as a type of hysteria. Interestingly, *Elaps corrallinus* is the only snake remedy in the rubric **'hysteria, menses, before'** although *Lachesis* appears in **'irritability, menses, before'**.

To conclude: abuse and grief can be in the background on an emotional level and suppression on any level. One cannot keep a snake down as they will always raise their ugly head – unless quelled with this set of specifically-targeted remedies according to the individual indications of the case.

Laurocerasus officianalis

Laurocerasus (cherry laurel) is recommended at birth when the oxygen supply to the baby's lungs has been compromised. This has a parallel with the remedy *Carbo vegetabilis*, both remedies sharing the symptoms of coldness and weakness. However, I believe *Laurocerasus* has a deeper impact than *Carbo vegetabilis* in preventing a trajectory of long-term resulting pathology on both the emotional, as well as the physical sphere.

In one case, a 22-year-old male could not separate from his mother, such was the effect of their shared trauma since the birth experience. He had been so underweight and vulnerable at birth that he had to be wrapped in silver foil for any chance to survive, and his mother detached somewhat from him at that point for self-preservation as his prognosis was so dismal. When the chronic case was taken, I learnt that he had recently been inadvertently responsible for an accident which caused a fatality. When he spoke about this, he could not produce any feelings whatsoever about what had happened.

On looking at the main emotional symptoms of the remedy based on lack of moral feeling – see rubrics **'moral, feelings, lacking'** and **'unconsciousness, coma'** (mental insensibility), it can be seen how he arrived at this point. For **'unconsciousness'**, see the Mind chapter under **'unconsciousness'**, and the Clinical chapter under **'coma, unconsciousness'**. [5]

After he took *Laurocerasus*, the patient was able to connect with those difficult feelings and process them accordingly. In such a case, I recommend high potencies such as 10M to reconcile such an early and implanted level of trauma. *Opium* may have been given first in a case needing this remedy, as it shares these two key emotional symptoms. However, the primal causation is specific in this case, which led me to select *Laurocerasus* as the simillimum.

Other important emotional symptoms under *Laurocerasus* include: abandoned feelings, anger when misunderstood, fear of insanity and weeping from criticism. However, this remedy is poorly represented in the repertory in rubrics for these symptoms.

In my experience, *Laurocerasus* is useful where a single twin has survived and the other twin died in the womb, which has an intensely traumatic life-long effect. This is even if the surviving twin is unaware of this loss, such is the power of the cellular memory. The life trajectory is blocked by such symptoms and the sufferer can often only break out once this remedy is given.

Laurocerasus is not an easy remedy to identify for a first prescription in a chronic case as it is well indicated in 'lack of reaction' cases; it is actually black type in the rubric *'reaction, lack of'*. However, once a patient's lack of reaction has been observed, it may be possible to trace the illness back along the time-line, which will reveal the early compromising trigger to the progression of disease.

This remedy is very deep-acting because it contains hydrocyanic acid – a powerful poison that can quickly lead to coma and death. This component explains *Laurocerasus's* action on the vagus nerve, undermining heart and lungs, and also the gut and uterus. The vagus nerve is rich in oxytocin, the bonding hormone, and this remedy seems capable of stimulating oxytocin, which might explain its powerful action when a surviving twin feels their loss at a cellular level.

Laurocerasus demonstrates that there is no such thing as a 'small remedy' – only a remedy limited in its proving. This often overlooked remedy could save the patient prolonged suffering as well as those around them where there are strong enough indications for using it.

Lycopodium clavatum

Lycopodium is becoming more and more important in contemporary life and increasingly indicated in younger people. This could be because today's society often pressurises children to excel, regardless of their individual academic development. [98]

The *Lycopodium* child has the mental capacity to achieve these expectations – they can be precocious and their mental capacities usually outstrip their physical ones. As they may be physically puny, they attract bullying, such is their unconscious 'expectation'. In turn, to compensate for their perceived shortcomings, they can easily be the perpetrator of such behaviour themselves – see rubrics **'dictatorial, despotic'**, where it is black type alongside *Lachesis* and *Nux vomica*; **'haughty, behaviour'**; and **'power, love of'**, where it is the only black type remedy. They may even take refuge in developing their academic prowess as a way of escape – see rubric **'precocity, children'** and **'escape, attempts to'**.

The level of pressure exerted on them to succeed saps their self-confidence. Anticipation builds up and they start to realise their main fear – of failure – (see rubric **'fear, failure, of'** where *Lycopodium* and *Nux vomica* are the only black type remedies in a rubric with many entries). This remedy often addresses issues such as dyslexia, and is indicated for low self-esteem with remedies such as *Anacardium* and *Lac caninum*.

So, one can trace the underpinning trauma in *Lycopodium* to **'domination, by others, ailments from'**, **'anger, ailments from'**, **'mortification, ailments from'** (this is often unexpressed – *Staphisagria* is not the only remedy here), **'fright, ailments from'** (black type), and **'grief, ailments from'** (one should not be restricted to *Natrum muriaticum* here).

In *Lycopodium*, (and *Anacardium* to some degree) the gut is the first target for their emotional unease. After all, there is a direct connection between the gut and the brain, based on the powerful

---

98   Chua, Amy (2011), *Battle Hymn of the Tiger Mother*, Penguin Group.

action of the vagus nerve which connects the two. [99] This means their digestion becomes weak and their insecurity is reflected in the bowels.

It is no coincidence that the liver is the organ targeted, as the liver symbolises issues such as anger and undigested emotions. Duodenal ulcers can develop, which can also occur in *Anacardium* and *Argentum nitricum*, other anticipatory remedies. Premenstrual tension complies with this remedy – the hormones being processed in the liver – connecting it to snake remedies such as *Lachesis*, which can act so powerfully here.

In *Lycopodium*, not only does the digestion become weak, but also the sexual organs, as all the energy is in the head, contributing to their insecurity in relationships. The original trauma is re-evoked when, for example, the patient needs to commit to a relationship. Due to their history, this may represent an impasse and they may feel the urge to escape – see rubric **'escape, attempts to, family and children, from her'**. They may have over-indulged in sexual pursuits in the past – see rubric **'sex, excesses, ailments from'** in the Generals chapter of the *Repertory*.

They may age prematurely due to lack of assimilation and burning out of the sexuality. *Selenium* shares this symptom, as well as the emaciation seen in *Lycopodium*. In *Selenium*, it is more likely to result from prolonged alcohol abuse, whereas *Lycopodium* works well in the early stages.

Lycopodium used to be thought of as a predominantly male remedy. However, with today's increasingly strong role of women in society, it spreads across the gender divide more and more.

Liver remedies generally have irritability on waking. *Magnesium muriaticum* is the most unrefreshed from sleep of all of them and shares with *Lycopodium* intolerance to milk.

Lycopodium wakes at 3-4am – typical times for liver disturbances. This is when the anxieties may surface in this remedy, reflecting

---

99   Bergland, Christopher (May 2014), How does the Vagus Nerve Convey Gut Instincts to the Brain?, *Psychology Today*.

onto the physical sphere. The mood also sinks after 4pm – see rubric *'crying, weeping, afternoon, 4pm to 8pm'*, where it is a single black type remedy.

The brain structures affected in *Lycopodium* include the limbic system where the mood is regulated and bonding takes place. This affects energy and sexual drive – *Chocolate* and *Sepia* share these symptoms with *Lycopodium*. The patient feels so defeated that they become resigned to their situation. The frontal cortex, where cognition is processed, in turn becomes affected as well as the hippocampus which involves memory.

The basal ganglia react, causing muscular tension affecting the nervous system which can lead to Tourette's syndrome in extreme cases. Other remedies here include: *Agaricus muscarius, Anacardium, Hyoscyamus*, and *Stramonium* – all remedies with strong emotional triggering symptoms.

Lycopodium is the only plant which absorbs aluminium. It is not in the rubric for aluminium poisoning but its symptoms may point to this as a contributing factor, and could explain why *Alumina* follows *Lycopodium* well, especially in old age when the memory may markedly decline.

The *Lycopodium* patient craves foods such as sugar and sweets – the very foods which can trigger their symptoms; the food one craves is often the one that aggravates the most. This might indicate a mineral deficiency in the organism or perhaps more likely the need for emotional sweetness, which is often lacking in their background.

Lachesis can complete the action of *Lycopodium* if the symptoms end up on the left side after starting on the right. *Chelidonium* can pave the way for *Lycopodium* to work, being less deep acting and opening up the verbal expression of the patient. *China* antidotes the ill effects of *Lycopodium* but is also complementary, especially in flatulence and bloating.

Lycopodium works well in a triad of *Sulphur* and *Calcarea carbonica*, in the order *Sulphur/Calcarea carbonica/Lycopodium* respectively.

In conclusion, this is an original and often overlooked polychrest at all times of life whose time has come for today's challenging world – especially for both young and old people.

Lyssin (Hydrophobinum)

Lyssin is also known as *Hydrophobinum* and is derived from the saliva of a rabid dog. This is a very emblematic 'Doctrine of Signatures' and conjures up wild images in one's mind. According to Noel Coward, "Mad dogs and Englishmen go out in the midday sun", but homeopathic provings disagree as, in fact, the *Lyssin* patient is severely aggravated by exposure to the sun. Not only do they find the impact of the sun's rays unsettling, but also anything they perceive as any type of disturbance to their equilibrium. Another example is noise – even the sound of someone eating an apple can make them incandescent with rage, so sensitive is their nervous system; see rubric **'sensitive, noise, to, others eat apples, hawk or blow their noses, cannot bear to hear'** where *Lyssin* is a single remedy. Convulsions can even be brought on by exposure to light or water. This over-sensitivity could be a reflex from earlier damage to the brain structures.

Self-mutilation is increasing nowadays at an alarming rate; other remedies such as *Mancinella* also indulge in such release of pent-up emotion although *Mancinella* is so impressionable it could easily be a copycat pursuit. In *Lyssin*, they could just as easily drive the knife into another person as themselves, such is their blinding drive to assuage their overwhelming anger in that moment. They need to be provoked to reach this point – being a severely syphilitic remedy, the effects can be ferocious to witness. See rubric **'impulses, morbid, stab his flesh with the knife he holds, to'** where *Arsenicum album* and *Staphysagria* are the only other two remedies. *Lyssin* also appears in the rubric **'mutilate, body, inclination to'**, where a greater number of remedies appears.

Water aggravates the patient; this relates to the shimmering quality from sunshine. See rubrics **'hydrophobia, fear of water'**, where it is black type; and **'fear, noise from, of rushing water'**, where it is in black type with *Stramonium*, showing the combined sensitivity to noise and water. Even drinking water exacerbates the *Lyssin* patient, perhaps forcing them to gag. They may bite if there is any sense of threat – main rubric **'biting, behaviour,** *desires to'* where *Lyssin* is black type. This threat may be imaginary – see rubric *'delusion, injured, being'/'delusion, insulted, thinks he is'/'delusion, tormented, thinks he is'/'delusion, wrong, he, has suffered a'*; judging by the number of rubrics here on the same theme, one can see how exaggerated this threat is in their mind.

In one case, a five-year-old boy was about to be expelled from school until he took this remedy. His mother had been ill in pregnancy with him, and could not as a result bond with him at birth. His spatial awareness was weak and he would invade other children's space with his overtly provocative behaviour. This behaviour is similar to *Hyoscyamus*, *Mercurius vivus* and *Saccharum officinale*, although it is less sexualised in *Lyssin*.

Another case is of a married man who had become so aggressive that his family was on the verge of walking out. His story was one of abuse from childhood, and the remedy had a dramatic effect on his temper and his ability to re-integrate domestic life to its former glory.

In recent years, with so many soldiers returning from the battlefront with post traumatic stress disorder, this remedy could come into its own with the history of deep primal wounding in the background of the case. If there has been no opportunity to debrief, the victim may persist in acting out the distress in everyday situations on their return to civilian life. The psyche is locked in battle mode so they are easily taunted by any perceived provocation to an unjustifiable level. Sensitivity to noise could be due to a blast injury they experienced during fighting. This is often an invisible wound but the effects are deep and hard to remove. (Natrum Sulphuricum is another remedy indicated in blast injuries.)

'Sympathetic, empathy, feels same pains as others' is an interesting rubric, with *Lyssin* and *Phosphorus* being the only two remedies. With *Lyssin*, it could be due to their over-developed sensitivity and 'there but for fortune go I' attitude, which may explain why this remedy can be strongly indicated in auto-immune diseases, such is the weakness of their boundaries. This remedy can be added to the rubric *'auto-immune diseases'*.

Staphysagria is related in its *'mortification, ailments from'* but is more likely to bottle up the effects: even if they were angry enough to lash out, it would not be as extreme as *Lyssin*.

The gloom of *Syphilinum* can be detected in *Lyssin* – rubric *'delusion, happen, something terrible is going to'* where the only other remedy is *Palladium*. So, the case may need to be backed up with a dose of *Syphilinum* to secure a cure, especially if 'maintaining causes' remain strong. Another syphilitic aspect is the ritualistic behaviour often seen in cases with a history of abuse or neglect. See rubric *'ritualistic, behaviour'*.

Lyssin is the rabies nosode, so can work well as a prophylactic for this disease and, in addition, can be indicated in support of the active state of rabies. Other important remedies for this disease are reputed to be *Belladonna*, *Cantharis* and *Stramonium*.

Lachesis is the closest analogue to *Lyssin* of the other remedies derived from animal poisons.

Magnesium carbonica

(Other main derivatives include: *Magnesium bromatum, Magnesium muriaticum, Magnesium phosphorica* and *Magnesium sulphuricum*)

There is a dream in the provings of the three major *Magnesium* remedies, *Magnesium carbonica, Magnesium muriaticum*, and *Magnesium sulphuricum,* which reveals the unconscious state of the patient needing one of these remedies: it is found in the rubric *'dream, forest, of a, going astray in a'*, where the only other major remedies are *Ammonium muriaticum, Pulsatilla*, and *Sepia*. This dream conveys the essence of the *Magnesium* remedies, feeling abandoned in a dark place – a feeling which is key to the patient's general state. The sense of abandonment goes to their core and often originated in the primal years of the life of the patient.

The *Guardian* newspaper published an article entitled, "Swedish children upset by parents' phone use" which exemplifies this rubric well. [100] It cites the fact that more than a third of children in Sweden's cities complain that their parents spend too much time staring at phones and tablet computers, leading doctors in the country to warn that children may be suffering emotional and cognitive damage. It says that even their language development could be affected by this phenomenon. This sense of neglect of which these children complain is a reminder of the *Magnesium* group of remedies. It is not just children in orphanages who may need these remedies, as was thought in the past, but children in some of the most advanced countries in the western world today!

An important rubric that features *Magnesium carbonica* and *Magnesium muriaticum* is *'deception, ailments from, friendship deceived'*. Nowadays, children can increasingly grow up unaware of their true origins due to adoption, paternity, or even IVF. This information, especially having been intentionally denied, still

---

100 Orange, Richard (October 31, 2013), Swedish Children Complain Their Parents Spend Too Long on Phones, *The Guardian*.

affects them at the cellular level. After all, it is often what is not expressed which hurts the most and, further down the line, the truth is often divulged by accident which can propel the victim of this misguided withholding of information into the true *Magnesium* state of feeling 'lost in the forest' without rescue.

As a result of these deep imprints, the patient does not thrive; the gut becomes impaired due to the lack of serotonin referred through the vagus nerve from the brain. [101] Later on, they might develop diarrhoea (*Magnesium carbonica*) or sheep-dung stools (*Magnesium muriaticum*). Milk aggravates the *Magnesium* patients and often leads to the type of bowel disturbances mentioned here. It is no coincidence that milk aggravates the child, as it represents the primal food supplied by the mother and is therefore so connected to the bonding process. Triggers on the emotional level include anger, fear, fright, and grief. Sea air can also bring on their symptoms.

Sepia is often given after childbirth but the situation could easily call for *Magnesium muriaticum*, for when the patient feels let down by her own female side. According to Jan Scholten, the *Muriaticum* element refers to the mother element. [51] This could be the implicit message they received about being a woman from their mother or someone who represents this role model figure in their lives. Manic depression is a feature of the remedy and can sometimes be unleashed post-natally, which is not surprising given the background described here.

The rubrics of the *Magnesium* remedies not only cover **'abandoned, forsaken feelings'**, but also **'anger, ailments after'**. So, if *Staphysagria* is considered for this latter symptom, the *Magnesiums* should not be overlooked (albeit they appear in plain type). This often-unexpressed anger may represent acting-out the family dysfunction in cases needing these remedies.

Both *Magnesium carbonica* and *Magnesium muriaticum* appear in the rubric **'indolence, averse to work'**.

---

101 McDaniel, Laura, *What is the Gut-Brain Connection?*, www.connectwc.org/what-is-the-gut-brain-connection.html.

Jan Scholten first introduced *Magnesium bromatum* in *Homeopathy and Minerals*, [51] breaking down its concepts into:

Magnesium – pacifism, aggression, fear of loss and pain

Bromatum – guilt, restless, escape, passion, instinct, psychotic

Interestingly, *Magnesium muriaticum* is black type in the rubrics: **'homesickness, nostalgia'** and **'hysterical, behaviour'**. Perhaps *Magnesium muriaticum* should be added to 'hysteria in a man', with the existing remedies: *Carcinosin*, *Crocus sativa*, *Medorrhinum*, and *Moschus*.

Magnesium carbonica has an interesting rubric, **'absent minded, writing while'**, with only three other remedies, two of which are obscure in context with this symptom: *Aconite*, *Kola*, and *Quassia amara*. This confirms *Magnesium carbonica* as a good remedy for learning issues, featuring in other comparable rubrics such as: **'mistakes, writing in'** and **'memory, weakness, of'**. The patient resists being touched and is worse when cutting the wisdom teeth.

On a physical level, *China officianalis* can be compared to *Magnesium carbonica;* the former is to loss of fluids what the latter is to exhausted nerves. Here, it resembles *Medorrhinum* which, like the other nosodes, is not well represented in the repertories. I had always thought of *Magnesium carbonica* as a primarily tubercular remedy, but this aspect of the mental picture also shows its considerable affinity with the sycotic miasm.

Magnesium muriaticum is often better indicated after childbirth than *Sepia* for 'post-natal depression' when bonding between mother and child is absent. This is when the 'uncompensated state' often reveals itself, and the woman cannot cover up her true feelings with all the turmoil in the hormones combined with the huge adjustment in care-taking demanded of her. There is a tendency to use *Sepia* routinely for this state but, when this rupture is rooted in emotional neglect within the mother's history, then *Magnesium muriaticum* heals in a more radical way. Not only does it reconcile the presenting situation with long-term implications for both parties affected, but can also act retrospectively, reaching back to the source of distress in the mother. Interestingly, this remedy does not appear in the rubric **'depression, childbirth after'** despite its strong indication for this state, whereas *Sepia*, naturally, appears in black type, with *Sulphur*.

Given that *Magnesium muriaticum* is a major liver remedy, and that hormones are processed in the liver, it makes sense that new mothers need this remedy because childbirth is a time when hormones tend to undergo marked turmoil, challenging the ability to adapt to changes. This has lifelong implications for the symbiosis between mother and child; disruption can damage their joint relationship long-term and can extend through the generations to follow. A woman with post-natal depression who needs this remedy often comes from a family background such as described above. The missing factor of transgenerational trauma commonly plays itself out in new mothers as well as fathers.

A family's story based on the *Magnesium* remedies was first published in an article entitled *The Missing Equation: Transgenerational Trauma.* [102]

102 Adalian, Elizabeth (September 2014), *The Missing Equation: Transgenerational Trauma*, www.hpathy.com/clinical-cases/missing-equation-transgenerational-trauma.

Mancinella venenata

Mancinella venenata is derived from the Manganeel Apple, reputed to be the apple Adam presented to Eve in the Garden of Eden. This hints at temptation and forbiddenness combined, portraying the split portrayed in its homeopathic picture. It belongs to the Euphorbia family, along with *Hura brasiliensis*, a remedy also discussed here. The Euphorbia family of remedies generally feel constricted, which comes across strongly in both these remedies, emotionally and physically. The skin plays a major role in *Hura, Mancinella*, and other Euphorbia remedies such as *Croton tiglium*. The neurosis on the emotional level is translated onto the physical level, especially in *Hura* and *Mancinella*, such is the extreme of these remedy pictures.

Mancinella is under-represented in both repertories and materia medica. I find that *Mancinella* lies between *Anacardium*, with **'domination, by others, ailments from'**, and **'thoughts, vanishing of'**, its tendency towards isolation – see rubric **'isolation, feelings'**, as well as neurotic skin symptoms, and *Stramonium*, where isolation is also highlighted, combined with clinging and terror. *Calcarea carbonica* shares its sensitivity to bullying and need for security, and *Phosphorus* with its suggestibility to fear and sympathetic nature. It reminds me of *Pulsatilla* in its vulnerability during changes, especially at puberty and at the menopause, but psychosis during these times is better covered by *Mancinella* than *Pulsatilla*. Although it is not in the rubrics **'crying, alone, when'**, and **'dwells on past, disagreeable occurrences'**, it resembles *Natrum muriaticum* in these characteristics.

The full-blown psychosis in *Mancinella*, with its 'splitting-off' and hearing voices, is rooted in the terror of some traumatic childhood experience. This could be from over-dominating parents or, conversely, where parents have been over-protective. One parent may be over-dominating while the other parent compensates by being over-protective. Nowadays, children can be over-exposed to violent films, perhaps without the parents' consent, and exposure to frightful images or bullying can trigger the *Mancinella* state.

Bullying in schools is actively discouraged nowadays, but it is still a phenomenon increasingly observed in wider society. Such a trauma experienced by a pregnant woman can be transmitted to her unborn child, resulting in newborns developing the baby blues, culminating in depression during the teenage years. [103] The amygdala, the brain structure responsible for regulating emotion and stress, is affected if the mother is depressed at this time of 'structural connectivity' in the foetus. This influence continues to affect the child and, in *Mancinella*, is exacerbated at times of change, such as puberty.

In one case, a six-year-old was sleepless for two weeks until he received this remedy, after seeing a frightening film. Without this intervention, he might have progressed to the full-blown *Mancinella* state as he had a controlling mother, and he resisted any situation which threatened to remove him from the family home. *Mancinella* needs the security of their own familiar territory (like *Baryta carbonica* and *Calcarea carbonica*). It is in the rubric, **'homesickness, nostalgia'** and **'homesickness, ailments from'**. The *Mancinella* child is easily unhinged, as this case demonstrates. *Phosphorus* is the obvious remedy for fear from seeing distressing images, but the *Phosphorus* patient can easily be talked out of their fears, unlike *Mancinella*, which is drawn to the dark side, like *Stramonium*.

Mancinella resembles *Stramonium, Anacardium, Arsenicum, Hyoscyamus, Lyssin, Staphysagria*, and *Tarentula hispanica* (of remedies discussed here) in self-mutilation, a growing current phenomenon. All these remedies share with *Mancinella* a lack of barrier to filter out and separate what belongs inside, and what belongs outside themselves. In *Mancinella*, the self-mutilation is often a way of replicating the behaviour of a strong cult hero, such is the patient's poor sense of identity as well as attraction to destructive influences.

---

103 Pearson, Rebecca M., Phd, et al. (2013), Maternal Depression During Pregnancy and the Postnatal Period. Risks and Possible Mechanisms for Offspring Depression at 18 Years, *Journal of the American Medical Association of Psychiatry*, 70(12):1312-19.

In another case, a precocious 15-year-old male presented with disabling depression. He became homesick on a school trip abroad when he realised he was different from his peers. Due to this new awareness, he became extremely sensitive to the bullying he was experiencing which was partly due to his precocity, but also to his increasingly overt effeminate nature. On returning home, he clung to his mother and wanted to know her every move. During the consultation, I learned that she had experienced a miscarriage prior to her son's conception and, as we spoke, she revealed that she had not processed the loss sufficiently and had rushed too soon into another pregnancy; as a result, her suppressed grief was transferred to the baby while in utero. She, albeit unconsciously, over-compensated, creating the smothering relationship that had built up between her and her son. No wonder she found it hard to let him go – as was intuited by him on a cellular level. By the son remaining unnaturally needy, their locked-in symbiosis was secured – a good example of 'transgenerational trauma'.

After receiving *Mancinella* 200c, he recovered from the feelings of depression and alienation by integrating the needy side of himself, which had previously been over-exposed. Over time, he no longer got teased at school and could follow pursuits which took him abroad and therefore away from home. This enabled him to develop his musical interests, which had formerly been suppressed as a result of the enmeshed dynamic between mother and child.

The background of these cases might explain why *Mancinella* appears in the rubric **'fear, homosexuality, of'**. A combination of these patients' sensitivity, timidity, and sympathetic nature make them vulnerable which, in turn, might create a leaning towards homosexuality or its opposite, a fear of homosexuality. Mancinella, the plant, is associated with evil in folklore and, historically, homosexuality has often been connected to the devil. This is reflected in the main and very distinct delusion of this remedy.

I have usually prescribed *Mancinella* for males, especially at puberty. In middle age, however, it manifests more in females, possibly due to the 'angst' the menopause brings. *Mancinella* is in the rubric *'sexuality, nymphomania, women, menopausal period, at'*, with *Lachesis* and *Murex*. An example of this is a 40-year-old woman who presented with extreme paranoia which led to her hearing voices. This state was triggered when her 16-year-old daughter told her about an attempted rape by a family friend. The patient was understandably confused as she felt her loyalties were torn between her daughter and the family of the perpetrator, and this confusion tipped her over the edge into feelings of paranoia. This outcome is reflected in *Mancinella's* sympathetic nature, combined with its susceptibility to terror, evidenced in this case by the traumatic image of the assault upon her daughter (a situation that could easily suggest *Opium* as the possible overlying remedy). *'Anger, ailments from'* could be the main underpinning rubric in this case.

Based on these cases, perhaps *Mancinella* should be added to the following rubrics:

- *'domination by others, ailments from'*
- *'fright, ailments from'*
- *'clinging, behaviour'*
- *'confusion, identity, as to his'*
- *'confusion, identity, sexual identity'*
- *'pining away from mental and physical, anxiety'* (*Aurum metallicum* is not the only significant remedy here!)
- *'precocity, children'*
- *'sensitive, children'*, and
- *'insomnia, anxiety from'*

Rubrics where it should be highlighted include:

- *'homesickness, nostalgia'*
- *'horrible things, sad stories, movies, ailments from'*
- *'mutilate, body, inclination to'*, and
- *'sympathetic, empathy'*

As the well-known rubric *'fear, devil, being taken by the'* is also a delusion, *Mancinella* is also in *'delusion, devil, taken, by, that he will be'*. This symptom can be translated into the rubric *'horrible things affect profoundly'*, which also helps to explain *Mancinella's* lack of discrimination when observing distressing images, as demonstrated in their draw to inflict injury on themselves.

The delusion and the fear of insanity are present because they might actually become insane, as seen in the following rubrics:

- *'delusion, voices, hears'*
- *'fear, ghosts, of'*
- *'insanity, madness'*
- *'memory, active'* (this is why images take hold so easily)
- *'memory, weak – do, for what he was about to'* (due to their preoccupation with this tendency)

In conclusion, some young men feel marginalised in today's culture and this is worse in the aesthetic *Mancinella* male. Society does not take into account that there are many ways a male can contribute – even if he does not fit into the stereotypical role. With the current rise of female success in the academic field as well as in the workplace, and in order to reconcile this imbalance, this remedy will probably become increasingly needed in the future.

Mancinella teaches us that we do not have to deny or suppress our vulnerability, a position which can lead to feelings of profound fear and fragility; if only society could appreciate that it is only human to be vulnerable. This remedy is a true saviour of sanity – one could go so far as to say 'mad but for you – *Mancinella'*.

Mercurius vivus

(Other main derivatives include: *Mercurius corrosivus, Mercurius cyanatus, Mercurius dulcis,* and *Mercurius solubilis*)

Mercurius is represented by *Mercurius solubilis* and *Mercurius vivus* as the main derivatives. *Mercurius iodatus flavus* (mostly used for right-sided throat infections), and *Mercurius iodatus ruber* (mostly used for left-sided ones) could be considered to be the lesser known derivatives. *Mercurius corrosivus* and *Mercurius cyanatus* cover a wider application than the *Iodatus flavus* and the *Iodatus ruber* derivatives.

The 'Doctrine of Signatures' hints at the elusive nature of the patient needing this group of remedies. When a thermometer breaks and the mercury inside spills all over the floor, however many attempts are made to gather it up, it just rolls out of grasp evading all contact with any surface. This is reflected in the planet Mercury 'going retrograde' – a well-known expression used when communications between people become elusive, difficult or interrupted.

A condition called alexithimia, for which the literal translation from the Greek is 'having no words for emotions', was first recognised in the 1970s (see Part 1, 'alexithimia'). This lack of emotional expression is key to the *Mercury* patient, often indicated by the degree of resulting somatisation of symptoms. It is evident that alexithimia contributes to psychosomatic illness, alcoholism and drug addiction, as well as 'post traumatic stress disorder'. The patient needing this remedy often hides behind alcohol to facilitate spontaneity of speech and overcome their timidity. They may be incapable of articulating feelings, become confused by questions related to feelings, have a limited ability to cry, a tendency to speak in a monotone and adopt rigid positions. Without the social context and real-world meaning provided by the right side of the brain, they can suffer mental problems as a result. [61]

Rubrics that illustrate alexithimia include: *'delusion, hell, suffers, the torments of, without being able to explain'*, where *Mercury* and *Lyssin* are the only remedies; *'answers, slowly'*, where *Mercury* is in black type; *'ideas, deficiency of'*; *'recognise, does not, his relatives'*; *'speech, unintelligible'* in the Speech chapter of the *Repertory*; and *'stupefaction, knows not where he is'*. The last two rubrics suggest that, after the remedy has been taken and in order for a curative response to take hold, the 'floodgates are opened' and the patient, and those around them, may find it difficult to adapt to the consequent emotional outbursts of feelings.

Stammering is an important symptom which illustrates the remedy's difficulty in communication (other black type remedies in the rubric *'stammering, stuttering, speech'*, in the Speech chapter, include *Belladonna*, *Causticum*, *Nux vomica*, and *Stramonium*).

Mercurius is an emblematic syphilitic remedy – indicated by the dark mood and aggravation at night, meaning symptoms are deep-seated and very disturbing to the patient. However, the remedy also belongs to the sycotic miasm with their spreading nature of skin disease and suppurations as well as learning difficulties and avoidant behaviour – the latter resembling *Thuja*.

Patients who need this remedy may seem emotionally insensitive but, on the physical level, they are extremely reactive, especially to changes in the environment and temperature.

The *Mercury* patient needs a strong trigger to cause them to withdraw. Fright and mortification are the main emotional ones and, due to their inability to articulate their feelings, these triggers can have a lasting impact. Alternatively, the emotional triggers could have occurred at the pre-verbal stage of development when the patient had no outlet to articulate their reactions. Lesser-known triggers on the physical level are head injuries and sexual excesses.

Impulses such as approaching a stranger on the street and grabbing their nose will leave the perpetrator of such a bizarre action unable to explain themselves. When tackled about such behaviour, they become worse for contradiction – see rubric *'contradiction, intolerant, of'*; and may even become paranoid – see rubric *'delusion, enemy, everyone is an'*; and *'delusion, enemy, surrounded by'*; *'fight, wants to'*; *'spit, desire to, in faces, of people'*; and *'suicidal, disposition'*; as well as *'suicidal, disposition, window, whenever he sees an open, or a cutting instrument'*, where it is a single remedy in italics. Perhaps *Lyssin* should be added to this rubric – both *Lyssin* and *Mercury* are in *'impulses, morbid, horrid'*.

Autism is a classic example of the type of 'state' seen in *Mercurius* patients. This is mirrored on both emotional and physical levels, as seen in their instability, poor communication, and maladjustment to the environment. In vaccine-damaged children, their fundamental susceptibility to the mercury in the vaccine components can trigger their 'state'.

Many illnesses afflicting these patients affect their oral cavity and around the throat chakra – the seat of the voice and communication. This remedy gives the patient the gift of articulating their feelings in a coherent way, thus saving the physical structures from intense suffering. This is not to overlook the damaged brain structures creating the 'state' in the first place.

The background to *Mercurius* lies in the inability to 're-inhabit' childhood memories, without which they do not have this resource to fall back on and build their character accordingly. It is as if one's memory becomes a major element in our identity. This is partly a social process based on parent-child discussion about the past. [28]

In summary, this remedy is frequently used in acute illness but often eludes the prescriber on a constitutional one – such is the 'mercurial' quality of the patient.

Natrum muriaticum

(Other main derivatives include: *Natrum arsenicosum, Natrum carbonicum, Natrum phosphoricum, Natrum silicata,* and *Natrum sulphuricum*)

The main derivatives in the psychic sphere are *Natrum carbonicum* (sodium carbonate) and *Natrum sulphuricum* (sodium sulphate), as well as *Natrum muriaticum* (sodium chloride – better known as common rock salt). *Natrum muriaticum* is considered the major polychrest in the *Natrum* group of remedies.

In the UK, it is all too easy to prescribe *Natrum muriaticum* to the exclusion of the other *Natrum* remedies as the UK population is widely considered to be emblematic of this remedy – introverted as a result of emotional hurt – see rubric **'love, disappointed, ailments from'** and **'dwells, on, past, disagreeable events'**. However, other *Natrums* may be better indicated in the case. *Natrum carbonicum* has a picture of over-sensitivity on all levels and resulting allergies – see rubric **'depression, diet, errors of'** where it is a single black type remedy: an emotional symptom conditioned by a physical trigger, which could be considered a 'strange, rare and peculiar' symptom in homeopathy.

In *Natrum sulphuricum*, the depression is deeper than both *Natrum carbonicum* and *Natrum muriaticum*, falling into the category of 'bi-polar disorder'. Thus, sleep disturbances in such cases respond better to *Natrum sulphuricum* than *Natrum muriaticum*. All these remedies are closed in their nature, but *Natrum sulphuricum* is the most closed of all three and may, in fact, be one of the most closed in the whole materia medica (alongside *Chelidonium, Kali carbonicum, Mercurius vivus,* and *Thuja* as important examples). The state in this remedy could have been induced by head injury.

Natrum sulphuricum, being such a grounded remedy, does not reach hysteria like *Natrum carbonicum* and *Natrum muriaticum* although, despite its introversion, *Natrum muriaticum* can actually reach a state of mania. Psychosis and paranoia do not appear in

Natrum sulphuricum, but *Natrum carbonicum* and *Natrum muriaticum* both appear in the rubric *'schizophrenia'* although not in *'paranoid'*. In fact, if *Natrum sulphuricum* had a rich interior world to escape into, the patient would not sink so deeply into dark depression. [28]

After a successful prescription of *Natrum sulphuricum*, the patient starts to express themselves; somatic symptoms found in this remedy, such as arthritis and asthma, are often relieved, and the patient is no longer driven to the ultimate despair seen in its picture, possibly culminating in suicide. For the rubric *'suicidal, disposition'*, *Natrum carbonicum* is plain type, *Natrum muriaticum* is italics, and *Natrum sulphuricum* is black type. This variation indicates the exponential degree of intention in each of these related remedies. When appreciating the materia medica to this degree of detail, it is easier to calibrate the case more precisely, and vital components are not overlooked which support the optimal functioning of the patient.

With such strong psychic forces in this group of remedies, it is inevitable that the gut can suffer due to its association with the 'second brain'. [3] As a high level of the neurotransmitter serotonin is located in the gut, it is no wonder that this group of remedies often have gut problems; *Natrum carbonicum* being the most sensitive. This distress travels from the top end of the stomach to the rectum – illustrated by *Natrum sulphuricum* with its infamous rubric *'cheerful, stools, after'*, where it is a single, black type remedy. Here again, as in *Natrum carbonicum*, one sees how the mood in the *Natrum* remedies can be significantly conditioned by the state of the gut.

Any skin symptoms suffered in the case could be a direct reflex from the anxious gut experienced by the patient as a projection from the emotional state, such is the link between the two, which is especially pronounced in the *Natrum* remedies.

In conclusion, this group of remedies can prevent one from literally being 'caught between a rock and a hard place'! One only has to think of the song by Simon and Garfunkel, *I am a Rock*, to be reminded of the degree of yearning experienced in the *Natrum* state.

Opium and *Morphinum*

Opium is derived from the poppy, Papaver somniferum, and its addictive and hypnotic effects are well documented, dating back to the opium dens in China. All homeopathic remedies derived from recreational drugs have a marked affinity with trauma in their provings: *Anhalonium* (Peyote), *Ayahuasca*, *Cannabis indica*, *Cannabis sativa*, *Coca*, and *Morphinum*. It is highly likely that a history of trauma precedes addiction, and the trauma must have been so profound that the only way to cope is to literally 'numb out' the pain in this way.

Nowadays, one hears about post traumatic stress disorder in soldiers returning home from overseas battlefields. In fact, records in the USA show that more returning soldiers commit suicide than actually perish in action, demonstrating the need for professional recognition and strategies to perceive and stem this predisposition from coming to realisation. [104]

As discussed in the Introduction, my work in former war-torn countries taught me that early childhood experience predominantly dictates the reaction to battle trauma, however dramatic the latter exposure. It all depends on susceptibility, which is conditioned during the primal time of development, setting the 'compass' for life. *Opium* is the main remedy to resolve deep and buried trauma which can be unconsciously re-evoked years later with exposure to a resonant image.

In one case, a woman had no memory of her early wartime experience, but the imagery of current war in her country of origin triggered complete paralysis of her mind. She did not understand this as her early exposure had not been spelt out to her, having occurred during the very vulnerable pre-verbal period of her life. However, she had to re-visit it with the support of this remedy for full resolution to occur, together with gentle professional counselling. Counselling is often helpful in these cases as so many

---

104 Pilkington, Ed (February 1, 2013), U.S. Military Struggling to Stop Suicide Epidemic among War Veterans, *The Guardian*.

realisations come together while the case unravels.

In *Opium*, the classic contributing keynote symptom is fear remaining after fright, only to be re-evoked when triggered by unconscious resonant images – as illustrated in this case. *Stramonium* shares this symptom and in fact often follows *Opium* well, when the realisation of the initial betrayal comes to consciousness.

The *Opium* patient can develop physical symptoms such as miscarriage, retained urine, or suppressed menstruation, as a direct result of sudden fear.

The mind can become dull and vacant – see rubric **'torpor, mental'**, where *Opium* is in black type alongside *Gelsemium*, *Natrum muriaticum*, and *Nux moschata*; and **'unconsciousness, coma'** as well as **'coma, mental instability'** in the Clinical chapter of the *Repertory*, where it appears in black type with *Helleborus*.

Due to the level of trauma exposure in *Opium*, this dullness translates onto the physical sphere with the rare symptom of painlessness. Other remedies sensitive to trauma such as *Arnica*, *Helleborus*, *Saccharum officinale*, and *Stramonium* also experience painlessness. *Morphinum*, on the other hand, reacts strongly to any hint of pain, in complete contrast with *Opium* and is, of course, used in its material form in orthodox medicine for pain relief in hospitals. *Opium* can antidote the effects of crude morphine used in this way. See rubric, **'sensitive, pain, to'** in contrast to *Opium's* **'painlessness, of complaints, usually painful'** – in the Clinical chapter of the *Repertory*, where *Opium* appears in black type with *Arnica* and *Stramonium*, and **'sensitive, want, of sensitiveness'**, where it is a single black type remedy.

Morphinum is a good remedy for the pain of shingles and over-sensitivity to the pain of childbirth, especially when the roots of early trauma are deeply buried, which could be described as a 'somatisation'. It is a wonderful 'lack of reaction' remedy for pain when nothing else acts or holds, e.g. after remedies such as *Hypericum* and *Tarentula hispanica* have been given.

In one case, a 64-year-old woman who had been paralysed by the shock of burns received in early life recovered her mobility with the use of *Morphinum*. She also needed other remedies later to support her emotional development that had been arrested at the point of injury; a phenomenon often found in such cases (see 1.1. Setting the Scene).

The *Opium* patient may not experience pleasure (like *Helleborus*) or, by contrast, may be exalted and talkative with a vivid imagination. These contrasting polarities resemble bi-polar disorder and are often seen in cases under the influence of alcohol and drugs.

Both *Opium* and *Morphinum* have a lack of moral feeling, which translates into lying – see rubric *'lies, inclination to tell, never, speaks the truth, does not know what she is saying'*; and *'untruthful'*, in which *Veratrum album* and *Opium* appear in black type, as well as *'deceitful, untruthful'* where *Opium* and *Thuja* are black type remedies. *Morphinum* is in italics in the last two rubrics.

Sleep symptoms may reveal the level of trauma in the background of *Opium*, seen in symptoms such as apnoea, sleep-walking (somnambulism), or snoring. *Opium* shares with *Apis* and *Lachesis* the symptom of sleeping into an aggravation. The patient is generally sleepy but can be sleepless from excitement, like *Coffea*.

Any brain disease such as epilepsy or stroke responds well to *Opium*, especially when the patient is in a coma-like state, the effects resembling opium poisoning in its crude form. This remedy can prevent brain damage where high fever persists and danger threatens. A history of head injury resulting in concussion might have contributed to the presenting brain disease.

The bowels may become paralysed resulting in absence of desire for stool – this could be due to a drug layer or as a reflection of the numbed emotional state.

There is often a lack of reaction to other indicated remedies, in which case both *Opium* and *Morphinum* can open up the patient to receive their simillimum once the trauma layer is removed, even after many years of remaining dormant, as shown in the cases mentioned above. Weakness may be a concomitant in the case needing *Opium*, as it is the only black type remedy in *'reaction, lack of, weakness, with'*. This could be seen as a peculiar symptom in the context as *Opium* is not generally a remedy associated with weakness.

Rhus toxicodendron

(Other main derivatives include: *Rhus diversiloba, Rhus glabra, Rhus radicans,* and *Rhus venenata*)

Rhus toxicodendron is derived from poison ivy – a plant which can easily spread along a path of its own making, at the same time emitting its toxic load along the way to those who come into contact with it. In homeopathy, the remedy is better known for its physical symptoms than mental and emotional ones, which happen to be quite distinctive and relate to its 'Doctrine of Signatures' for both plant substance and pattern of growth. The reason for the emphasis on physical symptoms, despite the fact that the mental and emotional ones are quite marked, is because the primal triggers to these states can so easily be overlooked. This is because they are not underlined when this remedy is presented, and the only way to identify them is to hunt them down through its key rubrics. These triggers include abandonment, anger and vexation, anxiety (often as a concomitant to the anger), fright, and mortification. Triggers such as anger, vexation and mortification usually lead to *Staphysagria* because *Rhus toxicodendron* only appears in plain type, compared to *Staphysagria* in black type. However, the rubric **'anger, ailments from, anxiety, with'** lists *Rhus toxicodendron* in plain type without *Staphysagria* in this rubric which shows that, if one uses a more general rubric without considering the concomitant, one can be misled when singling out the simillimum for the case, the anxiety being key to the way anger is expressed in this remedy.

The well-known physical symptoms in *Rhus toxicodendron* include 1) aching joints; and 2) skin eruptions, although *Rhus radicans* (1) and *Rhus venenata* (2), derivatives of *Rhus toxicodendron*, can often work better for the latter two symptoms respectively. These symptoms are often a 'somatisation' of unexpressed emotions which manifest in this way.

Depression is strong in the *Rhus* remedies and, if unaware and suffering from lack of expression, the patient can turn to drink to drown their sorrows, which affects their sleep and creates a wakeful picture at night, often dwelling on past disagreeable occurrences. Although this remedy is plain type in the general rubric *'dwells, on, past, disagreeable events'*, it is black type in the sub-rubric *'midnight, after'*, alongside *Natrum muriaticum*. This may be because they cannot bring these worries to consciousness during the daytime as they often escape through restless behaviour and gain relief by walking outdoors; see rubric *'depression, walking, air, in open, amel.'* where *Rhus toxicodendron* features alongside *Platina* and *Pulsatilla*.

The night time aggravation and degree of depression which can drive the patient to suicide indicate its strong syphilitic picture. The presenting symptom is often one of depression which masquerades as exhaustion to the patient, often due to this driven state at night.

There is a strong fear of being poisoned – which makes sense, considering the substance from which the remedy is derived. In general, if a remedy is derived from a poisonous substance, then it figures that there could be a projection of this state in the remedy picture. Other black type remedies in the rubric *'fear, poisoned, of being'* include *Arsenicum album*, *Hyoscyamus*, and *Lachesis*.

Rhus toxicodendron belongs to the same plant family as *Anacardium*, of which the emotional symptoms are perhaps better known than the physical ones, in contrast to *Rhus toxicodendron*. A restricted feeling in the physical symptoms runs through both remedies. Both are relieved by motion but this is more marked in *Rhus toxicodendron* in which the desire to escape is strong, even though it is only plain type in the rubric *'escape, attempts to'*. However, what is this patient escaping from? Could it be their 'early demons' that have not been brought to the surface? In the early stages, this just manifests as restlessness; however, as the pathology progresses, a type of paranoia seen in schizophrenic states takes over – see rubric *'schizophrenia'* with sub-rubrics *'paranoid'* and *'persecuted, that he is'*. Then, fear of being poisoned, fear of death, and delusion of being pursued by enemies can become marked.

Financial loss and preoccupation with business worries often predominate in the end, which are a reminder of *Aurum metallicum* and *Bryonia*. Of course, *Aurum metallicum* does not have the marked restlessness seen in *Rhus toxicodendron* although the suicidal drive is equally strong in both remedies. *Bryonia* has a more stable base and its pathology does not progress to such breakdown, because it does not belong to the syphilitic miasm, as do the others already mentioned. (*Bryonia alba* is closely aligned to *Rhus toxicodendron*.)

The conclusion here, as with all remedies, is that the trajectory to the final pathology is triggered in infancy, a factor that is especially overlooked in the general portrayal of the *Rhus toxicodendron* remedy picture. Subsequently, the resulting emotions often remain subdued until the syphilitic miasm takes hold later in life in the form of alcoholism. This, in turn, affects the brain structures until paranoia can take over, propelling the patient to a destructive end in the form of memory loss or suicide. If intervention with this simillimum takes place, this trajectory can be averted and the patient released from such possible outcomes. In the process, they are restored to optimum health to embrace the life which, hitherto, they may have been unable to appreciate due to a gloomy prevailing mindset that evolved over the years to culminate in these negative final expressions of disease.

Saccharum officinale or *Saccharum album*
(Other main derivative: *Saccharum lactis*)

What more emotive substance is there than sugar, from which this remedy is derived?

There is a contradictory attitude to sugar in our society – it is known to be harmful but it is used as a reward both to ourselves and others, often as a substitute for love. This replacement for love dates back to the bonding experience, which is so often sadly lacking; there may even be a history of abuse. A child might have been adopted or feels neglected by their parents. An early lack of symbiosis with a birth mother leaves an indelible imprint. If sugar has been substituted for true affection, the child grows up with this association embedded in their psyche and this can translate into eating disorders as the child develops (with remedies such as *Carcinosin*, *Hyoscyamus*, *Tarentula hispanica*, and *Vanadium metallicum*). In the remedy picture, *Saccharum* patients have a lack of boundaries with a bottomless pit of need for reinforcement and validation. This lack of boundaries translates into their relationships with other children where there may be inappropriate proximity of an aggressive and provocative nature. This provocation can present like *Hyoscyamus* or *Mercurius*, with signs of sexual precocity.

Birth by Caesarean section, with no struggle to come into life through the birth canal, could be a contributing factor to the *Saccharum officinale* state. Also, babies born by Caesarean section are often removed from their mothers at birth, which has a marked effect on the vital early bonding process. However, the susceptibility towards the expectation of instant gratification is probably already dormant in order to be evoked by this scenario.

There is an association between sugar craving and heroin addiction due to their joint connection to lack of dopamine, the pleasure-giving neurotransmitter. Sugar is said to be eight times more addictive than cocaine, which suggests *Saccharum officinale* could be a much overlooked and underused remedy for any major addiction, whatever its source. [105]

If a child on the trajectory towards addiction can be treated when young, this addictive progression could be arrested. The limbic system (the emotional centre), the part of the brain where dopamine is produced, can become undermined through repeated traumatisation. Resulting issues include isolation, pitifully low self-confidence, and absence of enjoyment. This effect on the limbic system feeds into the other brain structures as they are all inter-linked. Other remedies sharing these traits include *Adamas*, *Androctonus, Helleborus*, and *Plumbum metallicum* – all significant remedies for 'States on the Spectrum'. This might explain why the needs in the *Saccharum officinale* patient are so boundless. It is indicated in pre-menstrual tension, alongside *Chocolate, Lachesis, Lac humanum*, and *Sepia*, as this vulnerable time of the cycle brings out the primal neediness of the patient, with little ability for them to cover it up. *Chocolate, Lac humanum* (mother's milk), and *Saccharum officinale* are all remedies derived from basic favoured foodstuffs, and comply with this 'uncompensated' set of symptoms.

A strange, rare, and peculiar symptom of this remedy is 'painlessness' – a symptom it shares with *Opium* and *Stramonium*, both also remedies with a history of extreme trauma. It is as if the organism has been so brutalised that they have become anaesthetised to pain as a defence mechanism. This 'painlessness' could relate to alexithimia which is described in Part 1 and under *Mercurius vivus* and *Natrum sulphuricum*, where the patient is so cut off from their feelings that their inability to sense emotional pain is transferred onto the physical structure. Having studied the different brain structures, I believe *Saccharum officinale* is a true polychrest transcending the different brain structures, as well as *Agaricus, Anacardium, Androctonus, Baryta carbonica, Carcinosin, Helleborus, Hyoscyamus, Lyssin*, and *Stramonium*. [21]

The *Saccharum officinale* provings show the depth of toxicity matches the syphilitic miasm with its marked putridity and

---

105 Ahmed, Serge H., Dr. (2009), Is Sugar as Addictive as Cocaine?, *Journal of Food and Addiction*, 139:620–22.

destruction, not only of tissue, but right down to the bone itself.

In the *Encyclopedia of Remedy Relationships in Homoeopathy*, Abdur Rehman says that as *Saccharum officinale* is deep acting, it can be hazardous to give in high potencies. [91] There is a strong association with *Calcarea carbonica* with its craving for sweets and tendency to flabbiness, although this type of body shape may not be apparent in everyone needing this remedy.

Even in Hering's time (1800-1880), there was awareness that many chronic diseases of women and children result from the consumption of excessive amounts of sugar.

Saccharum officinale is a significant remedy in diabetes with its relationship with sugar and tendency to leg ulcers. There is often diabetes as well as cancer in the family history, as in *Carcinosin*.

Among recent writings on *Saccharum officinale* is Melissa Assilem's *The Mad Hatter's Tea Party*, in which she also analyses related food substances such as milk and tea. [106] The late Tinus Smits emphasised the importance of this remedy in the treatment of autism, as it can address the frequent concomitant gut symptoms of putrefaction which can undermine the case. [107]

In conclusion, this remedy is under-represented in the repertory despite having a full picture of its own. When a remedy such as *Magnesium carbonica* (the orphan's remedy) does not work or hold, consider *Saccharum officinale*: the neediness here is taken to a higher level in conjunction with our current materialistic age in the West – instant gratification without feeling rewarded and a trajectory towards the destruction of the syphilitic miasm.

---

[106] Assilem, Melissa (1996), *The Mad Hatter's Tea Party*, The Homeopathic Supply Company.

[107] www.tinussmits.com/3870/saccharum-officinale.aspx.

Stramonium

This plant is derived from jimson weed which grows in wasteland or graveyards. This is emblematic of the background to the nature of the patient needing this remedy. *The Scream*, the iconic painting by Edouard Munch, reminds us of the true bleakness and terror in this remedy picture. The isolation in the remedy picture can date back to the womb and birthing experience when connection to the maternal source might have been broken – perhaps the cord was tied round the neck of the infant or there was early separation for other health reasons. If this essential initial contact between mother and child is missing, a gaping hole leaves the patient exposed and vulnerable to repeated retraumatisation of a similar nature.

There are many delusions in this remedy; the unique one 'is always alone in a wilderness', where it is a single remedy and sums its picture up well, reflecting back to the origin of the remedy composition. Another significant delusion is 'imagined himself alive on one side and buried on the other' which evokes the level of 'split' experienced by the psyche, given this background. A history of abuse might have contributed to the prevailing emotional state.

The resulting neediness means the patient develops a clinging nature – see rubric **'frightened, waking, terrified, knows no one, screams, clings to those near'**, where it appears as a single remedy (in italics). This could reflect damage to the limbic system of the brain, the structure responsible for mood regulation and bonding. The need for company, combined with dread of the dark, is marked, and this can lead to nymphomania in extreme cases. *Crocus sativa*, *Hyoscyamus*, *Lachesis*, *Medorrhinum*, and *Platina* are important remedies which share this symptom.

The strong sense of paranoia and suspicion, which indicates damage to the temporal lobes, may result from a background of abuse. Other remedies with similar damage include *Anacardium*, *Androctonus*, *Arsenicum album*, *Cannabis indica*, *Crotalus horridus*, *Hyoscyamus*, and *Lachesis* – remedies that show a similar sense of split in various degrees.

Hahnemann observed 'painlessness' in *Stramonium* – a symptom which is also seen in *Arnica, Helleborus niger, Opium*, and *Saccharum officinale*, other remedies with a history of trauma. [108] It is as if the degree of psychic pain experienced in the past has acted as an anaesthetic to any physical pain. They may unconsciously resort to self-harm as a way of manifesting this state to assuage their feelings of numbness; see rubric: **'mutilate, body, inclination to'**. It is hard to pin down the *Stramonium* patient as the urge to escape is so strong, showing its relationship to *Belladonna, Hyoscyamus, Mercurius vivus*, and *Veratrum album*, which are all black type in **'escape, attempts to'**. In fact, *Belladonna, Hyoscyamus*, and *Stramonium* form a triad overlapping on many other fronts and originating from related plant species. All these remedies, alongside *Lyssin*, are black type for **'fears, water, of'** – it is as if its unfathomable nature makes the *Stramonium* patient feel ungrounded. There is also a dread of mirrors, as if viewing their reflection compounds their sense of alienation, as depicted in the painting, *The Scream*. This symptom is replicated in the remedy, *Lyssin*.

With the possible link between abuse and schizophrenia (see 'Schizophrenia' in Part 1 [74]), *Stramonium* should be considered as an early intervention to prevent this possible outcome. The trigger could also be due to other possible factors such as head injury or the ingestion of narcotics. In order for such a deep disease to be triggered, the level of early trauma must have been severe, whether emotional or physical. This is commensurate with the disease trajectory of this remedy and, if the susceptibility is triggered to this degree, the patient may hear voices – the extreme state of schizophrenia – see rubric **'delusion, voices, hears'**.

Anacardium is another remedy with a 'split' which can prevent the full-blown symptoms of schizophrenia developing. In the famous rubric of *Anacardium* – **'delusion, possessed, as if, by a devil'**, *Stramonium* is the only other black type remedy in this rubric.

---

108 Hahnemann, Samuel (1796), *Essay on a New Principle for Ascertaining the Curative Powers of Drugs*.

Mancinella resembles both *Anacardium* and *Stramonium* in its attraction to the dark side of life and strong sense of isolation.

Mercurius vivus is known to share the symptom of stammering with *Stramonium*, another symptom indicating a background of deep-seated distress and possible exposure to trauma during the pre-verbal stage of development. In *Stramonium*, the stammering may be more apparent – see rubric **'stammering, exerts himself a long time before he can utter a word'**, where *Stramonium* is a single black type remedy. In *Mercurius*, it could be masked under the guise of elusive communication.

Tarentula hispanica

(Other main derivative: *Tarentula cubensis*)

The word 'tarentula' conjures up the image of a predator ready to attack and poison the victim, evoking fear to the point of terror. A significant aspect in the behaviour of this arachnoid is its unpredictable movement – one minute the tarentula is still and the next it pounces with alacrity. In the 'Doctrine of Signatures', this summarises the behaviour of the patient requiring this remedy. They will not easily reveal this cunning side in the interview as the ability to manipulate is ingrained in their approach to life. (The snake remedies and the one derived from scorpion share with the tarentula an evocation of terror.)

The propensity towards movement is exemplified in the love of dancing. There is even an Italian dance, 'Tarentella', named after this spider – needless to say, it has a jerky and unpredictable theme to its steps. This remedy has great relief from music – see rubric **'music, ameliorates'** where it is black type, alongside *Aurum metallicum*.

These patients often have a seductive side which, combined with their deviousness, can predominate in the case. In one case, a young child was able to make unfounded allegations about their carer, such was their degree of precocity at an unusually young age. See rubrics **'delusion, assaulted, is going to be'** where *Androctonus* and one more obscure remedy are the only other entries; and **'hysterical, behaviour, lascivious'** (*Hyoscyamus* and *Platina* share this rubric). With the marked history of 'disappointed love', 'anger', and 'grief', it is no wonder that there can be this type of sensational cry for attention. Given also that the *Tarentula* patient is extremely sensitive to touch, one can perceive how this allegation was possible in this case.

This patient had asthma which the initial indicated remedy, *Lycopodium*, did not touch. However, when *Tarentula hispanica* was prescribed for the distinctive hysterical aspect of the case, the asthma resolved speedily. The intricacies of this case proved that such behaviour is indeed possible although not generally documented for this age group but, given the background and the full picture of this remedy, it was highly indicated. *Tarentula hispanica* is not the first remedy to consider for asthma, but – with the degree of manipulation in the background – it fitted the case. This illustrates the importance of prescribing based on the complexities of the mind which, when addressed, will also result in whatever presenting physical pathology responding to treatment.

Tarentula hispanica and other hysterical remedies such as *Crocus sativa* and *Hyoscyamus* also appear in the rubric *'eat, refuses to'*. What better cry for help than resorting to this type of self-destruction!

Paralysis is another symptom which can be triggered by hysteria in this remedy – if there is no-one present to observe, there is no limitation to their movement. However, when the patient is observed, they can manipulate paralysis. If the paralysis is addressed in isolation, a case of this nature cannot resolve. Possible triggers are: after the birth of a sibling or when the parents are divorcing and the focus of attention has been removed from the child. The unconscious mind acts to ensure that they rise 'above the radar' as the fundamental layer of 'disappointed love' has become exposed.

The nervous system is very much affected in *Tarentula hispanica* and this remedy acts well in cases of chronic pain, especially where the patient is driven to restlessness and absolute despair. For nerve pain, I recommend *Hypericum* in the acute, and *Magnesium carbonica* in the chronic stage. *Morphinum* is the most sensitive to pain (as mentioned in the *Opium* entry) and is a wonderful 'lack of reaction' remedy when nothing else acts or holds. *Morphinum* is so effective that it can actually work retrospectively after many years to unlock deeply traumatised cases when other indicated remedies have failed to act or hold their action.

The brain structure mostly afflicted in *Tarentula hispanica* is the anterior cingulate gyrus where primitive emotion is stimulated, and there is often an unbridled knee-jerk reaction to any perceived threat. This area can be triggered due to low levels of serotonin, contributing to 'in your face' ADHD, as seen in *Tarentula hispanica*, and other animal remedies already discussed such as *Bufo, Lachesis, Lyssin*, and *Scorpion (Androctonus)*.

A sign of the extreme tension experienced in *Tarentula hispanica* is pulling out of the hair, 'trichotillomania', a phenomenon which is documented increasingly in today's media. [109] This remedy could well be the simillimum here.

Tourette's syndrome, where the patient experiences uncontrollable outbursts of unprovoked shouting and contortions of the body, is well matched by *Tarentula hispanica* and other spider remedies such as *Mygale lasiodora*, which has a distinctive symptom – relief during sleep of all the symptoms. Other remedies for Tourette's syndrome include *Agaricus, Anacardium, Hyoscyamus, Lycopodium*, and *Stramonium*.

Tarentula hispanica goes deeper in *Nux vomica*-type cases where the organism is overworked and resultingly overwhelmed, which activates the nervous system and, consequently, 'all Hell breaks loose' as described above.

Tarentula hispanica is related to both the syphilitic and tubercular miasms. Its complementary remedy is *Arsenicum album*, which is more clingy and less chaotic than *Tarentula hispanica* in its manifestation.

In sepsis, its derivative, *Tarentula cubensis,* works well. It is a wonderful remedy, like *Arsenicum album*, at the end stage of life, when sepsis often contributes to the final demise of the patient, providing calm release.

---

109 *Trichotillomania,*
www.kidshealth.org/teen/your_mind/mental_health/trichotillomania.html.

Vanadium metallicum

The periodic table, where this element sits at number 23 in the Ferrum series, contains many clues to help us understand this remedy. Jan Scholten speaks of the Ferrum series being about duty, responsibility and 'grind'. [51] Vanadium sits between titanium at number 22 and chromium at number 24. Although titanium is known for its strength, vanadium is even heavier than titanium, and is a harder material; a factor that is often overlooked and is manifested in the action of the remedy. On the other hand, chromium, as a food supplement, supports the metabolism in conditions such as eating disorders or diabetes. [110] This has an overlap with vanadium which is an oxygen carrier and a catalyser.

As a *Metallicum* remedy, the *Vanadium* patient often presents with very weak energy.

Raised levels of vanadium have been reported in the tissues of patients suffering mania and depression, and the abundance of this mineral may be a causative factor in manic depression. [111] Lithium, the allopathic drug, seems to work by dampening down the action of vanadium in the system. The remedy, *Vanadium*, is especially indicated in anorexia and bulimia, illnesses that are increasingly common with all the demands of modern-day living. [51] Here there is an overlap with the remedy, *Chromium*, in its action on the metabolism. However, the background of anorexia is often one of a perfectionist drive – a feature often seen in minerals in this series. [112]

The perfectionism is illustrated in the fear of failure, as well as of criticism. Here, there are parallels with *Aurum metallicum* as well as *Carcinosin* which is also reputed for eating disorders, but the *Vanadium* patient presents in a much more rigid and dogmatic manner. This is a reflection of its hardness as a substance in its

---

110 *Chromium in the Diet* (2008), European Food Information Council.
111 Naylor, G.J. and Smith, A.H.W. (1981), Vanadium: A Possible Aetological Factor in Manic Depressive Illness, *Psychological Medicine*, 11(2):249-56.
112 Wade, Tracey D. and Tiggemann, Marika (2013), The Role of Perfectionism in Body Dissatisfaction, *The Journal of Eating Disorders*, 1:2.

original form through the concept of the 'Doctrine of Signatures'.

Behind anorexia, there is often a mental make-up of depression combined with obsession. The beauty of *Vanadium* is that it acts on both the emotional and physical levels simultaneously, thus addressing the manic depression behind the eating disorder and, at the same time, feeding the tissues with the missing nutrients which undermine the organism in such a destructive way.

Other conditions that comply with *Vanadium* include the early stages of tuberculosis, impotence, liver disease, AIDS, anaemia, arteriosclerosis, and liver disease. Comparable remedies include *Arsenicum album, Aurum metallicum, Carcinosin, China, Phosphorus,* and *Tuberculinum.*

The psychologist, Suniya Luthar, writes that the children of rich parents have twice the risk of developing mental problems as their less well-off peers. [69] These children were found to experience surging levels of neuroses, including eating disorders and drug abuse. Depression and anxiety, the drivers for such behaviour, occur at twice the normal rate in these children. The study concludes that the cause lies in the relentless pressure to succeed which many children cannot live up to, and results in isolation from their parents. [98] This background replicates the picture of *Vanadium metallicum* where eating disorders may result from such influences. The article continues that, in previous generations, children were less vulnerable to these types of pressures. It concludes by emphasising that it is not just parents who create this scenario, but also the community at large in the form of teachers, schools, coaches and peers. The Internet age does not make this any easier, where much resilience is needed to withstand the pressures from, not only one's peers, but also one's role models in society.

Veratrum album

(Other main derivative: *Veratrum viride*)

Veratrum album is derived from the white hellebore plant and belongs to the Liliiflorae group of remedies, alongside female remedies such as *Crocus sativa, Helonias*, and *Trillium pendulum*. In his book, *Insight into Plants*, Sankaran says *Veratrum album* complies with the Liliiflorae group of remedies in its distinctive picture of feeling as if in a tight corner and must get out of it by lies, boasting, and employing every means possible. [94] Heart remedies such as *Convallaria majalis, Lilium tigrinum, Sabadilla*, and *Sarsaparilla* also belong to this family of remedies.

The main sensation in *Veratrum album* is of being trapped and having to lie – see rubric **'untruthful'** (*Opium, Tarentula hispanica*, and *Thuja* are other significant remedies here) – and boast in order to escape from this – see rubric **'braggart, boaster'** where *Lycopodium, Platina*, and *Sulphur* are black type remedies and *Veratrum album* is in the sub-rubric, **'rich, wishes to be'**, with *Lachesis, Lycopodium*, and *Platina*. *Veratrum album* shares with *Platina* and *Sulphur* their alluring behaviour and egotistical conversation as ways of being included. There is also a fear of being excluded by losing their position in society, and *Veratrum album* is the only black type remedy in the rubric **'despair, social, position, of'**. This feeling of being cast out reminds one of *Hura brasiliensis,* where the feeling of ostracisation is even more extreme. In *Veratrum album*, to compensate for this feeling, there may be a delusion of being in communication with God.

The syphilitic aspect of this remedy shows in the propensity to destroy clothing – see **'destructiveness of clothes, cuts them up'**. *Tarentula hispanica* is similarly destructive.

Lycopodium, Platina, or *Sepia* are the usual choices for the symptom of despising one's children. However, *Veratrum album* is also in the rubric **'children, dislikes her own'**.

Phantom pregnancies could comply with the rubric **'delusion, pregnant, thought herself'**, which is a hysterical symptom acting as a cry for help. *Crocus sativa* shares this hysterical approach, as do other key remedies *Opium* and *Sabadilla*.

Anorexia – see rubric **'eat, refuses to'** – is another hysterical symptom with *Veratrum album* in black type and *Crocus sativa*, *Hyoscyamus*, *Opium*, and *Tarentula hispanica* as the main other remedies. There is usually a background of fright, grief, or scorn in the background of this 'disease'; the triggers must be quite extreme to engender such strong emotional reactions.

Erotic insanity is not confined to such remedies as *Hyoscyamus* and *Platina* – *Veratrum album* is also in black type. Note that *Crocus sativa* can be compared in the rubric **'kisses everyone, menses, before'**. *Veratrum album* also has lewdness and lewd talk, well-known symptoms of *Hyoscyamus*, and also *Stramonium*; see rubrics, **'sexuality, lewd'** and **'sexuality, lewd talk'**. *Veratrum album* also features in nymphomania, especially before menses/after suppressed menses, and puerperal; this is a reminder that *Platina* is not the only remedy to consider here.

Lying does not only apply to remedies such as *Opium* and *Thuja*. *Veratrum album* is very capable of lying in order to present an impression of authority; see **'untruthful'**, where it is in black type.

Veratrum album is a major remedy for collapse; compare it with *Camphor* for its coldness and weakness, and bringing patients back from the edge of life. *Camphor*, *Cuprum metallicum*, and *Veratrum album* make up Hahnemann's trio of cholera remedies. *Veratrum album* shares *Arsenicum album's* symptoms of sudden weakness and disabling diarrhoea and/or vomiting. Both remedies, as well as *Carbo vegetablis*, have the concomitant of coldness running through the picture. *Carbo vegetabilis* is indicated in extreme situations; in this case, in pathology primarily affecting the lungs but also the gut. Equally, there can be constipation in *Veratrum album*, where there is inactivity of the rectum as can also be seen in *Opium* and *Plumbum metallicum,* as well as the better known polarity of diarrhoea.

Veratrum viride is derived from the American hellebore plant and is equally intensely focused in its remedy picture, especially in the acute phase on the physical level. The plants are indistinguishable from each other when not in flower. *Veratrum viride* acts principally on the brain and arterial system of the organism and is a more obscure remedy than *Veratrum album*.

CONCLUSION

I hope this work will offer new insights to practitioners regarding the transgenerational approach to trauma. I found, when I started to adopt this approach, that it not only completely altered the outcome of cases, but also created more sustained healing. In addition, immediate family members and colleagues benefit enormously as they pick up on the changes that filter out to them in a vicarious way. It is almost as if the 'charge' is removed from what was hitherto a destructive dynamic.

In fact, case-taking undertakes a whole new meaning, as the practitioner can detect nuances which contribute to the mode of questioning and subsequent responses. By observing the dynamics between people in this way, the patient starts to heal as they make sense of the context to their suffering.

As patients reap the benefits, practitioners can also enhance their own development within this very exciting field, which can so readily be applied in homeopathic practice as well as in the practitioner's own 'story'. Hence, trauma is truly 'de-coded' and no longer infiltrates the patient's life – or the practitioner's, for that matter. By healing our own journey in this way, we can transmit the clarity gained accordingly to our patients, and the 'cure' becomes more than just the remedy – more a symbiosis of the remedy and this implicit message. Commitment is needed on both sides to pass through this 'eye of the needle', but the awareness gained in embracing one's true potential can have resounding results beyond all expectation.

Just as the 'Doctrine of Signatures' informs the action of plants in their healing process through their way of growth and subsequent development, the way trauma carries its message across the generations informs the ongoing future reactivity of the individual. The three-dimensional approach laid out in this book is aimed at diffusing this process so that life can be fully embraced with all the ongoing challenges it inevitably brings. After all, life is not a linear process by way of its very nature.

Homeopathy is one of the few disciplines which can work retrospectively to 're-calibrate' the trauma response which is so deeply embedded in the 'primal susceptibility'. As this process occurs, energy is made available to release the corresponding burden of physical ailments that are so closely entwined with the reactive state of the mindset.

Maya Angelou, the author of *I Know Why the Caged Bird Sings*, is quoted as saying: "You can never go home again, but the truth is you can never leave home, so it's all right." [113]

Of course, it is true that you can never go home again. However, by not re-visiting 'home', you are destined to repeat early patterns, often destructively, in future resonant situations. At the same time as never forgetting where you come from, the patient needs to know how to move on from that place and not be sucked into a similar vortex when similar challenges arise. If you can never leave 'home', then you are stuck there and can become infantilised by this entrapment. By integrating the primal blueprint which represents 'home', the individual can move on from it over the course of time towards self-discovery and personal growth, avoiding becoming enmeshed in the limitations it so lastingly instilled at the time.

In fact, as Maya Angelou expressed in the second part of her statement, "... but the truth is you can never leave home, so it's all right", the concept is that, by integrating the traumatic blueprint of childhood, it can then be safe to identify with 'home'. A person can then reverse the trajectory in a conscious way.

It is evident that Maya Angelou achieved this so well in her lifetime by reaching out through her eloquent writing which inspires so many. She clearly managed to transcend her early trauma in a truly compelling and transparent way for the benefit of others. This unlocked the key, not only to her full recovery, but her ability to empower others to embrace their history as a tool for growth and transformation.

---

113 Angelou, Maya (1984), *I Know Why the Caged Bird Sings*, Virago, New Ed edition.

So, by targeting trauma across the generations in each individual who presents for treatment, it is possible for them to revisit 'home' in a constructive and life-enhancing way. Thus, through the gentle art of homeopathy, this often intractable missing equation can be addressed. Only then can the patient achieve a lasting cure, which may have evaded them till such time. Its onward transmission should continue to echo down the line in tune with the drumbeat of time.

REFERENCES

[1]   Herman, Judith (1997), *Trauma and Recovery*, Basic Books, New Ed Edition.

[2]   Eizayaga, Francisco X. (1991), *Treatise on Homoeopathic Medicine*, Ediciones Marecel, 1st Edition.

[3]   Gershon, Michael D. (1999), *The Second Brain – Your Gut Has a Mind of Its Own*, Harper Collins Publishers.

[4]   Obissier, Patrick (2005), *Biogenealogy: Decoding the Psychic Roots of Illness – Freedom from the Ancestral Origins of Disease*, Healing Arts Press.

[5]   Murphy, Robin (2005), *Homeopathic Clinical Repertory*, Third Edition, Lotus Health Institute.

[6]   *Causes of Illness – 7 Emotions*, www.sacredlotus.com/go/foundations-chinese-medicine/get/causes-illness-7-emotions.

[7]   Scholten, Jan (2007), *Homeopathy and the Elements*, Alonissos Verlag.

[8]   Verrier, Nancy, MA (April 11-14, 1991), *The Primal Wound: Legacy of the Adopted Child. The Effects of Separation from the Birthmother on Adopted Children*, American Adoption Congress International Convention, Garden Grove, California.

[9]   Cyrulnik, Boris (2009), *Resilience – How Your Inner Strength Can Set You Free from the Past*, Penguin.

[10]   Miller, Alice (2008), *The Drama of Being a Child: The Search for the True Self*, Virago.

[11]   Boyd, Hilary (2012), *Thursdays in the Park*, Quercus.

[12]   Van der Kolk, Bessel (1998), Trauma and Memory, *Psychiatry and Clinical Neurosciences*, 52(S1):S52-S64.

[13]   Brandt-Rauf, Sherry I., JD, Mphil, et al. (November 2006), Ashkenazi Jews and Breast Cancer: The Consequences of Linking Ethnic Identity to Genetic Disease, *American Journal Public Health*, 96(11):1979–1988.

[14] Booth, Catherine et al. (January 2010), Infection in Sickle Cell Disease: A Review, *International Journal of Infectious Diseases*, 14(1):e2-e12.

[15] *Cyprus: How One Nation's Culture Influences Its Genes* (2010), www.geneletter.com/cyprus-how-one-nations-culture-influences-its-genes-16/.

[16] Dube, Shanta R. et al. (2009), Cumulative Childhood Stress and Autoimmune Diseases in Adults, *Psychosomatic Medicine*, 71(2):243-50.

[17] Goldberg, Rita (2014), *Motherland: Growing Up with the Holocaust*, Halban Publishers.

[18] Goldberg, Rita (March 18, 2014), London Reading, Waterstone's Bookshop, Hampstead High Street.

[19] Rodriguez, Tori (2015), Descendants of Holocaust Survivors Have Altered Stress Hormones, *Scientific American Mind*, 26(2).

[20] Janov, Arthur (2000), *The Biology of Love*, Prometheus Books.

[21] Adalian, Elizabeth (Winter 2010), Sculpting the 'Software' – Targeting Specific Brain Structures, *Homeopathy in Practice*.

[22] Doidge, Norman (2007), *The Brain that Changes Itself*, Viking Penguin Publishers.

[23] Negri-Cesi, P. (April-June, 2015), Bisphenol A Interaction with Brain Development and Functions, *Dose Response*, 13(2):1559325815590394.

[24] Strifert, Kim (2014), The Link Between Oral Contraceptive Use and Prevalence in Autistic Spectrum Disorder, *Medical Hypothesis*, 83(6):718-25.

[25] Hall, S. (2012), Journey to the Genetic Interior, *Scientific American*, 307(10):80-4.

[26] Dominguez-Salas, P. et al. (2014), Maternal Nutrition at Conception Modulates DNA Methylation of Human Metastable Epialleles, *Nature Communications*, http://www.nature.com/articles/ncomms4746.

[27] Rodgers, Ali B., Bale, Tracy L. et al. (May 2013), Paternal Stress Exposure Alters Sperm MicroRNA Content and Reprograms Offspring HPA Stress Axis Regulation, *The Journal of Neuroscience*, 33(21):9003–12.

[28]   Fernyhough, Charles (2012), *Pieces of Light: The New Science of Memory*, Profile Books.

[29]   Hellinger, Bert (2001), *Love's Own Truths: Bonding and Balancing in Close Relationships*, Zeig, Tucker and Theisen, Pheonix, USA.

[30]   Steiner, Rudolf, Bamford, Christopher, and Fox, Helen (1995), *The Kingdom of Childhood*, Steiner Books, Inc., Foundations of Waldorf Education, USA.

[31]   Stirt, Joseph A., MD (2002), *Quantations: A Guide to Quantum Living in the 21st Century*, iUniverse, USA.

[32]   Kiss, Enikő Gyöngyösiné, *Personality and the Familial Unconscious in Szondi's Fate-Analysis*, www.szondi.pte.hu/document/fate-analysis.pdf.

[33]   Holmes, Jeremy (1993), *John Bowlby and Attachment Theory (Makers of Modern Psychotherapy)*, Routledge Publishers.

[34]   Murphy, Robin (2006) *Nature's Materia Medica*, 3rd Edition, Lotus Health Institute.

[35]   Goodwin, R.D., et al. (2013), A Link Between Physician-Diagnosed Ulcer and Anxiety Disorders Among Adults, *Annals of Epidemiology*, 23(4):189-92.

[36]   Schmidt, Charles (March 2015), Mental Health May Depend on Creatures in the Gut, *Scientific American Mind,* 312(3).

[37]   Wilson, James L. (2002), *Adrenal Fatigue: The 21st Century Stress Syndrome*, Smart Publications.

[38]   Jung, Carl G. (1991), *The Archetypes and the Collective Unconscious (Collected Works of C. G. Jung)*, 2nd Edition, Routledge.

[39]   Bell, Michele (2003), *The Effects of Prematurity on Development: Process Studies: The Premature Birth*, www.prematurity.org/research/prematurity-effects1c.html.

[40]   Smith, Rebecca (April 18, 2014), Bullying at School Affects Health 40 Years Later, *The Telegraph*, www.telegraph.co.uk/news/health/children/10772302/Bullying-at-school-affects-health-40-years-later.html.

[41]   Bilsker, Dan and White, Jennifer (December 2011), The Silent Epidemic of Male Suicide, *British Columbia Medical Journal*, 53(10):529-34.

[42]   Harville, Emily W., PhD, and Boynton-Jarrett, Renee, MD, ScD, *Childhood Social Hardships and Fertility: A Prospective Cohort Study*, www.ncbi.nlm.nih.gov/pmc/articles/PMC4100793.

[43]   *Xenoestrogens Increase the Risk of Endometriosis* (March 3, 2015), www.bioidenticalhormoneexperts.com/xenoestrogens-increase-the-risk-of-endometriosis.

[44]   Nelson III, Charles A. PhD (October 2012), The Effects of Early Life Adversity on Brain and Behavioral Development, *Brain in the News*.

[45]   Van der Zee, Harry (2009), *Miasms in Labour*, Homeolinks.

[46]   Swaab, Dick (2014), *We are our Brains – From the Womb to Alzheimer's*, Allen Lane.

[47]   Lott, Tim (October 24, 2014), The Terrible Effects Of Postnatal Depression, *The Guardian*.

[48]   Bauer, Annette et al. (October 20, 2014), *Costs of Perinatal Mental Health Problems*, Centre for Mental Health, UK.

[49]   Lott, Tim (2009), *The Scent of Dried Roses: One Family and the End of English Suburbia – an Elegy*, Penguin Modern Classics.

[50]   Apter, Terri (2012), *Difficult Mothers: Understanding and Overcoming Their Power*, W.W. Norton and Company.

[51]   Scholten, Jan (1993), *Homoeopathy and Minerals*, Stichting Alonissos.

[52]   *The Barnes Basal Body Temperature Test*, www.regenerativenutrition.com/content.asp?id=574.

[53]   Zeman, Adam (2009), *A Portrait of the Brain*, Yale University Press.

[54]   Khandaker G.M. et al. (2014), Association of Serum Interleukin 6 and C-Reactive Protein in Childhood With Depression and Psychosis in Young Adult Life: A Population-Based Longitudinal Study, *Journal of the American Medical Association of Psychiatry*; 71(10):1121-1128.

[55]   Coccaro, E.F. and Coussons-Read, M. (2013), Elevated Inflammatory Markers in Individuals with Intermittent Explosive Disorder and Correlation with Aggression in Humans,

Journal of the American Medical Association of Psychiatry,
71(2):158-65.

[56]   Fairweather, Delisa and Rose, Noel R. (2004), Women and
         Autoimmune Diseases, *Emerging Infectious Diseases,*
         10(11):2005-11.

[57]   Herbert, Martha and Weintraub, Karen (2013), *The Autism
         Revolution: Whole-Body Strategies for Making Life All It Can Be,*
         Ballantine Books, Inc.

[58]   Bligh, Rebecca (2008), *Simon Baron-Cohen's Extreme Male Brain
         Theory of Autism,* www.academia.edu/2033271/Simon_Baron-
         Cohens_Extreme_Male_Brain_Theory_of_Autism.

[59]   Adam, David (2014), *The Man Who Couldn't Stop – OCD and the
         True Story of a Life Lost in Thought,* Picador.

[60]   National Institute of Mental Health, USA,
         www.nimh.nih.gov/health/publications/pandas/index.shtml.

[61]   Ornstein, Robert (1998), *The Right Mind: Making Sense of the
         Hemispheres,* Harcourt Brace and Company.

[62]   Rodriguez, Tori (July 2014), Emotional Ignorance Harms Health,
         Scientific American Mind, 25(4).

[63]   Cox, David (November 2, 2014), Could Eating Oily Fish Help
         Prevent Dyslexia?, *The Guardian.*

[64]   Filbey, Francesca M. et al. (2014), *Long-Term Effects of Marijuana
         Use on the Brain,* www.pnas.org/content/111/47/16913.full.

[65]   Collingwood, Jane, *Cannabis May Cause Schizophrenia-Like Brain
         Changes,* www.psychcentral.com/lib/cannabis-may-cause-
         schizophrenia-like-brain-changes.

[66]   Lewis, Marc (2011), *Memoirs of an Addicted Brain: A
         Neuroscientist Examines His Former Life on Drugs,* PublicAffairs.

[67]   McCrae, John (1915), *In Flanders Fields, the Poppies Blow.*

[68]   Matson, Johnny L., Sturmey, Peter (2011), *International
         Handbook of Autism and Pervasive Developmental Disorders
         (Autism and Child Psychopathology Series),* Springer.

[69]   Luthar, Suniya (2003), The Culture of Affluence: Psychological
         Costs of Material Wealth, *Child Development,* 74:1581-93.

[70]   Cavendish, Camilla (March 15, 2015), Parents are Inflicting Psychological Harm in an Educational Arms Race, *The Sunday Times*.

[71]   Waumsley, J.A., Dr, Chairwoman (2011), *Obesity in the UK: A Psychological Perspective*, The British Psychological Society.

[72]   Ellen, Barbara (July 13, 2014), The Overweight Deserve Help, not Sneers or Malice, *The Observer*.

[73]   Bastiaan, T., Heijmans et al. (2008), Persistent Epigenetic Differences Associated with Prenatal Exposure to Famine in Humans, *Proceedings of the National Academy of Sciences of the United States of America,* 105(44).

[74]   Sideli, Lucia et al. (June 2012), Do Child Abuse and Maltreatment Increase the Risk of Schizophrenia?, *Psychiatry Investigation*, 9(2):87-99.

[75]   Kelland, Kate (June 24, 2014), Study Finds Genetic Links between Schizophrenia and Cannabis Use, *Reuters*, US Edition.

[76]   Coghlan, Andy (April 2014), Keep the Body Well to Slow Alzheimer's, *New Scientist,* 222(2966):10.

[77]   Bauer, P., Larkina, M. (2014), The Onset of Childhood Amnesia in Childhood: A Prospective Investigation of the Course and Determinants of Forgetting of Early-Life Events, *Memory,* 22:907-24.

[78]   Finger, Elizabeth C. et al. (January 2015), Oxytocin for Frontotemporal Dementia: A Randomized Dose-Finding Study of Safety and Tolerability, *Neurology*, 84(2):174-81.

[79]   *Meares-Irlen Syndrome,* http://www.dyslexiasw.com/advice/all-about-dyslexia/meares-irlen-syndrome.

[80]   *Auditory Processing Disorder,* www.nhs.uk/conditions/auditory-processing-disorder/Pages/Introduction.aspx.

[81]   *Memory and the Brain,* www.human-memory.net/brain.html.

[82]   Hambidge, K. and Silverman, A. (1973), Pica with Rapid Improvement after Dietary Zinc Supplementation, *Archives of Disease in Childhood*, 48(7):567-8.

[83]   Bakan, R. (1979), The Role of Zinc in Anorexia Nervosa: Etiology and Treatment, *Medical Hypotheses*, 5(7):731-6.

[84] Wood, Janice (2012), Childhood Trauma Linked to
      Schizophrenia,
      http://psychcentral.com/news/2012/04/20/childhood-trauma-
      linked-to-schizophrenia/37610.html.

[85] Laing R.D. and Esterson, Aaron (1990), *Sanity, Madness and the
      Family: Families of Schizophrenics*, Penguin Books Ltd.

[86] Sass, L.A. (1998), Schizophrenia, Self-Consciousness, and the
      Modern Mind, *Journal of Consciousness Studies*, 5(5-6):543-65.

[87] Shariatmadari, David (August 25, 2013), A Book that Changed
      Me, *The Observer*.

[88] Adalian, Elizabeth (Winter/Spring 2013), Beyond the
      Constraints of Alumina: Unlocking the Key to Dementia,
      Homeopathy In Practice.

[89] Boericke, William, Dr. (1999), *Pocket Manual of Homoeopathic
      Materia Medica and Repertory*, B. Jain Publishers Pvt Ltd.

[90] Assilem, Melissa (September 1990), *Folliculinum: Mist or Miasm?*,
      www.homeopathyhome.com/reference/articles/follic.shtml.

[91] Rehman, Abdur (1997), *Encyclopedia of Remedy Relationships in
      Homeopathy*, Haug Verlag.

[92] Bratman, R. (2007), *Complementary and Alternative Health: The
      Scientific Verdict on What Really Works*, Collins Publishers.

[93] Ferrence, S. and Bendersky, G. (2004), Therapy with Saffron and
      the Goddess at Thera, *Perspectives in Biology and Medicine,*
      47(2):199-226.

[94] Sankaran, Rajan (2002), *An Insight into Plants, Volume I*,
      Homeopathic Medical Publishers.

[95] Vermeulen, F. (1996), Hura Brasiliensis, *Synoptic Materia Medica
      2*, Merlijn Publishers.

[96] Baldwin, James (1953), *Go Tell it on the Mountain*, Alfred A.
      Knopf.

[97] Baldwin, James (1956), *Giovanni's Room*, Dial Press.

[98] Chua, Amy (2011), *Battle Hymn of the Tiger Mother*, Penguin
      Group.

[99] Bergland, Christopher (May 2014), How does the Vagus Nerve
      Convey Gut Instincts to the Brain?, *Psychology Today*.

[100]   Orange, Richard (October 31, 2013), Swedish Children Complain Their Parents Spend Too Long on Phones, *The Guardian*.

[101]   McDaniel, Laura, *What is the Gut-Brain Connection?*, www.connectwc.org/what-is-the-gut-brain-connection.html.

[102]   Adalian, Elizabeth (September 2014), *The Missing Equation: Transgenerational Trauma*, www.hpathy.com/clinical-cases/missing-equation-transgenerational-trauma.

[103]   Pearson, Rebecca M., Phd, et al. (2013), Maternal Depression During Pregnancy and the Postnatal Period. Risks and Possible Mechanisms for Offspring Depression at 18 Years, *Journal of the American Medical Association of Psychiatry*, 70(12):1312-19.

[104]   Pilkington, Ed (February 1, 2013), U.S. Military Struggling to Stop Suicide Epidemic among War Veterans, *The Guardian*.

[105]   Ahmed, Serge H., Dr. (2009), Is Sugar as Addictive as Cocaine?, *Journal of Food and Addiction*, 139:620–22.

[106]   Assilem, Melissa (1996), *The Mad Hatter's Tea Party*, The Homeopathic Supply Company.

[107]   www.tinussmits.com/3870/saccharum-officinale.aspx.

[108]   Hahnemann, Samuel (1796), *Essay on a New Principle for Ascertaining the Curative Powers of Drugs*.

[109]   *Trichotillomania*, www.kidshealth.org/teen/your_mind/mental_health/trichotillomania.html.

[110]   *Chromium in the Diet* (2008), European Food Information Council.

[111]   Naylor, G.J. and Smith, A.H.W. (1981), Vanadium: A Possible Aetological Factor in Manic Depressive Illness, *Psychological Medicine*, 11(2):249-56.

[112]   Wade, Tracey D. and Tiggemann, Marika (2013), The Role of Perfectionism in Body Dissatisfaction, *The Journal of Eating Disorders*, 1:2.

[113]   Angelou, Maya (1984), *I Know Why the Caged Bird Sings*, Virago, New Ed edition.

PRINTED AND BOUND BY:
Copytech (UK) Limited trading as Printondemand-worldwide,
9 Culley Court, Bakewell Road, Orton Southgate.
Peterborough, PE2 6XD, United Kingdom.